More praise for Mark Russinovich and the Jeff Aiken series

"A very scary and too-plausible novel. *Zero Day* is not science fiction; it is science fact."   —Nelson DeMille

"In [Mark's] latest compelling creation he is raising awareness of the all-too-real threat of cyberterrorism."   —Bill Gates, on *Zero Day*

"To IT folks, Mark is every bit a hero as Wozniak, Gates, or Ken Olsen."
                                        —Doug Barney, *Redmond Magazine*

"Russinovich scares us all in this techno-thriller that gets the details right!"
                              —Mikko Hypponen, Chief Research Officer,
                                                  F-Secure Corporation

"An engaging writer who fearlessly tackles potentially brain-freezing topics."
                                        —*San Francisco Chronicle*

"Russinovich works for Microsoft and understands the world of computer software. He's able to convey complex technical information in easy-to-understand terms. Thrills and strong characters add to the fun. Fans of Daniel Suarez and other techno-thriller scribes should add Russinovich to their reading lists."   —*Booklist*

"Scarily plausible."   —*Library Journal* on *Zero Day*

"Top-notch geek lit."   —*Kirkus Reviews* on *Zero Day*

"A compelling story with thrills and chills to entertain you. I found it more plausible and fun than Dan Brown's *Digital Fortress*."
                              —*Seattle Post-Intelligencer* on *Zero Day*

ALSO BY MARK RUSSINOVICH

Zero Day

TROJAN HORSE

Mark Russinovich

THOMAS DUNNE BOOKS
ST. MARTIN'S GRIFFIN ❧ NEW YORK

THOMAS DUNNE BOOKS.
An imprint of St. Martin's Press.

TROJAN HORSE. Copyright © 2012 by Mark Russinovich. Foreword copyright © 2012 by Kevin Mitnick. All rights reserved. Printed in the United States of America. For information, address St. Martin's Press, 175 Fifth Avenue, New York, N.Y. 10010.

www.thomasdunnebooks.com
www.stmartins.com

The Library of Congress has cataloged the hardcover edition as follows:

Russinovich, Mark E.
    Trojan horse / Mark Russinovich.—1st ed.
        p. cm.
    ISBN 978-1-250-01048-3 (hardcover)
    ISBN 978-1-250-01049-0 (e-book)
    1. Cyberterrorism—Fiction.   I Title
    PS3618.U7688 T76 2012
    813'.6—dc23

                                                              2012028218

ISBN 978-1-250-04254-5 (trade paperback)

St. Martin's Griffin books may be purchased for educational, business, or promotional use. For information on bulk purchases, please contact Macmillan Corporate and Premium Sales Department at 1-800-221-7945, extension 5442, or write specialmarkets@macmillan.com.

First St. Martin's Griffin Edition: April 2014

10 9 8 7 6 5 4 3 2 1

ACKNOWLEDGMENTS

I'd like to thank John Lambert, David Cross, Frank Simorjay, and Scott Field—colleagues of mine at Microsoft—for reviewing drafts of *Trojan Horse* and providing valuable input based on their real-world experiences with cyber espionage. Ron Watkins provided me great input on the plot and character development and made helpful reviews of numerous drafts.

I'm grateful to Kevin Mitnick for endorsing the book with his foreword and to Mikko Hypponen for his blurb. I've learned a lot from both of them and am honored to have their names associated with *Trojan Horse*.

My thanks also go to my agent, Ann Collette, from the Helen Rees Literary Agency, who helped usher the book through the publication process. I owe thanks to Peter Joseph, my editor at Thomas Dunne Books, for believing in a sequel, for the insightful feedback he gave in his reviews, and making sure everything was covered for the successful publication and launch for *Trojan Horse*.

Finally, I want to again thank my wife, the real-life Daryl, for her continued support of my indulgence as a fiction author.

FOREWORD

It is Mark Russinovich's in-depth knowledge of Windows and how data traverses over the digital landscape that creates the chilling realism in the backdrop of *Trojan Horse*, the highly anticipated follow-up to his first novel, *Zero Day*. I've long said that people are the weakest link in the security chain (and, in the past, frequently taken advantage of this myself). In his thrilling tale, Mark shows us that malware remains a significant threat as the sophistication of malicious programs continues to grow. The bad actors still use the age-old technique of social engineering—the method of manipulating people into performing an action in order to leverage the help of the victim to exploit a security flaw in the application software that resides on their computer. When used together, these two attack methods can lead to devastating outcomes as they leapfrog over even the most resilient network defenses. No one is immune to social engineering, and even the most technically competent can easily fall victim to this method.

In today's world, it is rare that such an attack will merely affect one network. Once again, Mark makes us aware of how interconnected our systems are, and how their dependencies can be used to create havoc in our world. Geographic boundaries are no longer an obstacle for those wishing to cause harm. Our future wars may employ people on the battlefield as a last resort. The initial efforts will likely be fought digitally over the vast technology infrastructure that the Internet has created. It is now possible to have a virus weaponized in China, employed in Berlin on behalf of Afghanistan, and have the payload delivered in Sydney or the United States—masking origination, and making detection and accountability almost impossible.

Mark has created well-defined characters in Jeff Aiken and Daryl Haugen, whose challenges will absorb the reader. His attention to detail in both the technical and backdrop settings are realistic because they are closely related to real events exposed by the media. Even the nontechie will have no trouble understanding the well-explained technical details. The story line keeps the reader immersed, anticipating what will happen next, and the only difficulty comes in trying to put the book down.

Trojan Horse is a work of fiction, but it makes you think about the possibilities in the future as the sophistication of our adversaries continues to grow in response to narrowing gaps in security posture. I am both honored and privileged to have the opportunity of an advance read of Mark's latest work, and look forward to sequels in the future. However, after reading his book, even I am left wondering how prudent the decision was to open an e-mailed copy of the manuscript called "Trojan Horse.doc."

—KEVIN MITNICK,
SPEAKER, CONSULTANT, AND AUTHOR OF
THE *NEW YORK TIMES* BESTSELLER *GHOST IN THE WIRES*

MEMORANDUM

DATE: June 24
FROM: Rhonda MacMillan-Jones
Deputy Director, Cyber Security
National Security Agency
TO: Admiral Braxton L. R. Compton
Chairman, Joint Chiefs of Staff
Pentagon
RE: Confirmation

This is a follow-up to our conversation earlier today in which I confirmed the discovery of extraneous software embedded within the U.S. Pacific Fleet Command computer structure. This malware has access to the database that manages fleet deployments. It is highly sophisticated, unlike any we have previously encountered. At this time we do not know how it penetrated COMPACFLT computer defenses, how long it has been embedded, or the extent of the infection. It constitutes the most serious penetration to date by malignant software embedded from an unknown source within a highly classified U.S. military command computer system.

We share your suspicions that this malware was responsible for the ten-hour blackout experienced by COMPACFLT during fleet maneuvers off Taiwan nineteen days ago. Be assured that we are working with your staff and will do all within our ability to locate and remove every vestige of this Trojan from your system and that we will learn how it managed to insinuate itself into such critical software.

I wish to repeat that we do not yet know the scope of the penetration or the capacity of the malware to disrupt, or direct, fleet operations. We urge great caution in the interim. Though we cannot know its origin with certainty, the level of sophistication and the nature of its disruption indicates a nation-state with national security interests toward the United States.

cc: CoS, POTUS
        NSA, White House

INTERNAL DISTRIBUTION ONLY
SECRET

DAY ONE

THURSDAY, APRIL 9

CYBER PENETRATIONS REACH ALL-TIME HIGH

By Arnie Willoughby
April 9

Sophisticated computer penetration is at record levels according to Cyril Lester, executive director of the Internet Security Alliance. In a speech delivered at the association's annual meeting in Las Vegas, Nevada, Lester said, "Despite an increase in awareness by individuals and companies, malware, particularly in the form of Trojans, continues to find its way into computers at an alarming rate."

Though hackers still release what Lester described as "junk malware," advanced and highly sophisticated viruses are an ever-greater cause for concern. Most target financial records and a number have been highly successful in looting personal and bank accounts.

A new version of the Zeus Trojan, for one, recently penetrated bank security then silently stole more than one million dollars from an estimated three thousand accounts, according to Lester. "Authorities have been unable to trace the ultimate destination of the funds," he said.

The Zeus Trojan infected Windows machines through various exploits in Internet Explorer and Adobe Reader. It then lay dormant until the user entered his bank account. Through a technique known as keystroke logging it captured log-on information later used to access the account. If it was determined to hold at least $1,250 dollars the money was stolen.

Though not proven, the cyber operation is believed to have been orchestrated by an East European cyber gang.

Until recently, the Zeus Trojan was considered the most sophisticated and dangerous virus of all time, Lester said. That dubious distinction has been supplanted by Stuxnet, the mysterious virus which has targeted Iran's nuclear development program. Lester emphasized that even more dangerous malware is likely already implanted in computers worldwide. "We've scarcely viewed the scope of the risk we face," Lester said.

The Internet Security Association is funded by the major computer and software manufacturers in the U.S. Lester has requested a four-fold increase in funding.

1

YAKIMA, WASHINGTON
EASTERN WASHINGTON ELECTRICAL GRID
WAYK5-7863
12:47 A.M. PST

Scalpel."

The nurse placed it in the surgeon's palm firmly, without the slap portrayed in movies. The young patient had been brought in more dead than alive following a highway accident. She could not have been more than fifteen years old. Somehow, in the violence and extremity of the collision a knifelike blade of hard polymer had pierced her skull and embedded itself in her brain.

Her vital signs, however, were strong and given its position, if properly removed, the surgeon was optimistic for a satisfactory recovery. She was young, resilient, and the brain had an amazing capacity to restore itself at this age.

The surgery had already lasted for more than three hours. He'd removed a portion of her skull to give him access. He'd picked out bits and pieces of bone until she was clean. But this was the worst of it. Remove this bit of plastic from the young woman's brain and there was a very good chance she'd live. Leave it in place and she'd die. Make a mistake and she would be left functionally impaired or dead.

Dr. Elias Holt lifted his hand and prepared to make the delicate incision. Just at that moment the lights blinked, then a moment later came back to life. Holt waited in case it happened again. Nothing.

"We're on emergency power," Paul Sanders, the tech with the ACPM, or acute care physiologic monitoring system, said. "My data scrambled, Doc. I need a minute to reacquire."

Holt lowered his hand. There was no need to say anything. The technology this delicate surgery relied upon would soon be back up.

"All right . . ." the tech began, but just at that moment the lights went out and did not come back on.

Everyone on Holt's experienced team knew to freeze in place, to do nothing. In a moment, the power would be restored from the outside grid or the hospital's auxiliary system. A power outage was rare and Holt could not recall a time when he'd been left in darkness during surgery.

The Mount Rainier Regional Medical Center was a small hospital with just eighty-five beds. In recent years, it had added emergency care to its profile as part of a significant expansion. The patient had been brought here because the accident had taken place nearby and her condition was so desperate.

After twenty seconds of darkness the lights sprang on. "Paul?"

"Sorry, Doc, but I need to reacquire my data. It will take a minute or more."

"How's the patient, Allison?"

The anesthetist answered, "Stable. No change."

Holt waited, then asked, "Paul?"

"I'm resetting now."

Just then the lights went out again.

In the basement, the night supervisor was staring at his computer screen. He could make no sense of what he was seeing. The primary backup generator had started twice, then simply kicked off. There was no power coming into the hospital from the outside power grid. They were on their own and this should not be happening.

He'd been trained on the computer that controlled the power supply but hadn't done anything with the system since then. It was automatic, computerized. It ran itself. Just as he was considering actually doing something, the generator kicked into life a third time. He held his breath, hoping no surgery was underway.

Twenty seconds later the generator died again.

Kathleen Ficke left the Holiday Inn bar and walked to the elevators. The bar was closing and her night was finished. She punched the button and waited for the doors to pop open.

Ficke worked three or four times a month on such assignments for the Smart Agency. When she'd applied for the job, the owner had explained it to her in simple terms. "When a wife thinks her honey is fooling around, sometimes she wants proof, usually to get a better deal in the divorce. That's when they come to us. I get a good photo and send a woman of the right age into the hotel bar where the target's likely to do his drinking. She can't be too pretty or too plain; she can't be dressed sexy. In fact, I'll take a full body picture of you before you go out. You'll have the guy's photo. All you do is sit alone at the bar and drink a Coke. That's it. Don't talk to anyone, get rid of any man who tries to pick you up, including the target. We just want to know if he's with someone or if he hits on you. That's it. You file a report and I give you two hundred dollars. Want the job?"

The work had proven just as easy as he'd explained and the extra money had come in handy. She was tired and ready to go home. Her cat needed to be fed.

She'd spent two hours in the bar and during that time her target had consumed eight bourbons. He'd been at a small round table talking with two men he'd apparently met in the bar. Each of them had given her the eye but none had approached her, not like others.

The elevator doors opened with a digital chime. Ficke stepped in and a moment later so did her target. He glanced at her, slightly intoxicated, and punched the button for the fourth floor.

"You?" he asked.

"Lobby."

She stared straight ahead as the elevator began to move. He was over-weight and she could hear his labored breathing. His face was flush and his eyes watery. Now she could smell the booze.

Without warning the elevator stopped. There was the fading sound of dying machinery in the shaft. "Whoa," her target said. "Who turned out the lights?"

Ficke said nothing but was acutely uncomfortable at being stuck in an elevator with him. They stood silently until the wait extended uncomfortably.

"I saw you at the bar," the target said out of the darkness. "No luck, huh? Maybe he got held up. I've got a bottle in my room. Once this buggy gets going, come on down and we'll talk it over." He moved closer, so close the reek of bourbon flooded across her face. "What do you say?"

Engineer Doug Bradstreet watched the green lights flash past as Trans-American train number 435 plowed through the night at sixty miles an hour. The run had begun just ten minutes earlier when he'd cleared the switching yard in Yakima and now he was picking up speed before reaching the Pacific Coast mountain range.

He wasn't supposed to do that, of course. He'd been assured he had all the engine power he needed to make the climb, but he liked to build speed and hit the mountains as close to full throttle as reasonably possible. His two linked engines pulled eighty-three cars filled with coal intended for the TransAlta coal-fired power plant near Seattle. Bradstreet enjoyed the motion, the sense of power that came with giving the twin engines their head and letting them run.

The window was open and he leaned out every few seconds, relishing the rush of fresh air across his face. A series of green lights told him all was well ahead. He'd spent long hours this way, the green lights a seemingly endless stream. Just at that moment, the lights suddenly flashed red. Bradstreet eased back on the throttle. Flashing red meant the light system was off the power grid and running from battery power. He slowed, feeling the slight uphill grade suck the power from the train.

Then the flashing lights turned dark. Bradstreet cut the power to nil and the powerful train slowed until it came to rest atop the second of the five bridges the track crossed before reaching the mountains. He removed the microphone, punched the button, and said, "This is 435. I've lost signal lights and am stopped on bridge two. What's the problem? When will I get lights back? Can I proceed?"

"Stand by," came the answer. Bradstreet didn't know if the outage extended to his control, but even if it did the facility had a backup generator.

Bradstreet looked down into the chasm below feeling uneasy. He didn't like heights. He decided to ease the train off the bridge if he didn't get the go-ahead. Just then a frightening thought crossed his mind. He punched the button again. "Hey, Lenny! Is 389 behind me stopped? Lenny! Tell 389 to stop!"

Trans-American number 389 had been in the switching yard behind him. It was scheduled to run thirty minutes back but it had a light load and would have closed fast, depending on the light system to alert it when it approached 435.

"Lenny! Can you hear me? Lenny!"

At Mount Rainier Regional Medical Center, the generator continued starting then kicking off. The pattern had repeated itself eight times with no end in sight. The patient's skull was open, the deadly polymer still in place. Three flashlights were now casting the surgery in ghostly shadows. They were inadequate for an operation but alleviated the darkness.

"Doctor," Allison said. "She's starting to fade."

"Paul, do you have status?"

"I can't get power long enough to get a reading."

Dr. Holt positioned his scalpel. "I'm proceeding. I need all the light focused here, please."

What else is there to do? he thought. If he waited she'd die. The lights blinked off and he paused. When they next came on he'd have to work quickly. Do it wrong, he reminded himself, and she'll die anyway.

2

Guy Fagan finished his coffee as he read the e-mail from a colleague in Washington State concerning the surprise fourteen-minute collapse of the power grid in Yakima earlier that morning. No cause had been found for it.

WAyk5-7863 was considered one of the most stable in the nation. The Inland Empire, as the region was once known, was largely self-contained, walled off from the western portion of the state. Most of its electricity was hydroelectric with a bit of coal and nuclear thrown in, a perfect balance it was thought. The area had a predictable climate that placed no great demand on the grid. Economic growth in the region was anemic and the electrical supply had increased at a modest and easily sustained pace. There had been no similar collapse in years—none, in fact, that Fagan could recall.

It was odd and his colleague was speculating that it might very well have been caused by a computer glitch. That struck Fagan as most likely. Grids were increasingly dependent on computers and specialized software. They were complex structures, far more complicated than the public understood. In the past, during times of great demand, enormous areas had cascaded into darkness, events caused by nothing more than a fallen tree or a collapsed power line. They could take days, even weeks to meticulously rebuild. Electricity, the lifeblood of the twenty-first century, had to be in perfect balance between demand and supply. Computers made that job easier but in providing one more area of control they also made the grids more vulnerable.

Fagan had good reason to know. As a senior software engineer, he was relatively pleased with his position at PGTA. It was his second job out of college and he'd been steadily promoted over the last decade. Since inception, the company itself had deftly carved out a nice little niche for itself in the software industry. In its early days, it had provided generic software of various applications. Now, it produced a significant portion of the code used throughout the electric grid in the United States under contract with the U.S. Department of Energy. The transition had been complete when the company renamed itself PGTA, short for Power Grid Technology Applications, two years earlier.

Fagan himself was manager for the project, writing the code for any emergency override of the electrical grid in the event of an attack against a regional substation or its operators. His work was interesting and important. He took pride in that.

He had been assigned to this project after six years on the IT team that had maintained the security of PGTA's own systems and database. The company had received a number of awards for the protection it provided its clients. In its years of existence, PGTA had never experienced a serious penetration of its firewall. Not one. And that success was due in no small measure to Fagan himself.

He glanced at the list of unopened e-mails and spotted one he was expecting from DASS, Dallas Applied Software Solutions in Texas. It was a vendor with which he frequently did business, one of his more important sources of industry specific code. He opened the message.

At that moment the Trojan entered his computer, quickly finding its way through an unpatched exploit. It had ridden this message to place itself behind the PGTA firewall. There it unrolled into his computer's operating system, wrapping its tentacles around every function it was targeted to seek and control.

Before Fagan had time to read the message, his screen lit up with a brief flash. This stopped him short. *What was that?* Revisualizing the flash, he realized that he'd seen something like it before and for a moment struggled to recall when. Then he had it. It had been during his latest security training. The flash had resembled the antimalware intrusion detection warning dialog. Or something very like it. Regardless, he'd never before experienced such an event on any computer.

Better to be cautious than sorry, he decided. He opened the security software and was relieved when it reported everything was fine. Nothing to worry about. He paused for a moment, wondering if there was anything else he should do and decided there was not. He closed the program and returned to his message, not giving the incident another thought.

As he did, the Trojan guardedly acquired the source code to the power grid control software, blending its actions seamlessly into the activity of the computer so as not to attract attention. Before the day was out, the Trojan would also copy Fagan's e-mail list and the data files in his computer related to each e-mail.

Fagan liked to work a bit late, volunteer some time to the company. He believed it was the secret to his success. He'd never been one to watch the clock and bolt right at quitting time. Just after six o'clock he turned off his screen and headed out, his thoughts already directed toward the problems he'd face the next day.

Some hours later, when the PGTA offices were closed, the Trojan in Fagan's computer "called home," inconspicuously transferring the data it had copied. This launched it on a long digital journey from Menlo Park, California, to whoever had written the malware code, the person who was interested in shutting down significant sections of the U.S. electric power grid by remote command.

3

UNITED NATIONS OFFICE AT GENEVA (UNOG)
OFFICE FOR DISARMAMENT AFFAIRS
PALAIS DES NATIONS
5:47 P.M. CET

Franz Herlicher looked at his paper again with amazement.

He had of late noticed a creeping tendency to type the wrong word rather than to simply misspell the one he'd intended. He blamed the word processor's spell-checker for it. If he misspelled, it caught the error at once. Over the years it had served to improve his spelling dramatically.

But he'd noticed that now he often simply typed a similar, but incorrect word, with nearly the same frequency with which he'd once misspelled words. He wondered if a certain proportion of errors were programmed into the human condition and no matter how hard you worked to eliminate error, error always returned, one way or another.

But that wasn't the problem here. He'd not typed the wrong *word*. This wasn't a matter of inadvertently substituting "tenant" for "tenor" as he'd done earlier that day. No, in the paper he'd distributed he'd managed to mistype throughout it, altering the paper in subtle yet significant ways, finally changing the entire last *paragraph*, nearly every word of it. The reality was that his paper was no longer the one he'd written.

And Herlicher had absolutely no idea how that could be.

The problem had been pointed out to him by his colleague, Lloyd Walthrop, with the UK Foreign Office in London. His e-mail to that effect had been scathing and Herlicher was still blushing from the memory of it. Theirs had been a valued professional relationship and he wanted nothing to tarnish it. After all, Herlicher didn't intend to remain in dreary Geneva among the Swiss forever.

Educated at the Bavarian law facilities in Munich, Franz Herlicher had begun his career with a brief stint in Brussels, working for an odious Prussian he'd despised. When this chance to move to the United Nations came along he'd jumped at it. He'd been promoted to senior analyst within the Office for Disarmament Affairs and was assigned to draft the final committee report on the Iran nuclear weapons program. His first version had been well received with only a few minor suggestions for changes.

This was a break-out opportunity for him, he was certain. The report's conclusions would likely shape world events and it was not unlikely that the entire report, with his name on it, would find its way into the public domain. The best part was that even if the Western powers refused to act, he would still have garnered exposure that made the kind of career he'd always envisioned.

Herlicher had frankly been surprised when the committee had voted to take such a firm stand against Iran. He'd not encountered such assertion in the organization previously. He'd determined early on that the true purpose of the UN Office for Disarmament Affairs was not to prevent nuclear disarmament or to even accurately report nuclear developments within nations, but rather to evade commitment and responsibility. It was, he understood, the way of the world.

Don't stick your neck out or it will get chopped off, his father had taught him. Let the world take care of itself. If anyone was truly interested in stopping the proliferation of nuclear weapons they'd do something about it, not ask for more reports.

But something had clearly happened to change all that, at least for now. It might have been a sudden realization that a nuclear Iran was a threat the civilized world could not ignore, but Herlicher thought that unlikely. The world tolerated a nuclear North Korea after all. Or it might have been outside pressure, say from the United States, Britain, or even France, even all three behind the scenes, but again he doubted that was the case. The UN was largely impervious to such pressure. Since its inception it had become monolithic, driven by its own internal and self-serving dynamics.

The answer he'd been given over lunch when he'd discreetly posed the question of "Why now?" when the evidence had been there for years had caught him by surprise. It seemed so improbable that he doubted it could possibly be true.

"A source," the chairman had told him. "A source has come forward with irrefutable evidence."

"You mean someone came to us instead of the United States?" Herlicher had asked, unable to mask his shock. After all who could trust them? UNOG, for one, leaked like a sieve. Why come to them with such intelligence? Why not sell it to the Americans? That's what they were good at, buying up people and resources.

And why assume that ODA, as his office was known, would act? Its history suggested quite the contrary. Herlicher had been mystified by the explanation.

"Yes. He's an idealist apparently and very well sourced. We now know Iran is about to detonate an atomic device. We know where, we know the scheduled date. The evidence is beyond dispute. It has been decided that we will issue a timely and decisive report."

"Why?"

The chairman leaned forward. "Because if we don't, the source says he will go to the Americans and it will come out we had the information first. So it's going to come out one way or the other. Better us since it's inevitable."

Now that, Herlicher decided, made sense. ODA had in recent years been largely discredited. This would change that.

In his office Herlicher leaned back in his chair, then glanced at the wall where the window should have been, if only he were ranked more highly on the organizational chart. The old League of Nations had constructed the Palais des Nations in the 1930s. The imposing structure had been assumed by the United Nations after the Second World War and was now the European center for that international body. Some 1,600 employees filed into the enormous edifice each day. The building itself was situated in lovely Ariana Park and overlooked Lake Geneva with a magnificent view of the French Alps, neither of which Herlicher could see from his small office.

Should this report not live up to his admittedly high expectations, his plan was to return to the EU, hopefully in a slot above the evil woman he'd left behind. One of the men to help him with that transition was Walthrop, which was why the e-mail had been so difficult. Never before had words on a computer screen seared him with such force.

Herlicher finished his after-lunch coffee and reread the report once again. It summarized the facts leading to the conclusion. He'd asked Walthrop, confidentially, to run through it and let him know if he'd overlooked any aspect his final report ought to address. He'd been intending to curry favor with the man by giving him an advance peek but his effort had the opposite effect.

His first reaction to the e-mail had been to ask himself how the man could have misread his report so badly. Still, cautious as ever, Herlicher had gone to his "Sent" folder and clicked on the attachment to confirm what he'd sent. Perhaps he'd linked to some early draft or even a different report altogether. Something.

And then he'd seen it. In utter and total disbelief he'd stared at the report he'd sent. In shock, he'd printed the thing out and was now holding it in his hand. It wasn't the report he'd written. It wasn't the report he'd attached and sent!

A wave of paranoia swept over him. His immediate thought wasn't "How could this happen," but rather "Who was doing this to me?" And why? What possible purpose could this serve?

He'd immediately sent Walthrop an explanation but realized how futile it sounded. Someone had entered his computer, bypassing all security, and cleverly altered his words so that the report said the exact opposite of what he'd written. It was incredible. Herlicher struggled to gather his wits as he reconsidered the situation. Who would believe such a story? It was his report, sent from his office, from his computer. How could anyone tamper with it? And if it had been altered, why had he sent it in the first place? That would be the question.

Still, what else could he say? It was the truth. Someone had found a way to change his report. He didn't know how, or when, but *someone* had done it. He followed up by calling Walthrop repeatedly, but either the man was not in his office or he was refusing to pick up his telephone.

Herlicher sat in despair. He wondered if in a moment of insanity he'd really written it that way and now had no memory of the act. Perhaps in some kind of psychotic, self-destructive trance he'd made the changes. He struggled with the thought, earnestly trying to conjure a memory, anything that would suggest such an explanation. There was none.

Iran was poised to detonate a nuclear bomb in less than three weeks. That was the point of the report. That was what he'd written. There'd been no reason, no possible motivation, for him to have written anything else. He had no opinion on the subject, no reason at all for the report to say one thing rather than another. But the report now said there was no evidence to suggest Iran was about to do any such thing.

Herlicher went carefully through the printed report, making a point to highlight every change. When he finished he was surprised there were so few, no more than a dozen words spread throughout, two short sentences rewritten, then the new concluding paragraph. How long would something like that take? Given their totality it didn't seem possible anyone could have done it quickly.

He rose, instinctively straightening his tie as he did, and paced as he thought this through. Could he be actually suffering some kind of breakdown and not realize it? He'd read once that the deeply mentally ill had no idea they were deranged.

Was he crazy? *Ausgeflippt.* That was the German word for it. His mother had once mentioned one of her uncles in that way but he'd been under the impression the man's aberrations were a consequence of the war and his years in a Russian POW camp. Now Herlicher considered that perhaps that was what she'd wanted him to think. He could recall no other instance of mental illness in his family. Of course, his mother could have been lying.

Herlicher glanced at his door quickly. No one was there. Maybe someone had come into his office and made the change. He locked the door at night as instructed but he wasn't the only one with a key, and to be frank, sometimes he forgot.

Still . . . someone wanted him to look bad. That was the most likely answer. *Who could that be?* Though he'd been very careful during his time in Geneva there were always enemies, those who disliked him personally, those who sabotaged a colleague for fun, those with an agenda. And there was always the latent hostility toward all Germans you saw throughout Europe. No, any list would be very long and he was sure to omit someone.

Three others had keys officially but how could he know for certain where it ended? He was not the only one ever assigned to this office. They might have kept the key. That's what he would have done. Then there was the cleaning staff. Not all of them were Swiss. Some were Italians.

Then he recalled that he was supposed to lock his computer screen whenever he left his desk, but he rarely did so and it locked automatically after being idle for fifteen minutes anyway. The only way someone could have altered his report was to slip into his office while he was away and *before* the computer went into default mode and required the password.

Herlicher strained to recall the events leading up to the e-mail. What had he done? Had he left the office long enough for someone to make changes? He wiped his brow with his pristine handkerchief.

Now he had it. He'd left his office to use the restroom. He'd finished the final draft and decided to take a break before composing the e-mail to

Walthrop. He left the office and passed . . . Carlos Estancia, his supervisor. Why didn't he think of that immediately? It was so obvious. The man didn't like him. How many times and in how many ways had he shown that? But had Estancia popped into his office during the time Herlicher had been gone and quickly altered the report?

How long *had* he been gone? Herlicher considered it and was crestfallen at his conclusion. Five minutes. No more. That was simply not enough time for anyone to make the subtle changes in the report. And on reflection, the extent and quality of the alterations were certainly beyond Estancia's ability. The man was a moron.

Suddenly Herlicher collapsed in his chair. Now he remembered. He'd performed a final copy edit, then had sent at once. There had been no delay.

There'd been no time for anyone to sabotage his report. None. *Maybe, maybe, I really am losing my mind.*

4

LONDON, UK
WHITEHALL
FOREIGN AND COMMONWEALTH OFFICE
RESEARCH GROUP FOR FAR EAST AFFAIRS
5:33 P.M. GMT

Lloyd Walthrop was still angry with Herlicher. The man had called and left a voice mail and now had sent by e-mail an explanation Walthrop refused to read. The German was a cretin. Walthrop had always taken him to be a weasel but until now he'd assumed the man would deal with him honestly, at least until it was in his interest not to.

He'd first met Herlicher the previous year at a Madrid conference on the state of the Iranian economy. It was an area of official mutual concern. At the time he'd seemed a mild-mannered, if a bit paranoid, German bureaucrat. The only thing notable about him was that he worked for UNOG in Geneva. Even that wasn't especially significant until he'd let drop that his primary duties were with the UN Office for Disarmament Affairs and that he served on the committee tasked with producing any United Nations' status reports and recommendation on Iran's nuclear program. That had caught Walthrop's attention, as he assumed it was meant to.

Walthrop had been pleased at the contact. Since then, they'd exchanged e-mails and reports but in recent weeks he'd impatiently waited for a new nuclear report. Herlicher had been assigned its actual writing and that struck Walthrop as a coup for himself.

Though officially assigned to the Foreign Office, the key aspect of Walthrop's job was to gather intelligence from the various branches of the UK government and to funnel it to those who needed to know. Occasionally he acquired an interesting tidbit from an EU source and when he did, that was so much frosting on the cake. Unofficially, he'd been asked to pay special attention to the imminent UN report on Iran.

According to his sources, the situation there was coming to a head. More than one national intelligence agency was reporting that detonation of an atomic device in the Iranian desert was forthcoming. There was serious talk of meaningful international action. Iran had flaunted the UN inspectors and sidestepped sanctions for too long. His reading of the current state of the world was much as it had been just prior to Operation Iraqi Freedom and Operation Desert Storm before it: Something was going to happen.

Some of what Walthrop did was presented officially, though confidentially, but the greater part found its way to the necessary hands through informal back channels. From time to time he was called on to brief leaders in Parliament and the office of the prime minister. It had long been this way in British intelligence. He'd attended the right schools, knew the right sorts, and over the decades had demonstrated his loyalty and judgment. Outside certain circles he was unknown, and he very much preferred it that way.

He'd wondered at first if Herlicher had known his true position in the UK government but over the following months realized he did not. He'd targeted Walthrop for no other reason than he worked in the Foreign Office. But once Walthrop had indicated an interest in the German's work, the two had formed the sort of bond that existed between colleagues possessed with mutual needs. The Brit wanted to know what UNOG was going to report before it became common knowledge while the German was looking for a leg up in Brussels. One hand washed the other.

Walthrop turned back to the foolscap on his desk and reworked his report with a pencil. He knew it was all quaint, very archaic; his assistant chided him about it from time to time, but he simply couldn't think straight on one of those computers. He detested the things—and he didn't trust them. After all, the things were now connected, like so many tunnels from house to house, and the so-called firewalls and other security measures built in or installed failed to work with depressing regularity.

Not that Walthrop wasn't a man of the twenty-first century. He preferred travel by jet to the alternative and in the last year had developed an appreciation for video conferencing. He couldn't help wondering about the security of it all but was assured there was no issue and he was careful with what he said.

Still, all those bits and pieces of electronic data out there somewhere was troubling. Better if important information was set down to paper and locked away with a trusty guard outside. Walthrop didn't think of this as old-fashioned, rather as just so much common sense, though he had to admit there seemed a dearth of that in recent years.

One evening he'd expressed, once again, his dislike of computers. His wife had pointed out that his voice was carried by telephone with electronic pulses, that a telly was nothing more than a computer screen—to which he allowed that explained a great deal to his way of thinking. Why his war with the PC? she asked.

He'd explained it to her again. He knew his protestations sounded silly when uttered but there it was.

And, of course, there was another issue. What he wouldn't acknowledge to her was that he didn't type all that well. He'd only learned at university and had never been very good at it. The computer only made things worse by pointing out an endless stream of mistyped words and questionable use of grammar. He preferred to write his letters and reports out in longhand then transfer them by typing into his computer. It wasn't perfect, it was very slow, but his wasn't a fast occupation.

Whatever his reasons he was never entirely comfortable with computers. More than once when he'd opened an interesting attachment he'd inadvertently downloaded a virus. It had happened often enough for his lack of computer prowess to become a subject in the greater office. In fact, he'd had a bit of trouble with Herlicher's attachment as he recalled.

Earlier that day when it arrived he'd glanced at the subject line and felt a wave of satisfaction. At last! He clicked on the attachment, but instead of opening the file he saw the following:

OfficeWorks has stopped working.
A problem caused the program to stop working correctly.
Windows will close the program and notify
you if a solution is available.

Below the message was a button that read, "Close program."

Now what is this? he'd thought. Why would he want to close the program? And just how did Windows expect to get back to him? This was one of those questions he never got an answer to. And if Windows, whatever that was, could get back to him about this problem that meant Windows, or whoever controlled it, knew what was taking place in his computer. That was exactly what he was talking about.

OfficeWorks sounded familiar. He considered that a moment then, slightly embarrassed, realized it was the name of the office word processing program his division used. The bright kids from IT had assured him that almost everyone in the world used it. It was the best there was.

If it was so good, Walthrop thought, *why did it stop working?*

He closed his e-mail program. He'd learned that starting it up again usually fixed any problem he ran into. Then he'd gone to Herlicher's e-mail and double-clicked on the report. This time it opened without a problem. That was more like it.

He now realized that his response to Herlicher the moment he'd finished reading the report had been an indulgence. He'd been needlessly harsh and berated himself for it. The man might be a suspicious fool but he had his uses and now he'd cut him off as a source.

Of course, he'd misled Walthrop badly, and the Brit had made the mistake of confiding his expectations about the results of the pending report to the foreign secretary. Now his professional reputation, or at least his judgment, was at risk. Just the day before Walthrop had received a note reminding him to make available the advance copy of the UNOG report.

He should never have confided his expectations and with that realization he understood the true object of his anger: himself. He shook his head in wonder. Here he was at fifty-two years of age, and still relearning the lessons he'd thought he'd absorbed decades earlier.

It was, Walthrop decided, the excitement that had been the cause. He'd been eager from the moment when he realized he was being provided with an advance look at the imminent ODA Iran report. This was one of those tidbits for which he was famous within his circles. He'd let pride govern his actions.

Not that the UK government ministries gave the United Nations much credence. It had done nothing to stop the spread of nuclear weapons and technology and wasn't likely to in the future. But when the UN, of all organizations, condemned Iran by stating categorically that it was about to detonate a nuclear bomb he believed that would finally compel military action. At long last, the United States, Britain, and France were prepared to initiate a military strike to prevent a nuclear test and to cripple the Iranian nuclear program.

As Walthrop understood it, Iran had scheduled detonation of its first atomic bomb for April 26. The essential fuel to make the bomb possible would be processed and ready about ten days earlier. The UNOG report, Herlicher had told him, was due to be released on April 13. That would give the world powers just three days before the enriched uranium was ready, or thirteen days to disrupt the testing site if that was the plan. These were very short timeframes but for such a vital issue they were entirely feasible. Now what had looked like a near certainty was all at risk because the ODA had buckled at the knees. That was the only explanation he could see.

The thought of Iran with a nuclear bomb scared the daylights out of Walthrop. Ever since the Shah was replaced by fanatical clerics, Iran had been the primary source of financial support to Muslim terrorists the world over. The ongoing conflicts in the Middle East were primarily caused by Iran, which supported both Hamas and Hezbollah. Certainly, Israel did little to help herself but it was Iran constantly tossing petrol on the fire.

Supporting such terrorist organizations with state income was Iranian policy. As long as the mullahs held control of that vast nation with its enormous oil wealth, worldwide jihad would continue. And there were times when Walthrop was persuaded that he was one of the few in the Foreign Office who truly appreciated the inevitable consequences.

Once Iranians had the Bomb, Walthrop had no doubt they'd place it in the hands of nut jobs willing to use it. And if his colleagues in the government took any comfort at all from the thought that Iran would stop with bombing Tel Aviv and that the destruction of Israel would bring an end to this madness they were very much mistaken in his view.

Because Walthrop had not the slightest doubt that the second major city on that list was London itself.

He just couldn't believe that the UN was once again going to back away from the self-evident. Last week when he'd encountered Herlicher in the lobby of the UN building in New York, the German had confided that UNOG had received material from a highly placed source in Iran and that the report he was authoring would give a detonation date and recommend immediate action. Then he'd sent this monstrosity to him instead. More of the same endless dribble. What use was the man? What use, for that matter, was the United Nations?

Walthrop glanced at his e-mail and briefly considered opening Herlicher's new message. His telephone had rung three times since he'd replied to the report and he'd not picked up, letting it roll over to voice mail. The German had nothing to say he wanted to hear.

Walthrop sighed. It wasn't the end of the world—at least, not yet.

5

WASHINGTON, D.C.
GEORGETOWN
K STREET NW
3:21 P.M. EST

Jeff Aiken stared at the computer screen as he eased back in his chair. Outside, a gray rain fell as it had all day, the streets dark and slick. He'd returned from Atlanta the night before, preferring the comfort of his home to another night in a sterile hotel, and had worked remotely, running the final tests of his fix.

His financial sector client was a household name in the southern states. Malware had been detected by its in-house IT staff during a routine scan of the outbound network traffic from the servers. It had identified bursts of data directed at IP addresses somewhere in Russia. They had been unable to determine the origin of the traffic so Jeff had been summoned.

He'd spent three days in Atlanta. There he'd made a virtual copy of the server using a tool that took a "live" system and produced an image of it. With his forensic tools he located a rootkit-based virus. Rootkit was an increasingly common and very troublesome technique for cloaking viruses from standard detection. They were increasingly popular with malware writers. It had been their prevalence in the attack code two years before that had made the Al-Qaeda viruses so difficult to identify.

During his forensic investigation Jeff determined that the virus propagated from system to system employing a vulnerability, ironically in one of the major security suites, another household name, this one worldwide. He established that it was installed in all his client's systems. The IT department had discovered the hole and patched it pretty quickly but, as was the case for most corporate IT staffs, they'd held off installing the patch to make certain it wouldn't cause problems on their servers. The uninterrupted performance of the Web site and database was nearly always considered to be most critical. It was during that delay they'd been infected.

The good news was that the virus was a generic botnet host, not one of the newer, far more sophisticated versions designed to target the company specifically. It was the kind of broad digital aggressor every company encountered from time to time. They'd dodged a bullet because if a virus specifically targeted at them had penetrated their system, it would have caused financial havoc on the company's customer accounts.

Once he grasped the nature and extent of the infection Jeff had recommended that they utilize the best-case solution, which was to "repave" their system. This meant reinstalling the operating system and server applications, then restoring all the data from the uninfected backups. The CEO had balked at the downtime this would entail, calculating it would be both disruptive and expensive. Instead, Jeff had been told to cleanse the system.

Though faster and cheaper, this was the least certain approach. The enormous size and complexity of the system meant there were countless digital holes in which malware might lurk. Jeff could never be certain he'd cleaned everything. But he understood the practicalities of a functioning business; this was not a laboratory situation. And he understood that taking the system down to rebuild it would have created significant issues of trust and reliability with the company's clients.

No antivirus signatures had been established for the virus as yet. This was how the usual antivirus programs uncovered malware. As a consequence, Jeff had to do it for himself by defining a series of steps to purge the virus from the system. This malware-cleaning solution then became a script that the company could run on their live server. It would seek out the tentacles of the virus and surgically sever them, deleting its files after the malware had been immobilized.

He'd alerted his contacts in the antivirus security industry to the new virus and made his fix available once he'd developed it. His connections were extensive and he was widely respected in his field because of his work to advance the state of antivirus research and in creating effective countermeasures.

Jeff had run a test of his solution before leaving Atlanta and it checked out. He'd then left the system to the IT staff while he flew home. He'd just spent the day remotely running additional tests, really for his own peace of mind. It all looked good, but as he'd tried to explain, this approach always left bits and pieces of the virus behind like so much clutter scattered across a factory floor or piled in corners. Generally that was no problem, but do it often enough and you slowly contaminated the operating system in subtle ways that adversely effected its efficiency and security. Well, they'd been warned.

In the quiet of his house he heard a car drive by, its tires splashing as it passed through standing water. Finished, Jeff disconnected from the Atlanta system, then opened his accounting spreadsheet to calculate the bill.

Daryl was away—again. Since the events of two years before when they'd nearly been killed obtaining the codes needed to partially counter the force of a cyber-attack on the West by Al Qaeda, they'd been a committed couple. She'd resigned as director of US-CERT Security Operations located at Arlington, Virginia, and joined him in his private IT security company, Red Zoya Systems LP. The name was a takeoff on the zero day applications that had made the Al Qaeda attack so frightening.

Though neither of their names had surfaced in the media after blunting the Al Qaeda attack, within certain circles they were superstars. Word of their exploits, both accurate and wildly exaggerated, had spread throughout the cyber-security industry. The result was more work than they could comfortably manage.

Their fees continued to pile up in the bank as neither of them had the time to spend their income. They worked out of their Georgetown Redstone town house, though; on any given day one or both of them were out of the city or country on a project. They stayed in touch remotely, but the work tended to be all-consuming. Partly it was their nature, but it was primarily the demands that came with the job. By the time they were summoned the situation was always critical.

One snowy Sunday Jeff had contemplated just how many days they'd spent apart. He'd pulled out his calendar and made a dismal discovery that only confirmed what he suspected. In the last eighteen months, since they'd been set up here and been fully available for work, he and Daryl had spent a grand total of twenty-three days together. And on most of those days one or both of them had worked. He did not include one frenzied three-month period when they had largely worked from the office together on a special project as there'd been little interaction between them except as related to the job at hand.

He'd pointed this out to Daryl while she'd hurriedly packed for her next trip and she'd assured him they'd do something about it, that she *wanted* to do something about it—just as soon as she got back. That had been three weeks ago.

Jeff finished the tabulation, saved the file, then locked the screen with a sigh. This was no way to run a relationship. He sometimes wondered why he even bothered. Given the reality of their situation, he could only see one outcome.

Just then his telephone rang. He glanced at the number as he answered. London calling.

6

Ahmed Hossein al-Rashid left class ahead of the pack, stepped outside the building, and drew a deep breath. The wind flowed down the Vltava River valley, bringing with it the floral fragrance of the countryside. It was spring but there was still a hint of lingering winter in the air. The other students streamed about him, laughing, talking, smoking. He pulled a pack of Marlboro cigarettes from his pocket, turned his back to the wind, then lit up with a Zippo lighter.

Thirty-eight years old that month, with olive skin, thick black hair and mustache, he was a physically fit man who worked to stay that way despite his love of American cigarettes.

He liked Prague. Though a European capital, with the narrow, winding streets of the Old City and the ornate coffee shops rich with their pungent aroma, it reminded him of home. Of course, in most ways it was very different. The Czechs were a cold people, not especially friendly to outsiders. No wonder the Slovaks had broken away at the first opportunity.

Prague was, for all its appeal, a superb example of the decline of the West. The Czechs had given up having children, for one. If it weren't for immigrants like himself the population would be falling. Then who would there be to tax and pay for the lavish social programs and early retirement every Czech expected as a right of birth? And for all the churches that dotted the city, the Czechs were an atheist people—which in his view was even worse than the polytheism of most Westerners.

But his primary complaint was that he missed his own culture, the intimacy of his extended family. There were in Prague nearly 300,000 illegals.

With a population of just over one million it was impossible to move about without spotting someone from another country. There were, however, no more than two hundred Iranians in the city and Ahmed spent little time among them. Many had a connection to the long-deposed Shah and his regime, and Ahmed had no wish to be involved with them or Iranian politics.

An attractive blue-eyed, blond Czech, a student in his class, smiled at Ahmed as she passed. He could not recall her name but would make a point to sit with her next time. Some of these Czech girls liked a fling with a darker-skinned, exotic man from the Middle East. He was glad to play his part, though he had to be careful Saliha didn't find out. He needed to stay on her good side and she didn't like his roving eye one bit. Their relationship had cooled in recent months, though she was no less possessive.

Ahmed set out for his apartment, which was in a less desirable, but cheaper, part of the city. Forty minutes later the concierge nodded as he entered his building. A fat man with beady eyes, he rarely shaved or bathed. Ahmed had heard he was Hungarian, though he suspected he was actually a gypsy. He mounted the narrow stairs two at a time to the third floor. He unlocked the door, entered, closed it behind him.

Tossing his backpack on the coach, he opened the netbook on the table in front of the room's only window as he lit another cigarette. He checked for messages and there it was. He downloaded the attachment directly onto a new key-ring thumb drive, deleted the message, then for a few minutes scanned news from home.

Ahmed glanced at his watch, closed the netbook, then quickly made the bed. Saliha was due any minute and she hated dirty sheets, often sniffing at them as if she could detect the odor of another woman. Perhaps she could, if he'd be so foolish as to bring one here.

He'd just finished when he heard the door open.

DAY TWO

FRIDAY, APRIL 10

GLOBAL COMPUTER NEWS SERVICE

CYBERWARFARE'S PEARL HARBOR

By Alice Payton 04/10 11:50 AM EST Updated 1:45 PM EST

TORONTO, Canada—The mysterious computer worm known as Stuxnet is the malware equivalent to a digital preemptive attack, an increasing number of virus experts say. When first detected in July 2010, it was found to possess the potential to bring industrial society as we know it to a grinding halt. The self-replicating worm has been described as a stealth cyber drone, which seeks out a specific function of industrial software then seizes control. The bit it hunts for is embedded in the programmable-logic controllers, or PLCs, of Siemens programs. No larger than a pack of cards, PLCs tell switches when to switch, make machines turn off or on, and regulate the flow of liquids. In short, PLCs dictate the manual operation of the machinery we depend on. "Once you control the PLCs you are in charge," says Eugene Atwood, CEO of Digital Activation, Unlimited, in Toronto, Ontario.

Stuxnet is the largest virus ever unleashed and is also the most sophisticated. It gains access through thumb drives and once within a computer immediately conceals itself. Thereafter it seeks out the exact PLCs it wants, duplicating itself along the way. If it meets a dead end the worm simply sits there and does nothing but take up space. When it finds what it seeks it takes over. It is now believed to have been targeting the Iranian nuclear program from the start and is thought to be responsible for all but bringing that program to a standstill. Several Iranian scientists have reportedly been executed in the false belief they sabotaged the program.

"It is devilishly clever and fiendishly contrived," Atwood says. Stuxnet has steadily destroyed Iran's uranium enrichment effort, along the way infecting perhaps every one of the tens of thousands of computers initially employed in the program. No one knows the author of Stuxnet. Suspicion has been directed at the Israeli Mossad but some experts claim the CIA Cyberterrorism department may have played a key role. "It avoids collateral damage," Atwood said, "almost as if it was written with a lawyer looking over the designers' shoulders."

"The secrecy associated with Stuxnet is astonishing," said one expert, speaking on background. "This is especially so when you consider that key aspects of

Stuxnet were certainly farmed out to private security experts. Even they didn't know they were working on this project." He went on to say that a third rendition of Stuxnet is believed in certain circles to be under development. "If Stuxnet was Pearl Harbor, this next version will be Hiroshima," he said. "Iran is working against time to get its nuclear bomb detonated and the clock is running out."

Regardless of its origin, or whether or not Iran will ever effectively counter it, Stuxnet has been a game changer. "We crossed a threshold with it," Atwood says. "Malware and cyberwarfare will never be the same. I shudder to think what the future holds for a world increasingly dependent on computers and the Internet."

7

LONDON, UK
WHITEHALL
FOREIGN AND COMMONWEALTH OFFICE
RESEARCH GROUP FOR FAR EAST AFFAIRS
IT CENTRE
3:14 P.M. GMT

Graham Yates finished a review of the steps he and his team had taken with the infected computer. He straightened in his chair and waited for a response as Lloyd Walthrop looked on.

"Let me review this then," Jeff said, pressing to overcome his jet lag. "Mr. Walthrop received a document, which initially refused to open and crashed the program. That sent you an alert. On his second attempt, the file executed. The incident was so minor he didn't report it."

"That's right," Yates said. He was in his forties, trim, and dressed in the blue pinstripe suit so common to UK government offices. "We noted it, however. We've become very proactive in dealing with such events. Like any system that interacts minute to minute through the Internet, we've had problems with attempts to implant malware and have been the recipients of 'spear phishing' directed at targeted individuals."

Jeff had dealt with spear phishing before. It was a technique for spreading malware intended to steal sensitive information. After the recipients opened an infected document, it sought to trick them into disclosing usernames, passwords, and financial information. It did this by masquerading as something trustworthy the target dealt with frequently. It could be an e-mail or instant message. It often directed users to enter details at a fake Web site that looked and felt as if it were legitimate.

Yates continued, "We think, or strongly suspect, something's there.

Whatever it is has a bug that caused our monitoring of OfficeWorks to alert us to its presence." He cleared his throat. "This is potentially out of our depth. You are an acknowledged expert in this field and are generally familiar with our system. I should be asking if you've encountered contaminated OfficeWorks document files previously."

"Not long ago malicious PDFs were used to attack both Google and Adobe utilizing vulnerabilities and flaws in Adobe's Reader software," Jeff said. "Another, known as Operation Aurora, targeted Google's intellectual property. It's one of the reasons Google had so many issues with their presence in China. The Chinese have an ongoing army cyber warfare operation and Google is apparently a major target. RSA, the gold standard in digital cryptography with presumably the finest security in the world, was the victim of an Advanced Persistent Threat attack, which breached its security and stole very valuable authentication technology. It all but certainly was Chinese in origin.

"OfficeWorks is nearly universal. It's the most commonly used word-processing program in the world. The recent version is as bug free as anything anywhere. I've not heard of any significant problems with it recently. Is this attack restricted to Mr. Walthrop?"

"There have been no other incidents. We've initiated manual inspection of key servers to look for suspicious activity on the systems or in our network activity without finding anything. We know that hacking techniques are sophisticated enough now to hide in the noise, so to speak, making them very hard to discover."

Jeff suppressed a yawn. It had been a long sixteen hours since receiving the telephone call summoning him to London. He had called Daryl to tell her about the assignment. With a sinking heart he couldn't help but notice how distracted she was by her project when they spoke. It had been in that mood he'd hurriedly packed.

Since losing his fiancée in the World Trade Center attack, Jeff had initially found it impossible to move on emotionally. Only much later, when circumstances had put him together with Daryl, had he awakened. Their frantic chase to stop the Al Qaeda cyber-attack, putting their lives at risk in the process, had served to bond them in a remarkable way. The early months of physical recovery from their wounds, of buying the town house together and joining forces professionally had been as wonderful and satisfying as any he'd ever known, the ideal joining of a personal and professional life.

In this war Jeff and Daryl were one team in a million. Jeff was in his midthirties and though he spent most of his time in front of a computer, he'd played rugby at the University of Michigan and still ran almost daily when possible. After university, where he'd obtained his doctorate, he'd taught at Carnegie Mellon, then gone to work for the Cyber Security Division of the CIA. Since 2002, he'd had his own security company.

He'd first met Daryl Haugen when she'd been with the National Security Agency, then assistant deputy executive director and head of a team at US-CERT working for the National Security Agency, or NSA. Also a Ph.D., she was a year younger than Jeff, just over average height, slender, with a fair complexion and blond, shoulder-length hair.

When he and Daryl had been brought together two years ago in their pursuit of an Al Qaeda plot to inflect massive damage to computers and the Internet in the Western world their romance had begun. Jeff had not believed he could love again but there it was, as rich, as deep, as fulfilling as before.

Jeff had rushed to reach Dulles in time for a direct red-eye flight. On the plane he'd done what research was possible on the Internet, then slept fitfully, his thoughts turning repeatedly to Daryl. Was it real? Had it ever been? Did she really feel for him what he felt for her? Or was she going to leave him? Finally, he'd escaped from his thoughts into a restless slumber.

He'd arrived in London at noon local time, been ushered immediately through immigration and customs, then driven to Whitehall where he'd been greeted by Yates. Jeff had worked with Yates before, when Jeff had been with the CIA. The UK had its own spy agency, GCHQ, which increasingly specialized in cyber operations, but their inability to match industry salaries left them short-staffed, forcing government agencies to frequently bring in outside consultants. Though there were any number of experts in malware, few carried Jeff's security clearance. For those reasons he'd been summoned to London earlier in the year to deal with a complex infection of a portion of their network. That one turned out to be part of a generic botnet. Yates primarily maintained the intraoffice IT system and had very limited experience with viruses, other than in working to keep them out. His concern was not so much the file in question but the integrity of the system overall. He and his team could very quickly find themselves lost if they tried to tackle virus code itself and it turned out to be something serious. And there'd been enough significant problems in recent years to require that experts be brought in at the first sign of any new malware attack. It was simply too dangerous to allow new code to infect an entire system.

"Unless there is more, I should get started," Jeff said.

"By all means," Yates said, glancing at Walthrop, who nodded. "We've moved Mr. Walthrop's computer into a free office where you can work undisturbed. This way."

Not surprisingly the office was in the basement. Though it made no sense to place IT in desirable offices with expansive views, a window would have been a pleasant change, just once.

A man of about thirty was waiting inside. He extended his hand and introduced himself. "I'm Elliot Blake," he said. "I've been the one on this bug. I know you by reputation and am delighted at the prospect of working with you. I have a great deal to learn."

"Elliot's my best man," Yates said. "It was he who alerted me to this and advised against chasing it ourselves. I'll leave you to it. Don't hesitate if you require any services, any at all. Elliot can always reach me in seconds. It's good to see you again." With that and a light pat on Jeff's back for luck, he left them alone.

Blake was a slender man with black hair and glasses. After pointing Jeff to the coffee, teapot, and biscuits he dived in. "We've got the latest version of OfficeWorks and we update as a matter of routine. Until now we've had no difficulty with it. I'm assuming Mr. Yates briefed you?"

Jeff nodded.

"So here it is from my end. None of Mr. Walthrop's files are corrupted that we can detect. We're told the contents of the document he received from the UN office in Geneva are reported as *altered*." At this Blake made a face as if he had no idea what to believe. "I checked the digital signature and that just doesn't hold up. It's the one affixed in Geneva by the author. So I'd say the bloke in Geneva is lying. I ran the usual antivirus scans and came up with nothing. I even ran one for rootkits with no luck."

Digital signatures could not be altered. Period. Invented in the late 1970s, they rely on asymmetric cryptography. In cryptography, a secret code called a key is used to encrypt and decrypt messages, much like how secret decoder rings work. With asymmetric cryptography, a user has two keys that work in conjunction. A message encrypted with one key can decrypt a message encrypted by the other and vice versa. However, a message can't be decrypted with the same key used to encrypt it. With this scheme, a user can freely distribute one of the keys to enable others to send them encrypted messages that can't be decrypted by anyone else. The key kept secret is called a private key and the one given out is a public key, as if many decoder rings were able to encrypt messages but only one special decoder ring could decode them.

When used for digital signing, the signer uses a hashing algorithm to produce a shortened version of the message—essentially a unique summary—they wish to sign, and then encrypts the hash with their private key. This encrypted hash is the message's digital signature because it's a way for a user to digitally confirm that the message is authentic. Checking to see if a message is actually the one that the sender signed requires simply regenerating the hash of the received message and seeing if it matches the one obtained from decrypting the digital signature. Any alteration of the message, no matter how small, results in a mismatch. The security of the scheme is assured by the infeasibility of determining the private key from a public key by even the most powerful modern computers.

Increasingly, governments relied on digital signature software to protect the authenticity of documents and in many cases refused to accept attachments not digitally signed. It was the system by which everyone knew a document was genuine. So it seemed the man in Geneva must be lying.

"We make every effort to determine the cause of any crash rather than take chances. We've found no evidence of a virus in fact." Blake cleared his throat. "As I understand the process from this point on, to determine if the file is infected I have to trace data from the point of the crash, through God knows how many paths, each one potentially being the source of the vulnerability. Have I got that right?" Jeff nodded. "I've never done that before so you can see my problem. We want you to determine if there is a virus and if so, find out as much about it as you can, including who made it and what it's up to."

A corrupted file can be spotted, usually quite easily since it's visibly different. But an *infected* file was not necessary outwardly corrupt. It could look and behave in a perfectly normal fashion. Jeff asked which antivirus programs he'd run and Blake provided the names of the five most commonly used.

"You did right," Jeff said. "If this document is infected you could have a virus spreading throughout your network and exfiltrating data even as we speak." He pulled out his own laptop and looked for a place to put it. "Let's get started. Frankly, I'm dead from the flight but we'll see how much steam I've got left."

Jeff sat before Walthrop's computer and linked to it. Next, Blake stepped him through the document's folder and showed him the problematic file.

Jeff launched a Windows virtual machine on his own laptop to serve as the laboratory and a sandbox in which he could experiment while keeping the virus contained. His first step was to configure the machine to match the characteristics of Walthrop's as closely as he could. He then confirmed that his virtual machine was running the same version of Windows, including the updates. Then he installed OfficeWorks, also making certain it had the same updates as Walthrop's version and configured the program in exactly the same way. Every detail could potentially be significant if the malware was specifically targeted at Walthrop.

With his test environment ready, Jeff copied the infected OfficeWorks document into the virtual machine. He now unleashed a host of automated tools so that they were ready to watch for any sign of compromise. These were scripts, sequences of commands that executed other programs, or were operating system functions, stand-alone programs that picked apart the document searching for anomalies and signs of common attack vectors. In the old days, this had been done manually and the work had been both slow and tedious.

In his laptop's test environment where a potential virus could cause no damage he attempted to open the file. It made no difference if it crashed or not. If it did, then he could begin figuring out how to get OfficeWorks to work; if it didn't, he could skip that step and start figuring out what the virus was ultimately trying to do.

The file failed to open. This might indicate nothing of significance as the program could have a bug that was only indirectly triggered by this particular file. Or the problem could be malware that was trying to burrow into the computer, but had hit something unexpected and failed. That was what Blake and Yates feared. If that was the case, whatever was in there had encountered an environment for which it was not programmed, meaning there was a flaw in the malware's assumptions, causing it not to execute. For now Jeff would act with the assumption he was dealing with malware.

On his laptop were diagnostic programs that were the result of thousands of hours of work. They included the standard diagnostic and recovery tools used by everyone in his profession, but over the years he'd added a collection of very useful utilities. So valuable was the information that it was copied to several DVDs he'd secreted here and there, two of which were in safe deposit boxes. He'd once laughingly told Daryl he was thinking about having them insured.

"Okay," Jeff said, "let's first see if it's a fresh variation of an existing virus."

"Would that be good?" Blake asked.

"Oh yes, I can catch a variation pretty quickly and the fix is often a snap. We'll know soon enough."

New variants were the most common causes of infiltrations. An old virus became increasingly less effective as antivirus programs learned to sniff it out. The next step for the author was to alter it just enough to sneak in under the radar. Thousands of new pieces of malware were unleashed onto the Internet every month and the number was growing. Most were variations and such a variation was the most likely explanation for this problem.

Of course, no virus could actually alter an OW file, not without it looking like gibberish. Jeff didn't want to seriously consider the alternative.

"Elliot, what do you know about the man in Geneva?" he asked while he waited.

"Only what Mr. Walthrop says, which is that he's a civil servant with UNOG. They have a professional association. They both serve on an Iranian economic development committee."

Jeff was inclined to think it most likely the man in Geneva was lying, as the digital signature had not been altered. It was impossible, absolutely impossible, to alter an OW document and not change the signature since it was embedded in the file. It seemed a silly claim for someone to make but he'd seen and heard of much worse from so-called professionals.

He now scanned the registry settings. Most often, malware created new entries there. This told the operating system to activate the virus whenever the computer was turned on, or when the user logged in. He spent some time checking every suspicious program reference or bit of code he didn't recognize. Then he'd locate the code's file and confirm it originated with a company. Malware rarely had such information. In some cases he conducted an Internet search to locate information about the file. Sometimes the suspect file had already been flagged as malware. It was tedious but had to be done.

Jeff was pleased with the level of security he found on the system, though he'd expected nothing less from such a high-priority office. Still, he knew from experience that agencies and businesses that should know better often had appalling computer security. He routinely found antivirus programs that were no longer current. Most of the malware he located had slipped in because someone had left the door open.

The scope of the harm viruses caused was enormous and not generally appreciated by the public. What they saw in their personal lives wasn't the tip of the iceberg, not even the tip of the tip of the iceberg. Compromised government agencies didn't want to reveal the extent of the damage for obvious reasons. It was no different with businesses. Personal and financial data was routinely stolen. Internet crime netted well over $100 billion annually and there was no end in sight. Organized cybercrime operations in Eastern Europe were becoming more sophisticated every month.

The worst part, from Jeff's perspective, was that most individuals and companies had no idea they'd been hacked. Malware was so common he found at least some of it in nearly every computer network he examined. The only good news was that most did not do any great harm. It was obsolete or improperly designed, or cut off from its "bot herder" and left dormant.

Malware found its way into computers through two routes. The recipient inadvertently admitted the virus by opening an attachment or Web link, usually believing it was something it was not. Or the virus prowled the Internet, knocking on the doors of every connected computer, searching for vulnerability in an application or even within the operating system itself. Computers were so complicated any number of such vulnerabilities existed when software was released, whether new or an updated version. As they were discovered, usually because they'd allowed malware in, they were patched and closed. The problem with this approach was that there was always a period between infection and patching when bad things could happen.

Sometime later, Jeff said, "Okay, Elliot, I see nothing known so we can rule out the easiest solution. Whatever you've got is brand-new. Now let's see if we can get the thing to execute."

"You *want* it to work?" Blake said, sounding shocked.

"That way we can examine it for clues as to its origin and purpose," Jeff said. "I'd have a seat; this will take a while."

Once he'd started the process Jeff said, "Okay, it's almost certainly using a zero day vulnerability." Zero day was the term used to identify software bugs for which no fix existed because it had not as yet been discovered. Since a zero day vulnerability wasn't yet known it was the most effective device for spreading malware as any computer with the vulnerability was wide open to cyber-attack.

OfficeWorks had improved its security enormously in recent years and was perhaps the most vetted word-processing program in existence. It was coded and built with the latest defense-in-depth antimalware technologies and only a handful of exploitable vulnerabilities had been discovered in it since the release of the newest versions. It was also designed to isolate any malware into a digital sealed room to prevent contamination elsewhere. But for all its design sophistication and vetting Jeff was not surprised that a zero day vulnerability existed in its latest manifestation. Such programs were so complex with so many authors they were never entirely secure.

Zero day vulnerabilities were a worst-case scenario for those involved in cyber-security. It had been just such vulnerabilities that had made the massive Al Qaeda attack two years before so devastating, even though the efforts of Jeff and Daryl had significantly blunted its intent. Without them the damage, and loss of life, would have been much, much worse.

Jeff rose and poured a large cup of black coffee. He drank half, then placed it down. He set his wristwatch to a two-hour timer. He'd learned the hard way that at least once every two hours he had to stretch and walk about a bit if he was to keep at this. Most problems he solved demanded a single extended engagement typically lasting eighteen hours. At that point his mental acuity declined significantly. He suspected that wasn't going to work in this case, especially as he was already exhausted.

He sat down, took another pull of the black coffee, then loaded Office-Works into a debugger tool. A debugger is a program that enables a developer or, in this case, a security researcher, to control the execution of another program. It could be paused, which made it possible to step through individual CPU processor instructions, and it could be configured to pause when a specific instruction or set of conditions was satisfied. When the program was paused, the debugger enabled Jeff to view its state, including the value of all its variables. In many ways, it was like a dissection kit, letting him peer beneath the surface of the program, both observing and controlling its operation to unearth how it worked. He knew that all sophisticated malware had "anti-debugging" mechanisms, but he also knew how to defeat the most common techniques, including those that tried to prevent debugging in a virtual machine.

Once the debugger was running Jeff opened the suspect document. The debugger reported at once that OfficeWorks would not open; in so doing it accessed an invalid memory address, causing OfficeWorks to crash. So that he could more easily map the execution of the program to that point, he decided to run OfficeWorks under a special version of the debugger obtained from friends at Microsoft. It enabled him to "rewind" the program to earlier points. With this he began to step backward in the program to determine what OfficeWorks flaw the malware intended to exploit. It was as if the virus had been running an obstacle course, surmounting each barrier with ease until it came to the one it could not cross. Jeff's job now was to find that point.

This was one of the more painstaking phases of the overall process, requiring Jeff to type notes recording all the branches the OfficeWorks program followed and the values of the data it passed. He was searching for a spot where, if something was different in one of the values, OfficeWorks would follow a path resulting in a buffer overflow, a condition in which a bug wrote data beyond the region allocated for it. Most malware infections started with just such a buffer overflow, which would cause the program to inadvertently execute code it wasn't programmed for, code controlled by the malware's author.

Always daunting, this time the process was especially difficult and Jeff found himself slowly overwhelmed as the day dragged on. At one point Blake had a light meal brought in, at another he suggested Jeff join him for tea. All very English, Jeff thought, munching on one of the butter cookies they called biscuits.

Throughout the afternoon and into the evening the permutations exploded and the complexity of the paths was nearly more than Jeff could grasp. But at last he located an OfficeWorks execution that accessed data in the suspect document ultimately triggering the invalid access. This, he knew, was the malware's entry point, but there had been something about Walthrop's environment that foiled it. If things had been as the author wanted this would have executed the OW document.

He'd suggested to Daryl at one point that afternoon that he might need her help and she'd assured him that she'd have the time. Despite her evident distraction during their brief conversation she said she was down to the final stages with her project and would be leaving shortly. Hoping she was free and home by now he sent her a message on mIRC, an encrypted chatting program used when they worked together remotely. He briefly summarized the issue and informed her that he'd found the entry point.

"Here's the malicious data sequence," he finished. "See what you can come up with." The code within a virus often contained hints as to its origin, sometimes even about its author. Carelessness and vanity were two of their most powerful assets with any new virus.

A few minutes later her reply arrived. "Back home. Will see what I can do. Luv u."

Now Jeff used the debugger to change the value at the point where OfficeWorks referenced it to the value that would allow OfficeWorks to execute the buffer overflow as the virus was intended to do.

It worked.

He watched the malware expand and decrypt itself into the memory of OfficeWorks and then activate. This part of his job was typically satisfying since it usually meant the beginning of the end, the time when he'd find a solution.

But there was more to it than that. There was something fascinatingly malevolent about a virus as it revealed itself, like a cancer spread through an otherwise healthy system. It modified everything it wanted to control, even bits of code for which it had no use. It was arrogant and self-possessing. It was, Jeff often thought, almost alive.

This was where he'd see the anti-debugging techniques. If one was in play in the execution of a CPU instruction it would behave differently than usual. Another common tell was the execution of a long string of useless instructions, one that it would take days to step through the sequence. Such a sequence was integral to the malware's correct operation. Jeff had so much experience he knew how to spot these sequences and set "conditional breakpoints" that halted execution at key points, including one close to where the sequence was set to finish.

This virus installed itself in the memory of the OfficeWorks process, then reached out and inserted itself into a critical system process, one that kept Windows alive, performing background operations on behalf of the operating system and other processes. If things had been as the author wanted, the virus would now be in position to execute within OfficeWorks. He watched as it set a timer. That done, it quietly went to sleep.

"It's got a timer," he said to Blake with a smile.

"A timer?" he repeated.

"It set an alarm clock, a timer to activate randomly every twelve to twenty-four hours."

"Why would it do that?"

"Because it's harder to spot when it's asleep. But we're not waiting for it." Jeff overrode the timer and told the virus to wake up now. This allowed him to see what it did.

It was well into the night by now. The corridor outside had been silent for some time. Blake had glanced at his wristwatch repeatedly, finally commenting that the American sure seemed to work long hours. Jeff was exhausted but his breakthrough compelled him to press on. Over the next three hours he monitored the malware's execution using both the debugger and another tool that recorded every change the virus made.

With his monitoring tools Jeff searched for the saved or modified files it created. Seeing none he searched for an update to the registry configuration database, typical alterations done by all malware he'd looked at before. What he found was . . . nothing.

The virus left no tracks.

This came as a great surprise. Though this virus had been cleaner than most he encountered, until this moment he'd had no great respect for the author. The techniques he'd observed had been pioneered by others. But this was impressive. It was as if the malware had walked across virgin snow without leaving a print.

He had known this technique was coming and dreaded the day. Authors of malware knew that rootkit scans were becoming increasingly common and rootkits could no longer be relied on to conceal a virus. With this new technique the author was adopting a fresh, and very effective, method in the never ending race for digital stealth. As it spread, and it surely would, viruses would become increasingly difficult to locate.

This was the first time Jeff had seen it employed. If someone were to analyze the system at the point they'd see no sign of the infection. They'd have to know precisely where in the system process to look for the copy of the malware loaded into memory. That would be like trying to find a book in a major library without the Dewey decimal system.

He told Blake what he'd just discovered.

"You mean it makes no modifications to the system, so it can't be discovered?" Blake said. "I've never heard of such a thing. I didn't even know it was possible. How does it survive a system reboot?"

"This is a form of malware that leaves absolutely no detectable trace of itself when loaded, but for it to maintain its foothold through a shutdown it would have to download itself to a file and register the file to execute at the next reboot. After activating, it would delete the file from disk. That way, it is effectively invisible without resorting to rootkit techniques. Of course, if the system powers off without executing a shutdown, the virus won't survive, but that's a very small risk that the author was apparently willing to take. At least that's what it looks like to me. I'm going to reboot now and see if it actually happens."

Jeff left the monitoring tool running during the shutdown and subsequent reboot. He carefully examined the resulting activity log of the transition until after midnight. It was then he finally found evidence confirming his theory. That was what the virus did. Nasty. He stopped to mull the possibilities.

"Mr. Aiken," Blake said. "You fell asleep."

Jeff jerked his head up. "Sorry." He rubbed his eyes, then said, "Elliott, I need to sleep. Back after a few hours' rest, a shower, and some food. And call me Jeff, will you?"

8

Saliha Kaya stretched naked across the sheet, glanced at Ahmed snoring lightly beside her, then rose and quietly turned on the shower in the cramped bathroom. Once the water was hot she stepped in, luxuriating in the wet warmth. She had no shower in her apartment and took full advantage whenever she spent time here with Ahmed.

Recently turned twenty-eight, she was above average in height and had very long, black hair. Her traditional Turkish figure held more curves than was currently fashionable in magazines, and though attractive she could not be described as a beauty. She had a manner, however, that men found quite appealing.

Saliha was one of six children born to a very poor family in Ankara. Her father had worked in construction while her mother stayed home for the children. To help, she and her daughters made shawls, which she sold at the market. By the time Saliha was ten she could make a shawl blindfolded.

There'd been no money for more than basic school and with so many children Saliha had understood she must fend for herself as soon as she could. She'd waitressed for a time, spurned an offer to become mistress to an older banker, then traveled with a young lover to Prague, for a chance to see the world before it was too late. When their relationship soured and he'd returned to Turkey, she'd stayed on. Her appearance and personable manner had given her work in bars and the trendy clubs, which was where she'd met Ahmed.

She spoke no Farsi and he spoke no Turkish so, as was the case with so many international couples, they conversed in English. She'd once loved her handsome Iranian passionately but the flame of her love was slowly fading. Their time was coming to an end and if she found one more sign he was sleeping with other women she would end it abruptly, no matter how much he paid for her trips.

With the last of the hot water gone, Saliha turned off the faucets, then stepped from the shower and toweled herself carefully. She moved quietly into the single room, sat before an old mirror, and slowly combed out her hair, memories of her childhood flooding back as they always did at such moments. Her grandmother had lived with the family until just before Saliha left home. She'd loved her granddaughter's long silken hair, telling her it was a gift of Allah, one she should always cherish.

Saliha didn't know about God but men certainly liked it and every woman she knew was envious.

Ahmed moved lightly. She glanced at him through the mirror. He was a handsome man, with a fit body. He was quick, smiled easily, and was fun to be with. And there was the powerful physical chemistry between them. Whenever they were together they fell into bed at once. It was as if until after sex they couldn't carry on even a simple conversation. She'd never before experienced anything like it.

Saliha lived in a room in an apartment she shared with three other women who worked at the same club. She'd wanted to move in with Ahmed not long after they met but he'd resisted and now she was glad. It would make ending it much easier.

The question was when.

Her best friend had told her about Ahmed's love of European blonds. Then one of her roommates, Ayten, said that she'd seen him outside a coffee shop with a blonde and there'd been no doubt what was going on between them. Saliha had her own doubts even before hearing from her friends. This latest story was just so much confirmation. She wanted a faithful man. Was that too much to ask?

Then there was this business of Ahmed's. She'd stopped asking about it months before but it still bothered her. He was involved in something mysterious and probably dangerous. Attending college was clearly a cover based on the caution with which he lived. He paid cash for everything. That in itself was not so unusual, as few illegals in Prague had bank accounts, but he was a legal resident student and there was no reason for him not to have an account.

Also, she could never determine just where the cash came from. He received no checks, she was certain. The money just seemed to appear. He was occasionally lavish in his spending and yet he always had enough.

He never spoke on the phone in her presence. And he had at least two phones. With her it was always the same one. Another appeared whenever he was making these mysterious calls. She'd often wondered who he talked to because if he had friends, she'd never met them.

Then there were his mysterious trips. He'd simply leave without a word. Sometimes he was gone no more than two days, sometimes as long as two weeks. When he returned he made no mention of the trip, never brought her a gift. It was as if he'd never been away. It was strange.

At first she'd suspected he was involved with drugs in some way. Not as a dealer, of course, she'd seen no signs of that, and certainly not as a distributor, but . . . somehow. But as she'd come to know him she'd understood the absolute contempt he felt for drugs and drug users. Ahmed might enjoy women but in his own way he was quite puritanical. He didn't attend mosque every Friday but it was a rare month when he didn't go at least once, which was more than Saliha could say.

No, he was involved somehow in the black market. That had to be it. But what? She couldn't decide. Her latest theory was weapons, though she'd seen no sign of them and Ahmed had no gun, of that she was certain.

But she couldn't help wonder what would happen to her if she was ever caught running errands for him. Ahmed had promised that what she did was harmless but he would say that, wouldn't he?

She slowly dressed, watching him as she did. She pulled on her tight slacks, connected her bra behind her back, then slipped on a very tight white blouse. Finally she stepped into the high-heeled boots she enjoyed so much even though she towered over many men, even Ahmed, in them.

She returned to the dresser and idly fingered the key-chain thumb drive, balancing it in her hand as if she could somehow decipher its mysteries. What was on it? She'd never looked. She'd never so much as tried. She'd been concerned there might be some way for Ahmed to tell. He'd warned her that the information could only be accessed with a certain code and he had ways of knowing if she even opened the file. She slipped it into her pocket.

Saliha glanced at the dresser, then placed her hand on the cash. She didn't like it when he paid her like this, after sex. It made her feel like a whore, though the money wasn't for sex and they often slept together when she received no money at all. No, the money was for expenses plus a bit extra to buy things for Ahmed he couldn't get in Prague. She'd get the balance, her fee, when she returned.

With a final glance at Ahmed she let herself out, hearing the door latch behind her. She walked down the stairs, then passed out into the late-afternoon sun under the gaze of the Hungarian. She was used to that. She lightly touched the switchblade knife in her pocket, the one she'd carried since puberty. Just let him ever try and lay a hand on her. She slipped on sunglasses and strolled toward the city center.

DAY THREE

SATURDAY, APRIL 11

CYBER SECURITY NEWS

US DOD PRIME TARGET

By Dietrich Helm

DOD Is the Most Targeted Computer Network on Earth

April 11

Yesterday, Adam F. Dye, the U.S. Deputy Secretary of Defense for Cyber Security, reported that the DOD computer infrastructure is the most attacked digital target on Earth, receiving in excess of 100,000 cyber assaults annually. "I cannot say that we have been entirely successful in blunting all of these attacks," Dye testified.

Dye said that the entire DOD information system had been taken off-line for ten hours last year because of a major penetration. Had this occurred during a time of crisis the American ability to defend itself would have been significantly compromised. "This is the new face of warfare," Dye said.

Last year the U.S. Strategic Command reported there had been some 40,000 successful breaches, not attempts, on the DOD. Indeed, the computers of half of all U.S. government agencies dedicated to national security are known to contain malware.

"We are not winning the cyber war. The best I can say is that it is a stalemate," Dye said.

Congressman Robert Sanchez [D-CA] demanded to know how the most advanced country in the world, with the finest computers and engineers, could be in this state. "It's nothing less than gross incompetence," he said. Sanchez has argued for a significant reduction in the budget for the Department of Defense. "Are you saying we could lose a war without the enemy ever firing a shot?" he asked rhetorically.

Dye asked to conclude his remarks in a closed session.

9

LONDON, UK
WHITEHALL
FOREIGN AND COMMONWEALTH OFFICE
RESEARCH GROUP FOR FAR EAST AFFAIRS
IT CENTRE
1:54 A.M. GMT

Blake led Jeff out of the building with relief, mentioning that he still had a forty-five-minute drive home ahead of him. Meanwhile, Yates had booked Jeff into a boutique hotel just down the street, the Royal Arms, a converted Victorian mansion, which specialized in discretion. As he walked to the hotel, Big Ben pealed just down the river from Whitehall. A light fog drifted through the quiet streets, reminding Jeff of a Sherlock Holmes story.

The events of this last decade had only served to impress upon Jeff the increasing danger of the cyber world. Computers were under relentless and ever more effective attack, if not from some juvenile hacker looking to claim bragging rights, then from Russian mobsters phishing penetrations seeking financial information, Eastern European gangs out to blackmail companies through denial-of-service attacks, or the ongoing Chinese government campaign to gain security access and information in the West.

It was a never-ending battle, one that demanded increasing sophistication and proactive measures to effectively counter. The usual antivirus security companies that provided firewalls and scans were constantly playing catch up as they responded to each new attack only *after* it was launched and discovered. Though doing a reasonably effective job, they were essentially counterpunching. All kinds of malware made it into countless computers before being discovered and before a protective patch was prepared, then distributed. His latest client was just such an example.

Worse, the sophisticated tools needed to create malware were commonly available on the Internet. Any geek with basic malware knowledge could download components and cobble together a virus or Trojan, and many did. And now that criminal bands and certain rogue governments were in the malware business for real, the sophistication of each attack was increasing with each passing month.

There were, in general, three varieties of malware: junk malware like "scareware," malware aimed at stealing money or data to sell, and government espionage including cyber warfare. Such state-directed attacks were ongoing and surprisingly effective.

Valuable data on the U.S. Joint Strike Fighter project, the costliest weapon system ever built, was stolen directly from the Pentagon's computers. The Air Force's air-traffic-control system had been penetrated and the intruders downloaded several terabytes of valuable data related to its electronics and design. The Department of Defense's Secure Internet Protocol Router Network was infected for a time with specially designed software intended to disable the system in time of confrontation or conflict.

In the private sector, the situation was so bad that a major American manufacturer of computers had actually shipped a new product that contained a virus. Infections in iPhones and other cell phones, in every device commonly used in the twenty-first century were increasingly common. Their use for cyber penetration was only a matter of time.

The Royal Arms was nearly beside St. James Park. This part of London was rife with history. He'd like to come here with Daryl someday, when neither of them was on assignment. He wondered if they ever would.

Once in his room Jeff showered then sat in a comfortable chair and despite his exhaustion called Daryl. She sounded glad to hear from him, but then she always did. After he told her what he'd discovered since his e-mail, she briefed him on her examination of the virus code.

"It's tight, as far as I've been able to see to this point. I still have more to do, though," she said.

The heart, the digital soul so to speak, of the Internet and of computers was software code. Code was the magic that made everything work. Code produced the images, the colors, the words, everything.

Just as there were brilliant painters and amateurs, so it was with code writers. Anyone with a modicum of software knowledge could copy, paste, and modify bits of code. Script kiddies did just that, adding little of their own to the work, often surprised when what they'd cobbled together actually did something. Such junk sat in computers all over the world, sometimes clogging them up, often as not doing nothing but taking up space.

Then there was tight code that did what it was meant to do efficiently, cleanly, and with a minimum of space and fuss. Corporations typically produced such code, sometimes government agencies did as well.

Then there was genius code, code so good, so smooth, so effortless, it was like a brilliant work of art. This wasn't *that* good, Daryl told him, but it was very, very good indeed.

When she finished, Jeff said, "The author has really thought this through. When the system shuts down, the virus saves itself to a file with a name identical to one that's part of the primary antivirus suite used by the UK government, just in a different location."

"That's clever of someone," she said. "So if an administrator were to stumble on it and examine its properties they'd see ones that matched those of a legitimate file."

If suspicious, an extra check would typically be to verify the digital signature of the file, tamper-proof evidence that confirmed who it was produced by. However, despite the fact that all Windows components were digitally signed by Microsoft and many software vendors signed their software, the antivirus industry ironically had been slow to adopt the practice. The result was that this second check couldn't be performed in this instance because the author had been clever enough to hide the file in the one place where digital signatures weren't commonly used.

"The guy's pretty sneaky," Daryl said.

Jeff told her that he couldn't think clearly any longer and was going to bed. "Sleep tight," she said. He left a wakeup call for five hours later and was asleep at once. In his dreams he chased pixels across a screen, saw images of streaming code, and engaged in conversations with Yates about their virus that had never taken place. When the telephone rang it was as if he'd never left work, never slept at all, he was so weary. He showered, redressed, ate a continental breakfast, then set out for Whitehall.

The early-spring morning was fresh and invigorating. Big Ben pealed again. A bleary-eyed Blake was already in his office and waiting for him. "You look better than yesterday," he said as he led Jeff into the basement. "I'll let you get to it."

"There's no need for you to keep me company," Jeff said as he set his bag down. "I know where to reach you." Blake left, looking relieved.

Jeff picked up his cell phone and sent Daryl a message to let her know he was working. She came back at once. "Worked all day with no luck." Jeff did a quick mental calculation. It was nearly three in the morning in D.C. "As I told you, this thing is really clean, I mean *really* clean. Now in the chat rooms."

Malware creators often bragged about what they'd launched. There were certain chat rooms frequented by such authors and even if they did no crowing personally, it was not unusual for someone familiar with the new virus to chat about it, and the author. This often led to vital clues as it had before when they'd uncovered the Superphreak virus that led them to the Al Qaeda plot.

For Jeff, it was time to determine what the virus did when it went active. Utilizing his debugger again, Jeff focused on the system process hosting the malware parasite. This was a protracted, exhausting process requiring his full attention on the heavily obfuscated malware code. The author had worked hard at making it difficult to analyze. But after several hours Jeff made a key discovery. Every two or three days, after it awakened from its digital slumber, the virus generated a list of a thousand seemingly random DNS names and reached out onto the Internet. DNS, or Domain Name System, is the convention used to give the actual numeric addresses, like 192.168.122.12, human readable aliases, like www.facebook.com. Individuals and companies purchase names from domain-name registrars around the world and the registrars maintain mappings of names to the numeric addresses, called IP addresses, in databases on the Internet that software can reference to perform name translations.

The virus then worked its way through the list it generated, one at a time, again at random intervals lasting anywhere from ten seconds to one minute. The lack of regularity was designed to cause the queries to blend in with the usual network activity in the log files. In each case it was attempting to connect to a specific DNS. The purpose once there, Jeff knew, was to download instructions as to what the virus should do now that it was in the Walthrop computer with access to his files.

This was a technique the author had borrowed from the infamous Conficker virus that first appeared in late 2008. It was especially crafty since the author had to simply activate one address of the thousand listed at approximately the prescribed time and from it, deliver the instructions to the virus. The timing was structured into the malware system.

Antivirus investigators such as Jeff and Daryl, not to mention traditional law enforcement agencies involved in stopping cybercrime, lacked the resources and time to check the registrant of every possible domain name the malware was employing. Worse, it was easy to obtain a domain name under a fictitious or borrowed identity and most of the randomly generated names were in third-world countries, which lacked legal agreements with the Western nations and typically had few cyber laws.

He forwarded the address generation code to Daryl and asked her to research it for patterns when she had time. Maybe the names weren't as random as they first appeared. It would take hours to devise a way to fool the virus into thinking that the time to generate the domain names had arrived so she could scrutinize them in the meantime. Once that was accomplished she'd analyze the list, looking for signs, for patterns, for anything that would help. But she'd have to sleep soon. He wished she was here, working with him hand in hand.

Authors tried to be clever when designing a virus but they could not avoid leaving clues. Bits and pieces of old code were often cobbled into a new creation and the old code, created or used when the author was green, tended to be sloppier. Jeff and Daryl had once managed to find the street address in Moscow for an author based on just such a clue. She'd had no similar luck earlier with the code itself but Jeff was more hopeful she'd have some success with the address list. There was bound to be a pattern.

During these long hours Jeff observed the malware in detail, identifying new files it duplicated into the computer and locating files that had been modified using a Windows feature that tracked such changes. The virus appeared to be searching only for document files, including presentations and those in OfficeWorks.

This was the heart of what Jeff did. There was no glamour in it, but both he and Daryl shared a passion for the cyber hunt. They were detectives on the trail of the culprit and at any turn of the electronic corner within the computer they might uncover him.

Jeff lost all connection to day or night. Every two hours his watch chirped. He would stop, stand up and stretch, go for a walk in the hallways, find a restroom, and splash water on his face. Back in the office, he would pour a cup of whatever had caffeine in it, often eat something sugary, then return to his digital world.

He hated losing, hated it with an all-consuming passion. And he loved games. For him, uncovering the virus, unraveling how it worked, assessing what damage it had done, was the greatest challenge of all, as real to him at times as playing rugby.

He'd told Daryl once that at times like these the pixels in the computer, the code he read, were his entire world. He could understand how certain personalities became addicted to the cyber universe. As it became even more sophisticated, he occasionally wondered what the future for some people was going to be, locked away in their rooms, utterly lacking any normal contact with humanity, their brains directly wired into the network.

By afternoon Jeff concluded he'd learned all he could at Whitehall and told Blake to arrange a meeting as soon as convenient. He called Daryl, who he reasoned had to be even wearier than he was. She'd been working at very odd hours.

"You awake?" he said.

"Just barely. I'm living on coffee." She sounded tired. "I called Frank Renkin at the Company to see if he'd put his team on the DNS names. It was a big job." Frank was a friend of Jeff's from college where they'd taken a number of classes together. She knew him as well from her work with the CIA. Neither of them had kept in touch particularly but they all worked in the same field and ran into one another from time to time. They also customarily exchanged data they thought the other could find useful. What Daryl liked best was that Frank was happily married and had never made a pass. He'd landed with the CIA, working internal computer security.

"And how is Frank?"

"Very good. A third baby is on the way. They want a boy this time. He seemed a bit stunned at the thought. I don't think it's planned." Jeff laughed. "I called because he represented the government in the Conficker Cabal and might have information on new strains."

"Right. Our guy's using the same name-generation technique. Any luck?"

"Nothing off the top of his head," she said, "but he was glad to get the information. I also forwarded the code to him and he promised to get back as soon as his people compared it to what they have on Conficker. It's always possible it's the same author."

"Yeah. More likely our guy borrowed it."

"You know, I don't want to give our author too much credit but this seems to be a very well-thought-out virus. When I stepped through the code I didn't find a single hint of origin, nothing. It seems like he made a conscious effort to keep it clean. And there was something else. It doesn't have the feel of a single gifted author. I'd say several people worked on this thing." She paused. "There was also nothing in the chat rooms. Not a word. This thing's potential is so great you'd think somebody, somewhere, would be talking about it. It's as if it was created in a vacuum."

"Any luck with the DNS names?"

"I've just been looking over the results Frank's team came up with and can't help notice that the names are heavily biased toward those ending in Iran. In fact, nearly half of them produced by the algorithm fall under the Iranian namespace, ending in *.ir.*"

"That's either a very stupid move on the part of an Iranian author," Jeff speculated, "or a clue dropped to deliberately mislead us."

"Right. But there's no way to tell which at this point."

"You know, it's impossible for us to position ourselves to intercept a command coming to it. And if the author picks up we've accessed the thousand URLs he's using, he'll just add thousands more. And we still have no idea of the scope of this thing, how old it is, or what it does." Jeff paused. "What do you think it does?"

"It can do most anything really, but from what you've found it wants to access documents. That tells me it's snooping."

"A cyber spy."

"Exactly. Like a keystroke logger but much better." Loggers tracked the keys struck on a computer keyboard in a covert manner so that the victim using the keyboard was unaware they were being monitored. The information was then accessed by whoever planted, or had access, to the embedded logger.

"You know," Jeff said, "this guy in Geneva might not be lying."

"If he's telling the truth, the only way it can be is if someone used this virus to access an OW file in his computer and altered its language *before* Herlicher sent it with the digital signature attached to it."

There was silence. They both knew what that meant.

"Get some rest," Jeff said. "I'm wrapping it up here. The next step is Geneva if they want me, where malware on that end—if it's still there—might have more clues. I'll let you know either way. Thanks for your help and thank Frank."

10

LONDON, UK
WHITEHALL
FOREIGN AND COMMONWEALTH OFFICE
RESEARCH GROUP FOR FAR EAST AFFAIRS
IT CENTRE
3:32 P.M.

Just as Jeff's wrap-up meeting was about to begin he received an e-mail from Daryl.

> The Company says this is first it's heard of this virus and tnx us very much. They want to know if we've noticed how clean code is. I said we had. When we figure out what it does we're to let Frank know at once. If they figure it out first, he'll do the same. Finally, Frank wants us over for dinner when we get back home. It's going to be a girl this time and they want to brainstorm names with us. I take it this is some kind of new game they've come up with. Miss you.

Yates and Walthrop looked hopeful and expectant as they begin. Through the office window beside him, Jeff saw a heavy fog rolling across the city. "This is what I have so far," Jeff said. "The trail goes to UNOG, as you suspected. I need to access this Herlicher's computer to be certain and to see if I can learn more about what it's after."

Walthrop nodded. "Franz is very upset over this. Between our concerns, his desire to placate me and your reputation, I don't see a problem with access. I had Graham speak with his counterpart earlier today when it became apparent where this was heading from what Blake told me. They've been taking a look at Franz's computer. There is a greater acceptance of the need to move quickly when it appears digital defenses have been penetrated. Plus, as you saw, this involves Iran's nuclear program. OFDA at UNOG has a great sensitivity to this. Franz's superiors already know what has happened and are not happy. It appears the release of their report has been delayed."

"What is OFDA?" Jeff asked.

"Sorry. The Office for Disarmament Affairs in Geneva. It will source the report. They want nothing to go astray. They are under tremendous pressure."

He didn't volunteer why that might be the case and Jeff didn't ask. "Have there been other incidents since I arrived?" he asked. "These things rarely occur in isolation."

"Yes," Yates said. "We've had two more computers refuse to execute OW files. Before you ask, one was again from UNOG while the other was from the UN in New York."

"It's spreading," Jeff said. "Here's what I have. Yes, obviously the problem was caused by a Trojan. It's brand-new and uses a zero day. That alone makes it stand out. It is also stealthy, utilizing a new and devious technique to conceal itself. It also turns off and on at random, and calls home for instructions in a way I cannot block except by taking it off-line and that's no systemwide solution."

"That's distressing," Walthrop said.

"Is it targeted to us?" Yates asked.

"I think it is," Jeff said. "It's certainly not generic."

"I see. So what does it do?" Yates asked.

"It's designed for government espionage, in my opinion," Jeff said. "At the very least, its purpose is to read your files. And while I have no conclusive evidence, the pointers suggest the government employing it is Iran." Walthrop visibly reacted to the news but didn't comment. "As I said, I believe it gives access to content, but . . ." Jeff hesitated. How to say the rest?

"Yes?" Yates said to encourage him.

"I suspect it allows an outside source to edit documents."

Walthrop sat up straight in his chair. "What?"

"If it executes and gains access, the interloper can change the contents of an OW document," Jeff said. "This happens, of course, before the digital signature is applied. The document for all purposes appears genuine. Of course, if the author of the document reviews the copy he sent he'll catch the changes. That's unlikely, though. People assume a document is the same as when they last saw it on their computer."

Walthrop eased back in his chair. "So Franz may be telling me the truth. Let me collect my thoughts on this. You're saying that this nasty piece of code gives access to our documents and allows them to be altered?"

"Yes," Jeff said. "That appears to be the case."

"And I think it's a genuine document when I receive it?"

"Yes."

"How long has this been going on?" he asked.

"I can't say," Jeff said.

"My God," Walthrop said. "It may already have read, even altered, thousands of files." All his fears about computers were coming true. He knew, he just *knew*, it would come to this someday.

"What else do you have?" Yates asked.

"The clues suggest Iran, as I said. But that could be a plant intended to throw us off. This is a very shady digital world we're dealing with."

"I'm curious. Why did my computer have a problem the first time but then opened the file when I tried again?" Walthrop asked. "If Herlicher was infected, his computer had no problem with the virus."

"I don't know what security UNOG is using," Jeff said. "That's likely the reason. As for the other, my guess is there's a glitch in the virus. It crashed OfficeWorks the first time you tried but not the second, but in neither case did it successfully activate. I suspect that whoever wrote this code didn't compensate for at least one of the OfficeWorks security checks."

"Is there anything more to be done here?" Walthrop asked.

Jeff shook his head. "Blake is perfectly qualified to clean the Trojan out of your computers, if it managed to get onto any of them. He's got the code and he knows where to look if necessary. I'd say my next stop is UNOG, assuming I'm to continue with this. I still need to write the detection program for you and I need to find out how this thing works. Any virus that's exploiting a loophole in the digital signature system is a serious threat. But I'd need to access Herlicher's system to confirm that's what happened here."

"We and our counterparts at UNOG are agreed that you should follow up at Geneva," Yates said. "You can understand this is a potential source of friction between Her Majesty's government and the United Nations. They are eager to see that possibility eliminated. There's a Swiss International Air Lines flight leaving at six thirty this evening, which you can just catch. You'll be in Geneva later tonight. Thank you for your help and we wish you luck."

11

GENEVA, SWITZERLAND
UNITED NATIONS OFFICE AT GENEVA (UNOG)
OFFICE FOR DISARMAMENT AFFAIRS
PALAIS DES NATIONS
4:47 P.M. CET

Franz Herlicher entered his office, glanced about for any signs that someone had been in it while he was gone, saw none, then quietly closed the
door before sitting at his workstation. Carlos Estancia, his manager, had
summoned him earlier for a quick meeting. Ostensibly it was to inform him
that an expert was arriving from London to examine his computer.

Herlicher wasn't fooled. There was surely more to it than that. There
always was. He'd worked for the Spaniard long enough to recognize that
look. Estancia thought he had something on him and was just waiting for
the so-called expert to give him the cover he needed. UNOG had its own
computer people. Hadn't he been cooperating with them? Who said he
wasn't? Why bring in someone from outside?

Herlicher glanced at his computer. The techs had done some work on
it, then abruptly stopped. He'd been told to leave it alone but he couldn't
help wonder what was there to be found. Everywhere he'd browsed was
cached away in some electronic recess, at least that was what he understood.
He had no taste for pornography and if he had, he counted himself smart
enough to know their IT staff would catch him at it at work. It had happened to others. He didn't squander work hours browsing aimlessly; he
knew that was monitored as well. And he certainly never wrote anything
disparaging about the UN or the Office for Disarmament Affairs. That was
the last thing he'd ever consider.

Estancia had confirmed what the IT people had said, that his computer had been hacked. That was the word he'd used, suggesting by his manner that somehow it was Herlicher's fault, as if computer security wasn't a matter for IT. Didn't they have programs to prevent that sort of thing? Firewalls? They'd been told their Internet security was second to none. Yet, now Estancia was trying to make this his fault.

There was no question of taking this London expert at face value. Something much more significant was taking place. Was he the target? Herlicher wondered, or just a cog in a much bigger game? Was there any way he could know?

Estancia had said nothing about Lloyd Walthrop but it was clear to Herlicher that a document he'd sent the man had been the cause of the problem. The fact that the experts were coming from Britain suggested to him that Walthrop had his own concerns. Shouldn't that get him off the hook now?

Herlicher couldn't make sense of the disaster. Estancia, the techs, everyone seemed to be speaking in double-talk. He pressed his hands to his head, feeling one of his migraines coming on. This was all so complicated.

He abruptly straightened with sudden realization. Estancia knew he'd contacted Walthrop about the Iranian report; had *been* regularly contacting Walthrop. *And providing privileged information.* There'd been no way to avoid using his office computer for those contacts though they were against policy.

Herlicher turned on his screen and opened his e-mail program. He began systematically deleting every message he'd ever sent Walthrop.

12

MAKU, IRAN
IMAM STREET
HOTEL SEYHAN ADANA
9:58 P.M. IRST

Saliha Kaya stood back from the window as she stared at the dark street below. There were few streetlights and most of those no longer functioned.

It was always this way on these trips. Fly from Prague to Ankara, hire a car, drive in one long day to the border with Iran, wait to cross, then check into the hotel. The woman had come and gone. It was done, so why couldn't she sleep?

It was all exhausting and she didn't know how many more of these trips she was willing to undertake for Ahmed. The pay was good—not great but good—but the inconvenience was considerable. The flight itself was no problem. She enjoyed airplanes and she often met businessmen who gave her their cards, promising to help her find work wherever it was they lived. She knew what they meant but each card represented an opportunity. Her relationship with Ahmed was going nowhere and every time she went back home, she grew more depressed at the prospect of returning to Turkey.

Her father had died the previous year. Two sisters and a brother still lived at home with her increasingly aging mother. Though her other siblings gave what they could, it fell to Saliha to be the family's primary support. After all, she lived in the rich West and earned far more than the rest of the family combined.

She'd arrived from Prague in the afternoon, taken a taxi to the apartment where'd she'd grown up, and surprised her family, as she always did.

Ahmed had made it clear that she was never to announce her trips to any-one. The girls and her brother were as delighted to see their big sister as she was to see them. She had gifts they excitedly opened and it warmed her to see the happiness she could bring them.

The apartment was on the ground floor and there was a small garden in back. As a child she'd worked it with her grandmother, providing fresh veg-etables for the family during the summer and fall. Now that she was gone and her grandmother dead, the garden had turned fallow. With the death of her father, her mother had no time at all to garden. She'd been at the market when Saliha had arrived so she was playing with the children when her mother returned. She smiled warmly and embraced her daughter.

"You are so thin. Don't you get enough to eat?" she'd said.

Saliha had laughed. "It is the fashion in the West. And I am not so thin as that." She slipped folded bills into her mother's hand.

Her mother bowed her head, then said, "Thank you, my daughter. With-out you . . ." The rest she left unspoken.

Yes, without me, Saliha thought. What would the family do? Suffer, go hungry, struggle. Her two sisters would likely be forced into prostitution, her brother be turned into a pimp or thief or both. She knew. She'd seen it enough. She'd escape that fate but would they?

Her older sister was married to a truck driver, the oldest brother worked in Istanbul on the docks. He'd not married so he could give his mother as much of his earnings as possible. To do so he lived in squalor. But the time was approaching when he must look to his own future and begin to save.

That night, Saliha treated the family to foods they normally didn't en-joy, then helped her mother prepare dinner. Her two sisters had crawled into bed with her, whispering, dreaming until they'd all drifted off. As always it had been a wonderful visit, but too short. These were the best moments of her life.

In Prague, Saliha worked with young women who'd forgotten their families. Money that should have gone home was spent on expensive clothes, a nice apartment, trips. They dressed and behaved like whores and in the process Saliha watched them become hard and bitter. How could anyone turn her back on home? On her family? She didn't understand it.

Early the next morning Saliha set off to rent a car, telling her mother she'd be back in a few days with more gifts. Her mother stood in the door-way, watching her retreating figure, waving a final time as Saliha turned the corner.

The drive from Ankara to the border with Iran took all of a long, hard day. She drove north and east of Ankara until she joined E80, the Trans-European Motorway or TEM, a divided highway that began somewhere far away in Western Europe and ended just short of the Turkey-Iran border. It crossed the broad Anatolian plain, then wound through long narrow mountain valleys over ancient passes. As she ate up the miles driving at a brisk pace, the true life of so-called modern Turkey unfolded before her. Aged men on donkeys, children herding sheep, exhausted fields struggling to produce one more crop so a family wouldn't starve. She'd seen it all before and the more time she spent in the West, the more desperate and impoverished her native country looked.

In this region of Turkey, a woman traveling alone was a curiosity. Twice she pulled off the highway to take a short break. When she entered the adjoining small villages she ignored the disapproving looks she received from old men and women, the aggressive stares from young men.

Ahmed had cautioned her to mix up her routine, to take different routes. She'd done that the first three trips and disliked it as any other route took a full, grueling two days. Now she traveled the best and fastest route. The trip was demanding enough without adding his silly rules.

That afternoon as she traveled east, the mountains grew higher, the road become less well maintained and the region more primitive. When she neared the border, she turned down a narrow dirt road. After a short distance she stopped beside a lovely stream lined with poplar trees, shielded from the highway by heavy vegetation. There she opened the car doors and snacked on food prepared by her mother as she listened to the bubbling water. Spring was later here and the air was cool though rich with the fragrance of the mountains. In late summer, the nearby pomegranate trees would be heavy with fruit. Their scent was one of the few pleasures in these trips.

With a glance at her wristwatch, she sighed, went to the car, opened the trunk, then her luggage. She removed a bundle of clothes. She replaced her denims with an ankle-length dark skirt, slipping on a matching long-sleeved parkalike garment. She placed her denims back into the luggage, removed a head scarf, and closed the lid.

She'd scrubbed herself clean before leaving Ankara and wore no makeup, bore no fragrance of any kind. Now she looked like a proper Muslim woman. She'd better.

At sunset, Saliha reached the border with Iran, placing on her head the scarf as she pulled to a stop. She'd traveled often enough to be recognized by the guards. If a single woman driving a car in eastern Turkey was eye-catching, it was even more so in Iran. She'd explained that she was from Prague and that her Iranian boyfriend's family lived nearby. Whenever she traveled to Turkey he asked her to visit them to give gifts. Then she'd buy some of the things he could only get in Iran and carry them back.

The guards searched the car thoroughly as they always did, even examining the two gifts she'd brought with her from Prague to maintain the charade. After a short delay she was on her way for the final half-hour drive to Maku. It was an ancient capital of the region, today of modest size. Resting in a river valley, it was dominated by a castle.

Here, her instructions never varied. She was to stay only at the Hotel Seyhan Adana and wait. Once that wait had been a short hour, another time she'd sat in her room or the lobby for three days, but always a starkly plain young woman would meet her. This time, early that evening the woman spotted her waiting in the lobby. After brief words of greeting she thanked her for the gifts, gave her items for Ahmed, then took the key-chain drive. That was it.

Back in her room, Saliha carefully opened the packages and meticulously examined the contents. They consisted of regional canned foods unavailable outside Iran. She was not going to be arrested for smuggling. Satisfied they were in order she rewrapped everything, ate a light dinner of rice with a lamb kabob, then found herself pacing in her room unable to sleep. She had another full day of driving ahead of her but sleep just wouldn't come.

She looked again at the quiet street below. It was full night and almost no one was about. When night descended in Iran an oppressive darkness came with it. She felt like a prisoner in her hotel room.

It was the risk keeping her awake, she realized. She wasn't stupid. While she had no interest in politics she knew that the Iranian mullahs were at war with the West. She'd considered her boyfriend from every angle and found herself finally reaching the conclusion that he was somehow involved in jihad. It was the one answer that satisfied all her questions. It alone explained his caution, his discreet devotion to Islam, his secret time on his computer, his different cell phones, his private conversations, his mysterious trips, and the thumb drive he gave her for each trip to Iran.

She was smuggling information, something the mullahs didn't want to have sent to Iran by the Internet or mail, hence a courier.

But what kind of information? What could be so important as to go to all this trouble and expense? She'd spent hours driving here and back trying to solve the enigma. Still she had no idea but she now understood that was the way it was intended to be.

As Saliha prepared for bed, her thoughts wouldn't turn off. She was in no danger here in Iran, if she was correct, and the Turkish officials, with the nation's increasingly Muslim orientation, certainly wouldn't care about what she was doing. If the Czech government really minded, Ahmed wouldn't have legal status and they'd either expel him or at least be asking questions. She made these trips regularly and had never once been asked about them.

So, she thought as she slipped between the sheets, who was she afraid of?

The CIA for one, but most of all the Mossad, she thought with a shudder. If she was right, either or both of those organizations cared very much indeed about what she was doing and the slightest mistake by someone could point the finger at her.

Saliha feared them both. She didn't believe for one minute the stories she saw on television or read about a dysfunctional CIA. That was all misinformation. She'd heard about the CIA all her life, how it was behind every coup in the Middle East, every assassination. She had not the slightest doubt. There'd be no Guantanamo for her if the CIA got her. They'd cart her off to some hellhole where torture and rape rooms were stock-in-trade. She had no idea what the Mossad did with people like her but she was certain the CIA alternative was better.

No, she finally decided, this is too much. She knew she must stop this. One more trip and that would be it. And Ahmed must pay well for it.

DAY FOUR

SUNDAY, APRIL 12

CONFESSIONS OF A CHINESE HACKER, PT. 1

A 20-SOMETHING COMPUTER GEEK IN SHANGHAI SHARES HIS SHADOWY WORLD OF HACKING FOR PROFIT.

By Johnson Lam
Internet News Service
April 12

Like many Chinese, when dealing with a Westerner he uses a Western name, Victor. In his case, however, it's also meant to conceal his real identity. Though accented his English is excellent. He is slender, well mannered, neat. And he is very proud of what he does.

In fact, the need to brag is constantly at odds with a hacker's desire for obscurity. Though China recently passed tougher cyber security laws they are either lightly enforced or not enforced at all. But Victor fears that could change. "If you put a face to your story, I'll be in trouble," he tells me at a coffee shop not far from his small apartment. "If I stay anonymous, I'll get rich."

Victor had thought to be an engineer but before university graduation he became intrigued with the digital world of hackers. They are a close-knit group, swapping code, selling viruses, gathering information on computer exploits they can use. "All the big companies have many zero day vulnerabilities," he says. "I'm going to find one and use it to make a killing."

Victor tells me that three weeks ago he unleashed his own personally crafted Trojan in a phishing attack and now has a botnet of more than 5,000 computers. The virus harvests banking information and when he is ready he intends to loot the owners' accounts for all he can take. He's already set up a complex digital route for the money before it lands into an account he controls. "They'll never know what happened," he says with a laugh, as he lights a cigarette.

I ask if he's proud of being a thief. "It's not stealing. If you leave your wallet on that table and walk off, I'm a fool not to help myself? It's the same thing. They let me in. Why shouldn't I take it?"

Victor is consumed with hacking. He reads hacker forums and magazines, chats with other hackers, swapping information and ideas, and writes malware code. "That's the hardest part. But also the most rewarding," he tells me with a satisfied smile.

Unlike Victor, most hackers don't bother creating their own viruses. They just take them from Web sites and adapt them to their own use. Some of the most successful viruses are rented. That's right, rented.

Next: The Entrepreneurial World of Hacking

13

Jeff was awakened by pounding on his hotel door. Disoriented, he sat up in bed and slid his feet onto the carpet. He rubbed his eyes as the pounding continued.

He'd been exhausted by the time he reached his hotel room in Geneva. Just after the final meeting at Whitehall, he'd texted Daryl to confirm he was flying to Geneva. Then just before takeoff and after landing, he'd called but had gone to voice mail both times. He decided she was earning some well-deserved rest. Once in his room, he'd ordered a room service sandwich, taken a quick shower, then gone immediately to sleep.

Drowsy, stumbling like a drunk, he went to the door and checked the peephole. There she was, grinning at him. He threw open the door. "What are you doing here?" he said as Daryl walked into his arms. She felt good and smelled sweet.

"Hi, big guy," she murmured. "Couldn't let you have all the fun, now, could I?"

When he finally let her go, he carried her luggage into the room and set it down. "Really," he said, "how did you know where to find me?"

Daryl gave him a smile. "I'm a supersecret cyber agent, remember? I have friends in the CIA." She laughed. "I just contacted Frank, then he made a call. I was on a direct flight while you were still in the air. I was so beat I took a pill and slept the whole way." She glanced around the room. "No bimbos. That's good."

She pulled open the curtains. "Just look!" she exclaimed. Through the window was a lovely view of a well-tended park and beyond it the azure Lake Geneva backed by the Alps.

"Let's order breakfast," she said, turning back to him. "I skipped the one on the flight so I could eat with you."

"Sounds good. Go ahead while I take a quick shower."

Inside the bathroom, satisfied he'd grasped the idiosyncrasies of the shower handle, he turned the water on, waited a moment, then stepped in, pulling the curtain tight. The hot water bathed his body as he turned slowly. It was wonderful. It felt like a week since he'd washed. It was good having her here. Very good. Just then the curtain drew back and through the steam a naked Daryl stepped in.

"Want me to scrub your back?" she asked. "We've got time before food arrives."

As it was, they kept the waiter waiting as Jeff threw on a hotel robe and let him in while Daryl hid out in the bathroom. He signed, gave the young man a lavish tip consistent with his mood, closed the door, then rapped on the bathroom door. "Food's here. You can come out now."

Daryl had brushed her teeth and run a comb through her hair. Without makeup in the strong morning light she was gorgeous. They both dug into the American-style breakfast she'd ordered.

"This is a very nice surprise," Jeff said between bites.

"I'm just sorry it's taken so long. I really have been trying to get free. We can take a trip. With me here to help, you'll get it done in half the time, probably sooner since I'm faster at this than you are."

"Says who?"

"My mom." Daryl took another bite. "I can't help thinking the Iranians aren't sophisticated enough for this. I'm not saying some Iranian, somewhere, might not have the knowledge and be able to do this though it seems like a team creation and it's pretty clearly a government operation. I just don't see the mullahs managing it, do you?" Daryl no longer sounded tired. She was back on the chase. "In fact, I can't recall a single incident of cyber code coming out of Iran. How about you?"

Jeff thought a moment. "Nothing. And one of us would have heard if there existed an ongoing Iranian government department tasked for computer interdiction. From all reports their computers are under near-constant cyber-assault. I don't see them having the energy for this. Just think about Stuxnet and all the harm it's caused. They're awfully busy countering that."

Stuxnet was to date the most sophisticated Trojan ever invented. Commonly accepted to be a digital weapon devised and launched by an opposing nation, it had all but brought the Iranian nuclear weapons program to its knees. No one claimed authorship but nearly everyone in the cyber industry believed it was a product of Mossad and CIA working together.

In fact, Jeff and Daryl were all but convinced they'd worked on a Stuxnet-like project for three months the previous year. They'd been asked to submit a bid to Frontline Integrated Systems, or FIS, a specialized software company that worked almost exclusively as a vendor for various U.S. intelligence agencies. Their task was to locate zero day vulnerabilities in Android's wireless services, WiFi and Bluetooth. Android was the mobile operating system used by a large number of cell phones. Once the vulnerabilities were identified they were to develop reliable exploits. The self-evident though unstated goal was to create a hole through which malware could jump from other systems to Android phones, and vice versa.

Jeff and Daryl were committed to the practice of responsible disclosure, which meant that whenever they encountered a zero day software vulnerability, they felt morally obligated to advise the vendors privately so the holes could be patched before they became generally known. But in the world of cyber warfare, such vulnerabilities were extremely valuable. A government agency would not disclose them because the vendors would then patch them, destroying their value. The couple had resolved this seeming conflict after they accepted the nature of cyber warfare and because their contacts at the CIA and NSA adopted a policy of disclosing such vulnerabilities one year after discovery or when they were exploited by someone else, whichever came first.

It was a compromise, one that in an ideal world they'd not have made, but theirs was not an ideal world. Cyber warfare was the new battleground between the great powers and it was a war the United States and the West had to win.

They'd received the contract for Project Tusk for a flat fee with a bonus for every zero day vulnerability they uncovered. They'd found one vulnerability in the Bluetooth stack, two more in the core WiFi driver as well as another two in the GPS driver.

"Maybe they outsourced it," Jeff said as he buttered a second piece of toast. There were plenty of criminal groups around willing to do the work for a price. There were, however, inherent problems with that approach. If someone, even or especially a hired gun, learned enough about you to graft an attack on others it was not difficult for them to turn their creation back on their employer or resell what they created.

"Anything's possible, I guess. But can you imagine a hacker writing code that clean?" Criminal cyber-gangs in the former Soviet Eastern bloc nations had turned such operations into a vast illegal financial industry but their code was often sloppy and until now, always identifiable for what it was. Was it possible one such group had raised the bar so dramatically?

"It doesn't seem to get the Iranians very much," Daryl continued. "So they read this Herlicher's files, even altered a copy of the final report to say there will be no Iranian nuclear bomb. So what? Such a mistake can be explained and is sure to bring people like us on the scene as soon as they changed something important. From what I've read they just want to get their nuclear bomb detonated so they can get on with their quest to become a major world player."

"And then arrange for it to be used."

"That's right." She paused. "I've often wondered why there is so little concern about them getting the bomb. Look what they've done financing terrorist groups worldwide. Don't people see what they do? And even if by some miracle they don't turn it over to their terrorist minions to use, they'll bully their way into complete Middle East dominance. After all, when it was still called Persia, the country had a long history of controlling the region. What's it going to take to wake people up? A nuclear wasteland? The lights going out in their hometown for a month? Sometimes I just want to scream." She stopped, drew a deep breath.

"It's all right, Daryl."

"No, it's not!" she said. "That's why I'm so upset. Look, getting back to this thing, I think it's someone a lot more competent than Iran, someone with a more expansive agenda."

Jeff considered that as they finished their meal and dressed. It made a lot of sense.

"So, you give this another two or three days to figure this thing out?" Daryl said, her mood having lightened. Jeff nodded. "I was thinking on the way over that Italy is very romantic, according to all the books and shows. Rome, Florence, Venice. We can see the city in a gondola while you serenade me."

"You've got me mixed up with the gondola guy. He does the singing."

Jeff leaned over and kissed her. "You're a woman of wonderful surprises. I love you."

"Keep talking like that and I might go ring shopping."

He pulled her tight. "I can think of worse things."

As they left the hotel, the view of the shimmering lake and distant mountains crowned with white clouds was gorgeous. They had a clear view of the famous Jet d'eau, the enormous jet water fountain, visible from nearly anywhere in the city. Jeff had heard that Geneva was known as a dreary city but from what he'd seen it didn't seem possible. So far he'd found it quite charming, though he suspected his companion had something to do with that.

The Palais des Nations, where UNOG was located, was a brief walk up the Rue de Lausanne to the Avenue de la Paix, the Avenue of Peace. Jeff noted that there were no visible guards on the grounds or immediately outside the building. The entrance was some distance from the street, reached via a long concrete walkway across a vast expanse of well-tended garden. Exterior security was either out of sight or depended in large part on the inherent stability and law-abiding nature of Swiss society.

Henri Wille, the security chief, was waiting to receive them at Pregny Gate, the usual entry point for first-time visitors. He was in his forties, trim and fit, and looked every inch Swiss with blond hair, fair skin, and deep blue eyes. Though wearing a suit, on his left breast was a distinctive badge. As the designated Interpol agent for UNOG he'd been alerted by the UK Foreign Office of the arrival of two key computer security experts and had been instructed to see to them personally. Frank Renkin had already alerted Graham Yates that Daryl would be joining Jeff. He'd been delighted because her reputation, if anything, exceeded that of Jeff's.

After introductions, Henri asked Jeff and Daryl to go to a nearby room to have their photographs taken. A few minutes later they received a badge to wear whenever in the building.

"It will grant you near universal access," Henri said. "If you require anything at all related to security come to me directly." He wrote his cell number on the back of a business card and gave it to Jeff. He then escorted them to the UNOG IT office and bid them good-bye.

The head of IT was out of the country and they were briefed instead by his assistant who introduced himself as Nikos Stefanidou. Short, with a bushy mustache, he was not happy with their presence. "This is a matter I believe we are capable of handling but others have decided to the contrary," he said with clipped words. "I will do what I can for you." He'd not risen from behind his desk.

"You have the computer here?" Daryl asked. It was standard procedure to disconnect the machine from the network and move it to the IT center so no one could do anything to it.

"No, it has remained in Mr. Herlicher's office. He was told not to use it." Jeff raised an eyebrow but said nothing.

"Have you had other reports of infection in the building?" Daryl asked.

"I couldn't say."

"Does that mean 'yes, you have,' or 'no, you haven't'?" Jeff said.

"I couldn't say."

"I suggest we get working, then," Jeff said. There would be no help here. "Can we see the computer, please?"

Franz Herlicher, the German technocrat, was a weasel in Jeff's opinion. He'd given them each a curt European handshake and a quick bob of the head before turning his computer over to them with obvious reluctance. "I must attend a meeting, which will last several hours so you will have the office to yourself. Of course, I will make it available as you need thereafter. I only wish to cooperate and clear up this terrible misunderstanding."

"Before you leave, could you tell us what happened?" Jeff asked.

"I'm sure you already know. That's why you are here." Herlicher pulled himself upright.

"It will be useful to hear it from your perspective," Daryl said.

Herlicher looked at one of them, then the other, unable to decide just who he should address. "All right then," he said, deciding on Jeff. He was the man, after all, but with Americans you could never be certain. "I had finished a late draft of the report, which was essentially the final report, pending approval of the specific language by my superiors. I then forwarded it to Mr. Walthrop at Whitehall but what he—"

"He's part of the approval process?" Daryl asked.

Herlicher swallowed. "Not . . . not exactly. He's a colleague and this report was very important to him. I wanted . . . his input."

"Go on," Jeff said.

"There's nothing else." Herlicher looked exasperated. "I received this most horrid message from him—you can see it yourself in my computer—

denouncing me as a liar! It was very unsettling, I can tell you. I'm not accustomed to such language. It was simply awful! I e-mailed to assure him there had been some kind of technical mistake but he didn't reply. Then . . . then I checked the report and . . ." Herlicher stopped, apparently unable to continue. He took a white handkerchief from a pocket and dabbed his moist brow.

"Then what?" Daryl said, when it appeared he wasn't going to continue.

"The report wasn't the same! It had been . . . rewritten. It's quite impossible."

"Perhaps someone here made the change," Jeff suggested.

Herlicher shook his head. "I already considered that possibility. I always lock my office when I leave and only two other people have keys." Neither statement was true, of course, but Herlicher wasn't going to present any version of events but the most proper.

"Still, the room must be cleaned and no security measures are ever airtight," Jeff said.

"Yes, I see your point. We do have some . . . less trustworthy types working here in menial positions. But that wasn't the problem."

"How can you be certain?" Daryl said.

Herlicher had watched a number of American detective motion pictures. He understood the "good cop/bad cop" technique he'd seen in them. He feared that was what was going on. Did these two suspect him? Surely not. He'd been told their presence was confirmation of what he'd suggested, that something had penetrated UNOG's cyber defenses, that he was not to blame for what had happened. But that might very well be a lie. They might just be here to trick him.

He pulled himself upright. "I am absolutely certain our building security was not compromised. You see, after I wrote the e-mail to Mr. Walthrop, I attached the document. I then opened it and proofread it a final time. I always do this with important files. The moment I finished reading it, I closed the file and sent it, all but simultaneously. I assure you, the file I sent was the one I wrote. The problem must be at his end. Now, I must go to my meeting. I wish you well in your investigation."

"One last question," Jeff said. The man stopped. "You affixed the digital signature before sending the e-mail?"

"Of course! Always on official documents. Now, good day."

Daryl watched the man walk off in a huff. Still, what he'd said, if true, was most interesting. She moved to a spot where she could work as Jeff sat at the man's computer. Another windowless office, she thought, as she linked to the computer and booted it up. Maybe she should get a job as a park ranger or something.

"He's been deleting files," Jeff said within a few minutes. "Looks like communications with other agencies. Probably sharing things he's not supposed to."

"Jerk." She looked at her screen, which duplicated the one Jeff saw. "And he doesn't know diddly about how to hide it. Okay, Superman, let's see what you've got now that you've had a full night's sleep and been laid."

"Let's start with the obvious," Jeff said. He went to the folder containing the file and opened it. "See it?" He read it through. "This one is different from the one Whitehall received. It reaches a different conclusion. That's odd."

"How?" Daryl asked.

"Until now I'd been thinking the virus allowed the interloper to alter the file in Herlicher's computer. I'd assumed he'd sent it along without double-checking, placing the signature on it at that time. But this report is not the one Whitehall received. That makes no sense." Daryl drummed her fingers. "What?"

"Just thinking. What if the change was made after the report was attached? This e-mail program holds its own copy of the file. Hang on." Daryl opened the attachment with the message to Walthrop in the "Sent" folder. "Whoa," she said. "This one *is* the same as the one Whitehall received. It's altered."

"Let me check the signature." When Jeff was finished, he said. "Yup, the signature is valid and the same."

Neither of them said anything for a long minute.

Daryl spoke first. "Someone used this Trojan to access the OW file *after* it was attached to the e-mail and altered its language *before* the digital signature was generated." She paused, then said, "This is unbelievable."

"Let's get a handle on this thing," Jeff said finally, and the pair went to work. Because of what he'd learned in London the process went quickly and within ten minutes he had located the Trojan. "There's the nasty little thing," Daryl said, spotting it on her screen as well.

"What we're postulating is that this guy sends the correct file, but it's altered at the moment it's sent as an e-mail attachment. And there is *no evidence* it was been tampered with. Jeff, they didn't just change a word. They rewrote the report! How can you do that in the middle of an e-mail transmission?"

"I have no idea. Let's find out."

For the next few hours they worked at unraveling how their Trojan functioned. They discovered that it was not hard-coded with commands when it was created and embedded. While these would work in most circumstances to accomplish what the author wanted, such an approach did not permit any degree of flexibility. The virus could only do what it had been preprogrammed for at creation. Instead, the Trojan was sophisticated enough to be programmed with script-language, which gave the author enormous flexibility. This was why it was so aggressive and clever in seeking out a domain from which to receive updates and orders.

Searching further they found snippets of script in memory that enabled the Trojan to copy Herlicher's e-mail messages whenever they were sent. The copies were kept in memory for later uploading to the control servers. The Trojan then periodically probed the file servers he was connected to, grabbing any documents Herlicher could access.

For the rest of the day they pored over networking logs and reverse engineered the malware, stopping from time to time to brainstorm. At one point, Herlicher stuck his head in the office and asked how they were doing.

"What do we do about lunch?" Daryl said by way of answer.

"I . . . there's a cafeteria on this floor, that way. It's not bad. The cooks are French."

After Herlicher left, Daryl went for food and brought it back. They ate as they discussed their latest findings. "One of the unique characteristics of this thing," Daryl said, "is that it retains itself and any documents it copies in the computer's memory."

"We didn't find anything in the memory scans," Jeff said, biting into a croissant. Why were they always so much better in Europe than back home?

Operating systems like Windows use a technology known as virtual memory. Its effect was to give programs the illusion that the computer had more Random Access Memory, or RAM, than it actually did. It accomplished this by writing out infrequently accessed data and code to a paging file on the disk. When the program accessed that data or code again, the operating system simply read it back into RAM from the paging file.

"There's no sign of the document, either the original or altered one, in RAM *now*," Daryl said. "Maybe the operating system wrote a copy of it to the paging file when the virus had it in RAM around the time that it replaced the original in Herlicher's e-mail, but *before* the Trojan deleted the altered copy from RAM."

"Now that's original, and devious. Someone's put their thinking cap on."

For the rest of that day, they used a special tool Daryl had previously written for their forensic tool kit. It copied the contents of the paging file, something that wasn't possible when the operating system was running. They then copied the data to an external disk they connected to their laptops.

"Let's see," Daryl said. She launched the scan and a few minutes later discovered pieces of the altered document scattered around the file. This was extraordinary.

"So that was it, smart lady. Who said you were just another pretty face?"

"Yeah, right, smart aleck," she said, with a laugh. "We're lucky they didn't include turning off the computer in their pathetic incident response policy."

While what they'd found was not direct evidence that the Trojan altered the document, it constituted substantial anecdotal evidence. They also checked copies of the document on the file server and those backups were the original document. The copy on the e-mail server was the altered version, and they discovered more bits and pieces of the alterations in the paging file.

Daryl's laptop flashed an alert. "Looks like the Company wants to talk."

14

PEOPLE'S REPUBLIC OF CHINA
XINJIAN PROVINCE
URUMQI
PLA CYBER WARFARE CENTER
10:43 A.M. CST

Colonel Jai Feng scanned the three oversized computer monitors at his workstation, taking in the data with a single practiced glance. He lifted another Hongtashan cigarette to his lips and took a long pull, the strong smoke delivering a jolt of nicotine almost immediately. He lifted his cup of coffee, long cold, and drained it.

Feng was dissatisfied with the progress of his team. He was under relentless pressure from Beijing to produce results and it seemed to him everything was going much too slowly. Working for him were the finest computer minds in China. Everyone was proficient in English while a number, though too few for his needs, were fluent. They were highly trained, highly skilled, and dedicated to the work, if not for the greater glory of China, then for the greater advancement of their careers.

The problem, Feng knew, was that he was overextended. When he'd first taken control of the PLA's Cyber Warfare Center, the operation had been quite modest and expectations low. But as he expanded its scope, and demonstrated time and again the usefulness of what he was doing, both resources and demands had increased.

He'd realized the year before that he needed to reorganize but doing so would be a major interruption in his ongoing operations. This was no time for that. Matters were much too crucial to risk it. And, of course, there were laurels to be had, a promotion to receive if he left things as they were with him in sole charge. But once he split command the inevitable would happen. It was human nature. Those who'd been hired by him, advanced by him, those who owed *everything* to him would slit his bureaucratic throat in an instant to jump over him in promotion. Time enough for that *after* he was made general and relocated to Beijing.

Angry with developments in his two main projects, he pushed himself away from his desk and set off on one of his unpopular lightning tours. The warfare center occupied all five floors of the modern building though the heart of the operation was on the second, third, and fourth floors. The second was dedicated to military penetration. Feng's unit there enjoyed extraordinary success in penetrating the U.S. Department of Defense databases. Its most recent triumph had been the penetration of the U.S. Pacific Fleet Command computer structure. The fourth floor was where the malware was crafted. Bright—very bright—software engineers were constantly thinking down the road, anticipating the next moves, both theirs and their adversaries, and generating clean, effective product. Feng knew that his long-term success depended on just how good these young minds performed.

Today, Feng took the interior fire-escape stairs and emerged on the third floor. He was preoccupied with cyber operations and that meant this floor. Here, dedicated teams conducted widespread and often very specific information gathering from thousands of crucial targets. Whenever an area vital to China's interest was involved, a team learned everything they could about those involved. In this increasingly digital world, that was often a great deal indeed. Most helpful had been the development of a Trojan they'd implanted in various telephone networks, giving them access to the in-house tracking of individual numbers. The networks did this routinely to assist them in determining service demand at specific locales.

There were, however, two immediate cyber operations about which Feng was most concerned. Four days earlier, he'd watched an elite team conduct a test of their system implanted in the WAyk5-7863 power grid located in the eastern portion of the state of Washington in America. The Trojan had been meticulously placed there the previous month. His team had run tests until it was certain the malware would work as intended.

This was the most sophisticated power grid Trojan China had ever developed, and was key to Feng's long-term strategy. Its potential was so enormous that he had not breathed a word of its existence to anyone in authority. He had to be certain it did what he was promised, then it had to be meticulously insinuated into the entire American grid system.

Feng's work was much like defending against a terrorist attack, he often thought. No matter how many times a nation successfully thwarted such an attack, the terrorists only had to succeed once. In his case, no matter how long his Trojans loitered in the targeted computers, or how successful his mission, he only had to be uncovered once. Then the tree would fall, as his grandmother had often told him, and the monkeys would scatter.

Feng often cautioned his young geniuses to be careful. Youth was impetuous, he knew. Reining in such passions totally was all but certain to be impossible. Mistakes would happen, they had in fact already happened, but none had as yet come back to them. He was satisfied the carefully crafted and planted Trojan would not be detected. So much malware, from any number of sources, already permeated the grid's software that his in effect hid amid the trash. Through this technique they'd managed to hide and cover their trail, to muddy the waters so to speak, leaving responsibility pointed elsewhere if it came to that.

Or so he hoped.

Feng had selected the hour after midnight in his targeted area for the actual test, a time when the consequences would be minimal. He wanted nothing dramatic to happen. For that reason the test had to be short.

It lasted just fourteen minutes. And the effect had been as comprehensive as Feng had been assured. Yakima and the surrounding region had been plunged into darkness. In crucial areas backup systems had sprung to life but in many cases these had been poorly maintained or untested and they'd failed at the crucial moment.

Feng had been delighted, especially when shown a satellite image of the area, a black blot surrounded by pinpoints of light. Then the reports of deaths and accidents had come in. A train stranded by the power failure had been rear-ended by another. The loss of life was scant as these were freight trains but entire cars had plunged into a canyon. An engineer and four others were killed. And there'd been a hospital death, a patient who died during surgery when the power was extinguished. There'd also been auto collisions, people trapped in elevators—all the things he'd expected. And so far there was not the slightest suspicion that the Chinese had done it.

There was, as well, his UNOG penetration. For more than a year another special unit had labored to crack cyber-security at the United Nations. That itself had not been so difficult, as well as planting the various malware they required for their project. Handling it all with delicacy though demanded great care and restraint. Planning when and where to act was even more daunting.

They were now reproducing the keystrokes of dozens of UN officials and recently, through the use of an amazing bit of word-processing code, had begun to access their files directly. With this information they'd slowly determined the central players.

Now, the latest variation allowed his people to alter files. Just as significantly the digital signature could be delayed and set in place after the revised document was ready. He'd reported this development of necessity, cautioning it should not be used carelessly. Given time his people could cause enormous damage to the United Nations but he was limited in how fast he could perform such work.

Then, with this program barely underway, he'd been ordered to modify the Iran nuclear report. Feng had balked, pointing out that the deception would be discovered at once and his long-term plans thwarted. Though his best people were busy modifying documents within the UN computers in Geneva and New York, they had not yet achieved the desired penetration because he lacked sufficiently skilled technicians able to express themselves in the proper English.

But his objections had been overruled. Someone wanted to delay any military action against Iran, to give them just a bit more time to detonate their first nuclear bomb. Iran had assured them it was imminent. Feng knew better and told his superiors the reality as he understood it. While the Iranians were close they were still hampered by their infected computers. In some cases they'd been reduced to handling issues by hand on a whiteboard. If they could inoculate their computer system from this Stuxnet pestilence the final steps could be accomplished in a few short weeks. As it was . . .

Feng still burned at the thought of the error left in the latest variation of the code they'd embedded in UNOG. When it had followed the path to London it had not worked. A flaw in the exploit code had caused Office-Works to crash. That should never have happened. On top of it, they had sent the malware with the altered document. They should have sent it in an unaltered file to avoid drawing attention. Now, the entire project was in jeopardy. Those bright kids had failed.

His protestations to his superiors about employing the software in such an obvious manner were pointless, he realized. The botched work by his team had led to early detection regardless. He'd have to find out who'd made the mistake; Feng's instructions had been specific.

He just wished he'd had a little more time. Iran's nuclear program had been brought to a virtual standstill by this Stuxnet worm. His people had devised, then he'd dispatched in stages, countering software to Iran as quickly as it could be developed, and while it had slowed the damage Stuxnet caused, it had not stopped it. The worm was constantly morphing, altering its approach, infecting operational parts of equipment by planting itself within the control computers.

The most frustrating part of the process had been the refusal of those above to allow his team to send these patches digitally. He'd assured them time and again that there were secure e-mail routes or ways to download from the Internet that would never trace back to China. But the role his operation played in assisting Iran was considered highly sensitive, one in which plausible deniability was the paramount consideration. Because of the need for speed he'd persuaded them to allow the first step in transmitting the patches to be electronic. After that a courier, a mule, was used. It added two to three days to the transfer time but Feng had been told the decision was final.

Feng was worried. New versions of Stuxnet were periodically released and he was certain that another had been designed to reinfect any untainted new computers. Only Feng's software could prevent it. And this needless, senseless, delay of two or three days to give some aging party official a bit of ease only increased the likelihood that an exploit would be implanted. The last version of Stuxnet had been more destructive than the first. He didn't want to think about what was to come. Despite the best efforts of the Iranians, the strains managed to find a way in.

Iran's program had already been so damaged and delayed the country had taken the unprecedented step of replacing thirty thousand computers to get a fresh start. Feng had cautioned against this approach before his work on Stuxnet had reached a more developed stage but the Iranians were paranoid about the "air gap" again being penetrated as it had previously been by thumb drives. They refused to wait, convinced they'd solved the problem on their own with stricter precautions.

As a consequence, Feng had a team working feverishly on a comprehensive counter for the new Stuxnet strain they'd detected in the systems, which went to the heart of the worm. This counter could be patched into the fresh network to keep it free from infection. He believed they nearly had it, that this new megapatch would suppress any Stuxnet variation, though nothing was certain. Feng had wanted this patch to be in place before the UNOG Trojan was employed as its discovery would likely speed up deployment of the new Stuxnet variant before it was implanted. But he'd been assured the UNOG software would not be detected and had gone ahead; then the software had been disclosed by orders from Beijing and the incompetence of his own people.

The one thing certain in all this, and the cause of Feng's great unease, was that if things went wrong he would take the blame.

At the UNOG team work area, Feng approached the supervisor. "Tell me."

The young man looked up, startled by his superior's unexpected presence. "Someone is conducting a forensic examination on the principal target computer in Geneva."

A rush of acid bathed Feng's gut. "That is unfortunate." But to be expected, he thought. "Has he found our plant?"

"I can't say for certain. We're not able to follow his movements."

"Continue to monitor his work, but put a team on UNOG's recent communications and learn his identity. That is priority. You are to provide me with an update every hour until you have that. Also, inform me of just how much he has learned if possible."

"Yes, sir. The target sent an e-mail informing a colleague a cyber-expert was arriving from London, an American apparently. Someone disconnected the computer about the time he was scheduled to arrive so we've been blind. We'll remain on this and work our other sources."

Feng placed his hand on the young man's shoulder. "I know you will do your best. Put a team on the identity. That is crucial at this point."

Feng went to the elevators and returned to his office. If the forensic investigator was good enough he just might find their plant. They'd hidden it well, cleverly, but it existed in that computer. The cloaking they'd given it might be discovered despite the assurances of his people. He needed to stop this man at once. And for that he required a photograph and a name.

In his office, Feng sat at his desk and promptly lit another cigarette as he considered how to proceed. He glanced out the window and scanned the skyline of Urumqi, taking in the snowcapped Tianshan mountain range. Winter was passing yet the mountains were still clothed in a glowing white. Below was the usual urban haze, the pollution associated with progress throughout China.

Feng was from Kunming in Yunnan Province in southern China, just touching Vietnam. Known as the City of Eternal Spring he'd not fully appreciated its magnificent climate until he'd been posted to Urumqi. Despite its majestic view of the mountains and its historic location as one of the principal cities of the old Silk Road, this was an arid region, with long dry winters and long, even dryer summers.

Feng longed to be home in beautiful Yunnan. Except for his wife and son, all his family were there. But leaving all that was the price he'd paid to ambition. He was not alone in that regard. Nearly every man of today's China was required to give up a part of himself for advancement. There was no turning back now.

He glanced at his coffee mug and wondered just when it was he'd given up the wonderful teas of his youth. At some point he'd given in to the preferred drink of the West. Everyone in his generation on the rise had, he believed. Like American cars, coffee was a badge of personal progress.

Feng understood that the People's Liberation Army Cyber Warfare Center had been located here to remove it from prying eyes. Urumqi was tucked away in a corner of largely desolate western China. No foreigner could come here without attracting attention. Few in China, and fewer still abroad, understood that this was the nerve center of China's ongoing cyber war against the West.

In his view, one shared by the general staff and party leaders, what took place within these walls was on par with China's nuclear capability. In many ways it was superior, in Feng's opinion, as China could always deny it existed. Deniability was the cornerstone of everything his team did.

But not all of China's cyber warfare effort was under his control and that was a constant source of irritation. He'd argued repeatedly against the current approach, pointing out the inherent inefficiencies, misguided attacks, poor training, and overlapping efforts. More than once his team had penetrated a U.S. government computer with absolute stealth only to discover poorly written code implanted by another Chinese operation, one certain to be detected. And once alerted the IT team would find his as well. Worse, those other operations were not nearly as careful about not leaving behind trails back to China.

In the beginning, before the PLA fully appreciated cyber warfare's potential and launched its own program here, the military had encouraged private hackers to attack the West. This was much like the old system of privateers the French and British had used in time of war, when civilian ships were given letters of marque, authorizing them to prey on the enemy's merchant ships. The idea was to unleash against the West the potential of thousands of young Chinese, then glean the benefits.

These were the so-called Patriotic Hackers. They were freebooters authorized to be destructive, to spread malware throughout the West. No one knew what they did, really, and most of it in Feng's view was a waste of time.

Malware was now openly sold in Chinese Web sites. Companies marketing it even offered an end-user license agreement and twenty-four-hour support services. Cutting edge exploits were commonly available. In some cases, buyers could carefully customize malware to fit their particular needs. A new hacker could specify if he wanted his malware to log keystrokes, to capture remote screens, to steal financial data, to remotely control a system, or some other undertaking. Sophisticated malware was sold off the digital shelf for as little as twenty dollars.

Feng had complained about such blatant marketing and had been told there was nothing to be done about it, that such activities were part of the price China paid for a more open economic system. But he'd not accepted the explanation. Someone, somewhere within the government he was certain, was pursuing this course to make it easier for the Patriotic Hackers.

The PLA made its first tentative move toward control when it organized Information Warfare Militia units. These were comprised of students, scientists, and IT professionals in research institutes, IT firms, university computer science departments, and even private computer clubs in China. Since inception they had developed a relatively mature cyber network in the West.

These groups were incredibly careless in Feng's view. He'd spoken against them repeatedly. They maintained online journals were they openly discussed what they did. They had forums where they bragged about every penetration or new virus they'd created. True, they stole data, launched denial-of-service attacks, created digital havoc. All the while, they left evidence behind and failed to close the digital door too often, letting the Americans trace their penetration right back to China itself.

Not much came of that, of course. The Americans would complain, the Chinese would express shock that some of their young people would do such a thing and would promise to look into it. That was all. But it served to keep the Americans on their toes and it obstructed Feng's more productive efforts far too often.

Though Feng had demonstrated repeatedly that such an approach was now outdated, it continued. At the least, the Information Warfare Militia units should have been abolished when his center was created. Feng had argued, with some success, that they had to be controlled. In a time of emergency they might attack the wrong targets or overreact. He'd been listened to, but not enough. There'd been changes, but they were insufficient.

Feng lit another cigarette and took in the mountain view again. The problem with this location were the Muslims, who comprised a quarter of the local population. The largest group, the Uyghurs, had taken to rioting in recent years, demanding increased rights, even independence from China. Feng had no doubt agitators were stirring them up. More than two hundred had been killed in the most recent demonstrations, many more simply disappeared.

Feng couldn't look at a mosque, hear the call to prayer, or see a Uyghur in ethnic dress without feeling a wave of disgust. These people were Chinese, why didn't they act like it?

At forty-three years of age, with short cropped graying hair and a slight paunch, Feng felt he was at the height of his competence. He was a short man at five feet six inches, not unusual for his generation but still below the average. These young men, he noticed, were tall and lean, with that healthy glow Feng wished he possessed. This was especially the case with those who'd lived and studied in the United States.

We're making a new China, he often thought when regarding them, *one complete with a new man.*

He sighed. Despite his efforts against Stuxnet, his penetration of the American power grid, and his success with the United Nations, the American DOD remained his primary target—that and its extensive network of vendors. The Americans were still surprisingly lax with computer security but there were areas his very best people had been unable to reach. His superiors were becoming more and more insistent that he gain access. The Americans might wake up someday, that was always possible, but he was certain that by then he'd have gutted the DOD.

As for the UNOG penetration, he knew he couldn't keep the failures of his own people a secret. There were plants among his staff. Beijing would learn of his failure. His stomach burned and he reached for an antacid.

His computer chimed. He clicked on the message and there was a photograph and a name, followed by a detailed biography of the man. He copied the material, then alerted the necessary people and made his request.

Feng sat back and lit another cigarette as he waited for his stomach to calm. All that work and then this guy comes along. He shook his head. Life just wasn't fair.

15

Ahmed skipped class that morning. He was too tired to feign interest.

The blond Czech girl had exceeded his expectations in bed. He consistently found these Western women to be amazing. The only part of the experience he'd found unpleasant was discovering the large tattoo across her lower back bearing the name of an old boyfriend. Why did these women insist on marking themselves? And with a throwaway relationship? It was disgusting.

He showered, bundled the sheets and clothing to be washed later, then made breakfast. He lit his first cigarette of the day as he opened his netbook. He browsed several minutes, then promptly at 2:00 p.m. went to a Web site he entered from memory. It was down. He waited, then refreshed his browser. Still down. He waited a full minute this time, then refreshed again. There it was.

A porn site. He liked the pictures. He wanted to meet the man behind them someday as their taste was identical. But he wasn't here for that. In the lower left-hand corner of the page was a small link in the form of a pulsating green ball. He clicked and it took him to a forum, or rather what was laid out like a forum. He hit his print tab and a small, fast printer clicked to life. In less than a minute, the forum was in hard copy. As he started to back out of the page to take another look at the pictures the Web site went down. He'd just made it.

Ahmed turned off the printer and computer, removed the pages, and moved to the small table to analyze them. He glanced at the calendar. It was the fourth month in the cycle so he went to the fourth entry on the forum. It was the eighth day. He went down eight lines. The line read, ". . . real? I think the babes are hot, hot, hot. I think you should post at least six new photos every . . ."

The number then was "six." He moved his finger to the bottom of the forum, then carefully counted up six lines. He read, ". . . set up with phones for talk. I'd love to spend five hot minutes with . . ."

Phone. He straightened. Now that was something. He'd never been ordered to phone before—never.

Ahmed dressed, taking time to look good, pocketed cash from his dresser, retrieved a fresh pack of cigarettes, slung his backpack over his shoulder, then went for a walk. He stopped once for a coffee and studied the foot traffic from the way he'd come and spotted nothing. He went to a marketplace, wandered aimlessly, twice checking surreptitiously by pausing at windows and using their reflection. He emerged on the far side, then sat for more coffee and a cigarette. Again, he saw no familiar faces.

He'd expected none. He'd done nothing to attract interest since coming to Prague. He'd been very careful. Next, he took several short back streets, stopping again at a coffee shop he'd never been to for a sweet roll. He sat and ate, scanned back the way he'd come. He lit a cigarette and watched. Nothing.

Such caution had been ingrained in him before coming to Prague and Hamid reminded him during every visit to keep his guard up. The Crusader was everywhere and no one could be trusted. Not that there was anything special about him to attract attention. He went to his classes and was an attentive student. To the extent possible, he made his trips over long weekends in what would be the normal pattern for a student. He still visited some of the trendy nightclubs, especially when Saliha was out of town. It was best to appear secular.

He finished his cigarette and set off casually, shifting his backpack to his other shoulder as he once again scanned a narrow alley. Still nothing. He walked briskly to a small mall and went directly to a kiosk where he bought a phone and supply of minutes, paying in cash. Afterward, he made his way to Letna Park with its famous beer garden. Here he could sit alone on the grass well away from any pathway and observe the expanse all about him. A couple was taking in the spring sunshine but they were folding up their blanket when he sat down. Once they were gone he punched in the number.

Whoever he'd reached answered at once. It was a one-way conversation. Ahmed listened closely, locking the information into his memory, thinking he could detect Hamid's voice at the other end but wasn't certain. The man was a chameleon. The caller disconnected without pleasantries.

Ahmed rose and walked out of the park. Along the way he removed the SIM card, then took the extra precaution of dismantling the phone itself. He discarded the bits and pieces at various trash receptacles. As he crossed the bridge, he dropped the SIM card into the slow-moving waters of the Vltava River.

He made his way across town, stopping twice, once for a soft drink, but primarily to check his trail. Nothing.

He found the apartment building in an alleyway, one used by pedestrians. He'd told Karim to rent a place where he could blend in and the man had done a good job. There wasn't a native Czech in sight. On the third floor, Ahmed used the key he'd been given, then entered the tiny room. Karim was out. No surprise. He didn't get off work until five. Ahmed sat to wait patiently for the man to return, slowly working his way through his pack of cigarettes.

16

I want to advise you," Frank Renkin said, "that we've got a very effective word-processing-based Trojan and as it potentially involves your area you should know about it." As assistant director of Counter Cyber Research, he was responsible for informing the appropriate chiefs whenever anything came across his desk that might be of concern to their area.

Agnes Edinfield was chief of the Eastern Mediterranean Bureau in the Company. She was in her forties, fit if perhaps a bit overweight with short dark hair and dressed in a well-tailored dark pinstriped business suit. Though she had strong features she was a handsome woman.

"Which country?" she asked.

"Likely Iran—one way or another." Frank gave her a brief summary of what he knew, the gist of which was that it appeared that the UNOG report they'd been anticipating on the Iranian nuclear weapons program had been doctored by means of the Trojan.

Everyone involved knew the significance of the report. After stalling for more than a decade the United Nations had finally indicated it was prepared to move. Frank understood that a source had, for its own reasons, elected to leak critical documents directly to the United Nations Office for Disarmament Affairs in Geneva. The information detailed the groundwork for concerted military action against the mullahs had already been anticipated.

"What changes?" she asked.

"We understand this was to be the final draft. The report is scheduled for release tomorrow. Now we learn that it has been altered to say there is no prospect of an imminent nuclear test."

Edinfield grimaced. "Altered, you say?" Frank nodded slowly. "I take this as confirmation," she continued, "if any was needed, that UNOG's source had it right."

Iran already possessed a midrange missile delivery system and was not that far from a long-range system that would extend their nuclear threat into Western Europe. The mere existence of such a system would profoundly alter the European Union's position toward Iran and Israel. The immediacy of an actual nuclear test was the most vital problem either of them faced. Frank was not free to disclose it to her but the first test was reportedly in just two weeks. The Iranians had made remarkable progress since bringing their new computers online and establishing an air gap to protect them from Stuxnet. If nothing was done, all indications were that they'd be a nuclear power before the end of the month.

"We've not seen anything previously resembling this Trojan," Frank continued. "It's not like the infected PDF files we encountered before. In its own way, it's as sophisticated as Stuxnet. When you open an infected OW file, the Trojan enters the computer. There it uses an entirely new method to conceal itself. Very clever." He omitted the details. Edinfield would have no interest in them. "We've known this technique was coming for some time; now it's here. It's going to make our work much more difficult."

"I'm sorry to hear that. Where's it originate from?"

"We can't confirm a source at this point. But its creator seems to be using it to try to influence events as the time comes for the release of this important report on the Iranian nuclear program. This is very clean stuff, Agnes, unlike almost everything we've seen and my people tell me that in their opinion it's beyond the ability of the Iranian government. All of their computer expertise is dedicated to the nuclear weapons program and to combating the Stuxnet variants that continue to significantly hinder them."

"How did this come to your attention?"

Frank brightened. "As I said, according to the author of the final draft of the UNOG report, his document was altered."

Edinfield thought for a moment. "Can you do that?"

"Not without leaving tracks. In this case there are none."

"I suppose he could be lying."

"We'll know soon enough. I've printed you copies of the original report, as the author says he sent it, and the one with the changes he denies making." He laid them on her desk and Edinfield pulled them to her. "I had the changes analyzed. They systematically water down the report and finally give it a different conclusion altogether. They aren't alterations you can dash off in a minute. It took talent and real effort, as well as a very sophisticated Trojan, though we've still not cracked the core of what it does. We're just working around the fringes. I don't know how events will play out at UNOG. So far this is tightly held information but that won't last long."

"Good job. Let me know what you learn when you can. By the way, where did you get the info?" Edinfield asked. The source of such information often told her a great deal and was always something useful to know.

"Daryl Haugen alerted us. We got lucky. The virus had a bug that caused OfficeWorks to crash, which alerted the IT staff and prompted their investigation. If that hadn't happened, the altered document would be changing the course of events."

Edinfield paused as she searched her memory. "Dr. Haugen? The one who worked for the National Security Agency?"

"That's her."

Edinfield thought a moment. She'd been involved in blunting, nearly stopping, the Al Qaeda cyber-attack on the West not that long ago. A great job all around, one the Company should have done, not an outsider. Then more of the story returned. "Didn't she leave the NSA and go to work with Jeff Aiken?"

"They have a company, yes. The British Foreign Office brought Jeff in to troubleshoot this and they turned up the Trojan. Daryl has been working with him remotely and gave me a heads-up, passing along the code once it was identified."

"I'll have my people check into this from our side. Maybe there's been some chatter that will be useful to you. Thanks for coming."

Frank rose and went back to his office, feeling utterly exhausted. His team was getting to the heart of the Trojan, he was certain, but he still had a long night ahead of him. At his office, he instructed his assistant there were to be no interruptions for an hour. Inside, he stretched out on his couch, wondering briefly when he'd next go home.

DAY FIVE

MONDAY, APRIL 13

INTERNATIONAL PC REVIEW MAGAZINE

CYBER WARFARE, THE NEW BATTLEGROUND

April 13 10:30 A.M.

Palo Alto—The digital penetration of an adversary's computers is now a reality. Every major country uses computer malware for espionage. It allows them to gather intelligence more easily, quickly and cheaply than do traditional methods. But the line between digital espionage and cyber warfare has become blurred as nations have come to understand that such malware can be repurposed for interference, disruption and attack.

The continuing success of the Stuxnet virus against the Iranian nuclear weapons program has introduced a new age in warfare according to experts. "Stuxnet is a game changer," says Reginald Bradshaw, a London cyber warfare simulation specialist. "From the date of its introduction the modern world has never been the same. It's the digital equivalent of the machine gun or artillery." A better comparison might be the nuclear bomb because a concentrated Stuxnet-style attack has the potential to destroy a nation's industrial capacity, according to a yet to be released UK Whitehall report.

Until now viruses, Trojans and worms attacked the data within computers. These assaults have been designed to learn what the owners wanted kept private. In many cases financial information is obtained to allow the looting of bank accounts. But now highly sophisticated malware commands industrial machinery to self-destruct, in effect to commit suicide. The consequences can be catastrophic especially if the machinery is part of a nation's infrastructure or national defense network.

In response to this heightened threat every major country now commits resources to counter measures. The United States has the US Cyber Command, or USCYBERCOM, a part of the US Strategic Command. It is the umbrella organization for all existing U.S. military cyber warfare operations. Significantly, it has both a defensive and offensive capability. "The Americans are no longer strictly playing defense," Bradshaw says. "They've moved into offensive operations. These will be the most secretive in history as deniability is the hallmark of such attacks."

It is not too far-fetched, Bradshaw muses, to see a day when one nation will attack another through the Internet and in so doing deliver a knockout blow. "I anticipate seeing that within my lifetime," the forty-three year-old cyber expert says.

For more information, visit Leslie Washington-Tone.com.

17

Ahmed eased the Volkswagen Jetta down the street as Karim examined the passing houses carefully, searching for the address in the darkness. Ahmed was concerned that their actions go smoothly, especially at this hour. If they were forced to drive too often up and down this deserted street, someone would surely call the police.

"There," Karim said. "That's it."

Ahmed drove to the side and came to a stop. "Don't take long," he cautioned. "I'll drive once around the block. Be here when I return."

Karim eased out of the car, tossed his cigarette into the gutter, closed the door quietly behind him, and set off across the yard to the side of the house where Ali lived. Ahmed put the car back in gear and drove away as slowly as he dared, and made a succession of right turns down equally deserted streets before returning to the same spot.

No one.

He sat with the engine idling, wondering if he should make another circuit. He lit a cigarette to buy time. Hamid had drummed it into his head repeatedly that operations and agents were undone by just such stupid incidents. It was situations like this that drew the attention of the authorities. As he pondered what to do, knowing he had to make a decision at once, two figures emerged from the shadows.

Karim slipped into the front seat. *"Salam,"* Ali said, taking a place in the rear, placing a small overnight bag next to him. A wave of cold air swept in with them.

"Salam," Ahmed answered. He then drove off with a sense of relief,

turning the heater up slightly. Karim opened a fresh packet of cigarettes, turning to hand one to Ali.

Since meeting Karim, it had been a busy six hours. They'd left his apartment and walked to the car lockup around the corner where the gray Volkswagen Jetta was kept for such occasions. Every few months, the vehicle was replaced. One of Karim's responsibilities was to see to that and keep the car serviced and gassed. Once a week, he ran the engine for half an hour and checked the tire pressure.

The car had started at once and Ahmed had been pleased to see a full tank of petrol. He drove cautiously out of Prague, initially confused as usual by the heavy traffic, the lights, and complicated cross streets. Once on the E50, however, the traffic thinned, the drivers became more predictable. Thereafter the trip went smoothly.

On the way to Mannheim, Karim briefed Ahmed on his recent activities. He maintained a ring of agents in northern Germany. He supervised recruitment from various sympathetic mosques, arranging training and for providing the cash so essential to such networks.

His personal life certainly lacked excitement, and that, Ahmed reminded himself, was good. Boring was safe. It was important they remain in the shadows. Karim worked as a waiter in a restaurant that specialized in, of all things, American food for American tourists. He had no girlfriend, not wanting to risk a relationship with anyone, but he confided that once a week he went to a brothel where he spent time with the same Ukrainian whore.

"I would not marry her, of course," he said, "but for a whore she is very sweet, and most agreeable."

The two agents could not have looked more different. Karim was a slender man, quick and alert, whereas Ali was large, over six feet tall, and heavy. His network, with identical duties, extended throughout southern Germany. In fact, their primary function was to create and maintain their networks until the day when Hamid set an operation in motion.

Ali had worked a time at the Daimler AG factory, building diesel engines. But his necessary trips proved too frequent to continue a job with such steady hours. Now he was working as a handyman for several rich Jews. He found that amusing.

Though they passed close to the Swiss border, Ahmed stayed within the EU to avoid passport controls as long as possible. The longer they were out of the Swiss security computer system, the better. He didn't drive often. He enjoyed the sensation of the car, the calming drone of the engine, the muted whine of the tires on the smooth surface. They were moving across space in this comfortable cocoon. From time to time, he took, in the enormity of the road system, considered the opulence that made it possible, and wondered how much would remain in the promised caliphate. He wondered if he'd live to see it. He certainly hoped so. He hadn't joined Iranian intelligence to die for a cause. He was content to leave that to others.

Toward dawn it began to rain. Ahmed turned on the windshield wipers, which slapped back and forth in a steady rhythm. The road was soon slick with water and he eased the car into the right line to merge with the slower traffic. At the first major truck stop he pulled in for breakfast. They took a booth in a corner and spoke sparingly in quiet voices.

Two hours later, the trio cleared immigration and customs at the Swiss border. Only then, in the security of the moving car, did Ahmed tell Karim and Ali their mission. They listened intently, taking it in with professionalism. Unlike most of his agents these were not wide-eyed fanatics. They'd been trained for the long term, to stay in place for years. For each of them, this would be his first aggressive action in Europe, though they'd both dispatched operatives on assignment previously.

Ahmed slowed as he pulled into Geneva. They'd just missed the morning rush-hour traffic, which was a matter of luck and which Ahmed took it as a positive sign. He drove cautiously through the city streets. He'd never before been in Geneva and found himself at once disoriented. He pulled to the side of the road and removed a portable GPS device from his jacket. He input the address he'd been given and was soon on his way.

He left Geneva proper and entered the small town of Meyrin, though the two blended together as one. The first blush of spring was emerging from winter and the trees were filling with bright leaves. The building was located just off the Avenue de Vaudagne, near the commercial district in Les Vernes. The street's buildings had two stories and a number of them had taken up the ground-floor space with a narrow garage. The street was not the best, ideally suited for their purposes.

Spotting the address, Ahmed nosed onto the sidewalk up to the closed garage to be less conspicuous than stopping on the narrow street. He turned off the engine. "Remain here," he ordered as he climbed out, blood returning to his cramped legs at his first steps. He approached the building and realized it was abandoned. Perhaps a third of those on the street seemed to be. There were signs in French that he could not read but the message was clear: no trespassing, stay out.

He took the place in. The trees to either side were unkempt, overgrown, nearly concealing the structure. He couldn't tell what it had been from the outside. He peered through a dirty window and saw abandoned machines of some kind, looking archaic, like something out of the last century. He thought of leather. Perhaps a shoe repair shop. He moved to his right and found the narrow stone walkway up the right side of the building.

He went to the rear and stopped at a heavy metal door. It was as described. Glancing about the yard he spotted the flat stone like something out of a Christian cemetery. He wondered for a moment what it had once been, how it came to be here. With some effort, he managed to lift it out of the soil, then flip it over. Within the damp soft soil was a small container. He withdrew the key from it, then unlocked the door. The hinges needed oil, he noted, as he pushed it open. The door creaked so loudly Ahmed wondered if anyone nearby could hear.

Inside, he spent only a few minutes examining the room with its adjoining bathroom. This had been a storage room with an office space in the corner at one time. While there was no equipment here there were discarded bits and pieces of machinery scattered about, the large ones left leaning against the walls.

He located the canvas bag in a cabinet above the toilet, and checked its contents. Then he took time to urinate. Locking the heavy door behind him and using the key again, he entered the garage from the rear. Inside, he found the white Volkswagen Crafter van.

He went back to the Jetta. "All is well." He handed the bag to Ali, then started the car. He backed it onto the street and parked. Now he opened the garage door, Ali and Karim helping him with it. The van's tank was also full and it started at once. He pulled the van out and parked on the street. Then he pulled the Jetta into the garage, locking the door behind them.

Back outside, the men climbed into the van. "Someone likes VWs," Ali said and the men chuckled. Karim passed cigarettes around and they lit up in minor triumph. Though Ahmed had been assured all would be in readiness, he was relieved that it was so.

He drove the short distance to Route de Meyrin, taking a few moments to get used to the feel of the top-heavy vehicle. It handled well but differently from the smaller and more agile Jetta.

In less than ten minutes, the street took him almost directly to his destination. Traffic was moderate for a busy city and they attracted no attention. He soon found a parking lot near the street and across from UNOG that did not require a sticker. It was almost nine o'clock. He parked and killed the engine. Once certain no one paid them any attention, he reached into his jacket, removed several photographs, and passed them out.

"When will he be here?" Karim asked, studying the photo of the man carefully.

"I have no idea. We must be vigilant," Ahmed said.

"How long will we wait?" Ali asked.

"As long as necessary. We will take turns so as not to attract attention." He stretched behind him and pulled the canvas bag onto his lap. He reached inside, feeling the various objects, then extracted and handed over two cell phones. "Use these for communication sparingly, my brothers. We cannot know who is listening."

The men turned the phones on. They were HTC Heros, which used the Android operating system. They were generic, not tied to any specific network and had been jail-broken, meaning Ahmed could acquire any apps he required from anywhere. They were fully charged and immediately acquired a cell tower.

"This must go smoothly," Ahmed cautioned. "We are to attract no attention of any kind. No littering. This is Switzerland and they take that very seriously. Our orders are explicit about what we must do. You understand?"

The men nodded. Ahmed withdrew two small American revolvers from the bag, Smith & Wessons with short barrels. These were standard weapons, no silencers, no special alterations, nothing that would identify them as part of a foreign operation. "Put these out of sight. Allow yourself to be arrested as a common criminal if necessary. In no event make any hostile move to a Swiss policeman. You understand?"

The men nodded again.

"Allah is with us," Karim said as he pocketed his weapon.

Ahmed smiled, slipping a heavy automatic from the bag into his waistband. "Let us hope so."

PRAGUE 3, CZECH REPUBLIC
TABORITSKA 5
9:12 A.M. CET

At almost the same moment in Prague, Saliha opened the door to Ahmed's apartment and found it empty. She closed the door behind her, then placed the bag she'd brought back for him on the table. The small room was stale, smelling of cigarettes. It felt abandoned. She opened the window to let in air, then took the room in again, carefully.

Could he have moved without telling her? It didn't seem likely but if he were to end it with her that was how she expected it would be. She crossed the room and examined his closet. A small athletic bag he kept there was gone and so was a jacket. But most of his things were untouched.

Another of his trips. She looked around but found no message from him for her. That was no surprise. He liked his secrets and she was, after all, only a woman.

So . . . no money. Not now at least. He'd not thought to leave it out for her. Well, he'd pay her when he returned.

Saliha sighed, took one last look about the room, then closed the window and locked the door as she left. At the entryway, the gross gypsy, dressed in a ratty soiled undershirt, eyed her in such a way that she shivered.

18

Though used by the DOD, mIRC was not exclusive to it though it had modified the code to require both public and private key codes between parties, something that was usually optional. The system allowed secure communication between computers anywhere. All messages, or video for that matter, were encrypted en route, and then unscrambled by the receiving computer.

Daryl received the incoming message on her laptop. Jeff crowded over to her. It was, as expected, Frank Renkin, who often used video in contacting them. The picture was sharp, and revealed how tired the man was. It was very early morning there and he looked as if he'd worked all night.

"I see you found your man all right," Frank said with a grin after greeting them.

Daryl smiled. "Thanks for your help."

"Any progress?" Frank asked.

She nodded. "I'd say so. But we still have lots of unanswered questions. How about your team?"

"As I messaged you earlier, we found the self-deleting concealment software, the same as you. Very sneaky and a nasty sign if crackers are going to start using something that sophisticated. My big news is it appears the purpose of the malware is to copy any document the infected computer has and is able to alter it. Does that sound familiar to you?"

Jeff filled him in on what they'd come up with, explaining in some detail how the Trojan made it possible to modify a document in the middle of an e-mail transmission.

"The *what*?"

"That was our reaction. You send an attachment," Jeff said, "even check it before it leaves your computer, but an *altered* document arrives at the other end."

Daryl answered. "They must copy the file to their system, study and modify it, then send back the altered version. They have their version already in place to make the switch when the e-mail is sent. In the process they manage, in effect, to suspend the application of the digital signature. It goes on the altered document."

Frank thought about that a moment. "They must have had someone watching the development of this report for a while since I take it this Iranian draft report was a work in progress."

"The replacement is automated," Daryl said. "If a change is made in the document before it is e-mailed they'd be alerted and react accordingly. They might miss something changed at the last second but most of the time they'll accomplish what they want. And if it's important enough to them, then by watching any one computer continuously they can always do a substitution. But there's nothing to prevent them from actually altering the document within the infected computer at any time if that's what they want."

"You can see what this means, right?"

"It's bad, that's for sure," Daryl said.

"It means," Frank said, "that we can't know if a digital communication is an original so we can't trust *anything* we read that we've received by e-mail, even if there's proof it originated with someone you trust. Nothing, and that includes attachments. We can no longer take anything at face value. And then there's stored data. A document you read one day might read differently later. If the Trojan is in your computer you have no idea what's been changed, none. It spreads doubt and suspicion throughout all Internet communication. Can you depend on what you see? Are you being lied to? Or is it a Trojan?" He sighed. "So, who do you think is doing it?"

"Based on the sophistication of this thing," Daryl said, "we think China is the likely author."

Frank nodded. "That's where we've gone. It targeted UNOG and the British Foreign Office. We think it's the big boys in cyber spying, though we've found no direct trail as yet."

"Why would the Chinese care about a United Nations report on the Iranian nuclear program?" Daryl asked.

"My guess," Frank said, "since we're talking about Iran here, is that oil is the connection. China already has a well-developed nuclear weapons capability at a time when the mullahs are creating their own. Iran has lots of oil and China needs it."

Jeff and Daryl often encountered Chinese penetrations when working for government agencies or government contractors. On occasion, they were able to trace the "call home" feature of the virus to a server located in China; far more often they did not.

Chinese cyber penetrations were noted for the extensive reconnaissance that preceded the actual penetration. Before making the effort they gathered as much information about the computer system and the people using it as they could. They determined what data would be available and which additional networks they could infect when access was accomplished. Once inside, they moved with incredible caution so as not to alert the IT team.

To this end valuable data was most often moved to e-mail servers, since they handle large volumes of data. There, the stolen files were renamed to avoid suspicion, then were compressed and encrypted before being exported. In one case such an attack had utilized eight computers at U.S. universities as drop boxes before transmitting the stolen data from them. They then distributed it to more than ten countries before it was finally funneled back to the highly secretive PLA Cyber Warfare Center.

A Pentagon report said that the Chinese military was making "steady progress" acquiring online-warfare techniques, believing that its computer skills could help compensate for its underdeveloped military. It was usually not possible to make that final connection to China but the sophistication of the cyber-attacks and the nature of the data stolen left only one possible conclusion in many cases. One such Chinese attack on the computers at Oak Ridge, Tennessee, for example, had successfully obtained nuclear development data. DOD weapons programs were routinely extended. In one penetration, between ten and twenty terabytes of classified and highly sensitive data was downloaded. Considering that the entire Library of Congress consisted of twelve terabytes, the loss was enormous.

For all that, the most disturbing penetration was the Chinese systematic mapping of the American electrical grid. They'd dropped software all over it and no one knew what it was meant to do, or when it would be called on to do it. No sooner was it located and removed or neutralized than fresh code took its place, often not discovered for months. In the event of a national emergency, the justified fear was that some computer tech in China would send a command and the entire United States power supply would cascade into darkness. It might take weeks, even months, to rebuild and there was no knowing what might happen while most of the U.S. national defenses were blacked out.

"So you're suggesting," Daryl said, "that Iran is giving China low-cost oil in exchange for nuclear weapons assistance. And this cyber operation is meant to advance Iran's agenda?"

"It's a theory at least, though one beyond our purview. Let's see if we can link this thing back to the Reds. My report will pack more punch if we've actually made the connection." He paused, then asked, "Do you have any idea how many computers are already infected there and in London?"

"No," Jeff answered. "You should contact Graham Yates for that information, as well as whoever runs the show here. Go as high up as you can. The guy we talked to, Nikos Stefanidou, was noncommittal. We were just shown to the computer, which, by the way, they'd not even bothered to secure."

Daryl spoke. "If they can alter an OW file, they can change data also. Think about it. A tweak here, an alteration there, in the middle of a voluminous report someone relies on. We were just lucky this one was discovered. Who knows how much other data they've modified already? Or where? And what modifications have been made to the software that runs our critical infrastructure by inserting a backdoor? If that happens we have . . ."

"Disaster," Frank said, looking very weary. "You have disaster."

19

Jeff yawned, glanced at his watch, and decided to call it quits. He was getting nowhere. He disconnected his laptop. Daryl was sitting across the room working independently on her laptop.

"Let's call it a day," Jeff said. "I think we wrap this up tomorrow. I haven't found any more clues." When she didn't look up he said, "What are you doing?"

"Oil. Remember? Have you ever noticed how many reports on the Internet don't have a date? It's like they are written for a magazine or something with a date on the cover, and it never occurs to anyone that the article will exist forever on the Internet. Anyway, this report's kind of old but it's authoritative."

"About what?"

She looked up. "China and oil, remember? Okay, here goes. This caught me by surprise—China is the second largest importer of oil in the world, after only you-know-who. Its economy grows at nearly 10 percent and its appetite for oil is all but insatiable, growing at 8 percent a year. You see, they decided to go with cars instead of sticking with mass transit."

"Big mistake," Jeff said. "Cars are a dead end."

"Maybe, but you need an enormous infrastructure to support a thriving car industry and it is a quick way to provide jobs while giving the industrial base a huge boost. Plus, factories that produce cars can easily be converted to military needs." She gave him a cockeyed smile. "Remember that crack about cars when you go shopping for one next month. I've seen you trolling the Web sites. Anyway, within twenty years they'll have more cars than the U.S. and that same year they'll be importing just as much oil as we do. So here's the deal. They don't have it. Want to guess where they get it from?"

"The Middle East?"

"No surprise, huh? And who is their biggest supplier?"

"Iran. Right?"

"You guessed, but yes, that's right. They signed a deal saying if Iran would give them lots of oil, China would block any American effort to get the United Nations Security Council to do anything significant about its nuclear program. They've been doing a lot of deals with each other ever since."

He slipped his computer into his bag. "That explains a lot."

"Oh yeah, these two countries are very cozy indeed. Anyway, China gets most of its oil from Iran. And they don't just need oil—they need *cheap* oil because they sell the least expensive gasoline in the world. I think that's to keep everybody happy driving all those new cars."

"Let's go. I'm hungry."

Daryl closed her laptop and picked up her jacket. As she walked out with Jeff, she said, "China's also been helping with pipelines throughout the Middle East, selling weapons and dual purpose technology. They aren't just banking on Iran. The consequences for Saudi Arabia are a change in reality for them—and us. It got all its intermediate range ballistic missiles from China and I'll bet you didn't even know that Saudi Arabia *had* missiles, did you?"

"I guess not." Jeff nodded to the guards as they exited the building. As instructed, one promptly sent a text to Henri Wille to let him know they'd left.

It was a lovely night outside and Jeff paused to take in the invigorating air coming down from the Alps. The sky was clear and Lake Geneva twinkled with reflecting stars. "Look at that," he said, stopping a moment to take it in.

"Wow, very nice." She took his arm and cuddled. "Let's hang out here a few days before leaving for Italy, okay?"

"Sure, after we've written the detection program for Whitehall and UNOG. They'll need to repave after this."

As they took the long broad pathway leading to the road, Daryl continued. "The analysis is that if—when—Iran gets the bomb, Saudi Arabia will be compelled to call in its chits from Pakistan. Apparently they financed Pakistan's nuclear program with that understanding. That was pretty clever. Saudi Arabia can say it doesn't have a nuclear program but when the time comes to get bombs and the technology to support them, they just get it all from Pakistan. At the same time, China will sell Saudi Arabia ICBMs, the big boys. They will make the Middle East entirely nuclear. The very idea has everyone on edge."

"Then they should do something about the Iranian nuclear program instead of just talking about it."

They left the park surrounding the palace and stepped onto the sidewalk on the Avenue de la Paix. Their hotel was five minutes away.

Jeff glanced at a man talking on his cell phone, obviously waiting for a ride. Daryl cracked a joke and they laughed.

Just down the street a white Volkswagen Crafter crept slowly toward them.

It had been a very long wait. Morning had become midday then afternoon. There'd been a short rain around three o'clock. The men used empty water bottles in the rear of the van to relieve themselves. At one point Ahmed had taken a chance and sent Karim off for food and something to drink. Allah had been with them, according to Ali, and nothing had taken place during his absence. While he was gone Ahmed had moved the car's location in the parking area, knowing an occupied vehicle would inevitably attract notice. Still, he decided not to risk it again as that itself might draw attention.

During the rain he'd rebriefed the men, reminding them that the guns were only to be used against the target—no one else—and then only as a last resort. His orders had been quite specific. Iranian agents would have to operate in Switzerland in the future and it was important they not be seen as a threat against the local police and citizenry.

Ahmed wished this were all taking place in Prague, a city he knew intimately. He understood what he had to do, where he was to go, and how to get there, but if anything went awry he would be forced to improvise. In the crowded streets of a busy unfamiliar city, he would almost certainly be caught.

He did not fear prison. Prison would be acceptable, if necessary. In time, his people would find a way to get him out. They always did. No, what he feared most of all was failure. He'd rather be killed today than face that.

Ahmed Hossein al-Rashid, as he appeared on his passport, was born Ebrahim Abadi, though that was a name he used only in Iran. He was the son of a wealthy Iranian family whose money predated the fall of the Shah. As a consequence, his father had become a zealous supporter of the Ayatollah during the revolution once the outcome was apparent. Ahmed had joined the Iranian army just after completing his schooling. There he'd excelled. He'd been trained in special operations and counterintelligence. He'd been rapidly promoted to captain and assigned to the Iranian intelligence service known as VEVAK, where his training had been expanded to include torture. VEVAK's mandate was far-reaching, both domestically and internationally, and of all such Iranian operations it was the best funded and most professionally run.

Ahmed had done well since his assignment to Prague and recently had been promoted to major. His career choice often caused him to wonder if he'd ever return home, marry, and have a son. His father had asked him about that the last time they'd met and he'd promised that there was plenty of time for children, though he knew that was a lie.

Ahmed was ambitious and believed in a greater Iran. If he was not inwardly the zealot the mullahs wanted, he masked it carefully with a proper showing of devotion. At heart he was secular. He wondered if Hamid knew; he suspected he did. From what Ahmed had seen, most of the senior operatives in Europe were men like himself. The zealots were assigned the active roles in the missions.

The fact that he'd been ordered into the field along with Ali and Karim, his two best operatives, told him the value placed on this mission. It was an honor to be selected and he did not doubt that success would be rewarded, just as failure would be punished.

His first foreign posting had been to Prague. What he heard from Iran since coming to Europe troubled him. The mullahs were as corrupt as the Shah, and there was vicious, even deadly, infighting within the regime. There was no doubt the regime had lost the confidence of the people; that was obvious to anyone who cared to know. Another revolution was always a possibility. The mullahs, he believed, had squandered their chance.

Though he maintained a low profile and scrupulously preserved his cover as a student, about once a month Ahmed traveled to meet with his senior operatives, to dispense cash, to deliver instructions orally, and to learn how each network was progressing. He also served as a conduit for information he acquired through the Internet and forwarded to Iran by mule. For that he'd recruited Saliha. The trips kept him alert. His biggest challenge had been to be in constant readiness for when an operation came to him.

Ahmed glanced out the open window as he lit another cigarette. He was tired of waiting but he'd waited before. He'd learned through experience not to become impatient. Few operations actually came off and when they did they rarely developed as planned. That was the nature of his calling.

The men took turns waiting near the main entrance that ran through the park to the building. From there they could clearly see the exit. Throughout the day Ahmed had received periodic text messages informing him that the target was still at work inside. Then he was alerted that work had stopped. Perhaps he was taking a meal, or he might just be finished for the day. It was dark, and the building had long since emptied of employees.

Ahmed called Karim, who was standing watch, as if waiting to be picked up for a ride. "Soon, my brother. Pay attention."

The city was quieter, clearly less lively than Prague. He leaned forward, watching closely. "Be ready, Ali. Any moment, I think."

And there he was, walking with a woman along the broad pathway toward the street. Karim called him. "I see him. Do you? What about the woman?"

"Take them both. No more calls."

Ahmed started the van, slowly exited the lot, then eased onto the street. Traffic was light. As he approached he saw the couple pass Karim, who then casually put away his phone, turned, and followed.

"Get ready," Ahmed said. Ali grunted as he positioned himself. Just as he reached the laughing couple, Ahmed brought the van to an abrupt stop. "Now!"

Ali flung the passenger door open and leaped out. Ahmed pressed a button and the van's side door popped opened. He forced himself to look away from the action, down the street and into the rearview mirror to see if they were attracting attention.

Daryl screamed when she was grabbed from behind. She was swept forward, strong arms holding her tight in their grip. A large man ran at them and went straight to Jeff as Daryl was all but carried to the open door of the white van. She couldn't get her arms free but threw her foot against the passenger doorjamb and spun them off so the man holding her could not force her into the vehicle. She screamed again for help.

The man behind her grunted as he struggled, making no progress. Then another man was helping him and a moment later had her legs forced into the van and the two of them were holding her down, pinned to floor. Once she was under control, one of them left. Daryl struggled against the other man but he had both her arms pinned behind her, nearly to her neck.

The pain was excruciating and she feared he'd pushed her arms out of their sockets.

On the street the large man had bowled over Jeff, catching him completely by surprise. His carrier slid from his shoulder and the laptop skidded to the side. The men rolled on the sidewalk as Jeff fought. The large slowly man gained the advantage but he could not manage to get the American to his feet. That was when another man came over and pressed a gun to Jeff's head.

"Come, or I kill you, then kill the woman. We have her already." His voice was calm, too calm for what he was saying, with only the trace of an accent. "Stop, I said. Or you die right now!"

Jeff ceased struggling and a moment later was inside the van. The door slammed shut, then the man with the gun climbed behind the wheel, and drove off.

"Jeff!" Daryl said before someone clamped his hand over her mouth. She bit him. He cursed, then struck her hard. Jeff kicked the man, then kicked him again as he struggled to pull Jeff back.

The mustached man in front shouted something in a foreign language and a gun was pressed against Jeff's face. He could see Daryl, her eyes suddenly wide in fear.

The driver said, "Stop it or we kill you and dump your bodies. No more fighting. That is finished." Then he snapped an order in the other language and the couple were quickly bound with clothesline and gagged.

Ahmed pulled onto Route de Meyrin, melding with the evening traffic. He watched the mirror closely but they'd attracted no notice that he could see. He reassured himself that as problematic as the snatch had been, it had taken less than one minute. In the dark, it was not likely that it had been noticed, or at least not sufficiently to summon the police in time to do anything.

But he had to get rid of the van at once. Fortunately, he didn't have far to go. Within a few minutes he easily found the empty shop again. He pulled up to the garage, nosing the van nearly against the doors. He stepped outside, quietly closed the door to the van.

Nothing.

There were no sounds beyond the ordinary, nothing to see that wasn't there earlier. He moved to the street itself and as casually as he could looked in both directions while he lit a cigarette. His hand was shaking slightly.

Back at the van he rapped on the side door. This was the dangerous part. They had to get the couple into the back room without attracting attention.

Ahmed pulled out his gun, using his body to shield it from the street. "Cooperate and you'll be free in a few hours," he said evenly. "All we want is to talk to you. Struggle, we'll kill you and leave you here. You understand?"

Jeff nodded. Daryl glared at Ahmed fiercely. *I'd better be careful of her*, he thought as he moved aside to let Ali and Karim pull them out. They then pushed and led the couple across the front of the store, along the pathway to the rear where Ahmed joined then. He put his gun away, then unlocked and opened the heavy metal door.

"Inside," he said as the men shoved the couple in.

Once the door was closed Ahmed spoke to Karim. "Get the bag out of the van and bring it here. Then drive to the commercial district I pointed out earlier. You know where it is?"

"I do."

"Good. Leave the van with the keys in the ignition. Perhaps we will get lucky and someone will steal it. Leave the driver window open to make it easy. Drive carefully but not suspiciously. Then take your time returning on foot. Make certain you are not followed."

"I won't be."

"Good. Give me your gun."

"What?"

"Your gun. You are not a gangster. You have no need of it now."

Karim handed it over and went out to the Crafter. Ahmed heard it start, then move off. He turned his attention to the couple, thinking for a moment how best to do this.

20

GENEVA, SWITZERLAND
POLICE GENDARMERIE CORNAVIN
PLACE DE CORNAVIN 3
8:22 P.M. CET

Yvette Chappuis had just made the turn onto the Avenue de la Paix when she saw it.

She slowed her car, gradually pulling to a stop, and watched in horror as two men struggled with a young couple, finally forcing them into a white van. She was certain she'd seen a gun. As the van pulled away she lifted her cell phone and made a call.

A sergeant at the Police Gendarmerie Cornavin, just down the street near the corner of Rue de Lausanne at Route de Meyrin, was soon speaking with her. The report of an abduction was always to be taken seriously—this was, after all, Switzerland—but one within a stone's throw of his station and immediately in front of UNOG was priority. He took the vehicle description, handed the slip of paper to dispatch, and within two minutes of Yvette spotting the abduction an alert had gone out.

The sergeant then asked the citizen to describe what she'd seen in more detail, concluding the call by telling her an officer was on the way to take a statement.

Her call and the sergeant's quick response was the last bit of luck the Geneva police would have for some time. No cruising police car observed the right van, though fourteen were pulled over in the next hour. None contained abductors or victims.

It wasn't until shortly after midnight, many hours after the report, that a cruising Meyrin Commune police patrol car spotted the white Volkswagen Crafter van in the commerce center parking lot. The driver window was down and the keys were in the ignition. It had all the appearance of an abandoned vehicle.

The shift commander, Ulrich Spyri, went to examine the van himself. He stopped his car some twenty feet from it, then climbed out, stretching after so many hours in his office. He instructed the waiting patrol officer to search the extended area around the vehicle. It was dark, the sky overcast, the air chilly, clinging this hour to the winter so recently gone.

For centuries, Meyrin had been little more than a sleepy village. Then, almost overnight, with the construction of the nearby international airport it had ballooned to a population of twenty thousand. The commune police force saw to the routine duties of law enforcement: conducting patrols, maintaining order, enforcing traffic laws. And tonight they were assisting the canton police in locating a vehicle much like this one, reportedly used in an abduction.

Spyri walked slowly about the vehicle, playing his flashlight across the panels of white, examining each of the wheels carefully, bending down to look under it. Nothing.

Next, he carefully opened the left door and examined the driving compartment. Again nothing. He spotted the button for the side door and pressed it, heard the door unlatch and partially open. He went around the vehicle, leaned in, and took a long minute to examine the interior, moving his light from point to point. He spotted two liter bottles of a yellowish liquid, likely urine, and the discards from a meal for more than one man. He climbed in, held the flashlight low, then ran it slowly back and forth across the soiled carpet. "There," he said under his breath. He reached out and lifted something up with his fingertips.

Blond hair. This was the van.

At his car, Spyri called in, alerting the canton police and dispatching a forensic team. Afterward, he stood beside his car and looked slowly about. They could be far away by now. They might have made the switch here, then driven off and were well into France or Italy by this time. Or they were not that far from here at all, hoping the police net would be extended and overlook them.

Whichever it was, or if it was something else, he was certain his men had no chance beyond blind luck in finding the couple. No chance at all.

The van was soon traced to the name of Franco Rivaz, reportedly a resident of Geneva, but no one by that name lived at the address given. Then word came from UNOG security. They were missing an American couple, computer experts. They'd left the building shortly before the abduction and never reached their hotel. A laptop had been recovered from the sidewalk near the street in front of the exit. The British Foreign office had been alerted.

The Geneva Gendarmerie remained on the case, joined by the canton police as well as by a detail from the UNOG Police de la Sécurité Internationale. One of those was Henri Wille, who'd learned of the abduction by telephone and had assigned himself to the team sent to locate them.

"They were a nice couple," Henri said, shortly after meeting Spyri for the first time.

"We're doing our best," Spyri said. "Maybe we'll find them."

By now every officer in the region was on the lookout for the young couple or anything of a suspicious nature that might lead to them. But without more information, without an address, or even a part of the city in which to focus, there was little hope they would be found.

Henri drew a deep breath. "Sometimes miracles happened."

Just then Spyri's cell phone rang.

21

Frank Renkin drew a sharp breath at hearing the news. When he could speak, he said, "Are we certain it was them?"

"Regretfully, yes," Yates said. "There is no doubt."

"Any luck?"

"The local police located the van that was used but have absolutely no idea where they were taken. I hold myself responsible for this. I never imagined that something like this could happen."

"Who would do this? Is it a street crime of some type?"

"In Geneva? In front of UNOG? Hardly. No, I'm afraid we must conclude that it is a result of whatever it is they were investigating. It's very troubling."

"How would anyone know who they were? Or that they were at UNOG? Or for that matter, what they were working on? This information has all been tightly held."

"Yes, it is another reason why I'm so deeply distressed. It suggests we have a leak of some kind. I can't think of any other scenario that fits. Mr. Aiken was kidnapped within one day of arriving in Geneva. All he did was sleep at his hotel and work at UNOG. Yet someone knew who he was, presumably what he was up to, and was able to snatch him. And Dr. Haugen, who was with him."

"That all seems a bit of a stretch," Frank said. "This could be completely unrelated."

"I believe we must assume my analysis is correct until we learn more. I don't see any other alternative. It seems to me that whenever we deal with the UN it leaks like a bloody sieve. I hardly know where to start."

Frank thought a moment, then said, "Maybe our leak isn't someone, but some*thing*."

There was a pause. "You're suggesting that our system is penetrated beyond this most recent incident?"

"Not yours, but perhaps UNOG's."

Yates seemed to moan. "I hope that isn't true. I'll request their IT people get on it."

"They'll be in ass-covering mode." Frank wondered if the Brits used that expression.

"Yes, they most certainly will," Yates answered, and Frank could hear the smile in his voice. "I'll have to see how much pressure Her Majesty's government can bring to bear. I'll inform you of any developments as soon as I learn of them. I know you were friends with them both."

They worked on the latest version of Project Elephant, publicly known as Stuxnet, Frank wanted to say. Elephant was the most secret project Frank had ever participated in. He and his counterpart in the Israeli Mossad had established the framework for the work and over the years it had gone well. No more than twenty software engineers knew everything and they served primarily as coordinators. Each aspect of Elephant had been parceled out to trusted individuals to write a specific portion of code. The control center was responsible for bringing it all together and arranging its release.

The first version was known in-house as Trunk. Once it was identified it had been given the name Stuxnet by the cyber security world and in the media. Version two of Elephant was known as Ear. It was publicly called Dugu. Now the third variant, Tusk, was out. When identified, Frank suspected it would be known as Stuxnet3, though it might receive an entirely different public name.

Somewhere in Israel, a team of bright boys and girls was projecting Project Elephant into the future, keeping it well ahead of the response curve. More versions were under development, a seemingly endless stream from what Frank could tell. No one knew with certainty where it would all end. For now, Project Elephant was carefully controlled and target specific. But the same system could be used by those less cautious. When that happened, the digital equivalent of an atomic bomb would be unleashed with devastating consequences.

Jeff and Daryl were the brightest. They'd asked no questions though he had no doubt they knew what they were working on. But what they knew paled when compared to how much they could conjecture based on what they'd seen. *You have no idea how important getting them back is,* Frank thought. But he could say none of this.

Frank disconnected with a sinking heart. "Were," Yates had said. They were dead already in the Brit's mind.

Frank gritted his teeth. After a moment he left his office and went in search of Agnes Edinfield. He discovered her in a meeting. *What else?* Frank thought. Meetings were first and foremost the Company's cottage industry.

Thirty minutes later, a tired-looking Edinfield emerged from the room, clutching a sheath of papers. She spotted Frank. "The Iranians are causing trouble all over the place," she said to him. "More evidence they're funneling weapons and money to Hezbollah. What's up?"

Frank moved to the side of the hallway out of earshot and said, "Jeff Aiken and Daryl Haugen have been kidnapped in Geneva."

Edinfield processed the information with a slight frown, then said, "They were still working on the OW bug?"

"Right. They'd traced it to a computer at UNOG. Daryl flew to Geneva and they've been working there. I had a video conference with them about it. They told me that they were nearly finished."

"What did they learn?"

"We believe the signs point to China. The British Foreign Office reports a penetration. The virus uses a bug in OfficeWorks that lets it get into a system when a user opens an infected document. We got lucky because a glitch in the virus caused OfficeWorks to crash, which alerted the Foreign Office IT staff."

"How about our end?"

"I'm still a day or two away from issuing an in-house alert. We want to really nail this thing first. We've reported the OfficeWorks flaw and notified US-CERT, of course." This was the operational arm of the National Cyber Security Division. Its primary objective was to create a strategic framework to prevent cyber-attacks against the U.S. computer infrastructure. The actual solution to the flaw would come from the company that made Office-Works.

Still, countless millions of computers would remain unprotected until the patch fixing the flaw was rolled out, something that could take a week or more. And then many IT staffs would delay applying it until they'd tested it, meaning that it could be a month or two before the door this cyber-attack used was even partially closed.

"Has this thing infected our networks?" Edinfield asked.

"We don't know yet. About Jeff and Daryl . . ."

Edinfield looked embarrassed for a moment. "I'm sorry. I'm exhausted. That should have been my first question. Have they been located?"

"No. A search is under way."

"What was it? Some kind of street crime?"

"They were abducted by three men just after leaving the UNOG building. It appears to have been planned."

Edinfield paused before continuing. "You're suggesting it has something to do with their work at UNOG."

"We can't dismiss the possibility. We've reached a time when experts like Daryl and Jeff are no longer immune to physical violence."

She seemed to recall something just then. "They weren't working for us, were they?"

"No. The British Foreign office hired them."

"Could there be a connection back to us?"

Oh yes, Frank thought. "They were working on this thing that potentially involves China, Iran, and the UN report on Iran's nuclear program. It's not my area of expertise, but my understanding is that the major powers will take military action if that report says they are about to detonate a nuclear device."

Frank paused to gather his thoughts, then continued. "As I say, it's not my area but let's accept that Iran is about to do just that—that is, detonate an atomic bomb, with all that means to the world. Let's say they only need just a little bit of time. If they can sabotage this report, delay UNOG issuing it or prevent the UN from speaking with a clear voice, then they'll buy valuable time."

"That sounds very speculative."

"Not so much, actually. The existence of this Trojan and the changes in the UNOG report suggests there's something to it. Now the team uncovering and tracing the virus has been abducted, right under the noses of the United Nations."

Edinfield nodded. "I get your point. One interpretation is that Iran is about ready to explode a nuclear bomb. That's consistent with the reports I've been reading."

Frank cleared his throat. "There is a bit more you should know. Some months ago, their company—meaning Daryl and Jeff—performed work for Frontline Integrated Systems on Project Tusk. They spent about three months locating zero day vulnerabilities in Android's wireless services,

WiFi, and Bluetooth. This was contract work for the Company. It was segregated so they don't know what project they were working on but they've been around. They know it was for us."

"How important is the work they did?"

Frank hesitated, then decided to tell her. "Crucial." He instinctively lowered his voice. "I can't say the name, Agnes, not without clearance, but think about it. I will say the project directly relates to what we were just talking about."

"Relax, Frank. I've not been briefed but I've heard rumors about Stuxnet3; even heard the word *Tusk* related to it. I get the picture. This is really bad. Really bad. Do you think that is why they were abducted?"

"I have no idea but we have to recognize the possibility."

"I agree. We need to get them back and safe. I'll do what I can, Frank. Thank you."

22

Once Karim left to return the van, Ahmed told Ali to go into the abandoned shop and work area facing the street. "Find a dark place. Be certain you are not observed," he said. "Any patrolling officer knows this building is unoccupied and if you are seen he will be immediately suspicious. But if a patrol car stops or you see officers on foot, I want to be warned." Ali nodded, then went into the front room. He was a good man and Ahmed was confident he'd be careful.

He looked back at the prisoners. They appeared calm, sitting on the concrete floor, near the far wall, too frightened to speak from what Ahmed could see. Now he considered exactly what he would do if Ali burst into this backroom with word the police were outside. He'd been taught to plan ahead. Focus on the task at hand but always know what to do next.

Shooting their way clear would be futile and was against orders. He smiled. No, he'd cut the prisoners loose and pretend they were old friends having a visit. The police would not believe it, of course, and the Americans would give a different version but a lawyer could make something of it in court. At the least, it would be better than finding them tied.

With this in mind he took a few minutes to improve their appearance, adjusting clothing, straightening hair. The man said nothing but the woman told him to, as she put it, "Go to hell and keep your hands to yourself!"

Next, Ahmed set the room in order. Afterward he cleaned himself up in the bathroom, then made the room even more presentable. As he worked, Jeff and Daryl exchanged looks of concern and confusion. It seemed an odd time for housekeeping but anything that delayed the next step Jeff considered a positive.

Ahmed took a seat and waited. After a bit there was a gentle rap at the door. He rose and admitted Karim into the room. "Any trouble?"

Karim shook his head. His jacket was wet, and water dripped from his nose. "It's been raining. It just stopped. I don't think anyone saw me walking. And I took a long way."

"Good. Watch the prisoners but say nothing."

Karim nodded in reply as he crossed his arms and assumed a position by the door.

Based on the messages he'd received, Ahmed knew the man was a computer expert of some kind. He didn't look like it, not at all, but Ahmed accepted what he'd been told. He was fit, almost like an athlete. He appeared nothing like the computer types Ahmed knew in Prague.

Ahmed had no idea why Hamid cared about the man but he'd been instructed to find out what he was doing in UNOG. In particular, he wanted to know of any progress he'd made. He'd been given no instructions about what to do with him in time but since his orders had been to kill him if abduction wasn't possible he didn't doubt what that would be. They'd not been told to wear masks. Once drained of information, once Hamid was satisfied, the outcome was inevitable.

His instructions had made no mention of a woman. It didn't matter. He'd taken her because he couldn't leave a witness behind. He assumed initially that she was someone the man had met in UNOG, perhaps an employee there, but her passport said she was an American and her address was the same as the man's. A wife? A girlfriend? Perhaps a colleague as well.

Ahmed decided on a direct approach. They didn't appear to be trained agents and this was the simplest way to find out if they were. He'd not laid a hand on either of them except for what was necessary to take them from the street and to bind them. There was time for violence later.

"Mr. Aiken, what work do you do?" he asked quietly.

"Why don't you go to hell?" Daryl snapped.

Ahmed smiled. *Now there's a fierce one*, he thought, wondering for an instant how he could use that to his advantage. "I was speaking to the gentleman."

"I *know* who you were talking to. Turn us loose. Now!"

Ahmed smiled. This was absurd. Is that what American women were like? Ordering men about? Demanding they perform? It explained a great deal if that was the case. "You must be silent or I will be forced to gag you again. It is not pleasant. Movies make it look as if it is nothing but we know otherwise, don't we?" The idea was to form a bond with them, as strange as that seemed. Given time—though Ahmed doubted they had enough—the captives would become friends, or at least very friendly.

"Don't tell me what I know and don't know! You people are criminals and the police are going to catch you, so you might as well turn us loose and get out of here. You haven't much time. The police are searching for us everywhere right now!" Daryl glared at Ahmed.

"It's all right," Jeff said. "There's no reason not to answer his questions. We have nothing to hide." *Tusk*, he thought. *I hope they don't know about our work on Tusk.*

Daryl gave Jeff a withering look but said nothing. While she'd had Ahmed's attention Jeff had searched the floor behind him for something, anything, and came up with what felt like part of a drill bit, or at least a fragment of hard metal. With it he'd begun methodically working on the knots binding his wrists. Now he stopped as the mustached man was looking directly at him. "I'm a computer security technician," Jeff said. It occurred to him that it might be possible to keep Daryl out of this.

"What are you doing for the United Nations?"

"A computer virus was sent by someone at UNOG to an office in Britain." Jeff could think of no reason to mention the UK Foreign Office until necessary. "I was locating it and fixing the problems it created."

Ahmed wrinkled his forward. "Surely, UNOG has people who can do that."

"It's a very sophisticated virus and it's new. I'm a specialist. It took some effort to discover it and determine its properties," Jeff said.

"Still, it makes no sense to spend so much money. And why would Britain use Americans? They also have people for such work," Ahmed said. This had to be CIA. He could think of no other answer. Abducting this man, the priority given the assignment, now made sense.

Daryl sighed as if Ahmed were stupid. "It had the potential of causing a great deal of harm. You understand *that*, don't you?"

"You do this work as well?" He already suspected as much about the woman.

"Go to hell," Daryl said.

Ahmed stopped for a moment. This was remarkable. He'd never encountered a woman like this before. He wondered if she were mentally deranged in some way. Either that or she failed to understand what was taking place.

"You found this virus, then?" he said to Jeff. "And fixed the problems?"

"We found it," Jeff said. "We were nearly finished here and planning to leave soon."

Jeff eyed Ahmed. He had no idea how rough this was going to get. These were clearly men capable of greater violence than they'd already demonstrated. He just wondered what it would take to convince the mustached man and didn't like where that thought took him.

Ahmed nodded. "I see." He drew a packet from his pocket and lit a cigarette, realizing as he did that he'd made the woman even angrier. *Perhaps if I blow smoke in her face she'll cooperate,* he thought.

He stood smoking, wondering what else to ask. The man's answers were straightforward enough. Finally, he told Karim to watch carefully while he went outside.

In the backyard, rain dripped from the overarching trees. Ahmed pulled an unused cell phone from his pocket and turned it on. When ready, he punched in the number. After several seconds a voice came on, sounding very much like Hamid, but you could never be certain.

"We have him and a woman who I think is a colleague working with him," Ahmed said in English. The American eavesdropping computers were programmed to focus on Farsi, he'd been taught.

"Problems?"

"No. All is well so far." He told him what he'd learned.

"So they found it and a fix is under way?"

"That is what he says. I think it is likely the truth."

"That is unfortunate. We just didn't move fast enough. All right, so be it. Use whatever means you require to confirm the information. They may be misleading you. Just make certain they are not lying."

"All right."

"If there is a change in the story, let me know."

"What am I to do when finished?"

"It isn't decided but they will not be released, obviously. He is valuable so take care of him. Do the same with the woman. For now it may be enough to keep them away, especially if they've lied to you. There is something more. I am sending you a photograph, a name, and a home address." He told Ahmed what he wanted done. "For the couple, move to the next stage. Learn what they know of the virus they were working on and who else knows about it. Be certain."

When the call was finished, Ahmed took the phone apart and removed the SIM card. The phone itself he broke up and scattered into the shrubbery in the rear of the lot. As for the card, he glanced about, then went to the patch of dirt where the key had been concealed under the flat stone. He broke the card with a rock, then pushed it deep into the soft, moist soil and smoothed the surface.

Unlike some he knew, Ahmed had never enjoyed torture. It was occasionally necessary and his instructor had carefully taught him how to use it to best effect. He looked heavenward into the cloudy sky. He heard the sound of a jet landing not far away, the slight sound of distant traffic. There was the lightest sprinkling of rain against his face. For a moment, he thought of home, of his sister whose wedding he had missed. He sighed and flipped his cigarette to the damp ground.

Inside, Jeff rubbed the metal against the cord steadily, careful to give nothing away. What he feared most was dropping it, certain the sound would be noticed. Whatever he had—he thought it a broken drill bit—it cut into his fingers. He pushed the pain out of his mind, telling himself not much longer. He could feel the wet of his blood.

The problem was what to do once his hands were free. His feet were still tied. He'd tried to communicate what was happening to Daryl and thought he'd succeeded but she was now ignoring him. That's what she'd do if she understood, but also if she had no idea what his facial expressions had meant.

The heavy door creaked open and in stepped their interrogator. Jeff stopped. This one with the mustache was much cleverer than the other two, and far more observant. He watched Ahmed speak to the man guarding them, then nod toward Daryl. The big man went to the woman, grabbed her by her shoulders, jerked her from the wall, sitting her upright.

Ahmed looked on, then squatted in front of Jeff. "Mr. Aiken, I must determine if you have told me the truth. It is necessary. I do not wish to harm you or the woman but . . ." He shrugged.

"I *have* told you the truth," Jeff said quickly, trying desperately to stop what he knew was coming. "If there is *anything* else you want to know, just ask. Neither of us has any reason to lie to you. Just don't . . . don't hurt her. Ask me. Please."

Ahmed stared at Jeff for a moment. *A man of considerable courage*, he thought, *though he has yet to be tested.* "I understand," he said.

Ahmed rose, went to the bag, and removed an unused heavy plastic shopping bag. He carefully unfolded it, then went to Daryl and stood behind her. She craned her neck to look back at him. Jeff started to shout, then was dumbstruck as in a single practiced motion Ahmed slipped the bag over Daryl's head, cinching it tightly around her neck.

Daryl shrieked. It was the most frightening sound Jeff ever heard. The bag muffled the sound only slightly. Ahmed stood behind Daryl, holding her head in the vise of his two hands while the other man held her strongly by her shoulders.

"What else have you to add?" Ahmed asked Jeff.

"Stop it!" Jeff shouted. "Stop it! I've told you everything!" His hands were all but free. "You're killing her."

Daryl was no longer making a sound. Instead, she sucked air hard now, the heavy plastic moving back and forth in front of her mouth.

"No, Mr. Aiken. *You* are killing her with your lies."

"What do you want?" Jeff shouted. "Just tell me. I'll say it. Tell me what you want to hear!"

"The truth. That is all. Are you really finished with your work? Truly?"

Daryl was slapping her legs against the concrete floor. The men held her fiercely. The plastic before her mouth was going back and forth more rapidly. Jeff worked the bit furiously, the pain now so sharp he could no longer ignore it.

Just at that moment Ali hurried into the room. "Police outside," he said.

"Did they see you?" Ahmed asked.

"No."

"Let's look. Karim, watch them." Then mercifully, he pulled the bag from Daryl's head. "You two be quiet or we kill you at once. There will be no rescue." Ahmed and Ali went into the next room.

The man released Daryl and she toppled to her side, taking deep breaths, her face bathed in sweat. Jeff looked at the man who was eyeing him steadily as if he knew something.

Ali led Ahmed down a short hallway, then to his watching spot and pointed. It was a good location, deep in the shadows. A patrol car was stopped across the street, the engine still running. The lone officer inside was looking at his lap, as if writing something. The men watched patiently, unmoving. Finally, the car eased slowly away.

"Stay here," Ahmed said. He turned to go back into the rear room just as he heard noise come from down the hallway, on the other side of the door.

The moment the mustached man had left the room, Jeff freed his hands. He'd given Daryl an affirmative look. She was still breathing deeply and he feared she was too distracted to help. Instead she said, "You there. I'm thirsty. Give me some water."

Karim shook his head as if he spoke no English.

"Water," she said slowly. She licked her lips. "Thirsty."

The man nodded in comprehension, then looked about. Spotting the carry bag he reached inside and came out with an unopened plastic bottle of water. He unscrewed the cap, then went to Daryl, leaned down, straightened her to a sitting position, then placed the bottle to her lips.

With his hands, Jeff pushed himself erect as Daryl butted the man with her head. Jeff dove at Karim and knocked him over. The man fell hard. Jeff sat on the floor, grabbed at the cord holding his ankles together, and was able with some effort to sweep it off his feet, taking his shoes with it. On his feet he lunged at Karim before he had a chance to get up and struck him hard across the jaw. Just as he turned to Daryl, the door to the other room opened.

"Run, Jeff. Run. Now!" Daryl said. "Get help!"

Jeff hesitated, looked at her in desperation, then turned to the heavy door and pushed it open. Ali was on him in a flash but Jeff had the door open and was outside. Ali came after him, dragging his arm, and shouting in a foreign language. Jeff turned and punched him in the face as hard as he could, striking him directly on his nose. The man cried out and released him.

Jeff turned to his right and fled in his thin socks down the narrow pathway into the street. Quickly orienting himself he spotted a busy street not far away and began running toward it, expecting the sound of a gunshot any second but none came. When he looked back, the street was empty.

For a crazy second, Jeff thought to return to rescue Daryl. But he didn't have a prayer of success against three armed men. So he turned and ran for all he was worth down the middle of Avenue de Vaudagne to the Route de Meyrin, praying he could find help in time at this time of night.

His socks were quickly worn away, then the skin of his feet. He sprinted. Running harder than he'd ever run in his life, praying this was the right choice.

DAY SIX

TUESDAY, APRIL 14

CYBER SECURITY NEWS

OUR DEADLY HIJACKED DRONES

By Dietrich Helm

Military Drones Turned on U.S. Troops

April 14

A leaked classified report confirms what has been rumored for some months. The drone aircraft on which the U.S. military has become so reliant has been successfully turned against our own forces. Use of all drones has been suspended pending a comprehensive review.

The United States military has placed increasing reliance on remote, semiautomated surveillance and weapons delivery systems. Their security has long been a matter of major concern. "I fear the day the enemy takes control of one," an army sergeant in Afghanistan said last year on condition of anonymity.

Though the government isn't releasing figures, it is estimated that well over three hundred insurgent leaders have been killed by rocket attacks launched from unmanned aerial drones since Operation Iraqi Freedom. Thousands of insurgents have been similarly killed. Roving drones armed with Hellfire rockets are operated from mainland America. The rockets are unleashed by the press of a computer key.

According to the report, a common software program such as SkyGrabber, which can be bought for less than $30 off the Internet, allowed insurgents to hack into the drone cameras and control system. This was possible, sources say, because though the system cost billions to develop and build, no antivirus software was ever installed in its operating system. The U.S. military ignored repeated warnings about this shortcoming.

The report reveals that last January a drone in Afghanistan was turned against American forces. Its rockets reportedly killed eight Special Forces. The drone had been launched for an attack on an insurgent stronghold but the U.S.-based operator lost control of the craft. The deadly attack took place a few minutes later.

"It will cost millions to fix and delay the use of drones for months if not a year," one informed source reports. "Software security measures should have been installed from the beginning. It's not as if this was an unexpected turn of events."

The overriding question is just how many Americans will die as a consequence of this failure. The Department of Defense has declined comment or confirmation of the leaked report.

Tags: drones, Afghanistan, friendly fire, insurgent hackers

23

Gholam Rahmani glanced at his wristwatch and realized he was running late. Moving about in central Madrid at this hour was always a problem and he should have allowed more time to reach the meeting. Pedestrians crossed the busy streets without regard for the cars inching along. Madrid had grown from a traditional pueblo and the city center had retained that small town configuration with its narrow winding streets and low buildings.

Rahmani eased back in the taxi and reminded himself not to worry about it. This was Spain and though these were Iranians with whom he was meeting they'd surely been contaminated by the chronic tardiness characteristic of Spaniards. He'd be lucky if the rest were even there. He drew an American cigarette from a pack, lit and decided he should simply relax.

As executive director of the Frente Democrático Iraniano, or FDI, headquartered in Rome, he made at least one of these fund-raising trips to Madrid each year. The FDI was one of the oldest organizations in opposition to the ruling mullahs in Iran. From his office in Italy he maintained the FDI's Web site and confidential forum, connecting Iranian ex-patriots from across Europe.

The organization received the ongoing attention of VEVAK, Iran's intelligence service, and Rahmani's rise to the directorship had been in part due to the assassination of two predecessors. This was the price expatriate Iranians once loyal to the Shah were forced to pay to return their country to freedom, to release it from the iron grip of theocracy.

The fall of the Shah had been disastrous for the Rahmani family. At the time he'd been living with his father in Rome where a new branch of the family's successful Persian rug export business had been established. But most of the family's wealth was in Tehran as was the rest of the family. When things appeared sufficiently settled his father had returned to bring them out, leaving his nineteen-year-old son to tend affairs in Rome. Rahmani had never heard from his father again.

It had been several years before he received word from his mother informing him that his two younger brothers had died as martyrs in the war against Iraq and that his two sisters had both been married and were now widowed for the same reason. She cautioned him not to return and instead to do all he could to someday find a way out of the country for the family, but most of all to take care of himself. That was his only contact with his mother. Afterward, she and his two sisters were lost in the unsettled time that followed the end of the war with Iraq.

The taxi driver tapped his horn to alert three talking women, then stopped beside the four stout pillars planted in front of the two-story building. These were meant to prevent anyone parking here. Rahmani stepped out, paid the driver, then went to the front doors. One of the young women seemed to pay close attention to him and he turned his face away. In the lobby he punched the elevator button for the third floor and waited. He heard the motor engage above, then felt the slight sense of movement as the small elevator descended to him. He glanced surreptitiously outside and noted that one of the other women was taking a photo with her cell phone. He would be in the picture.

He sighed. Nothing to do about it. They were likely harmless anyway. He glanced at his watch. Just after nine o'clock. Not so bad after all.

Rahmani was a diminutive man, though all his features were well formed. He stood just five feet five inches. His hair was luxurious and long. A source of pride, he kept it carefully combed. A closely cropped beard concealed the acne scars of his youth and he wore heavy-rimmed glasses. His usual dress was a dark business suit, though he wore a tie for occasions such as this.

He was greeted as he stepped from the elevator, the man speaking Farsi. They shook hands, then Rahmani entered the meeting room and found it almost full—an excellent sign. Nearly everyone turned to face him, most smiled and nodded in greeting. It was an older crowd with a scattering of young faces, adult children of men and women who had died in exile. For every woman there were three men. He walked to the front and stepped up on a slightly raised platform. There was a lectern and behind it a row of seven folding chairs.

Rahmani was urgently required at the office in Rome and he'd asked to advance the starting time for this meeting, so such a large crowd had come as a pleasant surprise. A woman of about fifty, slightly overweight and a few years old than he, greeted him.

"You see?" she said. "I told you they would come. Everyone is very excited to hear what you have to say." Her name was Zarah and she'd taken over local leadership of the Iranian community in central Spain when her father had died three years before. She'd proven less effective and contributions were down since then but she was enthusiastic. She wore too much makeup in Rahmani's view and smelled vaguely of sandalwood. "I know you must leave so I suggest we start at once."

Rahmani nodded and took a seat.

There were perhaps just fifteen thousand Iranian exiles living in Spain and they were by and large an affluent class. They'd always been generous to the FDI. This though his three largest donors had all died the previous year, two when they were struck by cars, the third having gone missing while sailing, his body later washing up on a beach near Tariff.

As Zarah introduced him in glowing terms his mind returned to the three women outside. It wasn't like the VEVAK to use women but they were changing their ways. He knew this community was watched and he was all but certain his donors had been murdered. It took courage to oppose evil.

Perhaps it was like that pizza parlor about which he'd read in Jerusalem. It was a special target for suicide bombers and over the years the slaughter had been enormous. But the parlor was always rebuilt and always well attended. The young Israelis refused to be driven away, refused to surrender to the terrorist. This was like that, Rahmani thought.

Zarah was done speaking and he stood to a round of strong applause. He acknowledged old friends in the crowd, then began with an update of FDI's activities this past year, followed by an account of his travels on behalf of the cause. He reported events within Iran that it was unlikely they'd heard. The mullahs kept a tight lid on the country but the FDI had its ways.

The most significant news from Iran was the progress it was making with its nuclear program. Everything else in the country was falling apart. With but a single gasoline refinery in a nation awash with oil it was necessary to import refined gasoline by tanker. As Iran's economic condition declined through corruption and mismanagement, there were constant shortages and long lines at service stations. And that was just an outward sign of the chronic deficiencies in nearly everything.

Even the vaunted nuclear program was experiencing serious setbacks. The virus attack surely initiated by Israel had significantly set back the production of enriched uranium. The nation's single nuclear power plant was very much an on-again off-again operation. But as badly as the program was progressing, at least it was progress, if that's how you chose to see it.

Iran will have the bomb soon, Rahmani told his audience. Very soon. And when that happens everything will change. His audience turned sober at the thought. He'd discussed the likely consequences with them before and they were informed people. They knew.

Within Iran, even some of those in opposition to the mullahs took pride in the prospect of their country becoming a nuclear power. India had the bomb; so did Pakistan and Israel. Why shouldn't they? The bombing of nuclear facilities by either America or Israel would anger many Iranians who otherwise despised the nation's rulers. It could very likely unite the nation in an unpredictable way.

But no one in this audience wanted to see Iran with the bomb. It would solidify the mullahs' hold on power and spread more tyranny throughout the region. It could very easily lead to the first nuclear war.

A counterstrike could not be prevented. The United States was pledged to respond with nuclear weapons if they were used against Israel. Israel itself could nuke Iran. Even if the Iranians managed to knock out Israel's land-based capability with a sneak attack, there were Israeli submarines with nuclear-tipped rockets cruising off the coast of Iran. And they could not be stopped.

What would the inevitable retaliation do to Iran? It would certainly destroy it as a modern nation; cast it back into a new dark age from which it would never arise in their lifetimes. And in so doing, leave it open to foreign aggression. Iran had been invaded and occupied before, and would be again Rahmani was certain.

Without a nuclear bomb the current regime was trouble enough for those listening to him. They had worked hard to establish themselves in Spain. They maintained a low profile, struggled daily against the stereotypical belief they were Arabs, an unpopular group in Spain. They struggled as well to make it clear that they opposed and were victims of the mullahs, not supporters of the theocracy.

As always Rahmani wrapped up on an optimistic note. He didn't practice the art of frightening people to give. The money should come from the heart. In traditional fashion a fedora was passed and most laid checks or envelopes into it, though a number gave euros. Rahmani would record the cash for the organization's private records but the money itself would go into his pocket to pay his way. This kept it from the Italian tax authorities.

He finished with his customary farewell. "We will see a free Iran again. I believe it. And you should believe it as well." He smiled broadly. "Be sure to give us your current address for our newsletter."

Afterward there was a crush of hands and of words of deep gratitude. Before leaving he pocketed the updated register, then with a warm smile set off. Outside the women were gone. Rahmani took a taxi directly to the airport. On the plane no one seemed to pay him special attention, nor did anyone as he went to get his car.

By that afternoon, he was at his office. He placed the revised register in his safe, making a mental note to update the computer database later. He glanced at his watch. There was much to do and very little time.

24

MEYRIN, SWITZERLAND
MAIRIE COMMUNE DE MEYRIN POLICE
RUE DES BOUDINES 2
9:34 A.M. CET

Ulrich Spyri entered the police station with a scowl. He'd allowed himself to have hope in what logic and experience told him was a hopeless situation.

"Where is he?" he asked the desk sergeant.

"In the common room, sir."

"I'll be there if anyone needs me." Spyri was buzzed from the waiting area into the hallway leading to the offices and holding cells of the police station. He walked the short distance to the common room. Inside were three tables with chairs, a pair of vending machines, a joint use refrigerator, a microwave and two toasters. Someone had placed travel posters along one wall with pictures of distant and sunny climes.

When the American had been picked up on the Route de Meyrin by a patrol car not long after midnight, Spyri had him rushed to the station. His feet were bleeding and he was struggling to compose himself. He'd been bandaged and provided with a pair of shoes. For all that he'd been through, he gave a good recounting of the kidnapping, of his extraordinary escape, and an accurate picture of where he'd been held and how to get there. He'd conveyed the sense of urgency they all felt.

Within minutes Spyri was confident he knew where the woman was. His lieutenant had been furious as they'd waited the few minutes for the tactical team to prepare for the rescue. The old shoe shop wasn't three blocks from the police station.

The raid had taken place very quickly and with typical Swiss precision. And to no avail.

The woman was gone. So were the three men.

The forensic team had meticulously combed the van they'd discovered but so far had produced nothing of use. The problem now was that Spyri had no idea what vehicle they'd fled in. They'd questioned everyone living or working along the street but no one had seen anything. With the border to either France or Italy not ten kilometers away they were surely already out of the country and had been by the time the raid was launched. He'd immediately sent an alert but had no expectation it would succeed.

Jeff was sitting at a table with a blanket across his shoulders. A female officer had been assigned to remain with him as experience had shown a woman had a calming effect in such situations. Spyri took a chair that gave a small squeal as he moved it and sat facing the American.

"You've been told?"

Jeff nodded. "Yes. I'm disappointed but relieved you didn't find a body. Do you have any leads?" There were two Band-Aids on his face, three more on his hands. The laces to his oversized shoes were untied. He clutched a mug in his hand.

"We've sent an alert to all the neighboring countries. We routinely work with them and they will treat it as if the crime had been committed within their jurisdiction. We've also notified our own police in the unlikely event they've remained in Switzerland."

"What did you tell them to look for? Three men and a woman?"

"I'm afraid so. That's all we have presently." The American looked exhausted. Well, he would be.

There was a rap at the door and Henri Wille from UNOG entered the room carrying a black athletic bag. Spyri gestured at a chair. "You two met before, I think?" Spyri said. Jeff looked up and nodded in recognition.

"I am very sorry for this, Mr. Aiken. Your government and employers have been informed. I want you to know we are doing everything we possibly can to find Miss Haugen."

"Thank you." Jeff drank the now cold tea, then said, "Let me ask you an important question. If they were going to kill her, wouldn't they have done it where we were held? Then they'd leave? They wouldn't take her to kill her later, would they?"

They would if they wanted to question her first, Henri thought, glancing at Spyri, who by his look had reached the same conclusion. "We can't know what they plan," Henri said. "They are criminals, terrorists from what you've told us. We just must do all we can to find her. Has anything more come to mind since the police last spoke to you?"

"Nothing. I keep reliving it over and over, wondering if I shouldn't have tried to get her myself."

"You did the right thing," Henri said. "It was three against one. And they were armed. You'd have had no chance." No one said anything for a long moment, then Henri continued. "We found this at the scene of your abduction." He reached into the bag and extracted Jeff's laptop bag. "We've assumed it was either yours or your partner's."

"It's mine," Jeff said. "I could use it right about now."

Henri glanced at Spyri, who shrugged. He handed it over to Jeff, who took it with alacrity. He'd lost his cell phone during the abduction and never expected to see his laptop again. He removed the computer and flipped open the screen.

"We'll leave you for a bit, Mr. Aiken," Spyri said. "If I hear anything, anything at all, I'll let you know at once." He glanced at the female officer, indicating she was to remain. She nodded in understanding.

Outside in the hallway Henri leaned against the wall and let out a deep breath. "Rough," he said when Spyri had closed the door. "I'll be tagging along for now," he said. "I'm the Interpol contact at UNOG and I've received instructions to stay on this until she is recovered." Spyri nodded. "Don't look so grim," Henri said. "You did your best."

"I don't feel any better for it."

"I understand but you've got one of the two who were abducted. That's better than anything you could have hoped for a few hours ago."

Once the WiFi connection was established, Jeff immediately sent a message summarizing events to Frank Renkin in Langley, copying it to Graham Yates at Whitehall. Frank replied at once.

Good to know you're with us. Our best wishes for Daryl's safe return. Get some rest.

Frank

Suddenly overcome, Jeff placed his face into his hands in thought and exhaustion.

"Can I get you something, sir?" the woman asked from her place.

"No. I'm . . . just tired is all."

"We have somewhere you can lay down. I think it would be a good idea."

"Not yet. Thank you."

He went back to Frank's message and hit "reply." He asked for his assistance, unofficially if necessary.

I understand. If a friend can't go to the wall for you at this time what's he good for? You know I'll do what I can. Just be discreet. I'll get back to you ASAP. Don't do anything foolish.

Frank

Next, Jeff sent a message to Bridget Evans, Daryl's best friend at the National Security Agency where she'd once worked. Worldwide electronic surveillance and encryption were their specialty. To his relief he received an immediate message of sympathy and assurance that she'd do what he asked. "But it's my job if you aren't careful," she'd written.

Jeff closed the computer. "I'd like to go back to my hotel room, if that's all right. There isn't any point in my hanging out here from what I can see."

She stood up. "You're feeling all right, then? Shock can linger."

"I'm fine. I'd just like to get out of a police station and into a warm bed. I need to sleep and turn my mind off."

The woman nodded, stood up, and went out into the hallway. There she found Spyri, who was saying good-bye to Henri. He returned to the common room. "You're quite sure, Mr. Aiken?"

"Yes, I'm sure. This is now a police matter. I need to get some rest and I have to contact her family yet. I'm not looking forward to it." Actually, Jeff had no intention of contacting Daryl's family. He'd let her do that once he had her safely back.

"Very well," Spyri said. "Officer del Medico will drive you to your hotel and see you to your room. I will be in touch when we have any word at all."

It was not yet lunchtime when Jeff entered the ultramodern hotel room. Spyri had placed a uniformed officer out in the hallway as a precaution. To Jeff's surprise, he found it somewhat comforting to be back. It reminded him of a happier time, not that many hours ago, when his own world had been safe and he'd been with the woman he loved. It also seemed to him he could smell Daryl's fragrance, though he realized that was foolish. The room had been cleaned, the large bed freshly made. A light jacket Daryl had left out was now neatly folded atop her suitcase. He lifted it lightly and held it to his nostrils. There it was, her scent. He *had* smelled it.

Jeff placed the laptop on the desk and plugged it in to recharge. When he and Daryl had first moved in together she'd written a program that allowed the other to track his or her cell phone. That way they always knew were the other was. Since they traveled so often they'd found it a convenience. Plus, if either lost his or her cell phone, which Jeff had a tendency to do on occasion, they could find it.

He launched the app and his heart sank when he saw there was no signal from her phone. He checked for his own. The same. The phones weren't just off since they were programmed to report their position every fifteen minutes even when on standby. They were destroyed.

Next, Jeff checked messages and found none relevant. Though he had no appetite he picked up the room-service menu, used the telephone, and placed an order. He'd need the energy.

While he waited for the food, he stripped off his soiled clothes and stepped into a very hot shower. He let the water play over his body as he tried to control his thoughts. The last time he'd done this, Daryl had joined him and the memories were still vivid.

He stepped out of the shower and as he toweled off he inadvertently caught a look of himself in the large mirror. There was a bruise along his entire right side, two dark bruises on his face, as well as a number of small cuts and lacerations. He'd taken a beating.

He brushed his hair, then his teeth, and just as he put on the oversized bathrobe the doorbell chimed. He let the waiter carry his meal in and place it on the small table in front of the large window with two facing chairs, signed for it, then closed the door. He checked for messages again.

Nothing.

Jeff sighed, turned on the television for noise, then listlessly ate the meal, forcing himself to nearly finish the plate. Afterward he placed the tray outside, closed the door, then checked again for messages.

Still nothing.

He tried desperately to think of what else he could do. Rest, he decided. He could rest. He moved the computer to the bed and placed it beside his head, activating the chime and turning the volume all the way up. He lay back and closed his eyes, doubting he could sleep but within seconds had fallen into a restless black hole.

25

ISTANBUL, TURKEY
RED DRAGON RESTAURANT
YEDEK REIS SOKAK 13
KAVACIK MH.
11:52 A.M. EET

Rush hour was beginning and Wu Ying glanced across the terrace. Located atop a five-story building, his restaurant delivered a commanding view of the ancient city. The terrace was more than half full, a welcome sight as the weather had recently been cold. The Red Dragon was noted for its outdoor dining. In the near distance was the blue Bosporus, looking more inviting from here than it did on close examination. Flowing from the Black Sea into the Mediterranean, with the effluent of this metropolis of 12 million, it was an all but open sewer.

Today promised an early spring. Wu wondered if it would take or if winter would return. He glanced at the azure sky but found no answer there. Buds were thick on the carefully tended potted shrubbery, a handful of flowers revealing the first signs of blossoming. A good sign.

Customers had come out today to take in the view and enjoy his fare. There was laughter and the steady chatter of any successful restaurant, music to an owner's ears. Still, they were dressed warmly against what could on occasion be a chilling breeze from off the water.

The kitchen behind Wu was a zoo right now, contrasting sharply with the controlled pace and casual elegance of the terrace. The waitresses were dressed in body-hugging red cheongsam dresses embellished with elaborate golden embroidery. These had a closed neck and short sleeves. On their trim bodies the sight was subtly erotic, as the original designers had intended. His waiters were all young, slender, handsome men brought from mainland

China, like all the staff. Everyone and everything was efficient. Wu would have it no other way.

Originally from Shandong Province, China, he'd lived in Turkey for nearly ten years now. Besides the Red Dragon, he also owned the Great Wall in Ankara, and he divided his time between them. It was in Ankara where Wu had his residence, a modern condo situated above the city's chronic pollution. He had good managers at both restaurants but experience had proven they both required his attention.

Wu lit a cigarette near the railing so the sea breeze would carry away the smoke. This was Turkey and every adult and half the children smoked, it seemed to him, but enough antismoking tourists frequented the Red Dragon to make him cautious.

Wu watched an American couple across the terrace laughing. Each was overweight and their voices dominated the eating area. His father had told him that in time he'd likely resettle to America or perhaps Vancouver in Canada. Wu wondered if he'd like it. The thought of living in either place repelled him. But the Chinese were world settlers, more widespread than the Jews or Armenians. His time would come, he knew.

He reminded himself that he'd not expected to like Turkey. When his father first told him this was where he'd start the family business Wu had been miserable. Not even Europe, he'd thought. He'd expected France or one of the other Western countries. In the worst case, he'd thought he'd end up in South America, Rio or Buenos Aires. But Turkey!

It was neither East nor West. It was Muslim as well. He'd pictured himself living behind a guarded wall, cut off from a sterile city, unwelcome and alienated.

The reality had been the precise opposite. Turkey might be Muslim but it was a nominal designation. They didn't take it that seriously despite its overtly Muslim president. The ruling Justice and Development Party was traditionally conservative and presented a public secular face. It was a mixed-race nation, a unique melting pot in which the Middle East, Central Asia, Southern Russia, Greece, and central Europe had intermixed. Istanbul in particular was a city that took its pleasure seriously, which was why the capital had been moved to dreary Ankara. Wu had found a wonderful life in Istanbul.

And being part of neither Europe (though a member of NATO) nor the Middle East, Turkey was uniquely positioned as the crossroads for this vast region of the world.

Li Chin-Shou came out of the double doors, carrying a large tray of steaming food and headed toward the loud Americans. Perhaps thirty years old, he was remarkably fit and played his part well. As he set the plates down for the approving couple, he glanced about the terrace, taking it all in.

Though trade with China had increased this last decade and there were more Chinese here than ever it was not possible for Wu to move about Istanbul unnoticed. The Chinese had been in Istanbul for more than a thousand years but they were still a small minority. Unless you worked for the Chinese government in some capacity or operated an export import business, it was assumed you worked in a Chinese restaurant. So it was, the world over.

And that was just fine with Wu. The less attention he drew, the more he fit a stereotype, the easier his life was. He drew the last of his cigarette, then held it in his hand until he could dispose of it. Every smoking customer, it seemed to him, casually flicked their discarded butts over the railing. Each day he had one of his staff apologize to those who lived below before cleaning up the litter.

His father had known what he was doing. Istanbul was a world banking center, appreciated by the Arab oil moguls and international traders of all sorts. From here, Wu could safely and discreetly distribute the family's growing fortune. No less than once a year he returned to Beijing to visit his family, always returning with a stash of American dollars and euros. China might be a growing economic and military power but its future was uncertain. Every family of prominence planted adult children out of the country to establish roots and to squirrel away the family fortune.

And from here, he had ready access to Europe. It seemed, as well, that all those who really knew what was going on found their way here. The name players on the world stage rarely landed in Istanbul but the second-tier players, the money and power brokers, all did, most having a second home here. This was the true crossroads of the world, the gateway between East and West, as it had always been.

He felt a tingle in his pocket, turned toward the rail, and took out his iPhone. It was his father.

26

LANGLEY, VIRGINIA
CIA HEADQUARTERS
EASTERN MEDITERRANEAN BUREAU
1:49 P.M. EST

Agnes Edinfield stirred from her early-afternoon nap. She rose from the chair and went down the hallway to the restroom to refresh. There had been a time when she'd worked straight through her long day, rarely taking a break. But in recent years these postlunch naps taken in her chair at her desk with the door closed had become a daily habit.

Back at her desk she reviewed again the hard copy of Jeffrey Daniel Aiken's file. She'd never met the man, knew little about him beyond management scuttlebutt. He'd been one of those who claimed to have uncovered the Al Qaeda plot to destroy the World Trade Center and attack on the Pentagon. There'd been a lot of those Monday-morning quarterbacks in the Company in those days.

Sadly, Edinfield thought there was a lot of truth in the claims. She'd personally found the entire event very disturbing. In Aiken's case, he'd left the Company, and started his own computer security firm with which he was proving quite successful.

Though she knew Daryl Haugen no better, Edinfield had at least seen her several times and was aware of her very favorable reputation. She'd done good work at the NSA and was missed. Now she was Aiken's partner, and from appearances they were a couple.

Edinfield had spoken to Frank Renkin that morning and received what initially sounded like good news: Aiken had somehow managed to escape his captors. A Europe-wide manhunt, if that was the phrase, was under way for Haugen, who had not managed to escape. The Swiss police were treating their abduction as a terrorist act. Renkin had said nothing about Tusk, so for now it seemed whoever had taken the couple didn't know about it. She made a mental note to be certain Aiken was asked explicitly about his interrogation.

The part of Aiken's file Edinfield found most interesting concerned events two years earlier in Paris. There'd been a shooting of two Saudi nationals, brothers, who were believed responsible for the cyber-attack against Western computers and the Internet. Aiken and Haugen had been involved in that, keeping valuable information to themselves, not informing the proper authorities of the threat, then precipitating a gunfight by their actions. That was Edinfield's interpretation of events, which she admitted were sketchy. The confidential aspects of the story that were known were certainly intriguing but the file left a great deal unstated.

How a woman with the credentials and background possessed by Dr. Haugen could allow herself to be manipulated into some kind of Wild West shootout was beyond Edinfield's comprehension. Given events their due, it might have been an unexpected development. But such an outcome was to be anticipated when amateurs went beyond their expertise. Had the couple gone to the authorities the two brothers would have been apprehended and interrogated where much more would have been learned about their actions. In that event, it was likely that far more of their cyberattack could have been blunted.

But Aiken, acting as some sort of vigilante, had prevented any possibility of such an outcome. Instead, he'd left behind two dead bodies and had destroyed Haugen's reputation in the process. She'd left government service not long after, perhaps of her own volition, perhaps not.

Edinfield reread Aiken's history, then closed it again. The man had played football in high school, rugby in college—hardly the activities of your usual computer geek. There was something there, perhaps an unfulfilled desire for action, an appeal to danger.

Edinfield opened her intraoffice e-mail and typed a message to Renkin.

Subject: UNOG

Thank you for keeping me informed of the situation at UNOG. Be certain to advise me of ANY development ASAP. I am most interested in following events.

A. Edinfield

Next she sent a priority one message to her contact in Geneva.

27

PRAGUE 3, CZECH REPUBLIC
HUSINECKA 12
3:09 P.M. CET

Ahmed eased the Jetta into the rented garage, then killed the engine with a sense of relief and exhaustion. He sat for a moment with his hands resting on the top of the steering wheel and closed his eyes. He flexed his body, releasing it from tension. He couldn't remember the last time he'd been this tired.

Outside, Karim glanced along the street, then closed the two wooden garage doors behind them. He turned and opened the trunk where Daryl lay bound beneath a blanket. He pulled her up to sitting position, not gently but not roughly, either. She was drowsy and murmured a complaint. With considerable effort he lifted her from the trunk and stood her up against the vehicle.

With a sigh, Ahmed opened his eyes, exited the car, and walked to where the pair stood. Karim was holding the woman as if she might topple over. "I don't think she can walk," he said.

Daryl looked terrible. Her eyes were deeply set, ringed with dark shadows. There was a bruise on her left cheek. She was blinking slowly but her eyes remained mostly closed.

"She must," Ahmed said. "Your place is close and we are going to walk there." He'd wanted to drop the woman off with Karim but the narrow alley where his apartment was didn't allow a car. It was just around the corner though.

Ahmed moved closer to Daryl and spoke. "Wake up now. You must be awake."

Daryl's head rolled from side to side and she did indeed look as if she was about to fall over. Ahmed slapped her once, then again harder. It had no effect.

Ahmed grimaced. "This may take a few minutes. Try walking her back and forth to get her circulation going." He moved to the double doors and peered out. He could see no one.

The drive from Geneva to Prague had taken twelve long and nerve-wracking hours. Ahmed had made no plans to bring a hostage from Switzerland and had been forced to improvise. When the other American had managed to fight his way clear and flee on foot Ahmed had called both Karim and Ali back from their pursuit. Karim had argued they must find and kill him at once before he had time to reach the police.

But Ahmed didn't think that was possible. They weren't that far from a main road and he'd had an entire day to note how well policed Geneva was. No, the only choice was to leave—at once. He'd told Karim to load the car, then took Ali aside for his next assignment. Ali nodded in comprehension, picked up his small bag, embraced them both, then set out on foot.

The most immediate decision had been what to do with the woman. He'd considered killing her but there was little point in that now that the man was gone and could give the police their descriptions. And no matter how careful they'd been, one of them might have left behind a fingerprint. A murder would only heighten the intensity of the manhunt. He seriously weighed leaving her behind to be found but decided he still needed answers. And as long as he had the woman, the man would be focused on finding her, not on his work. No, he had to take her with them.

He took the couple's cell phones out to the backyard as he considered how to get out of Switzerland and into the European Union. He wondered what valuable information there might be in these little devices. He couldn't risk it though; he knew they could be traced. He removed the batteries, then the SIM card from each and destroyed them. For good measure he crushed everything else under his heel, then buried the lot.

Fortunately, the man hadn't seen the car. The border control into Italy from Geneva was generally lax but he didn't want to have to depend on that. Regardless, they'd have to stop, present passports, and undergo at least some level of scrutiny.

He had no choice but to smuggle the women into the EU and he had no time to figure out something clever. Not wanting to cooperate, stalling for time, Daryl had fought them but to no avail. As Karim held her, Ahmed found his medical pouch, located the syringe, then injected her. Then they'd taken her out to the backyard and into the garage where they'd lifted the already groggy woman into the trunk of the Jetta. Just to be safe, Ahmed told Karim to bind her up and to tape her mouth. In training he'd noted that similarly drugged subjects often snored. He'd tossed a blanket across her; then satisfied she was no threat he closed the trunk lid, opened the garage doors, and eased the car onto the street.

It was a high-risk option, one he'd only undertaken because the operation had been such a botch to that point. They'd produced their operation passports to reenter the EU as they were the only ones they'd used to enter Switzerland. He hadn't wanted to risk their day-to-day identities in the Czech Republic so had left those passports behind. He'd considered using the French passports he and Karim held but the car was registered in Prague and it would have raised questions.

The passports didn't have their cover names or a connecting address and would be destroyed once they were in Prague but they did have their photographs. Ahmed doubted that made a difference but with computer technology you could never be certain these days. It would take time he reasoned. The computers might be lightning fast but a human mind had to put two and two together, then set the technology in motion.

But he'd be known now. He could no longer remain anonymous. He could change his appearance but again computers made matching images much easier even if he wore a beard or glasses. That was something else he'd have to confess to Hamid, likely one disclosure more than his career could bear.

Walking her back and forth had helped. Daryl was more alert now. "We must walk a short way, Miss Hagen," Ahmed said. "I will kill you if you cause any trouble. It is a short distance. You understand?"

Daryl nodded. "I'm very thirsty," she said.

Ahmed gave her a long look. "As soon as you are in the apartment. Now straighten your clothing," he ordered, "and your hair." When she was finished he told Karim to go outside and when the street was clear to call for them.

"Let me go," Daryl said, licking her lips. "I won't tell anyone."

Ahmed smiled. "The man has already told the authorities. But that is far away. To answer your question, I will let you go, but first you must answer all my questions."

Daryl nodded, too exhausted to put up an argument. Somewhere in the back of her mind a dim memory named Tusk stirred uneasily.

28

MEYRIN, SWITZERLAND
MAIRIE COMMUNE DE MEYRIN POLICE
RUE DES BOUDINES 2
4:14 P.M. CET

Ulrich Spyri sat alone in his office. He picked up his small coffee and took a sip as he reviewed the list in front of him. In his time at the Mairie Commune de Meyrin police station he'd had few contacts with UNOG security. It represented an international agency after all, the largest in the world, and considered itself to be above mere local police. Henri Wille had proved a surprise.

"My neck's on the line here," Henri had told him.

"Surely they don't blame you. The couple was kidnapped from the street."

"That's how I see it but there will come a time when it will be argued that someone made a mistake and it's likely to be me who gets the finger."

"What were they doing here?" Spyri asked, expecting no answer.

Henri paused a moment. "I don't know the details but they are highly regarded computer security experts. They were working on a special project." The man, he told Spyri, was a former employee of the American CIA while the woman had worked for the even more elusive National Security Agency. They ran a cyber-security business routinely employed by both private companies and national governments. Henri had no doubt their abduction was related to their work.

Spyri had tried to question the American on that very subject but he'd been too distraught and concerned for the woman to answer his questions. Not long after, he'd asked to go back to his hotel.

Spyri had alerted the border-crossing checkpoints even before the failed rescue attempt. When the rescue team reported back their failure to find the woman he'd issued a standard Swiss nationwide alert. He next ordered a door-to-door canvass of the immediate neighborhood, which was broadened in scope as the day progressed.

Though the American had been surprisingly detailed in his description of the three men there was really nothing remarkable about them. Thousands, perhaps tens of thousands, of similar appearing men lived and traveled routinely in Switzerland. Spyri had put out the descriptions without success and that was how he suspected it would remain.

The forensic examination of the van and of the abandoned shoe repair shop had produced nothing of use. There'd been a few smeared fingerprints, blond hairs from the woman, darker hairs likely from the men, but nothing of help.

Spyri picked up his telephone and called his assistant. "Any word from the border yet?"

He had placed a request to have every bit of traffic that passed through from midnight to four this morning meticulously examined. His gut told him his men would be somewhere in that data but without a car description and a name it was going very slowly. Hundreds, perhaps thousands, of entries had been made in that short time span.

"They've been through every vehicle," his assistant said, "and so far have found nothing suspicious. They've reviewed each passport scanned. I'm to receive copies of those that even generally match Mr. Aiken's descriptions. You should get them at any time."

Spyri hung up. Maybe the American would recognize a photograph. You never knew. He glanced at the telephone and considered calling DAP again. It had been several hours. Though neutral, of necessity Switzerland maintained a counterterrorism service. Early on, Spyri had made a request through normal police channels to the Federal Office of Police asking for any information concerning a terrorist cell operating in the Geneva area. He expected nothing to come of it. National police response in Switzerland was notoriously slow. The Service for Analysis and Prevention, or DAP as it was known, was also responsible for investigating organized crime and money laundering. Spyri wasn't even certain they'd have the kind of information he needed.

In any event, the clock was ticking and he was all but certain that time had already run out for the woman. Spyri could not escape the feeling that something more was going to happen. He just hoped it wasn't the report of a body being found.

29

The e-mail chime woke Jeff. There from a Hotmail account was the response from Bridget, Daryl's NSA friend, containing the access information he'd asked for. "Be discreet," she had cautioned.

When the Internet first became a reality, politicians insisted on calling it the Information Super Highway. The phrase had quickly turned into a joke. Though it was accurate it scarcely grasped the true scope of the digital world that now seemed to run or monitor almost everything in the West. Entire airplanes, office towers, bridges, even ocean liners were designed by computer and constructed based on their designs. All but totally automated factories run by computers were commonplace worldwide. Any nation with the right natural and labor resources could have a predesigned factory dropped into place and fully operational in record time, all made possible because of computers.

And because of the Internet, distance largely meant nothing. These factories and nearly everything in between were digitally connected. American company call centers located in India and elsewhere were scarcely the tip of the iceberg. The only place where physical distance was meaningful was when it came to shipping and there were more than enough freight forwarders for that. If the right balance of resources, labor, and production costs was made against the cost of shipping, factories in the most remote corners of the world were profitable.

And there were other tasks that computers did very well indeed and at extraordinary speed. Databases were one of them. It wasn't just that the entire Library of Congress could fit on a single chip, it could as well be generally accessed and rapidly searched for specific information. A wealth of knowledge was readily available to anyone with a computing device who wanted to bother.

And now with scanners, even from a distance, certain types of data could be collected and stored automatically and remotely. In Western Europe and North America, police cars were increasingly equipped with an automobile license plate reader, which acquired every car license plate it encountered at lightning speed then ran it through a computer to see if the vehicle was reported stolen. The same system allowed officers to run plates of cars even before they pulled the vehicles over. The officer could run a driver's-license check of the registered owner or he could program the system to do that for him automatically. What this meant was that the officer, in most cases, knew as much as he wanted about the operator of the vehicle before he ever stopped the car.

The previous year, Jeff had worked on a portion of the European Union's TALOS system, Transportable Adaptable Patrol for Land Border Surveillance. Largely robotic, it was designed to handle surveillance and was becoming the EU's primary border-control monitoring system. The entire network was meant to be automated in the extreme. Conventional border-protection systems are based on expensive ground facilities installed along the entire length of the border complemented by human patrols. TALOS was meant to be more efficient and flexible.

The completed network would have both aerial and ground unmanned vehicles as well as roving robot vehicles, all supervised by a command and control center. The ground component would consist of a system of watch stations and primary-response patrols. The system was designed to be mobile and adaptable to local conditions of border length and terrain.

The design and implementation of the project had been extensive, involving experts from more than one dozen institutions, eight EU nations, Turkey, and even Israel, which had the most experience with such matters. And while this aspect of it was intended to reduce reliance on human patrols, the greater vision was to extend it beyond mere electronic border-camera surveillance.

With the credentials Bridget had provided, Jeff logged into TALOS. He spent several minutes surfing its interior to refresh his memory of its structure and to learn what he didn't already know. He was not surprised at how unchanged it was since he'd last had a look. Despite widespread illegal immigration into the European Union, there was no sense of urgency about implementing the project to its full capability.

He soon located ASSET, Advanced Software and driver Support for Essential Road Transport. As was the case with so many patrolling police cars, all European Union entry points possessed such cameras and every car entering the EU was recorded and basic computer checks run on its history. It made bringing stolen cars into Europe more difficult than ever and when an alert was out for a certain vehicle it could be stopped or tagged for follow-up when it entered.

France and Germany in particular also possessed an extensive network of highway cameras, which made it possible to track a vehicle on the major highways and often within the cities themselves once they'd been identified and marked.

Every passport of someone entering the EU was also scanned and if the individual arrived in a passenger vehicle, the two databases were linked. In other words, the driver and occupants of a car were matched to that car. Even if the system was not set up to do that automatically, the two sources could be readily matched if you had the right access codes and knowledge of the system.

Jeff had fled his captors shortly after one in the morning. The police rescue team had located and entered the building around two thirty so that was his starting point. He assumed the captors had left the country at once, which meant they'd have crossed no later than three in the morning. One hundred and twenty minutes. A check of the map displayed three major routes immediately out of Geneva into a foreign country.

Two major routes entered Italy, one veering east, the other west and quickly led into France. The third was a lesser road and took an indirect route before crossing the border also into France. Once in the EU, there would be no more passport controls. Two hours, in the dead of night. Jeff typed the query into the database analysis path using the ASSET syntax and crossed his fingers as he pressed ENTER. There had to be a manageable number. There *had* to be.

Six hundred thirty-eight. That was what he had to work with, assuming Daryl's abductors had fled Switzerland. He had no idea what vehicle the men were using, so next he matched the vehicles to the scanned passports.

Nine hundred and four passports.

He stopped to think. The vehicle he wanted would be multipassenger so he dropped all single-passenger vehicles. That left 246 cars and trucks, which gave him another idea. He could always come back if what was left proved a dead end. He dropped the passports for large commercial trucks. It was possible they'd had one lined up but unlikely. Now he had 187 scanned passports.

And that he could manage. Before starting, he picked up the telephone and ordered a large pot of American coffee.

He'd seen their faces. That had been their big mistake.

He also knew there was only one reason why they'd allowed it. They'd intended to kill him. And they intended to kill Daryl. The only question was when. With that grim foreboding, Jeff began scanning the passports photos, willing himself to take his time, to get it right.

30

GENEVA, SWITZERLAND
UNITED NATIONS OFFICE AT GENEVA (UNOG)
AVENUE DE LA PAIX
5:08 P.M. CET

Franz Herlicher closed the door to his office, carefully locking it behind him. Since the events of the last few days he'd become conscientious in following standard security protocol. Now he set out with briefcase in hand.

Work had been hell. The status of his report was up in the air since no one could be sure what data was authentic and what had been tampered with. The documents, pictures, e-mails, and other evidence they had that Iran was on the verge of detonating a device was being reviewed by the department's staff and they found more and more original material that appeared to have been modified, sometimes in major ways and sometimes in subtle ones. No one was sure anymore what was real and what had been doctored. He was determined that his months of work not go to waste and this huge opportunity for advancement and recognition be missed and was urging his superiors to circulate the copy of the report he'd verified as unaltered, but he was meeting resistance. They couldn't publish a report with such implications without all the supporting data being in order, certainly not with their records in a state of disarray.

Then there was the consternation caused by the abduction of the two Americans. When he'd first learned the news, he'd not believed it. He'd never heard of such a single incident taking place anywhere near the Palais des Nations. What troubled him was the rumor he'd heard during lunch. According to the grapevine, security believed the kidnapping was related to their activities. As they'd been working in his office, on his problem, Herlicher couldn't help wondering if he was at risk.

When the thought first crossed his mind, he'd dismissed it as absurd. He knew nothing about viruses and that sort of thing; that's why they had experts. But as he prepared to exit the building, he wondered if the Arabs knew that. Maybe they'd want him as well. Maybe the altered report had made him a target. They could have been Iranians. Outside, he stopped and checked the grounds carefully. The late-afternoon light was fading. Every tree cast a nearly black shadow. Anyone could be hiding there.

Several colleagues glanced his way and he realized his behavior was arousing suspicion. There'd be talk if he just stood here with his back to the building. He joined the stream of employees taking the walkway to the street and tried to put a smile on his face.

Ali Kharrazi was tired. He'd hardly slept in the last forty-eight hours. Yet he had much to do before he'd get any rest.

He still burned with humiliation at the American's escape. True, he and Ahmed had been in the other room when the man had managed to get free and assault Karim. But Ali had believed he should have had no difficulty subduing the man. Instead, he'd managed to be struck in the nose, a blow that still hurt. He was uncertain if his nose was broken but the skin had turned ugly shades of purple.

After receiving his orders and leaving the abandoned shoe shop, he'd moved quickly away from the busy streets into a quiet neighborhood. He'd found a darkened house, placed himself in the black shadows beside it, and after keeping a nervous vigil he'd fallen asleep. He was awakened at dawn as the family inside stirred, and he quietly set out on his quest.

With daylight and the return of normal city activity, Ali was no longer concerned. His passport was good, he had cash in his bag and a change of clothes. If stopped, he'd say he was looking for work and though that was technically illegal it was not something the Swiss police would arrest him over. They'd just check the stamp on his passport and warn him about the law.

He stopped at a workers' café to eat, feeling much better with a full meal in his stomach. This operation was rushed. There'd been no time to properly plan it. His escape would depend on confusion and a measure of luck. He was not concerned. What mattered was success; what took place after that was in Allah's hands.

At the café, Ali made inquiries and by noon was in possession of a used Ford Focus. It was suffering from a serious rust problem and had high mileage but it ran well. Next, he drove about the city to become accustomed to it and the car before heading to his destination. He was careful to avoid passing more than twice through his target area. The streets were narrow and complex. He identified routes but was concerned about recalling them at the crucial moment. He decided on another course of action. He drove back to the industrial regions and the lower-class residential areas. He checked the proximity of busy streets and public transportation.

Late that afternoon, he parked near the Place du Marché and waited. He wondered if this assignment was punishment for botching the earlier mission but dismissed the thought. It was important, and, he concluded, had been made necessary by their failure in allowing the man to escape.

Workers on their way home were now filling the sidewalks as they exited the sleek multicolored tramway. Ali waited until the streets were bustling, then took another look at the photograph he'd been sent, fixing it in his memory. He left the car and made his way to the address. There he stopped and scanned the men walking along the sidewalk, especially those approaching the building, careful not to be seen as doing so.

His situation was awkward. Standing within this well-dressed crowd of mostly blond-haired Swiss, Ali was aware of how he stood out. It was important he look like a laborer of some sort here to meet someone or maybe waiting for a ride. He couldn't simply stand like a statue. He used his phone frequently, pretending to text. He had to wait at or very near this spot because this was the only place he could be reasonably certain his target would appear.

To mask his intentions, Ali moved away from his position from time to time, walking a short distance up the sidewalk, then back, pacing easily as if searching for a car. But he always returned to the one spot from which he got a clear view of every man.

Herlicher had boarded his usual tram for Carouge, the suburb where he lived. Carouge was unlike any other part of Geneva. Originally controlled by Sardinia, its colorful three-story buildings retained a strong Mediterranean appearance. It was a quiet district, known for its artists, old-style cafés, and a certain small-scale nightlife that appealed to Herlicher.

At the Place du Marché, he climbed off the tram and walked the short distance to the Rue Jacques-Dalphin. He then turned onto his own narrow street, experiencing the first sensation of relaxation from work.

A heavyset olive-skinned man stood before him. "Franz Herlicher?" he asked with a becoming smile.

"Yes?"

Ali pressed the revolver against the man's torso and pulled the trigger three times in quick succession. The sound was explosive and those nearby recoiled reflexively away. A woman screamed as Herlicher fell to the sidewalk. Ali turned away from him, pushing his hand with the gun into his pocket as he did.

Guido Thury, gendarme with the Commune de Carouge police, was driving past in his white police car with its distinctive broad orange stripe, when he heard the noise and spotted the trouble. He jerked the car to the side of the road, riding up on the sidewalk, then bolted from the vehicle even as he reached for his handgun. Those were gunshots!

Ali was running toward Thury, back to the Place du Marché where his car was parked. It was a short distance and he estimated it would take him less than one minute even with busy pedestrian traffic. Once in the car he'd drive a distance, ditch it, then make his way to the immigrant quarter on foot. All he needed was a bit of luck during this crucial minute.

"*Arrêtez!*" Halt! Thury shouted at the running man.

Ali barreled down the sidewalk, knocking people left and right as he did, finally moving into the narrow street to give him a clear run.

"*Arrêtez!*" Thury shouted again.

Ali spotted the officer, brandished his gun, and gave a shout as he rushed at the officer. Thury crouched, held his pistol with both hands, and fired once into Ali's chest.

Ali staggered but kept moving, slowing with each step, his gun clattering to the cobblestone. After a few steps he was walking awkwardly, then he drew to a stop. He felt as if a heavy hammer had struck him. There was no pain but now it was as if all the air had been knocked from him. He willed himself to keep moving. Only in the car would he be safe. He took a step, then another, then dropped to his knees in an attitude of prayer.

There was more screaming very close. Behind, he could hear heavy footsteps. He placed his hand on his chest and felt a hot flow. He tried to breathe and it was as if a tight belt was choking him about the chest. He toppled face forward.

Everything around him slowed. He could no longer hear. The man who'd pointed a gun at him was beside him, mouthing something. Their eyes met for the first time. Ali moved his lips as if to speak. Thury knelt and moved his ear to the man's lips but there was no sound except a harsh whisper, as he heard for the first time the death rattle.

31

The system at the Italian border, Jeff discovered, was for the security officer to scan the passport of each incoming person. This produced an image of the page containing the photograph, which was stored along with the information that of the database search produced. To move people as rapidly as reasonable the system was limited to wants and alerts.

As the physical passport was scanned when the officer pressed it to a screen the quality of the photographs varied but was generally poorer than Jeff had anticipated. He had thought that the system would enable Italy, an EU country, to immediately access the passport database of each involved nation, especially if it also was part of the EU. That would have produced a clearer image but that was not the case.

The difficulty it presented him with was that because of the indifferent quality one dark-haired man in his thirties of a certain weight tended to look pretty much like another. He also could not discount the possibility of the use of glasses or presence of facial hair in photographs intended to make a visual search such as this more difficult if not impossible.

After several minutes, Jeff organized a system in order to speed the process. He passed through the 187 photographs with relative speed, noting those that roughly fit his recollection. He immediately discarded the obese or excessively thin, those with blond hair, and all women. He copied each of the other photographs and placed them in a separate file within his computer. This process consumed nearly two hours.

He then slowly went through the likely fifty-six photos in his computer, taking his time, trusting his instincts. It took half an hour to view them again and not one jumped out at him. The problem he realized was that he was searching for three men or any one of them. His mind could not conjure a single face and attempt to match it to what was on the screen. He had to recall three images.

He stood up and paced the room, trying to devise a means to make this happen. He could think of no additional screening device so sat back down and worked his way through the photographs, discarding once again those he was certain were not who he was looking for. When he finished he was down to a tentative nineteen.

Now he went through them very slowly, reminding himself that these men were professionals and would have made an effort in their photograph to present as bland an impression as possible. He thought of glasses again and paid special attention to the eleven wearing them.

And there he was. Jeff stared at the photograph, looked away, then stared again. He took a long drink of coffee. That was him. He was wearing glasses and sported a bushy mustache but that was the leader. His pulse quickened. One step closer to saving Daryl.

He examined the others again. Nothing. He went to his discards and then, almost at once, found another. He was much thinner and very young-looking in the photograph. This was the bigger man, the one who had stood guard over them. He looked diminished in the picture, as if it was the photograph of someone related to him.

Jeff segregated these two files into another folder. Now he went carefully back through the others until he was satisfied his third man wasn't there. What did that mean? Was he assuming too much? Were these two leaving Switzerland innocently, leaving Daryl behind guarded by their confederate? Or was the third man smuggling her out of the country some other way, perhaps across a thinly guarded part of the border in some rural region?

He stopped and reminded himself that there was no way he could know what was taking place. He could only make his most educated guess and act accordingly. He was certain that time was against him. He had to take chances.

Neither of the two passports had raised an alert with the border security officer. The names and addresses were certainly aliases and false leads. What he did note was that both passports were from the Czech Republic, though their names were Middle Eastern. He performed a quick Internet search. Both addresses were for modest hotels in Prague. He ran the names. There were no matches.

Now what? The car. The two passports were matched to a VW Jetta. When he checked he found that the ASSET system had automatically produced the registration and found the car clean. All it showed Jeff was that the country of original was the Czech Republic.

And that was it, nothing else.

Jeff rose and rubbed his forehead. What to do? What *could* he do? For all he knew, Daryl was right here in Geneva. That certainly made a lot of sense. The leader and one of the men had left the country, leaving her guarded by the third man. That was the simplest explanation.

Would they have risked smuggling her out in that car? Could she have simply been bound up and in the trunk? Would they have been so reckless?

He went back to the computer. There was no indication the vehicle had been searched but he didn't know if such a record was kept.

What to do?

He glanced at the security officer's code, which was the same for the two men and the car. He entered the number and located the sequence of the officer's scans for his shift. He moved to the time slot for the scans. The officer had spent thirty-four seconds on the two men and car. There'd been no search.

Jeff rose again, feeling restless. In his work, all the action was on the screen. He was accustomed to focusing his attention there. Now, an instinctive desire for physical movement all but overwhelmed him. He wanted to do something, *anything*, rather than wait in this room. He sensed that in such a compulsion lay danger, the very real risk of making the wrong decision.

He couldn't bear the thought of abandoning Daryl if she was nearby, but what if she was in Prague, waiting for him to come for her? What should he do? The tension and uncertainty was nearly more than he could stand.

There was a knock at the door, which startled him. He crossed the room and opened it to reveal a woman in police uniform. "Mr. Aiken. I've been asked to have you come with me."

"Why?"

"I don't know. Please come. I am told it is urgent."

32

GENEVA, SWITZERLAND
COMMUNE DE CAROUGE
RUE JACQUES-DALPHIN
6:07 P.M. CET

As the officer slowed the car to a stop, Jeff spotted Henri Wille standing within a circle gathered in the narrow adjacent street. The area had been cordoned off. In the fading light of the dying day, enormous work lights set ablaze the scene where the police stood; farther away down the narrow street, bright camera lights shone on reporters speaking into microphones.

"This way," the woman officer said as she opened his door.

There were bystanders but for the most part those present struck Jeff as officials of some sort or media. Henri spotted him.

"Mr. Aiken. Thank you for coming. I am sorry to say I must ask you to identify someone for me. He is dead. You understand?"

"A man?" Jeff's voice shook with emotion.

"I'm sorry if I've upset you. A man, of course. We have no new information at all about Miss Hagen. When you are ready?" He gestured toward a covered body.

Jeff nodded and walked over. A uniformed officer reached down and revealed the face, set in a grimace, the eyes mercifully closed.

"Yes. That is one of them." Jeff experienced a sharp satisfaction followed at once by a sense of loss. He'd never learn anything from him now. "What happened?"

"He was shot by a police officer. This way," Henri said, leading down the narrow street. "This man was waiting here and shot Mr. Herlicher to death as he was coming home."

"Herlicher is dead?"

Henri nodded. "Frankly, it had not occurred to us that Herr Herlicher might be in danger. Do you have any idea as to why one of your abductors would do this?"

"Daryl and I were working on a virus found on Herlicher's computer, so you have that as a connection. The virus was a potential security risk and unique. When they questioned us, that's what they wanted to know about."

One conclusion was self-evident to Henri. Someone of Middle Eastern origin was very worried about this computer virus. And they didn't want it interfered with in any way. Kidnapping computer experts and killing a UN official struck him as extreme but that only served to impress on him how serious this was to someone.

"Did either of you mention Herr Herlicher's name?" Henri asked. "It would be understandable if you had, under the circumstances."

Jeff thought. "No. His name never came up."

"You're certain?" Henri asked.

"Absolutely. Had they more time and asked it would have come out. We aren't heroes but we never reached that point." Then a thought occurred to him. "Perhaps Daryl mentioned him after I left."

"Yes," Henri said. "That's likely it, then."

"Are the local police making any progress searching for Daryl?" Jeff asked.

"I regret that they are not," Henri said. "Though she may still be in Switzerland, the local police think it most likely she was taken out of the country last night before they had time to raid the location you gave them. The officer in charge has requested the passport and vehicle records from the Italian and French entry points and hopes to have that information soon. It may prove valuable. He will need you to examine the photos at that time."

For an instant, Jeff thought about telling him that he'd already done that. He hated to see the police waste their time but Bridget put herself at risk to give him access. "Is there anything else you need from me?"

"No. Thank you for coming. I will confirm your identification for the local officers. Just stay in your room."

"I'll wait for your call."

The same female officer drove him back to his hotel. Once in his room Jeff returned to his computer. He sent the information he'd developed to Frank, surmising the Company would have the most ready access to the data he was after. He also brought him up to date.

Jeff quickly packed. He'd left cash, a credit card, and their passports in the room safe as he always did. He paused with Daryl's passport in his hand, then placed it with his. She'd need it. He had to believe she would need it again.

Jeff now knew why the third man had not left Switzerland. He also knew with absolute confidence that the other two had taken Daryl out of the country. They would not have assassinated a United Nations official in Geneva and risked the heightened manhunt to follow unless they had already spirited her out of the country. And while he could not know with equal certainty where they'd gone—they would surely have access to safe locations throughout Europe—he believed they were in Prague.

But what if the vehicle proved a dead end? Jeff had thought of little else since sending his message to Frank. He logged onto his laptop and pulled up the scan of the passports again. What on them could he trust? He'd forwarded the names and addresses but was certain Frank would turn up nothing of use. The photos—those were real. And with facial recognition programs, a computer could generate a small selection of likely matches. But the process was time consuming and he had no time. The trick then was to narrow the search field.

He had no idea how long it would take to scan every Czech passport or identity card but knew it would be too long. No, he needed to reduce the field significantly. But how?

He looked at the passport of the leader again searching for something, anything that would help. Occupation. In Czech, the man had listed *studentka*, repeated in French as simply *student*.

Jeff examined the man again. He didn't look like any student he'd ever seen. But it might just be the cover he was using. It was surely a common one for agents. This time he sent the file to Bridget, asking her to conduct the facial scan of every college and university ID in Prague. When that was done she was to extend it to all of the Czech Republic. He hoped the NSA would have access to that data or know who would.

He didn't wait for a reply. He had no time. She was bright and she knew what he needed.

Jeff quickly checked flights from Geneva to Prague and found none that were direct, most having a stop in Frankfurt. He booked a flight he could just make.

Now, how to get out of the hotel without the police stopping him . . .

In his office at the Mairie Commune de Meyrin Police, Ulrich Spyri's assistant gestured to attract his attention. He waited until Henri finished briefing him on the shooting and death of the murderer, then disconnected. He looked up.

"Italy has given us access to the border scans you requested. I've e-mailed you the link. I've checked the names."

"Any luck?"

"Nothing. There were no alerts last night during the time period you requested."

"All right. Let's get the American over here to look at the photos. Any names used by the kidnappers are likely aliases anyway."

Spyri poured himself a cup of coffee but when he lifted it to his lips he realized it was rank. He dumped it out as well as the last bit in the pot, then waited as a new batch brewed. He poured the coffee, added white powder since there was no milk in the refrigerator, then raised the cup again. Before he could drink his assistant rushed over to him.

"The man is gone!"

33

Colonel Jai Feng, dressed in mufti, lit another cigarette, and glanced casually at his watch. The meeting had been scheduled for 6:00 and now that he'd arrived, the real waiting began. The longer he was made to sit, the less important he was. The sober assistant in a trim navy Brooks Brothers suit gave no hint.

During the four-hour flight from Urumqi to Beijing, Feng had planned for this meeting. Mei Zedong, Deputy First State Counselor of the Communist Party, had been his patron almost from the beginning. Zedong's rise in the Party had preceded Feng's own advancement in the People's Liberation Army. Indeed, Feng had risen in the shadow of the always more powerful and politically astute Zedong. Theirs was an unofficial relationship and not widely known, though by no means meant to be a secret. That would have attracted too much interest in paranoid Beijing. Such associations were the lubricant of the Chinese government and accepted as necessary. Still, they met after regular work hours and Feng wore a gray business suit.

Though his orders to assist the Iranians had come to Feng through military channels, it was Zedong who had alerted him months in advance. This had given him valuable time to prepare and show his best to his official superiors from the very beginning. Now Feng had a coup to present to Zedong and was eager to get on with it.

He'd regretted the necessity of a face-to-face meeting as every hour he was away from his office was a risk but he was unwilling to chance an electronic communication of any sort. Events were moving rapidly and he did not trust his immediate subordinate to let him remain in charge for very long. Feng would be back behind his desk by lunchtime tomorrow, and that was not a moment too soon in his view.

At eighteen minutes after the hour the assistant lifted his head and informed him that the deputy was ready to see him. He'd received no communication that Feng could detect. It was as if the prescribed time had passed. Still, he'd waited less than twenty minutes and that was a good sign his star was still ascendant.

And why shouldn't it be? His Cyber Warfare Center produced more intelligence than every other department in China. His people had penetrated the American Department of Defense and stolen countless documents that had allowed the Chinese Air Force and Navy to leapfrog ahead in design. And because of him, China knew the precise American response to every potential confrontation. No government in history had ever had available such broad and accurate intelligence about their principal adversary.

But in Feng's view it was not even necessary to consider any of that. Just look at what his people had managed within the United Nations alone. It was without parallel. For the last few months, the Politburo had known every secret of that massive bureaucracy. And his department had just launched its most sophisticated operation, a Trojan that changed everything.

Zedong remained sitting as Feng entered the room. He reached across his desk to shake hands. "Can I get you anything, Colonel?"

"Perhaps some water, Deputy." To Feng's surprise Zedong rose, crossed to a wet bar, and poured a glass of water. He handed it to him, then took his place behind the desk. Zedong was perhaps five years older than Feng, and at least two inches shorter. Squat in appearance, resembling a toad as much as anything, he smiled constantly, a trait common among senior Party officials. Chinese culture held that the shorter the man, the more devious. That had been Feng's experience. But Zedong had always dealt honestly with him. And so it would be until the day he did not.

"You have something urgent, I believe?" Zedong said.

"Yes. The penetration of UNOG in Geneva with our new cyberweapon is all but complete and we are rapidly gaining access to the United Nation's headquarters in New York."

"So I understand. I recently read a report from your superior, General

Ming, saying the same thing. You are to be congratulated. Everyone is most pleased at this point."

"We have also gained total access to the UN Office for Disarmament Affairs. This is how we learned the contents of the final report."

Zedong smiled. "Which you altered."

"Which we altered. The objective as outlined for us was to delay the release of the report. Given how the United Nations operates we were told this would insert paralysis for these crucial weeks. Our plan, which succeeded, was to make the alteration at the crucial juncture. However, at our moment of greatest success the trouble started." Zedong's smile faded ever so slightly. This was the first he was learning of this. Feng gave him a succinct briefing of events, reporting in an even voice the detection of the latest Trojan, pointing out that it meant little in the end as altering the Iran report had made discovery certain. He focused his remarks on the American man.

Zedong considered the information before speaking. "This man was a threat?" he at last asked, with a measure of disbelief.

Feng nodded. "He discovered our code in Geneva with surprising speed." He omitted mentioning that his team had determined that the man had first identified the Trojan in London.

"This is an unfortunate development."

"I had his photograph and identity forwarded to our contact with Iran. Initially we didn't know the woman was with him. We only learned that after they were both picked up. Their operatives seized the couple as they were leaving the UNOG building. Their purpose was to learn how much they knew and how many others had been advised. And to halt the work."

"It also alerted the United Nations."

"Yes." Feng paused. "A few hours ago these same operatives killed a UN official. He was the author of the report."

Zedong straightened in his chair and was no longer smiling. "This is getting out of hand. Those people are lunatics. How protected are we?"

"Very. There is no direct connection between us and the Iranians. You will recall that we use a cutout. And the code was carefully vetted. It has no provenance leading back to us."

"Let us hope so." Zedong took a moment to light a cigarette. After drawing on it he smiled, then said, "I warned my superiors that you cannot alter such reports without alerting those involved."

Feng resumed his briefing. "We continue to alter documents as we speak. No one in the ODA will trust or believe anything in their computers.

It had been my hope that it would take months, even years, for them to un-ravel what we have unleashed. They might never have figured it all out. And we are reading nearly everything, most especially their communications. I could use twice as many people to handle the flood of information."

"I do what I can but there's no time to train them even if qualified people could be found on short notice."

"Our access is going to be short lived in any event," Feng said with res-ignation. "As they now know about the Trojan they will find a way to block it. I have a team devising a new penetration route but they will be on guard. As a consequence, it will never have the benefits for us I had envi-sioned."

Feng lifted his glass and took a long drink as he watched Zedong think. "Colonel," Zedong said finally, "I must tell you that there is criticism about your penetration of the United States Department of Defense. The infor-mation flow has slowed dramatically and certain key data long requested has not been produced."

Feng placed his glass down. "They are getting smarter. The easy days are over. Our job is more difficult but I'm confident we'll obtain every-thing that has been requested."

"I'm glad to hear that."

"This brings up another matter we've discussed previously. These Infor-mation Warfare Units, the so-called Patriotic Hackers, has anything been done to stop them? They make our job very difficult. Their carelessness in-creases security against us. Surely, with the success our sophisticated opera-tions have enjoyed, those who make these decisions understand that the time for such groups has passed."

Zedong nodded slightly. "I agree but progress is slow. Others control them and broadcast their every success. It is a way to cover them with glory and advance their careers. And certain people don't want to see you alone in this area. They fear too much power in one man's hands."

Feng bristled slightly. "I have always served the Party faithfully."

"Of course. But you understand."

Unfortunately, Feng understood all too well. Zedong glanced at his watch, a Rolex and a gift from his son the previous year. Feng cleared his throat as if to announce he had something important to say.

"You recall Stuxnet?" he said.

"I've read your reports." Zedong said with a smile. "And, of course, I read the *New York Times*. What about it?"

"It is my understanding that the Iranians have advised they are making considerable progress and believe they will be ready with their device in the immediate future. This was why I was ordered to alter the report."

Zedong grimaced. "Our latest information is that they have once again overstated their capability. Stuxnet2 crippled them far more than they admitted. They could be close, but . . ." He shook his head, then asked, "How effective do you believe their new air gap measures are?"

"Better than before. They prohibit thumb drives and outside computers. But we have no confidence in their measures. They are inept in that regard and we are starting to detect signs of a new version of Stuxnet. The Iranians report nothing but then they usually learn of such matters when their programs fail utterly or we tell them. But"—he thought a moment, then said—"now that the CIA knows we altered the UN report they will conclude Iran is very close. They are certain to accelerate release of this latest version."

Zedong stared out the window and when he spoke it was more to himself than to Feng. "If this new version does to the Iranian program what the previous ones did there will be no nuclear test. I will have to answer for that failure."

"We have an omnibus Stuxnet countermeasure."

Zedong looked at him sharply. "How effective is it?"

"We believe 100 percent. It will enable them to quarantine Stuxnet. Then it is just a question of how proficient they really are in the final stages of their program."

"They claim a few weeks at most. You're certain?"

"It works in all our tests and I assure you we've made them very tough."

"And if they've changed the virus?"

"Our countermeasure assumes the key elements of the Trojan remain essentially the same. Short of an entirely new design, this will stop it."

Zedong nodded approval. "Pass it along to your contact for transportation."

"We can just e-mail it the entire way. There are very effective ways for doing that. It will be much faster." This was an old disagreement between them.

"Absolutely not! It has been decided that there must be intermediaries. We will use the standard method."

"There's something I'd like from you."

"Yes?"

"When the Iranians seized the Americans we believe they took their laptop computers. They will have invaluable information for us. This couple works on all kinds of high-security programs, both in the private sector and within Western government security agencies. There will also be information telling us what they know about our Trojan that could be very useful. I want the computers. It is even possible, perhaps likely, they have done work on the next version of Stuxnet."

"I can't see the Iranians making good use of them."

"Nor can I. This is a small price for giving them the countermeasure."

Zedong nodded. "Pass on the request with your countermeasure. I'll work this end. Before you leave give me all the information you have about this couple and the Iranian operatives, if you know. Where are these computers?"

"In Prague, we believe. I have printed everything for you." Feng removed the report and placed it on the desk.

Zedong picked it up. "You've done well, Jai. Very well."

As Feng left, Zedong stared again out his window into the eternal smog of the Chinese capital. The Iranians couldn't be trusted in this. Once they knew the Chinese wanted the computers they'd deny having them. Or only produce one. He sent his assistant home, then scanned Feng's report in the outer office. At his desk he sent an e-mail to his son, attaching the document.

"Get the computers," he wrote. "As quickly as you can."

34

Daryl lay unmoving, willing her breath to remain in a slow deep rhythm. She knew her captors were suspicious. She had no idea how long she'd lain on the mattress, a few hours at least as the sun had first rested on her leg and had now moved on. She could smell cooking oil and strange, though not unpleasant, aromas coming from somewhere. From time to time, she'd risk raising an eyelid ever so slightly to catch a glimpse of the room and the two men.

It was a grim place with bare walls. Opposite her was a small wooden table with facing hardback chairs. There was, she was certain, a small kitchen area out of sight. Before her was a ratty couch, facing a wall with a small flat screen television sitting on a largely empty cheap bookcase.

As for the men, her primary watcher was perhaps thirty years old, slender. At first glance he'd seemed undersized but she'd determined if that were true it was only slightly. He sat in one of the chairs and faced her but he became restless and bored from time to time. He'd wander, usually returning with a coffee, which was how she'd decided the kitchen was above her head.

The other man was the leader. She couldn't place his age but he was a few years older than the other, with olive-colored skin, very black hair and a moderate mustache. There'd been just a single glimpse at his black eyes and she'd perceived a quick intellect and a certain animal cunning. He moved with athletic grace and seemed very fit despite his chain-smoking. In fact, both men puffed away with abandon, the smoke forming a visible cloud in the room.

The pair conversed quietly in a Middle Eastern language. It did not sound to her like Arabic, which she'd heard enough to believe she'd recognize. But it might be Arabic spoken with a strong regional accent. She thought of what other languages it could be and came up with Turkish, Armenian, and Farsi. She had no idea what Turkish sounded like and Armenians were Christian, hardly likely to be terrorists. She had no idea what Farsi sounded like but she'd come to believe that these men were Iranian. They had the most to lose from what she and Jeff had discovered.

Not that it made any difference. She was a prisoner and though they'd not yet killed her, she could not see any other possible outcome. She could remain a prisoner or die. So she would not remain their captive and if she was killed attempting her escape, that was better than to be taken like a lamb to the slaughter.

Neither man had so much as groped her. And that heightened her fear; not that she wanted to be touched or raped. God no! For now they kept their distance, treated her like professionals. But she had no doubt once the smart one had stripped her of every bit of knowledge she possessed, they'd kill her. She'd seen their faces.

She tested her wrists behind her back again. Were they looser? She couldn't tell. She was careful not to work the binding of the rope as it would alert the men that she was awake. For a moment she yielded to hopelessness. She could see no way out of this and despaired at the thought.

Still, Daryl could not help but cling to the hope of rescue. It was engrained in her. The dark moment passed; a resignation to her death was simply against her nature. When Jeff had managed his escape, she'd allowed herself to hope. Surely he'd find a policeman and help would come.

But this leader had moved with lightning speed. He'd sent one of the men off on foot, then ordered the other to wipe the place down quickly. The few items they'd brought into the room were taken outside, then within three or four minutes they'd hoisted her to her feet and given her that first injection. She'd been unconscious almost at once.

She had no memory of the next time period. It could have been two or three hours, or ten for that matter. There'd been the black hole of unconsciousness, then a surreal state during which she'd felt the road passing beneath the car, sensed the closeness of the trunk in which she lay. For a while she'd been certain she would choke because her mouth was taped shut and she'd had to will herself to remain calm.

Then the trunk lid was opened with a flood of stinging light. One of the men spoke to her but she remembered nothing of what he said, the tape was removed, and she immediately felt the prick of the needle again. And so it had gone until they'd trundled her from the car to this room where she lay, knowing the worst of her ordeal was yet to come.

For all this, she clung to hope of rescue.

But who would save her now? Jeff was in Geneva and while she had no idea where she was, it had taken a long, hard day's driving to get here so it was far away and in another country. No one locally would be looking for her.

No, if she was to live she had to escape. She could not depend on anyone but herself.

Daryl knew the questioning would soon begin. The leader had been about to start earlier, telling her he knew she was faking it, but instead he'd stalled. She could hear the exhaustion in his voice. She'd listened as he'd made a telephone call to a woman and left a message in English. It sounded like a girlfriend but there'd been something else that suggested to her a business arrangement. Not a prostitute, but something else she was certain.

Then he'd received a call and for the last five minutes had been deep in conversation with someone who was clearly his superior. The other man had glanced his way uncertainly several times. These two were in trouble with someone—that was easy enough to decipher, as was the reason.

They'd let Jeff escape.

Which meant it was going to go very hard on her very soon. They had to make up for their laxness and they'd do that, she was certain, by squeezing her mercilessly.

She wished she could sleep. She'd like nothing more than to escape this moment and her rising fears.

Only after moving the American woman to Karim's one-room apartment had Ahmed realized it was not suitable. This was a contingency he should have thought about previously. While the street here was occupied primarily by immigrants, so few of whom would want to summon the police, the screams of a woman would likely overcome that reluctance. And to learn what was necessary, he could not be certain she'd not find a chance to scream. He'd tried persuading himself but the place wouldn't do for what came next.

If only she weren't so stubborn.

He'd told her when they dropped her on the mattress that he knew she was faking it, and in fact he did. But what was he to do here if she refused to talk? He'd asked Karim if there was somewhere else they could take the woman later this night, after it was dark, somewhere secure and isolated. The man had shrugged.

Ahmed couldn't blame him for the oversight. There'd never been the need before. Prague was the command center for Central Europe. Operations were meant to be kept away from it. A safe house in the country, far from neighbors would have been ideal and not that difficult had he arranged for it earlier. But not now, not on short notice. And every time they moved the woman their exposure increased.

Ahmed was becoming convinced he should have just left the woman in Geneva. Taking her had been a risk and though so far he'd got away with it, having her was a hindrance to his every move. Maybe he should just kill her and get it over with.

But what to do with the body afterward?

This woman was not his only concern. There was Saliha. He had no idea if she'd returned from Turkey. He'd called her repeatedly but she was not answering. Damn her! He never should have mixed pleasure with business. She was jealous, that was clear enough, and now she was punishing him for her suspicions. He'd already left two messages and refused to leave more. He didn't want her to know how important she was to him.

He'd been under enormous stress since leaving Prague and there'd been little time for rest. The long drive from Geneva had nearly done him in. He'd not trusted Karim to drive, knowing the poor level of his skills, so he'd had to do it all himself. With the woman in the trunk there had been no choice.

His great temptation now was to leave the woman with Karim, collapse into his own bed, and deal with all this in the morning. He tried to think why the situation was urgent but it was as if his mind was filled with cotton.

He'd received a call, and though he did not recognize the voice, he had been certain who it was. Hamid.

"Where are you?" the man had asked in English.

"Prague. With my man and the woman." His answer was in Farsi so she would not understand. Hamid switched when he spoke next.

"The American?"

"Yes."

"Tell me." Ahmed gave a cursory briefing of the essentials. There was a long pause then Hamid said, "The one man is dead in Geneva. So is ours.

Shot to death by police. It is all over the news. There is endless speculation about what this means. Terrorists are identified as the suspects and security throughout all Europe has been increased."

Dead! Ali dead! Ahmed didn't want to believe it. The man been so steady, so dependable.

Well, it had always been possible, as it was for any of them. Still, though Swiss security was sophisticated, the police forces there were not accustomed to hunting down suspects with great speed. It was a soft country, with soft ways. Ahmed had expected Ali to slip away. He was beginning to think this operation was ill starred.

"How did the American get away?" Hamid asked. Ahmed told him. "That is not an explanation I can pass along, brother. Truly. It will not be accepted. You've been careless. I've never known you to be so careless."

That, Ahmed knew, was very true. He was surprised himself. "I have the woman," he offered as a consolation.

"Careless again. You should have seen to her in Geneva. Taking her with you was too great a risk."

"It worked."

"Perhaps. Or perhaps the police are watching you right now."

Ahmed took a drag of his cigarette before answering. "She has important information. I will get it."

"That is good." There was a pause, then Hamid said, "There is a vital message on its way to you in the usual manner. Your person must transport it at once. It is essential, more important I believe than what you might learn from the American. See to it at once." He paused as if weighing what to say next. Finally, "It will stop the Zionist interference with the computers. You understand? You have surely read of the virus attacking our program. Do this successfully and all will certainly be forgiven, for very soon thereafter the world can no longer abuse or neglect us."

When Hamid disconnected, Ahmed returned the phone to his pocket. He lit another cigarette as he eyed the American woman but his thoughts were on Saliha. Damn her!

35

As Saliha walked along Lupacova Street on her way to Ahmed's apartment, she glanced at her phone again. The same two messages. He was back in the city and eager to see her. Well, even if she was eager to get paid, he could wait the way he'd made her wait.

In the early-evening darkness, the street well lit, she stepped along at a steady pace, her long dark hair flowing over her shoulders and down her back, her black, leather, high-heeled boots clicking on the stone pavement of the walkway. There was a slight chill as spring had not yet turned to summer and she wore a matching leather jacket she'd bought in Ankara the year before.

She didn't like thinking about Ahmed. It made her unhappy. She'd once loved him passionately and imagined a life with him. She'd never before experienced such feelings. But during their first year together she'd come to realize that he was not faithful. She'd lied to herself about that. Her roommate, Ayten, had told her what she'd seen and she was right. A man who strayed always strayed. There was no stopping it. A woman could close her eyes to it, but if she did, she lived a lie and her life was never truly what she pretended it to be.

Yes, he was a lovely man and his fingers and lips were magic on her body but, though she was young, she knew there was more to a life together than wonderful lovemaking. Still, memories of warm summer afternoons wrapped in his arms, the church bells announcing the hour, the shutters thrown open, the flutter of the pigeons and the river breeze occasionally wafting over them nearly overwhelmed her. She wanted nothing more in such moments but to yield to fantasy, to imagine Ahmed was faithful and always would be, that they could have a life together.

But how stupid could she be? Dreams weren't reality and recent events had brought the real world back into her life once and for all.

She could not ignore this business he was in. The worst part was he'd put her into the middle of it. How deeply was she involved? In how much danger had he placed her—repeatedly? She had no way of knowing. She could ask but he would only lie to her. What risk was she taking for this unfaithful lover?

And perhaps it was all a pretense on his part, an emotional device to get her to do his unquestioning bidding. She didn't want to think him capable of such deceit but what else could she conclude? She'd come to realize that almost nothing he'd said about himself was real. For all she knew, he already had a wife and family in Iran. She'd heard such stories from other women. Why wouldn't it be true in her case? Was she so special?

You don't know what you don't know, her grandmother had often told her as she repeated the lessons of life to her lovely granddaughter while combing her hair. You can stare at the mountain all day but you cannot discern what is on the other side.

But don't learn too much, she'd murmur as if repeating a catechism, don't know things you don't need to know. Too much knowledge, the wrong *kind* of knowledge, can destroy your life. Don't ask what you shouldn't know, don't learn what isn't your business. Such was one great secret of life she had learned and impressed upon Saliha.

Ahmed wasn't involved with drugs or the black market—he was a spy. There could be no doubt. His secretive trips, the mask he put over his face when he received certain messages on his computer, his stern businesslike manner when he downloaded the encrypted files onto a new chain thumb drive, which he would give to her with great solemnity.

She'd never pressed him for answers about all this. Though she'd expressed curiosity initially, his evasions had alerted her. She no longer asked, not seriously at least, and she'd long since given up any expectation of an honest answer.

Always, she realized, there'd been an implied threat behind her trips, the hint that something terrible would be done to her if she failed to carry out the assignment properly. She dismissed that initially as so much showmanship, a Middle Eastern man telling her he was the boss, but now she knew better. She was at risk and not just from the CIA or Mossad.

She turned the corner and walked to the entrance of the building where

Ahmed lived. She entered the code and passed through the doors. The Hungarian, if that's what he was, emerged from his doorway as if he'd been lurking there. If anything he was dirtier than ever, his soiled undershirt his only covering above well-worn trousers. He'd not combed his bird's nest of hair or shaved in several days. He leered at her and said, "What do you want?" His tone announced he considered her a whore.

"None of your business," she answered, and walked toward him to pass.

He reached out with his hand and attempted to grab her arm but she moved quickly aside, nearly jumping to escape his clutch. Now she smelled him and realized he was drunk. He lurched toward her again but before he could take proper hold Saliha had her switchblade out.

Snap! She pressed the knife to his neck.

The man froze, then pulled back. Saliha glared at him, staring him into intimidation. "Touch me again," she hissed, "and I will cut your balls off, not that they are any use to you, old man."

With that she stepped away and started up the narrow stairs.

This had to end, she told herself. Just look at the situation Ahmed placed her in just to get her money. For that was her only reason in coming here. There would be no last trip. No, she was done with that. She'd get her money and never see him again, or the filthy man at the landing. She shuddered to think what he'd do if he ever got her in his power.

She knocked at the apartment and waited. When there was no answer she let herself in. The room was dark, exactly as she'd seen it the last time she'd been here the previous day. If Ahmed was back, and his messages said he was, then he'd not come here yet. So where was he? At one of his secret meetings, she decided, as she sat down to wait, not bothering to turn on a light. She removed a fresh packet from her purse, opened it, tapped out a fresh cigarette, and lit it. She drew the first smoke into her lungs with great pleasure, held it momentarily, then forced it through her nostrils. She closed her eyes and willed herself to relax.

Ahmed looked at Karim and said, "Watch the woman. Be careful with her. We've made mistakes and they are not happy. You understand?"

Karim nodded.

Ahmed considered telling him that Ali was dead but decided not to mention it, not yet. He couldn't be certain what the man might do to the woman in revenge.

He picked up her bag, which contained her computer. Hamid thought there was valuable information in it, not that Ahmed could understand the technical aspects. In the hands of experts the laptop was potentially a gold mine of data, more important than what she told them even. Maybe dumping her body was going to be the easiest solution after all.

He nodded to Karim as he let himself out. *No mistakes*, he said to himself as he stepped outside. There must be no more mistakes.

Saliha finished another cigarette as she waited. She realized that she was now feeling the full weight of adulthood and of her greater responsibilities. All that had gone before now had been an extended childhood. Her sister had called earlier that day with bad news. Their older brother had lost his job on the Istanbul docks. It was time to grow up, really grow up, and stop playing the adult, behaving as if her life was hers alone to live.

Saliha placed her face in her hands and sighed. How she missed her grandmother. How she missed the sweet innocence of her youth, the false security of their home. How she longed for life to be easier—but that was not to be, she knew. She was fortunate to have choices. Her English was very good, she'd been told; her looks would hold for some years yet; she was bright and she was not lazy. Given the opportunity she could be a productive employee anywhere in Europe.

She heard steps on the stairs outside and wondered if it was Ahmed. Would she have to sleep with him again to get her money? What if she did? This was the end of it for them. She stabbed the cigarette into the ashtray and instinctively straightened her hair.

And if it happened, it would be a way of telling him good-bye.

36

Slipping out of the hotel in Geneva had proved surprisingly simple once Jeff was ready. The guard in the hallway outside his door was nowhere in sight. Likely he'd just stepped away for a moment. Jeff had grabbed his gear and walked quietly to the backstairs and descended all the way to the parking garage. Again he found no guard. In fairness, he realized they were not holding him prisoner but looking to protect him from harm. Their focus wasn't on him.

He'd walked up the car ramp to the street, turned to his left away from the entrance, and a few minutes later climbed into a taxi parked at a stand. He'd made the flight only because an increase in the security level had backed up passenger boarding and all flights were delayed.

He'd not had to change planes in Frankfurt, taking the time to consider his actions as sleep was out of the question. Once in flight, an air of calm spread through the cabin. Jeff closed his eyes with fatigue. He could hear the muted tinkle and clatter of the cart as the attendants moved down the aisle, taking orders and serving drinks.

He couldn't shake the thought that this was all a waste of time. Police professionals and intelligence agencies were searching for Daryl; why did he think he could succeed where they failed? She could be anywhere right now—anywhere. The evidence on which he was acting was flimsy at best. He had absolutely no real proof Daryl was in Prague.

He ordered a double bourbon, surprising himself. He typically drank very little and then only wine. The liquid stung as he sipped it, the taste if not pleasant not unpleasant, either. When he finished, he felt a hot glow in his gut that slowly spread throughout his body as the tension eased from him.

Yes, Daryl could be anywhere. She could very well be dead. But the trail led to Prague. And even if the police and intelligence agencies were looking for her they were also occupied with a thousand other tasks. No one was more motivated to find her than Jeff because no one else loved her as he did.

The plane landed without incident. As soon as he could, Jeff booted his laptop to connect but found nothing from Frank. He put his computer away, made a mental note to buy a new cell phone, then filed out of the airplane and made his way to an Avis rental counter. Thirty minutes later, he had keys. But before going outside to claim his car he located a hot spot. And there was the message he'd hoped for.

The car is registered to Václav Morávek. The address is Jezkova 564, Prague 3. That is an unspecified commercial site. The name on the vehicle is a dead end and likely fake. Call the local police, Jeff, and let them handle it. You write software, remember?

Frank

Nothing from Bridget. He kept himself from sending her a reminder. She already knew how urgent this was.

Jeff drove out of the airport. He cautiously followed the GPS instructions, which still managed to confuse him repeatedly once he reached the crowded city center. There the old streets were short, extending only a city block. Though it was late the city had the sense of just coming alive and pedestrians crossed streets with casual care. More than once his eye was drawn to a young couple walking arm in arm, lost in their own world.

It was nearly midnight when he spotted the address. Afraid to slow, he drove by, went around the corner, promptly found himself lost, shut off the GPS system and its nagging voice, and finally made his way back to Jezkova Street. This time he slowed a bit as he went past but still could not make out what was at the address. It was an old building, with several large wooden doors, but that was all.

He drove in circles in the nearby area as he considered his next move. Frank might well have been right. Jeff had already withheld important information from the police in Geneva to protect a source, seriously handicapping official efforts. Then he'd taken off before he'd identified the photographs for them. He suddenly realized that by his actions he made it impossible for them to know who to look for or where to go in their search.

What would the local police do if he went to them? Once they contacted Geneva they'd probably detain him.

No, he'd made his decision. Now he had to play out his hand. If this was a dead end then he'd tell the police what he knew—if he was able.

A car pulled away from the curb, giving him a parking spot that he backed into. On the sidewalk, Jeff took a moment to orient himself. He walked back the way he'd been driving and after a few minutes located Jezkova Street. Though it was not crowded there were a number of pedestrians and he blended in while strolling by the address. He still was unable to make out what it was. There were no offices, from what he could see. It looked to him as if residences were on the second and third floors, which was the case throughout the street. His heart raced and for a moment he wondered if Daryl was being held there.

At the corner was a tiny shop where sundry items were sold: cigars, cigarettes, mints, magazines, toilet articles. He bought a magazine, thinking it might be useful as a prop, then a bottle of water and two candy bars since he had no idea when he'd eat next.

"Excuse me," he said to the young woman behind the counter, "but can you tell me what business that is down the street?" He hoped she knew more than the few English phrases her job required.

She raised her head. Her hair was dark and short. She wore stylish glasses. He formed the impression she was a student. "What business?"

"Let me show you." He smiled and went toward the door. She moved from behind her counter without hesitation and walked outside with him. He pointed to number 564 just down the street. "There, with the old wooden doors."

"Ahh," she said then smiled. "It is a lockup."

"Lockup? I don't know the phrase."

"You know, for cars."

"Like a garage, you mean."

"Like that. Few apartments here have parking so you must pay for a place. You understand?"

"Yes, I do. Thank you."

"Anything else?"

"Would the owners live close to their lockup?"

She nodded. "If they can." She shrugged. "I can't say."

After thanking her Jeff walked back to his car. What to do? He started the engine, pulled away from the curb and through the rearview mirror saw another car dart into the spot. He made several turns then drove down Jezkova Street again. The young woman was closing up for the night. He drove as slowly as he dared.

How often, he wondered, could he risk driving down this street? Maybe he should park nearby and watch the location from on foot. He couldn't see anywhere convenient for that, though. He kept driving, taking his time. He feared he'd attract police attention if he kept this up.

Jeff glanced at his watch. He'd risk an hour. If he couldn't find a parking spot from where he could watch the location for the night he'd park somewhere and risk a vigil on foot.

As he drove he wondered how he might contact the Geneva police and forward to them the photograph of the men he'd recognized. But he could not figure out a way to do that and keep Bridget out of it. What had he done by rushing off to Prague? Shouldn't he have at least waited to view the photographs for the police, pointed out the two he knew *then* flown to Prague?

The thought tantalized him but he sensed that time was an issue, that taking those few hours might prove fatal to Daryl. Well, he thought, it made no difference now. The fat was in the fire. He'd made his choice and would have to live with the consequences.

Finally, on his fifth or sixth time down the street—Jeff no longer could keep track—a parking spot magically appeared. He rushed to it, pulled the car in, then killed the engine. By turning just slightly to his right he could make out the lockup, as the girl had called it, from the corner of his right eye and not seem to be watching it.

He cleared his mind of all unpleasant thoughts. After a bit he ate one of the candy bars and drank some water. The street and city slowly become quiet and without realizing it he lay his head across the back of the seat and fell into an exhausted sleep.

37

Saliha sat smoking as Ahmed worked his new computer. He'd had a laptop he'd brought with him that he'd removed from a carrier and sat on the desk beside his old one. Nothing had gone as she expected since he'd arrived and been surprised to see her waiting—pleasantly surprised. They'd all but leaped into bed and now she was disgusted with herself. Why was she always so ready for him? She'd never been like that before.

Worse, he still hadn't paid her for the trip even though he examined the personal items she'd brought back for him with approval.

Saliha rose and went into the bathroom where she turned on the water, then prepared to take a shower. Ahmed no longer thought of her, not after, and was instead engrossed in his new computer. In that way he was like every man she'd ever slept with. They wanted a woman for one thing and that was all. She stepped into the hot water and considered what to do next. Or rather, how to tell Ahmed she was finished with these trips and still get paid. She'd wait until after getting the money she decided, then tell him. She'd never seen him lose his temper. Tonight might be the first time.

With the shower running in the background Ahmed stared at the computer screen without comprehension, his mind far away. His conversation with Hamid had disturbed him deeply. This whole operation he realized had been a botch from the first. He wondered now how many problem areas existed about which he knew nothing. The police could be searching for him this very minute. He had no way of knowing. He should have thought more carefully of the possibilities. That was what he'd been taught.

He'd simply driven to Geneva and kidnapped the couple. Those had been his instructions but it was assumed he'd consider every eventuality and take the necessary steps. Up to that point it had appeared a straightforward operation. What he'd not done was plan for likely scenarios and devised a plan for each. He'd had good men, access to others. It should not have been a problem.

It occurred to him that like his men he'd been in the field for too long, that his life in Prague was too easy. The edge he'd once possessed had been dulled by soft Western living and now he was paying the price.

Still, Hamid understood operational problems. He was a field agent himself, one of the best and knew how events could easily spin out of control. Ahmed's instructions had been vague and that always meant that the outcome was unpredictable as was the path in getting there. Hamid might truly be angry, even questioning Ahmed's ability, but he was a reasonable man aware of local difficulties. Ahmed had been under extreme time constraints. Hamid knew that.

Ahmed closed his eyes and pinched the bridge of his nose to release the pressure. He was being too hard on himself. Except for the escape, which had not been his fault, he'd done pretty well. He'd improvised, adjusted to changing circumstances and completed the mission. Mostly.

No, Hamid was not likely all that unhappy except possibly for Ali's loss. Good agents were hard to replace. The council's opinion was another matter altogether. These were men Ahmed did not know, faceless administrators who moved pins on maps, made decisions in meetings with an excess of enthusiasm, men who in their deepest soul cared not one whit about Ahmed or any of his agents.

He shook his head against the gathering despair he was feeling and told himself it was the result of his exhausted state. He needed to sleep then deal with the woman. But first there was this other matter. Hamid had told him it would make all right so he drew on his final reserves.

He turned to his own computer and checked his e-mail account again but found nothing. He lit a cigarette as he listened to the shower, his mind conjuring up an image of Saliha.

He'd been enormously relieved to find Saliha waiting for him. He'd feared she'd broken off or was playing some kind of woman's game and would make him search for her. Given the urgency of the mission he had to send her on he had been very concerned as he had no back up for her. But there she'd been.

After sex, though, she'd turned petulant. He didn't understand women. They were always like that after. He tried checking messages again. Nothing.

He'd have thought himself too exhausted for sex but the moment he laid eyes on Saliha he'd been ready. He realized it was the adrenaline of the mission, the closeness of failure, even of death. He'd rushed through the preliminaries, or perhaps it was her who had rushed. Now his fatigue had returned and he was so sleepy he could hardly keep his eyes open.

He checked messages. Again nothing. This was nonsense. How urgent could the message be?

He glanced at the woman's laptop. He would get the password from her first thing then skim the machine for data before turning it over to his computer expert. Unfortunately the man wasn't in Prague.

Ahmed closed his eyes as he sat, nodding off almost at once. The water stopped. He jerked awake. He checked his messages and there it was. *At last*, he thought. There was a coded message, the first time one had come with the attachment. He pulled over a sheet of paper and pencil and worked the code used in such situations.

Keep the computers safe. We want them.

Ahmed glanced at the woman's computer. So someone else understood how important it might be. But he had only the one. What would Hamid think when he learned?

Ahmed was getting a headache. He again pinched the bridge of his nose. The pressure wouldn't go away. He inserted the small thumb drive and transferred the attached file directly into it. Once it was loaded he closed the computer off then removed the drive.

Saliha was humming as she patted her damp hair. He could just make out the sight of her through the partially open door and though he felt no bodily urge for her at the moment the vision was fulfilling just to see.

He had to sleep. There was no getting away from it. He'd send Saliha on her way then lay down for a few hours. After that he'd return to the woman. That was the way it had to be. He'd muffle her and do what had to be done at Karim's apartment. He had no alternative.

Saliha stepped out of the bathroom and began to dress. She saw him holding the thumb drive. "What's that?"

"I need you to make another trip."

"I just got back."

"I know, but this is urgent."

She snapped her bra into place. "You haven't paid me yet for the last trip."

"I have your money."

"I'm sure you do but *I* don't have it and we aren't talking about another trip until I've been paid."

"This is important."

"It's always important, Ahmed. My money?" She held out her hand suddenly aware that she was dressed only in her bra and panties. For an instant she wondered if he'd toss it at her like she heard some men did to their whores.

Ahmed pulled out his wallet and counted bills. He handed them to her then said, "Okay now?"

Saliha counted the money, then shook her head. "My miscellaneous expenses. You didn't pay me for them last time either, remember?"

Ahmed made a great effort not to show his anger. "How much?"

She pursed her lips. "A thousand euros for both trips. It is a bargain because I think I spent more."

He handed her the money. She nodded approval then began dressing.

"You must leave immediately, as soon as you can make arrangements," he said.

"No. That was my last trip." She eyed him carefully, searching for any warning sign that he might explode. "This is too dangerous."

Ahmed suppressed a sudden surge of anger. "Dangerous? What are you talking about? You are doing nothing illegal."

"Oh? What is on that drive you hold in your hand? I watch you with the computer. It is very important."

Important, Ahmed thought. The CIA and Israeli dogs had crippled his nation's nuclear program with their computer virus. If what Hamid said was true, the code on this key chain would change all of that. "It is just information I need to get home." Do this, he'd been told, and all would be well.

"Then e-mail it the same way you got it. Okay?" Ahmed said nothing. "You see? It is important and it is dangerous for me to have it. I understand and I am finished with this."

What to do? Ahmed's mind raced through the choices. Take her into his confidence? That was out of the question. Threaten her? No, he couldn't make that last for the duration of the trip and she traveled alone, unsupervised. A woman like this would just vanish, reinvent herself in another European city. She must get offers from visiting men all the time. It was too easy for her. He hesitated at the thought of humiliating himself in front of her but could think of no other way.

"This will be your last trip. I promise," he said. "And I will pay you double."

Saliha looked at him carefully. Once more might be all right. That's what she'd decided in Turkey before changing her mind once she was back in Prague. "Four times more. You must double it again or I won't go." Eight thousand euros, that was what she wanted, plus her road expenses.

Ahmed slowly nodded agreement and she realized she could have demanded even more. What was this she was to carry? How dangerous could it be? "And half now, the rest when I return."

He nodded again.

"So? Get the money. I need to sleep if I'm to leave in the morning."

Ahmed went to his dresser drawer and withdrew the cigar box where he kept his open reserve. There were three hiding places nearby but he'd have to leave to get to one of them. He was certain he had enough. "Here." He gave her the money.

As she counted the bills Saliha said, "There's no flight before tomorrow morning. I know the schedule by now. The first flight never leaves before nine. And I have to call work."

"Make the flight reservation. You can spend the night here." Ahmed was suddenly fearful of letting her out of his sight.

She gave him a wicked smile. "I know what you want," she said. "But promise you'll let me sleep after, all right?"

The last thing Ahmed had been thinking about was sex but as he watched her at his computer making the reservation he felt himself stir. *I'm weak*, he thought a few minutes later as he joined her in bed. *No wonder I behave so foolishly.*

DAY SEVEN

WEDNESDAY, APRIL 15

CONFESSIONS OF A CHINESE HACKER, PT. 2

By Johnson Lam—*Internet News Service*
April 15

The Entrepreneurial World of Hacking

In Eastern Europe and Russia, hacking is a digital way of life. Râmnicu Vâlcea, a small city in the Transylvanian Alps of Romania, is devoted to cybercrime and has become rich because of it. Officially the government disapproves. But in China, hacking is both a patriotic cause as well as a lucrative endeavor. And though the Chinese government claims to be cracking down on it, there is little sign of that in Shanghai where I meet with the young hacker who calls himself Victor.

Though he once set out to be an engineer, Victor was drawn into the lucrative world of hacking. "For a few dollars I bought a hacker's manual," he says as he chain-smokes cigarettes. "It showed me how easy this was and taught me simple penetrations. But that was just the beginning."

Shanghai hackers form circles in which they brag about their latest techniques and conquests like jaded Casanovas of old. And though cyber security companies are constantly upgrading their product they are reactive by nature and so always one step behind. "I'm saving my list of zero day exploits that will make me rich," Victor tells me. He already has more than five thousand computers in his own botnet and once the number is sufficient to make him rich, he'll launch his attack and loot their bank accounts. The money will travel a tangled and untraceable digital route until it lands in a bank account he controls.

"After that I'll move on." I ask what he means. "For now the government doesn't care but they will in time. Anyone who stays in that game long enough could end up with his head chopped off in a football stadium. No, there's a safer and more interesting way to make money from hacking."

Victor explains that he plans to design hacker code, then rent it out. Most hackers can't be bothered to write their own programs. That involves actual work and according to Victor most are lazy. No, they either copy commonly available code from open Web sites or they rent them. "The best ones cost money but they are worth it. Once you have your botnet in place or have gained access to a single big account you need the very latest code to really get rich. That's what I'll do. I'll even take a piece of the action as the rental fee in some cases." He smiles at that, intrigued by his own thought process. "It will be fun, safe, and profitable."

But despite his claim that he will loot his botnet accounts just once, get rich, and walk away, Victor admits that he is intrigued by the prospect of another big theft. Ten billion dollars is gambled online every year, worldwide. Victor has crafted a code that he says will give him a slice of it. "Ten percent is possible," he says with a smile. "It depends on timing. How to do it is not the problem."

It is estimated there are more than ten thousand such hackers in China alone.

38

Wu leveled the SportCruiser LSA at 1,500 meters, adjusted his heading, then eased back in his seat. He listened to the steady drone of the engine, studied the controls until he was satisfied, then scanned the outside darkness. To his left was the black Sea of Marmara, to his right the glimmering lights of Istanbul. The SportCruiser was limited to two occupants and beside Wu sat Li Chin-Shou.

When Wu had received orders from his father in Beijing to retrieve two computers, he'd moved as rapidly as he could. This couldn't be like last time. His father, Mei Zedong, had instructed him to seize the computer of a certain Uyghur leader in Istanbul that contained the names of many Uyghur activists in Xinjian Province. It had been a fiasco. The man had been home when Wu had been told he was out. Worse, he'd managed to pitch his laptop from the balcony and they'd never been able to locate it afterward. Wu ordering the man's death had created an unpleasant police inquiry that fortunately never led directly to him. He had been officially reprimanded and personally shamed by the failure. Not much later, Li had been assigned to him.

Since learning to fly, Wu had come to know the staff at the Sabiha Gökçen Airport on the outskirts of Istanbul. He was generous with them and on the rare occasion when he wanted to take off at night, they asked for no more than a small contribution to make the runway available to him. Taking off in the dark with just the runway lights was no problem but he never wanted to attempt a night landing.

Wu had stumbled onto the utility of the SportCruiser quite by accident. He'd briefly seen a French diplomat who'd offered to take him aloft
in the sport ultralight she'd flown over from Paris. To his great surprise the
craft had been nothing less than a slightly downsized general aviation airplane. But because they were classified in the same category as a powered
parachute or aluminum framed and fabric ultralight, they were viewed as
a novelty by governments and escaped most aviation rules.

The craft were uncomplicated, designed to be simple to fly. Constructed
of metal and state-of-the-art composites this model had a low wing and a
bubble canopy. It was painted white and silver. A license only required
twenty hours of instruction. The planes could be had new for under
$100,000; half that for a good used one. The manufacturers had been quick
to see the opening and a number of them were now constructing planes
such as the SportCruiser, which was in every way an airplane. The official
limitations on their use were not much at all especially as they weren't enforced. Though the official ceiling was 10,000 feet to keep them from inter-
fering with traditional airplanes Wu had taken his to over 25,000 feet with
no problem. But he was content to cruise at the official level, even lower, so
as to attract no attention but still have the capacity to overfly any European
mountain range. He could, and often did, fly at very low altitudes, not only
below radar but also beneath any kind of normal observation.

The craft cruised at 222 kilometers an hour and was designed with a
1,120 kilometer range. Wu had extended that to just under 2,000 kilometers by installing an additional gas tank in the rear compartment. The instruments were basic though adequate and with a portable GPS device
Wu had no trouble navigating. He used an ordinary cell phone for communication. Though the craft's landing gear was fixed and it was officially limited to daylight and so had neither landing nor running lights, it was in
every important way a sturdy and reliable airplane.

To utilize the craft's extreme range, as he was doing tonight, meant a
grueling ten-hour flight. But taxing as it might be, it greatly improved his
flexibility as well as his ability to move about undetected. For one, Wu was
not restricted to general aviation airports with all the bureaucracy and record keeping that entailed. With a very low stall speed, the plane could
land most anywhere that was flat, including grass fields. With little advance
planning, Wu was able to land essentially where he wanted, quickly refuel,
then fly on. And when he reached his destination, he utilized the obscure
modest airstrips outside all major European cities where no records were
kept of landings and takeoffs.

By avoiding regular general aviation airports he was also not required to check in with aviation authorities or, for that matter, to even maintain radio contact while in the air. He faced no passport checks, no meaningful controls over his movement. If he did come to the attention of authorities, he presented his passport and explained he was flying on to some city with exotic ladies of the night. A lewd wink later, he was gone as the Sport-Cruiser was refueled and made ready for his departure.

Before realizing its usefulness he'd bought the SportCruiser LSA to commute between his restaurants in Ankara and Istanbul. It enabled him to cover the distance in just over two hours; otherwise he faced a seven-hour drive. He'd quickly logged two hundred hours in the plane to improve his ability and confidence. He'd flown at night twice before against the eventuality of such a flight. Though illegal, no one was checking, not if he departed from an unsupervised airport. Flying without running lights, shrouded in the darkness, he was all but invisible. He'd timed his arrival for morning, as before, and his landing would arouse no interest.

The wind was relatively calm tonight. The land was a vast stretch of darkness below, the cities of any size glittering, the expanse between black and fathomless. The engine droned steadily and it was possible for him to lapse into a near trance as he held the craft on course. From time to time, he scanned the instruments and confirmed nothing had changed.

Li had arrived from China some months earlier. He was a highly trained and motivated agent. He was also very bright and though he worked as one of his waiters, Wu could not help but question why such an able agent had been assigned to him. He wondered if he was being watched. After all, he worked in a relative backwater of Chinese intelligence and few demands were made on him by Beijing. An occasional agent dropped by to receive cash, information was funneled through Wu, and he was required to file monthly reports. But that was all. It was possible for him to go weeks at a time and forget he was a field operative.

Wu had originally been stationed in Istanbul because of its large Uyghur population. This was a Turkic ethnic minority that had begun arriving from China in the late 1930s. In 1952, several thousand Uyghurs fled China's communist regime into Pakistan and the Turkish government stepped in and brought 1,850 of them overland to Turkey. The new arrivals were settled in the city of Kayseri in central Anatolia and were given jobs and citizenship.

The kinship between the Turks and Uyghurs was self-evident. You could fly east from Istanbul, get off the plane in Urumqi, and make conversation to some degree. The average Turk felt enormous sympathy for and an affinity with the Uyghurs.

But in recent years, Ankara has become increasingly wary of antagonizing Beijing over the fate of the minority. The two countries had recently signed a $1.5 billion development deal and more were in the pipeline. Now, no more than a few hundred Uyghurs trickled into Turkey each year, and they would apply to the local office of the United Nations High Commissioner for Refugees for refugee status, where they were treated no differently than an Iraqi or a Sudanese. More often than not, they were given temporary travel papers and sent on to receptive third countries such as Canada or the Netherlands.

But there remained a significant Uyghur minority in Ankara and Istanbul, one that was heavily involved in opposition to the Chinese government. Agents were smuggled in and out of China routinely, even receiving training here in Turkey. The Uyghur independence movement was simply waiting for the day when the communist hold on China finally snapped and distant regions such as the Xinjian Province began to break away.

Wu's first official assignment, the excuse his father had used to get him placed here, was to watch the Uyghur dissidents in Turkey. A significant number, he'd learned, was nothing more than terrorists, licking their wounds in a friendly country while gathering resources. And for all the claim of neutrality toward the Uyghur, they were after all Turkic, and the Turkish government could not help but given them assistance. It might not be the government's official position but unofficially they turned a blind eye to the Uyghur independence movement.

These days, Wu assigned the agents under him to maintain a watch on the Uyghur dissidents. He stretched, yawned, then glanced at Li, who was sleeping. They'd talked little on the flight, a bit about home, more about the restaurant and Istanbul. He was not a talkative man.

Toward the east, Wu could make out the faint blush of dawn. They'd be there soon.

39

Tap! Tap! Tap!

The rapping on the window roused Jeff from a deep sleep. He blinked, then looked outside. He saw a baton and a man in uniform. Police. He rolled down the window.

"*Nemůžete spát zde!*"

"I'm sorry," Jeff said. "I don't speak Czech." He could see the officer now, a young, slender man wearing a black leather jacket and peaked cap.

The man switched seamlessly into English. "I said that you cannot sleep here. Not like this. Find a hotel. Okay?"

"Right," Jeff said. "Thanks. I was just tired." He started the engine, then rolled out onto the quiet street. He wanted to stay, wished he could think of some way to make it happen. Given the officer's demeanor he was certain the offer of a bribe would have landed him in jail. As Jeff passed, he looked again at the lockup. No change.

He drove down the street, then made a series of turns that took him out of the crowded city center. When he reached a residential district he went down a narrow street until he found an open spot and parked. He turned off the car and leaned back in the seat. He'd been lucky to last as long as he had without attracting attention. And what had he accomplished by sleeping? For all he knew the car was gone by now.

He glanced at his watch. He opened his laptop, finding six wireless connections, two of them unsecured. He went online and checked messages.

Attached are four likely matches attending school in Prague. Assuming you've seen the culprit I'll let you decide if one is your man. One does have an 83% probability.

Any word on Daryl? Tell me you're being careful. And cover my tracks, please. I need my job.

B

Attached was a document with four photographs and the data to go with them. All looked to Jeff to be of Middle Eastern origin. One was his man. He was wearing a light beard, was younger, and looked innocent, but Jeff would have recognized him anywhere.

Ahmed Hossein al-Rashid was the name. Iranian. With a local address. If it wasn't still good it would be recent and Jeff was optimistic that with it, the face, and the name he could run his man down. If he had enough time.

He quickly sent the information to Frank, telling him this was Daryl's kidnapper and requesting any information the Company had on him as quickly as possible.

Prague 3, Taboritska 5 1001/27. Jeff entered the address and went to the map. It wasn't that far from where he'd staked out the lockup. He made a mental note of directions, then started the car. It was possible Daryl could be there. If not, perhaps Ahmed would be, and given how Jeff felt, that would be very satisfying indeed.

Daryl lifted her right eyelid ever so slightly. The man sat in a straight-backed wooden chair, which he'd leaned against the door. His arms were crossed and he was asleep.

Despite the gag over her mouth, she'd nodded off herself after the other man had left. Awake now, she listened to the sounds of the building and determined it was still night though surely getting close to dawn. There was no clock in view. She closed her eye and willed herself to think.

Why hadn't she been questioned? They'd been quick enough to torture her in Geneva so why not now? It was the question she couldn't forget and though she didn't want to face the reality that when the other man returned she'd certainly be tortured again, *why* he was delaying bothered her. She couldn't help fear that something even more terrible was being arranged for her.

One thought was that this apartment wasn't suitable for their plans. She'd heard others through the walls, even some people walking and laughing just outside on the street. The place wasn't secure. But they'd surely have one that was and she suspected that was the reason for the delay. The other man, the boss, had gone off to make arrangements and get some rest. But he'd be back.

She tested her wrists. They were no looser than before and she despaired she'd ever wiggle her hands free. She felt behind her with her fingers but her movement was very limited and except for touching the wall she'd found nothing that would help.

Her feet were a different matter. Once her captor had nodded off, she'd started working her legs up and down; slowly her ankle ties had become slacker. She had no idea if she could get her feet free, and even if she could there was little she could do afterward with her hands tied. The man had the door blocked and though he was asleep she'd noticed he reacted to every little sound. If she wasn't very careful she'd wake him up.

Steadily, and slowly, she continued working her hands and feet.

There was nowhere to park on Taboritska 5 so Jeff was forced to find a spot three blocks away. He locked the car, then set out in the predawn darkness toward the address. He stopped at one store window, straightened his appearance in the reflection, then moved on. The day-old beard was now a fashion statement so he wasn't concerned with attracting attention.

Once again he was torn with indecision. Should he call the local police with what information he'd developed? If he did, how long would it take for them to act? They'd surely check with Geneva and Jeff didn't want to consider what the Geneva police would say about him cutting out on them. When the officer learned that Jeff had information he'd withheld, the situation would only get worse. Withholding such knowledge might very well be a crime in Switzerland. Knowing governments, the situation could easily end up focusing on his behavior, ignoring what he'd come up with.

And just what was that? He was certain he'd identified the face of one of the abductors. NSA, as the result of an illegal use of resources, had produced an address in Prague. He'd identified the vehicle the man had driven and the CIA had given him the address in Prague it was registered to, also information he'd obtained illegally. Both Bridget and Frank were out a mile on this. How could he come forward now with what he had?

He couldn't. He'd made his decision and both he and Daryl were stuck with the consequences. No, going to the local police was out of the question, not until after Daryl was safe or he had no other alternative.

Jeff turned down Taboritska 5. The streetlights were still lit but toward the east he made out the first blush of dawn. The city was starting to come alive. Taboritska 5 was a residential street, not the best neighborhood but certainly not the worst. The few people out struck him as foreigners and that made sense. Ahmed, as he'd come to think of the face in the photograph, wouldn't want to stick out. He'd select a street with other immigrants.

Then he was passing 1001. He slowed a little but didn't stop. You had to be buzzed through and the number 27 suggested to Jeff that the apartment was on the second floor though he had no way of knowing that for certain. He walked on to the corner where several people were already gathered at a bus stop and stood with them so as not to attract attention.

The sky was growing light as the city awakened. What to do?

Ahmed slid from the bed and went into the bathroom. He started the shower, not bothering to close the door. He wanted Saliha to wake up. She needed to get going if she was to pack and catch her morning flight.

As he stood under the hot water he felt as if he hadn't slept at all. He was exhausted. Every problem he'd taken to bed was still with him, and in the bleak light of a new day they appeared as intractable as they had in the black of night.

Well, he'd solved one issue. Saliha would be on her way and the key chain would arrive in Iran the day after the next. And none too soon. It was vital that Iran detonate its first nuclear bomb and take its proper place in the world. He had no doubt that Hamid was correct in his assessment. All she had to do was get to Iran, turn it over, and then all the mistakes of the last few days would be washed away. In fact, he could expect a reward, even a promotion, for his part in transferring this essential information.

Ahmed stepped from the shower and began to towel off. Regardless, he'd deal with the American woman this morning. It was no longer vital but if he could extract more information from her so much the better. Letting her go was out of the question. She knew him; she knew Karim. She was bright and he wouldn't be surprised if she hadn't picked their names out of their Farsi conversations.

No, her fate was sealed.

It would make his task this day simpler as it was easier to get information when it didn't matter what you did to someone. Once you cut off body parts, subjects always talked. Something in their nature knew it was over and they wished to die in one piece as much as they could. It was part of the primitive in us, Ahmed decided.

And it was a shame. She was a pretty woman—and tough. He wasn't going to enjoy any of this but it had to be done. Karim would take care of her after. And that's when he'd tell him Ali was dead.

As he dressed, he glanced at the woman's laptop. Safer to leave it? Or take it? He decided to leave it just in case something went wrong at Karim's.

"Saliha!" he said. "Get up. You have to go if you're going to catch your airplane." Saliha groaned, rolled to her side and pulled the sheet over her head. "Come on!" he said. "Up!" He reached over and pulled the sheet off her. "I mean it."

Saliha opened her eyes, squinted against the morning sunlight now streaming in the window, then slowly climbed out of bed and made her way to the bathroom. Ahmed sat at his computer and sent a message that, when read, would be interpreted to mean that his mule was on her way. That should make Hamid happy.

Next, Ahmed put the pot on and prepared morning coffee. By the time it was ready, Saliha was finished with her shower and was sitting on the edge of the bed, preparing to dress. Ahmed glanced at his watch. He needed to leave. He handed her the USB key chain. As she reached for it he seized her wrist. "Make no mistake."

She started and pulled back, then arched her eyebrow. "When have I ever made a mistake?"

"Don't start now."

Saliha wrenched her arm free, then stood up and confronted him. "Don't ever touch me like that again, you understand?"

"Just make the trip." He met her eyes and held them. "Don't forget I know where your family lives." He saw the fear. "Now hurry."

Jeff had moved down the street and returned to the bus queue three times, careful that the waiting passengers had turned over and there was no one to remember him from earlier. The city was alive now, a busy workday in the middle of the week, nearly everyone in a hurry.

He'd risked as much time as he could watching the apartment building. He'd seen four people leave, presumably for work. That was his way in. But he hesitated. He knew he had no time to waste but still he struggled with his decision to act alone. He was not a trained agent. What if he managed to get Daryl killed in his attempt? What if he was killed and she was left to her fate?

One of the men in line gave him an odd look and Jeff realized he'd been waiting there earlier. He glanced at his watch then set out up the street. He'd go around the block and enter the apartment building from the opposite direction. It was time. He just hoped it wasn't past time.

Ahmed opened the door to his apartment building and stepped outside. He paused and looked at the sky. It was going to be a good day. The street was bustling with activity and he realized he'd taken longer to leave than he'd intended to. He set out for Karim's apartment at a brisk pace. He had a great deal to do this morning, none of it pleasant. Better to get it over with. Fortunately, it was not far.

Jeff came around the corner of the building just after Ahmed passed from sight. He went to the entrance of 1001 and stopped. There were two rows of eight intercoms and buttons, so sixteen apartments in all. The building was four stories high so there were likely four apartments to each floor. The number 27 made no sense to him. If it was on the second floor, it should be 20 to 24 or some variation of it, or so it seemed to him. He reminded himself he wasn't familiar with how apartments were numbered in Prague or if there was even a standard system. And he seemed to recall that floors were numbered differently than they were in America. The second floor was the first floor and so on.

He stepped off the porch and assumed a position against the wall, doing his best to blend in, behaving as if he was waiting. He glanced at his watch.

It took two minutes but a woman of middle years came out of the doorway. Jeff rushed by her, grabbed the door, and let himself in. She never looked back.

The building smelled of fried food, unusual odors Jeff couldn't place. The entryway had not been swept in some time. Bits of paper and dust were gathered in the corners.

Jeff stopped inside the doorway. He couldn't just knock on the door once he'd found the apartment. How to get into it? As he was puzzling that out an enormous man wearing a tattered undershirt stepped from the apartment beside the door. *The concierge*, Jeff thought as the man looked him up and down.

"Do you speak English?" Jeff asked. The man slowly shook his head. "Number twenty-seven. You understand?" Again the man shook his head. Jeff thought a moment, then on the wall wrote the number "27" with his finger, then with a look inquired about it.

"Ah!" the man said with a strong odor of garlic. He stood perfectly immobile.

Jeff reached into his pocket, took out his wallet, and removed a $50 bill. He held it up. The man shook his head, then held up two fingers. Jeff reached into the wallet and pulled out another $50. With a smile the concierge let him enter, then watched Jeff mount the stairs.

Number 27 was at the end of the hallway on the third floor. Jeff approached quietly, then placed his ear to the door but could hear nothing. He turned the doorknob and found it locked. He drew himself back and slammed into the door.

Without warning, the rope the man had used to bind her ankles snapped free and Daryl could move her legs. She quickly looked at him. He was still sleeping, even though sunlight was now streaming in a window. He wouldn't stay asleep long.

She moved her arms again but could still find no give. He'd done a much better job there. What to do?

Karim closed his mouth, then sighed. She shut her eyes and waited. Would he be able to see she'd freed her legs?

She eased her breathing, fearful he could hear her. She wished she wasn't gagged. She'd never felt more uncomfortable in her life. Again she pushed at it with her tongue but to no effect. A moment later she heard the front chair legs drop to the floor, then the man get up and walk away. There was a pause, water ran, then she heard him urinating.

This was it, she decided. This had to be it. The other man would return any minute. With her hands still bound, she had almost no chance against Karim but she stood no chance at all against the two of them.

She pulled her legs up, then managed to get herself on her feet. It was harder than she thought and took longer than she wanted. The man was still urinating. She moved to the door, turned her back to it, and groped for the doorknob. She got a hand on it but before she could turn it, he came out of the bathroom. Spotting her, his eyes grew wide for a moment, then he lunged at her.

Daryl leaped away from the doorway, kicking over the chair as she did. She backed up, keeping an eye on Karim, who came straight at her.

Daryl had never taken a course in self-defense though a friend at the office had once urged her to join her in one. But she'd played soccer growing up and the moment he was in range she kicked him in the side of his face, striking him so hard he almost fell over. Before he could recover she kicked again, this time going for his torso. Karim grabbed at her leg but she jerked it free.

He backed up, then scowled and came running at her. This time, with all her strength, she drop-kicked him in the groin. The man fell to his knees. Daryl ran to the door and gripped the knob.

Saliha had wanted to fall back asleep once Ahmed was gone. She was exhausted. She suspected it came from having to deal with Ahmed now that she'd decided what he was really up to and what he had her involved in.

The building had turned quiet now that the rush of residents to leave for work had slowed. She lay back down rather than dress, but the sun shone directly into her eyes and it was impossible to sleep even a little. Plus, she knew she had to get moving. The plane was leaving that morning and she still had to hurry to her apartment to pack.

She'd sensed that Ahmed was going to do something he found distasteful. He'd been sharp with her before when he'd had something unpleasant to do. Men were like that, taking it out on their women.

At some level, she decided, Ahmed also seemed to have sensed the change in her and was responding. Maybe that was it. His behavior frightened her and once again she wondered just what information she was carrying. Though he'd always impressed upon her the urgency of his business, he'd never before treated her like this.

Perhaps she was being paranoid and his reaction had nothing to do with any of that. Maybe it was what she carried that had him so on edge. Something very important was happening and she was a central player in it.

For the first time Saliha wondered if she had more to fear from Ahmed and those who worked with him than she did the CIA or Mossad. *I should just vanish*, she thought. *I can dye my hair, change the name I use, move to another country. He'd never find me.* It was a great temptation.

She picked up the key-chain thumb drive and held it in her hand as she reviewed her options. Just *how* valuable was it? And to whom? Maybe that was a better course. Iran's enemies might pay a great deal for what she had, much more than Ahmed promised for this trip.

She realized she'd made a mistake telling him this would be the last one. Once she came back there was no reason for him to give her the rest of her money. That had been foolish. It was time she started considering Ahmed as he really was and not as her lover, certainly not as someone she could trust.

Who could she contact about the key chain? The idea all but overwhelmed her in its audacity. In the movies it was always so easy to attempt something daring and the actors knew just where to go. But she realized she had not the slightest idea how to go about it. And once she had, once the situation was out of her control, they'd have her, in a way Ahmed never had.

Who could she trust? The CIA? The Mossad? Turkey's National Intelligence Organization, the Milli İstihbarat Teşkilatı . . . MİT? No, she was nothing to them. And the last was a joke. They had no money and would most likely simply toss her into a prison brothel.

She put the drive into her purse. At least she was something to Ahmed. Maybe not what she'd once thought but something. He was a tender lover and until that morning he'd always been kind to her. No, she'd stick with Ahmed despite her fears and complete this final mission.

Saliha sighed, stood up, and began dressing. At that instant there was a loud noise at the door, then another, then a third, and suddenly it sprang open and a wild-eyed, disheveled man charged into the apartment.

Daryl found that the knob was impossible to turn. Worn by years of use it was slippery in her sweaty hands. She grappled with it repeatedly as with horror she watched the man slowly gather himself, then stagger to his feet as if drunk. Spotting Daryl at the door he all but dove at her.

Daryl darted away, avoiding his grasp as she savagely worked at her bound wrists. She was sucking air through her nostrils while her tongue pushed against the gag. She was desperate to scream for help and to draw an unimpeded breath of air. As it was, the fight took place in all but dead silence except for the scuffle of their feet on the hardwood floor, and the rattle and scrape of furniture as one of them bumped against it.

Karim came at her with a lethal look in his eye. She kicked him again, this time with her weaker left leg, hoping to catch him off guard, but instead he grabbed the slower and less-powerful limb. Only by falling to the floor and twisting away was she able to pull it from his grasp. Even then, she did not expect to be so fortunate next time. He was still woozy from her first hard blow.

Karim dove at her again as she rolled away, then managed to awkwardly get to her feet, kicking him once hard in the face when she stood erect. Getting up had been difficult. She mustn't go down again. He was nearly against the door so she backed toward the tiny kitchen. She knew this couldn't last much longer. She'd been lucky so far but that luck wouldn't hold, she knew.

As she feared there was no rear door. The only way out was through the front. She grimly turned to face the man as he came at her, more slowly this time, with greater respect, his nose bleeding profusely, a stream of blood pouring down his shirt. He was angry now, muttering what could only be obscenities in his native language.

Daryl slid along the short counter but there was nowhere to go. She doubted she could find a way by him, and even if she did she wouldn't be able to open the door before he got to her again. This was hopeless.

"Get out!" Saliha snapped in Czech, clutching her blouse to her breasts.

Jeff looked about the small studio, moved quickly to the bathroom, glanced in, and saw they were alone. "Where's the woman?" he asked in English.

Saliha wrinkled her brow. American? "What woman?" she answered in English. "Get out of here or I'll scream."

"Is Ahmed your husband? Your lover? Where is he?"

She looked at him quizzically. "What do you know about Ahmed? Is he seeing your wife?"

Jeff backed away from the woman so she wouldn't feel so threatened, taking a careful look as he did. Most women would have already screamed by now. She was a cool one.

"No, no, nothing like that. Ahmed kidnapped my wife," he said, simplifying his relationship with Daryl. "He's got her in Prague somewhere. I thought she might be here. I'm sorry to have startled you. But I think he's going to kill her."

Saliha stared into his eyes intently, then sat abruptly on the bed. This was terrible—everything she'd feared about Ahmed was true. The man before her was clearly desperate and also obviously not a criminal. "He's my boyfriend," she said. "Or was. I'm . . . Anyway, it's over between us now."

Jeff drew a deep breath to calm himself. "I have to find him. It's my only hope."

"Where did he kidnap your wife?"

"In Geneva."

"So far? How did you find him? Why aren't the police here?" She looked at the door as if expecting them to barge in.

"I don't have much time."

"Tell me."

"I used a computer, traced the vehicle he was in, found the forged pass-port he used, got this address from his student records. Please. Please." He said the last imploringly, forced to beg as a final resort.

"And the police?"

There was no time for this, but what choice did he have? "They were moving too slowly in Geneva so I got the information myself. I used friends with access and couldn't share the data with the police without getting them in trouble. I have to do this on my own."

That made perfect sense to Saliha. The police were slow and, in her experience, corrupt. In Turkey you never went to the police to solve any-thing. You summoned the men of the family and they took care of it to the extent they could. She looked at Jeff more closely, saw his anguish and his commitment. She wondered if any man would ever love her enough to do what this man was doing.

"I don't know where he went. He just left. I'm surprised you didn't see him in the hallway. He's doing something important." She paused. "Some-thing I think he doesn't like very much. He's not a bad man. But he is"— she searched for the word in English—"devoted, I think."

Jeff was panicked. He could search the apartment but how long would it take? And in the end would the terrorist have been so foolish as to leave the address he needed here. No. Think. Think!

Karim moved slowly, filling the kitchen, it seemed, to Daryl. With every passing second he was gathering himself and she knew this short altercation was going to end very quickly. She worked along the counter until her hands encountered something hard, which she latched onto, having no idea what it was. She reached the back wall and could go no farther. She tried moving whatever she'd grabbed around to scrape at the binding on her wrists.

Just then the man rushed Daryl, seizing her and encircling her with his arms, then holding her fiercely against him. "Stop it," he said with a thick accent. "Stop this. Or I will hurt you."

Daryl squirmed in his grasp, but he held her like a vise, his breath rushing across her face. She twisted and turned, but it did no good. Then she reared her head back, and with all her might butted her head into Karim's nose. With a yowl Karim released her and pulled away as she fell to the floor. Karim jumped up and down and continued to yowl, his hand pressed against his bleeding nose.

Daryl struggled to get to her feet, her hand holding on to the hard object she'd taken from the counter. She was certain it was a knife. One end was sharp and she realized that she'd cut herself in the fall. Her feet slipped repeatedly on the slick floor as she pushed herself against the wall, trying to edge up, to obtain the leverage she needed to stand erect without the use of her hands.

Karim was cursing in a foreign language. Now he met her eye and said in English, "I will kill you for this, you whore. You hear me? I will kill you slowly, and enjoy every second of it." He came at her now, more cautiously, one hand to his bleeding nose, blood streaming down his chest.

Daryl was on the floor and realized she'd never get to her feet now. There was no room and no time. Just then he did a belly flop on her, forcing the air from her lungs, his two hands now around her neck.

Daryl twisted away, then back toward the wall, trying to pin him against it so she could keep turning and force his hands away. He was squeezing her so tightly she couldn't draw a breath through her nose and with the exertion of the fight she was becoming light-headed.

But Karim was having none of it. He released her throat just long enough to grab her shoulders and press her flat to the floor, then moved up to use his body weight and knees to hold her down. Then he deliberately took her neck again in his bloody hands and squeezed, blood dripping from his nose in a near stream, falling on her face, into her eyes.

"What's this?" Jeff said, pointing to a laptop sitting on the desk beside Ahmed's computer.

"Ahmed brought it back from his trip. I've never seen it before. He was trying to work on it but was frustrated with it." Her voice became more forceful. "I have to leave. I'm going on a trip and have a plane reservation. Okay?"

Jeff opened the computer. It was Daryl's. "Sit down," he said sharply. "This is my wife's computer! You can leave shortly but right now I need you. My wife's life is at stake."

Saliha didn't sit. She glanced at the door and wondered if she could make it. Perhaps. She started putting on her clothes.

What to do? "His phone!" Jeff snapped. "He has a cell phone and you have the number." She nodded. "Give it to me."

"Why?"

"Because I can find him with it. Hurry."

She gave him the number and he scribbled on a sheet of paper. There were ways to trace the cell phone's location, he knew, but he immediately thought of Frank and Bridget. Either or both of them might have or could obtain access to the cell towers in Prague and triangulate the location of the cell phone. The police did it routinely, so did the cell-phone companies to track the areas of greatest demand. Most cell phones even had a GPS component which made finding their location very precise. They might very well be able to go directly into one of those systems but how long would it take? Were either of them available?

"You're certain you don't know where he was going?" Jeff demanded.

"I already told you that," Saliha answered angrily. She was slowly collecting her things. "I'm leaving," she said.

"No," Jeff answered, standing and quickly moving to block her way. "I already told you that I need you to stay with me. I need your help and I can't have you warning Ahmed."

She laughed. "We're finished. I won't warn him. I believe you. I really do."

"I need you to stay with me and not use your phone. Once I've located him you can go. I promise."

Saliha thought about that a moment, then looked at her wristwatch. She had some time. Sitting on the edge of the bed, she lit a cigarette as she watched the man open his own laptop and begin typing.

Frank, he'd decided. The Company could do this fastest. As his fingers raced over the keyboard his entire demeanor changed. He no longer had that haunted, desperate look. Watching him, Saliha could now understand how he'd been able to track Ahmed from Geneva to this apartment. And she believed he'd find him now.

40

Immediately after receiving Jeff's mIRC message with a name and address of the kidnapper, Frank Renkin opened the Company's Distant Horizon Cyber Watch [E], or DHCW Europe, database. Another version designated [A] was employed for Asia. Near Horizon was used in North America. He entered the name Ahmed Hossein al-Rashid. Almost at once a page opened with the same address: Taboritska 5, Prague 3, Czech Republic. It was the right man. Then he carefully read just who exactly Jeff had run up against.

The first tier on the man was the Known File. It had a photo and physical description. It gave his age as thirty-five, said he was a registered student, had legal status, and was Iranian. There were no established bank accounts. No wife. No job. The Known File listed only what was regarded as fact. Not much and that in and of itself raised an alert to those in the business.

Frank now moved to the Projected File. This was not speculation or rumor. The information here was the result of careful analysis and in his experience was rarely wrong, as far as it went. He leaned closer to the screen as he absorbed what he was reading. There was a 93 percent chance this Ahmed was an Iranian operative, probably of VEVAK; a 67 percent likelihood he was an organizer.

Jeff had found a big one. The name was a cover but an effective one as there was no information on his true identity. No other intelligence agency would confirm having information on him. He'd been in Frank's system for just over one year and was not under physical surveillance,

With a smile, Frank noted his own department had an ongoing operation against the man. He opened that file. *Now this is interesting*, he thought. Cyberterrorism identified one computer he routinely used. He was known as well to have two cell phones.

The man's phone calls were not being recorded, at least not by the CIA, nor was his computer messaging being read, but the traffic of each was monitored. It was continuously assessed to determine if his threat level should be increased. Given the evaluation of his digital traffic there was no doubt this man was an Iranian intelligence agent and at least a midlevel supervisor. His activities were limited to Central Europe and he'd not been connected to any terrorist event. He was scarcely on the Company's radar.

This was as far as Frank had gone when he received Jeff's second message.

Urgent, urgent, urgent Frank. Not a second to waste. Find the physical location of the cell phone with this number in Prague. 243 750 191 Daryl is likely there. Please! Hurry!

Frank grimaced and returned to the cell phones. The number matched one of those Ahmed used. He checked their status and read that the Company had inserted a bit of malware into both cell phones that allowed them to track his location as long as he was within range of a cell tower. This was, if Frank's memory served, made possible by a zero day vulnerability in the Android system Jeff had identified. Ironic.

So their locations were continuously monitored and when he checked they were moving in unison as he'd expected. Frank typed a response.

Target phone is in motion. Now on Krasova Street. Will advise of address when it stops. Be careful. Call police.

41

Wu Ying eased back on the stick and slowed the engine, maneuvering the SportCruiser into a slow glide at an easy fifty kilometers per hour, just above stall. There was a slight wind from his left and he watched his approach carefully. Li, awake now, sat next to him unconcerned, facing straight ahead as the countryside passed beneath them.

Wu had selected a small airstrip for his landing. Private planes sat in two lines outside modest-size hangers and the terminal itself wasn't much larger than a house. Though protocol didn't require it, he'd contacted the airport by cell phone and been told no landings were expected. Takeoffs were under way but were few and well spaced. He was just instructed to watch for them. This was standard for such airstrips.

Wu lowered the flaps and slowed the plane even more. The runway came toward him and then they were over it. As the craft eased down, it encountered the ground effect and seemed to hover until after a long moment it dropped through, then touched in a near perfect landing. Once the plane had slowed to the speed of a walk Wu gunned the engine and made his way to the parked airplanes. He pulled his into line and killed the engine.

He and Li opened their doors and stepped out. Wu was grateful to stretch in fresh air after the long flight. A small truck came up and Wu gave instructions to have the plane refueled and serviced. He handed the man more cash than necessary to see it was done immediately. With cash there'd be no record. He had no idea how soon he'd need the plane.

The men walked into the terminal and went to the counter. "Taxi?" he asked.

"I will call," the young woman said. "It should only be a short wait. There is a canteen you can use."

Down the hall was a room with various food dispensers. Wu and Li bought hot tea and croissants. They sat in silence as they ate and waited.

"Krasova Street," Jeff read out loud. "Take me there," he said. "It will be faster. You know the city." And he could be certain she didn't warn her boyfriend.

Saliha punched out her cigarette. "All right, if you insist. It's not far. I'll take you to the street but then I go, all right? I will promise not to call him. You will have to trust me. That is our deal."

Jeff nodded, then said, "That's what I said. Let's go."

A dark fog passed across Daryl's eyes and for a moment she drifted away. She willed herself back, then fought against the man, trying to twist out from under him. He held her even more forcefully, blood all but streaming on her.

Finally, knowing she had only seconds she turned with all her power and almost managed to squirm out from under him though his hands never left her throat. She'd been working her wrists continuously all this time, never giving it a thought, instinctively seeking to free her hands. As she lay nearly on her side, the binds suddenly broke. With the last of her strength she moved her arm free, maneuvered the knife, then struck blindly at Karim, her stab feeling more like a blow. She had no idea how deadly the knife was so she pulled it back and stabbed again, then again, then again.

Karim released her and screamed, clutching his side. With his other hand he struck her across the face and Daryl blacked out.

Saliha knew where Krasova Street was but had never been to it. The man urged her along and they moved at a near run. He kept slightly back but beside her. She considered if she should even go through with this. Out of the apartment, in the open, she reconsidered the situation. She didn't know this man. He claimed his wife had been kidnapped by Ahmed yet he didn't wear a wedding ring.

True, she had her suspicions about Ahmed but she was surprised she'd been so quick to believe the worst about him. Maybe it was true, after all he'd been very rough and threatening with her, but for all she knew this man was even worse. Because his story had the force of conviction didn't mean he was telling her the truth. Men rarely did.

Then a thought crossed her mind: What if he was a CIA agent? What if the Americans were after Ahmed and had concocted this story to get to him when they'd not found him at his apartment?

As quickly as the thought came it vanished. The CIA would have enough agents to do the job; they wouldn't send just one man. She'd looked. No one was following them. The Americans would have known Ahmed was not home and would already have his phone number. They had the resources. No, she decided, he wasn't an American agent.

She looked back quickly at him over her left shoulder. Maybe he was an Israeli, a Jew. She shuddered at the thought.

"This is it," she said at the corner. "Krasova."

It was a narrow street. Foot traffic only. "Here," Jeff said, taking her arm. He moved them to a doorway where he could open his laptop.

Saliha glanced about, confirming the man had no operatives with him. She needed to get away. She had a plane to catch. She looked at the pedestrians on the busier street they'd been on, examining each carefully.

There was a text message from Frank.

Krasova 702/34

Jeff pasted the address in Google Maps. "Just down this street, I think." He closed the laptop. "This way."

"Tell me," Saliha said, not moving, "are you a Jew?"

"What?"

"A Jew. Are you a Jew?"

Jeff laughed. "No, I'm a fallen Catholic."

"Ah. Like me. Only I'm a fallen Muslim."

As they turned the corner Saliha saw an opening and without giving it any more thought suddenly bolted away, running into the traffic, making her way quickly to the taxi stand across and down the street. She was gambling that the man was really looking for Ahmed. He wouldn't risk chasing her with so many people around and risk attracting the police.

Just as she reached the taxi stand she glanced back and couldn't see him. She looked farther along the street and there he was moving quickly, staring intently at every building as if searching for an address. She stepped into the taxi and gave the driver her address.

Saliha hesitated, then pulled out her cell phone. If something happened to Ahmed she'd never get the rest of her money. She pressed the speed-dial number.

Daryl slowly came awake as if climbing out of a dark and very deep well. It was utterly quiet in the apartment. She had no idea how much time had passed. She looked at the angle of the sun and decided it had only been a short while. She moved her hands to her face and with some effort, worked the tape, then pushed the gag from her mouth. She lay there breathing the rich air, grateful to be alive.

When she finally moved she realized she was wet with something sticky. Then it came back to her. Blood. Still on the floor she turned her head. Across the linoleum kitchen floor was a long, broad crimson streak. At the end lay Karim, unmoving. Slowly, cautiously, Daryl rose to her feet. The cut across her right palm hurt like hell.

The knife was gone. She glanced about the kitchen searching for a weapon in the event Karim was able to attack her again. There was a heavy old-fashioned cast-iron coffee grinder resting on the counter. She took it and approached the man. When she reached him she stopped, listened closely, watching him. No sound at all came from him. And his body never moved. He was dead.

Maybe.

Daryl went behind him, then tentatively reached forward with her left hand and poked him to see if he'd react. He didn't. Now she poked him even harder. Nothing. She took him by his shoulder and with some effort rolled him onto his back.

She shot upright. Karim's eyes were open and glazed over. She'd never seen anything like it.

Daryl backed away, bumped into the fallen wooden chair, straightened it, then sat, holding the coffee grinder on her lap like a purse. She'd never seen a dead man before, not like this, not out of a casket and in a funeral home. Then the horror of what had just happened struck her.

She'd *killed* him.

Daryl sat, contemplating the thought, waiting for the reality to engulf her, for the sense of regret, of guilt, then realized she felt none. The man deserved it. It was him or her and she'd been lucky enough to make it him.

Finally, her numbed mind started to function normally. *Get out,* she thought. *You've got to get out of here. The other one will be back at any time.* She stood up and moved toward the door. Just as she reached for the doorknob, she saw it turn and an instant later the door opened.

Wu instructed the driver to drop them two blocks from the address he'd been given. His father's information had been complete, the result of the considerable research skills of the Cyber Warfare Center. He had a description, several photographs, this address, and more. With luck he'd find the laptops at the man's apartment; with more luck he'd simply surrender it. If not, he had Li.

Taboritska 5. 1001/27. Here it was.

The street entrance was locked. Though Wu didn't intend to waste time he was not especially in a hurry. He could afford to wait. Just then a gross man waddled down the stairs and caught his eye. Wu gestured for him to open the door.

The concierge held the door open a few inches. He spoke in English as he didn't know Japanese or Korean or Chinese, whatever it was these two smiling men were. "What do you want?"

"We need to see the gentleman in apartment 27," Wu said.

The Arab, the concierge thought. *He is very popular this morning.* "Perhaps."

Wu understood at once and removed a twenty Euro note from his wallet. The concierge snorted. "You'll have to do much better than that. Ahmed is a friend of mine."

Wu doubted that very much. He pulled out a one hundred Euro note, an enormous extravagance. The man nodded. Wu held out the note and it vanished into the man's palm. He swung the door open. "Upstairs. Three flights. On the end."

"Is our friend home?" Wu asked.

The concierge shrugged, then vanished through his own door.

Wu went to the stairs and the pair moved rapidly up. Only Li carried a weapon. He drew out his automatic and stood beside the door, his back to the wall. He looked to Wu and nodded. Wu reached out and tried the doorknob. It moved. The door had been broken open. Li took the lead, entered, then called out for Wu to join him.

The place was empty.

"Search," Wu ordered. "We're looking for laptops, external drive, thumb drive, anything like that. Be thorough." The two men set about methodically searching the apartment.

Jeff had the right building but triangulation only worked so far. Frank could not give him an apartment number. Once inside he'd have to figure out where Ahmed was on his own.

Jeff examined the building carefully. It was four stories high, any number of apartments. How to close the odds? If he started knocking on doors he was bound to arouse suspicion. If he asked the wrong questions or appeared desperate it would have the same outcome.

He went to the entrance, which he found locked. On the side were three columns of six with names and buttons. Three of the name tags were blank, others were stricken through with handwritten names scribbled over. They were all incomprehensible to him. Of the remaining neatly printed names all appeared Czech, or at least Western.

A middle-aged man wearing the work clothes of a laborer came out the door without looking at him. Jeff caught the door and entered.

Now what?

Ahmed stepped into the room and stopped, stunned at what he saw. His phone rang at that moment but he ignored it. The furniture was scattered everywhere, there was blood on the floor, Karim lay near the kitchen looking dead, and the American woman was standing on the bloody floor holding something, her mouth wide open staring at him with utter shock.

"What have you done to my friend?" he demanded, moving toward her.

Daryl screamed, then shouted, "Help! Help!" as she lifted the coffee grinder to strike him.

Jeff heard the muffled sound from the foyer and bounded up the stairs, taking them three at a time. The shouting stopped, then resumed. As he moved he heard the sound again from above. On the fourth floor he was certain he was there. But now there was no sound at all. He moved quickly down the hallway, pausing to listen at each door, examining them for any sign that would help.

At the last door on the right he heard voices, agitated. One a man's, one a woman's.

Daryl.

Jeff grabbed the door handle just as he heard a struggle inside. The door was not locked. He opened it, rushing in at full speed. There was a man holding Daryl against the wall by her shoulders. Hearing noise he turned, but at the same moment Jeff dove into him.

The three went down in a pile, rolling about in the blood, unable to do anything effective because of the limited space. Ahmed never went about Prague armed and had not expected to need a weapon to get what he required from Daryl. The man was a giant, it seemed to him. The woman was crazy; there was no other description for her. She grabbed his right arm and was holding it firmly while the man was working to pin his left.

Ahmed struggled and pulled his arm free momentarily and struck Jeff hard against the side of his face. There was a scramble beside him as the woman struggled with something, then a black object struck Ahmed on the top of his head, then again, then again until finally he stopped fighting. Dazed and confused he lay there as he heard voices, seemingly distant. Then he was being manhandled and he felt himself being tied up. He opened his eyes for the final indignation as Daryl stuffed a soiled rag into his mouth, then tied it in place with a stark look of satisfaction.

Ahmed watched as the couple embraced, tried to focus his thoughts, then passed out.

"My God," Daryl said. "I never thought I'd see you again."

"Are you all right?" Jeff asked, never so relieved in all his life. If he'd lost Daryl he had no idea what he'd do.

"I'm . . . I'm all right. Very tired and, frankly, pissed as hell. And it looks like I killed one of our friends," she said, pointing at Karim. Her hand suddenly hurt and she lifted it up. "I cut myself."

Jeff took a look, glanced at Ahmed who was unmoving, then went into the bathroom. There were no bandages, nothing of use. In the kitchen he opened each of the drawers, finally finding an unopened roll of paper towels. He went back to Daryl who was sitting, exhausted, on the old couch by the window.

"This will have to do for now," he said as he sat beside her then pulled off several large sheets and pressed them to her bleeding palm.

"How did you find me?" she asked in a near whisper.

Jeff gave her a brief summary including the young girlfriend who'd fled at the last moment. "I was very lucky."

"It was about time we had some. Then the police don't know you're here?"

He shook his head. "I'd have burned Frank and Bridget if I told them. The police were on the same path but moving too slowly."

"Government."

"But without me to identify this man they don't know where to look. By the way, the third guy's dead, too. He killed Herlicher in Geneva, then was shot to death by the Geneva police."

Daryl's eyes turned cold. "Good. I'm sorry for Herlicher, though I doubt he's any great loss to humanity."

"Daryl!"

"You try getting kidnapped, tortured, smuggled out of the country, drugged, threatened, then fight your way out and kill a man in the process, and then see how it changes your perspective." She looked at Ahmed as if considering his future but said nothing.

"You did well," Jeff said, holding her again.

"I think he's coming around," Daryl said.

42

Wu stood back and slowly examined the room as Li methodically went through it again. The only computer belonged to the man who lived here, Ahmed Hossein al-Rashid. Wu would take it just in case. Li had found a cache of key-chain thumb drives. They looked unused but he'd take them as well. Otherwise he hadn't found what he'd been sent for.

"Collect it," he ordered. Li placed the items into the man's computer bag, which was decorated with a large logo of a local soccer team.

Wu lifted his phone. This Ahmed had been the subject of extensive interest to the PLA and the information Wu's father had passed on to him had been detailed. He didn't know why the man was important to China but he knew there was some vital connection to justify such an effort. Using a special app designed for agent use, he keyed in the man's cell-phone number and immediately acquired a location with an address. He entered his current address.

"He's not far," he said staring at the screen. "I think he took the laptops with him. Ready?" Li nodded and the two men set out.

This was just Wu's second field operation and he'd botched the first. He'd not asked if Li had field experience. It was better if the man thought he knew everything about him. What mattered was that he not make any mistakes and look foolish.

On the ground floor the concierge was waiting for them, blocking the exit with his large presence. He held a very heavy walking stick, more like a club, laid casually across his chest. "I should call the police," he said. "You're stealing from a tenant." He indicated the bag Li carried. "You have no right."

He wanted more money Wu knew. Would it buy his silence? The man should have been happy with what he'd already received. And if he paid, knowing now how he was, he might still call the police. After all, he had to explain to the tenant what happened to his apartment.

The man continued, "I told you Ahmed is a friend of mine. He expects me to look after things for him." He slapped the club against his chest gently.

Wu turned to Li and spoke in Mandarin. "We cannot trust him."

Li nodded. In a flash he leaped on the hulking man. Before he could respond Li had struck him against his neck. He toppled over like a felled tree, the club clattering to the floor. Wu looked outside. No one. Without speaking, each man took an arm and dragged the concierge into his apartment. Li immediately searched the rooms, then returned shaking his head. They were alone.

Wu straightened. The apartment had a vile smell. So? What to do? Tie him up and leave him? Wait for him to wake up and give him more money? Every possibility had risks.

Li looked over expectantly. Wu shrugged. "Kill him."

43

Groggy, Ahmed slowly opened his eyes and glanced around the room, taking a minute to recall where he was and what had happened to him. He spotted Karim lying not far away, dead. His two best agents, killed within a day of each other.

He looked up and there was the tall American couple, holding one another, looking down at him in a way he'd never hoped to see.

So this is what it's like, he thought. *To be on the other side.*

"Do you think the police are coming?" Daryl asked. "We've made a lot of noise."

"I don't know," Jeff said.

"Maybe we should just go."

"We need some answers, I think." Jeff crossed over to Ahmed.

"There's a dead man here," Daryl said. "I don't know where we are but I don't want to have to explain what happened."

"We're in Prague. And you're right." Jeff looked at Ahmed. "I'd say we need a very good reason to leave this one alive, wouldn't you?"

Despite himself Ahmed knew he'd given away his momentary agitation and fear. So, they were going to kill him. What else could he expect? It's what he would have done if the roles were reversed.

Jeff had no intention of killing the man but knew it was to his advantage for him to think it likely. He glanced at Daryl. Given her state he wasn't so sure of her intention. He knelt down.

"You see your partner there, dead? That will be you if we don't get some answers. I'm going to remove the gag but you have to nod your head to show me you understand. If you make a sound I will just kill you and to hell with the information. *Do* you understand?"

Ahmed nodded. Jeff reached forward and slowly untied the cord holding the gag in place. He pulled the dirty rag out and waited as Ahmed drew several deep breaths.

"What's this all about? Tell me everything," Jeff ordered.

Ahmed hesitated but only briefly. There was, he realized, no point in resisting in the extreme. They already knew a great deal from Geneva. "I was instructed to take you and learn how much progress you'd made in your research. That was all. I only took the woman because she was with you."

"Who gave you orders?"

Ahmed allowed himself a small smile. "I can't tell you that."

Jeff considered the nonanswer. The man was Iranian; Iran was all but at war with the United States and poised to detonate a nuclear bomb at any time if reports were accurate. Only the CIA and Israelis, through the very clever use of a Trojan, had managed to cause any significant delay, or the program any real damage. If this was an Iranian operation, then that meant the Trojan he and Daryl had been researching in London and Geneva was Iranian.

And that made no sense at all. It was far too sophisticated.

"What do you know about what we were researching in Geneva?"

"Nothing. It is not my field."

"What did your superiors want to know?" Daryl asked, steel-eyed.

Ahmed refused to look at her. "They didn't say. Just to find out how much you knew."

"Ahmed," Jeff said, using the man's name intentionally to let him know he knew it, "Iran did not design this virus. We know that. Who did?"

Ahmed wondered the same thing himself. "I have no idea. That is not something I would be told."

"What do you do in Prague?" Daryl asked.

"I'm a student."

Jeff said, "Don't be foolish, Ahmed. I can find a plastic bag in the kitchen. Do you think I've forgotten what you did to Daryl?"

Ahmed eyed the man carefully. No, this one might threaten him but he did not believe for a moment he would kill him, or even torture him, not enough to make a difference. No, it was the woman he feared. There was a coldness there now that he'd not seen when they'd first taken her. What was the point in withholding what they wanted to know? It was of no use to them.

"I supervise people and occasionally carry out orders."

"You mean you're a terrorist," Daryl snapped.

Ahmed laughed. "Hardly."

"You kidnapped us. You were going to murder me."

"Of course I wasn't going to kill you. I do not kill, I do not bomb. We gather information. That is all, I assure you."

"Get the bag, Jeff," Daryl ordered. "This SOB is lying." She moved much closer to him and squatted down. As Jeff went into the kitchen she said in a low voice, "Let's see how you like it. I'm going to enjoy this."

"All right, all right," Ahmed said. "I will tell you everything. It is not so much. I supervise, like I said. We do this and do that, not so much."

"And that woman?" Daryl said. "What about her?"

"What woman?"

"The one I found in your apartment," Jeff said returning with a plastic shopping bag.

"Saliha, you mean? My girlfriend. What did she tell you?"

"The way this works is, *we* ask the questions. What does she do for you?" Daryl asked.

"She's my girlfriend. What do you think she does?"

"That's right, smirk," Daryl said. She glared at him a moment, then snapped, "Give me that. He needs to learn manners." Jeff handed her the bag. Daryl deftly slipped it over Ahmed's head without preamble and closed it around his neck.

Ahmed reflexively drew a deep breath, the bag sticking across his mouth. He felt claustrophobic and in the grip of a panic attack. "All right, all right," he said, his voice muffled by the plastic. "I'll tell you." She held the bag a moment longer before removing it. "Every few weeks I receive an e-mail. I copy the attachment to a USB key chain. She takes it to Turkey, then on to Iran."

"A mule?" Jeff said. Why would anyone go to all that trouble to transfer data to Iran? It made no sense.

Daryl was there already. "Why not just e-mail it?"

"I don't know. I just follow my instructions."

Daryl moved to slip the bag back in place.

"All right, all right. They want no trail back to them from Iran."

Jeff suddenly remembered. The woman was leaving on a trip. "Is she traveling for you today?" he asked with sudden comprehension.

Stupid woman, Ahmed thought. *Talking to this man.* If he denied it the bag would just go over his head again. And at some point the woman might not remove it. "Yes. But she is gone by now. You can't stop her."

"What's she taking this time?" Jeff asked. Something big, he was certain. That would explain a great deal.

Ahmed, who viewed himself as the ultimate pragmatist, felt his chest unexpectedly swell with pride. These two were weak like all Americans. Soon enough America would have to deal with a reborn Iran. "Stuxnet. You know about it, don't you? You would in your field. She's taking the fix to it. Soon, my friends, you will see a bright fireball in the Iranian desert and not long after . . ." Ahmed smiled. "It is already too late."

Two Chinese men walking briskly in central Prague drew a few stares, Wu noticed. He slowed their pace and cautioned Li to not look so serious. "We are tourists or perhaps businessmen. We must not hurry."

The morning-rush time was over and traffic was not as heavy as when they'd come into the city. Wu decided against a taxi. It would be just as fast to walk. Ahmed, he understood, was an Iranian operative stationed in Prague. He served a vital though unspecified role that benefited China. His status as an agent had been obvious by the nature of the apartment. It had been too clean for a normal single man, with none of the usual things Wu would have expected to find. A complete set of furniture for one. It was as if the man had just one foot in, the other ready to bolt.

Wu understood perfectly. It had taken him several years before he laid down the kind of detailed life someone living permanently would. Still, he kept a small bag in both his apartments, one in Istanbul, one in Ankara, and at a moment's notice could be out the door. He'd noticed one in this man's apartment. In addition, Wu rented a safe house in both cities, listed under another name, paid for in cash—apartments no one knew existed. And he had two passports beside his official one, each bundled with a supply of American dollars and euros.

Wu checked his phone as he walked. The cell phone he was tracking had not moved. "The next street," he said to Li, who nodded in response. A few moments later they were at Krasova 702/34. The entry door was locked.

Wu rejected forcing it. "We'll wait," he said. He moved onto the street and kept the door under casual observation as he input the building address. It was listed in the man's database as belonging to a known associate. Three minutes later an elderly woman came up, fumbled with her key, and opened the door. They quickly followed.

Wu glanced at the numbers on the ground floor. "The stairs," he ordered. "Quickly now."

"I didn't like leaving him," Daryl said on the street, "even if he did tell us about his girlfriend." She'd taken a few minutes before leaving to wash up, removing as much blood as possible, combing her hair.

"What should we do? Kill him?" Jeff asked.

Daryl didn't answer. Her hand really hurt. She lifted it so she could take a good look. "We need to find a store or pharmacy. I have to fix this, get clothes, and get rid of this blood." The paper towels were soaking with it.

They spotted a small pharmacy within two blocks, though drawing worried looks as people made way for them on the sidewalk. They looked as if they'd been in a fight. Jeff bought what he needed while Daryl waited discreetly outside. There were bloodstains all over her. The pharmacy sold tourist T-shirts. He bought one for her. *I ♥ Prague!* Once her hand was properly bandaged and she'd ditched her blouse for the T-shirt, the couple took a taxi to Saliha's address, which Ahmed had surrendered.

"Do you think we can catch her?" Daryl asked. She picked at her pants. There were stains on her thigh but these were not obviously blood as they had turned brown.

"I don't know. Maybe. But she seemed in a hurry earlier and I delayed her."

After Jeff paid for the taxi, Daryl said, "Let me talk to her, woman to woman. You've already threatened her and she ran away from you."

"All right. But I'll be nearby, just in case."

The building was newer than the one they'd just left. The entrance was open and there was no concierge. They took the elevator to the fourth floor. Saliha's apartment was the second on the left. Daryl knocked as Jeff placed himself with his back against the wall just beside her, ready to move at the slightest provocation.

A woman answered the door, opening it three or four inches. *"Jo?"*

"I'm looking for Saliha," Daryl said with her winning smile.

"Oh. You just missed her."

"That's really too bad. Could I talk to you?" Daryl asked. "It's very important."

"About what?" The door moved as if she was about to close it.

Daryl held up her bandaged hand. "About Ahmed, what he did to me. About the danger Saliha is in."

There was a moment's hesitation, then the voice said, "Come in."

Ten minutes later Daryl emerged from the apartment smiling. "Come outside," she said as she walked passed him toward the elevator. On the street she led him around the corner. There was a bench and she sat down, Jeff joining her.

"Her name is Ayten. She comes from Istanbul. She worked with Saliha at the same club for a while but now works somewhere else. Three women share the apartment. She doesn't like Ahmed. She saw him with another woman and told Saliha he was cheating on her. She said Saliha makes trips to Ankara every few weeks to see her mother but Ahmed pays her so the trips are really for him. She doesn't know why. She says Saliha was very upset when she arrived; said a maniac had tried to kidnap her." Daryl stopped, gave Jeff a quick kiss and said, "Hello, maniac." She drew a breath then continued, "Saliha wasn't going to go on any more trips she'd told Ayten, but Ahmed is paying her a lot of money so this is the last one."

"Is that it?"

Daryl smiled brightly. "Of course not. I have Saliha's address in Ankara and her cell number. I also have her last name. Kaya."

Jeff beamed. "Excellent."

"So what do we do? If we contact the police, which one do we call?" Daryl asked. "And what do we tell them? I don't want to explain the dead body back there. And you don't want to say how you were able to find me."

That, Jeff thought, *is a very good question*. What counted was that he *had* found her, but in the rescue he'd painted himself into a pretty corner. The police in Geneva were going to be very upset with him. And at the least, here in Prague Daryl would have to account for the dead man. In an ideal world there would be no question of self-defense. She was, after all, a kidnap victim and the man had been one of her abductors.

But this wasn't an ideal world and Jeff knew nothing about the Czech legal system or politics. Ahmed and the other men were Iranian operatives so the Iranian government would be applying pressure once they knew what had happened. Would the Czech government stand up to an emerging nuclear power? Or would it fold and take the easy way? It was likely Daryl would be held at the least and it was not out of the question she'd be charged with a crime of some kind. He told her what he was thinking.

"I'm not sticking around," she said. "I need to get out of Dodge immediately. We both do. I'll text any answers to questions the Czechs might have from the safety of an undisclosed location. What will the Swiss police do about you, do you think?"

"I don't know. They're upset with me, I'm sure. Maybe more."

"We're victims in this. And we aren't without friends."

"Maybe. I can't be certain that's how they'll see this."

"Well, it doesn't matter, does it? We're getting out of this country before that body is found. And we need to stop this woman if we can, don't we? She'll be in Turkey today. Once there she'll just vanish. No one will be able to find her." She thought a moment then said, "What about just calling her? We've got her number."

Jeff shook his head. "She's not going to listen to me and she doesn't know you. It will just alert her and she'll move even faster."

"Maybe it will scare her off. She doesn't sound very committed to this last trip."

"I don't think we can take that chance, do you?"

Daryl thought a moment then said, "She's probably at the Prague airport waiting on the next flight to Turkey. How many can there be? Let's worry about the rest after we've found her."

44

They'd done a good job, Ahmed realized. He was tightly bound and not going to be able to get loose. The worst part was Karim's body lying not that far away. Ahmed twisted and turned away from the gruesome sight.

How long would he lay here gagged? Did Karim ever have visitors? It was possible he could lay like this until he died. Now that would be a truly miserable death.

He'd told too much, he reminded himself. They hadn't even tortured him. The mere threat was all it had taken. He was disgusted. But it was that woman. He'd have stood up to the man, he'd seen his humanity and had been willing to risk that he'd not take those final steps. But the woman . . .

He'd never seen anyone like her. He'd read somewhere that in earlier times the worst fate of any captive was to be turned over to a tribe's women. Now he understood. After what he'd done to her she'd been capable of doing whatever was necessary to him, and very likely enjoying every minute of it. He hoped to Allah he never laid eyes on her again.

He twisted himself again and tested his binding. She'd tied him up, of course. He could already feel his hands growing numb.

And what to report to Hamid? He would want to know what they'd done to him to make him talk; worse, he might require he return to Iran for examination, so Ahmed couldn't risk lying. Karim and Ali were dead. While he couldn't reasonably be blamed for Ali's death whose assignment had come directly from Hamid, he would be blamed for Karim's. The killing in Geneva had carried no great risk; the worst outcome other than failure would have been Ali's capture. The Swiss police were not known for using violence needlessly. He wondered what Ali had done to get himself shot. Or had it been some kind of terrible accident? Either way, the target was dead and that counted more than the life of a single agent.

Karim was another matter. Twice a prisoner had managed to escape, first the man, then the woman. In the process his Geneva operation had been disrupted and now his second operative killed. How was he going to explain it?

His hands were numb now. He might lose them if he just lay here. Then he had it. He should have thought of the solution sooner. He twisted, then twisted again, and began making his way slowly across the floor like some exotic insect. It was exhausting. He'd rest, then do it again, each time moving an inch or two toward the far wall. He'd reach it eventually. Then he'd point his feet toward the wall and start kicking. Eventually someone would come. At least he hoped someone would hear him and come.

Just then the door flew open and in rushed two Asian men, the first brandishing a pistol. They took in Karim's body and Ahmed in a single professional glance, then checked both the tiny kitchen and wardrobe for anyone else.

Wu closed the door while Li checked the man lying in blood. In Mandarin he said, "Dead. An hour I think."

Wu moved to Ahmed. "Your friend?" he asked in English.

Ahmed nodded.

Wu recalled the photo he'd seen in the file. "You are Ahmed Hossein al-Rashid." He said it as a statement of fact.

Ahmed hesitated, then nodded.

"We are friends. I'm going to remove your gag and untie you. We are friends." He told Li to see to it while he took a seat at the table in one of the wooden chairs. Once Ahmed was free Li all but carried him over and planted him in the other chair.

"Get him water," Wu ordered. "How do you feel?"

"I am fine."

"You've had a rough go of it, it's obvious. What happened to your friend?"

"Who are you two? Why does he have my computer?"

Wu smiled. "My name is George, his is Hanson," he lied. "We're here to retrieve those two laptops you got from the American couple. You should have received a message to keep them safe."

China. That was no surprise. Ahmed had long suspected what he was passing along could only be coming from China. "I only had one, the wom-an's, but it's gone."

Li came over with a glass of water and placed it in front of Ahmed. Wu told Li to help him as he couldn't use his hands yet. Li lifted it to Ahmed's lips and he gulped the water down eagerly. "More." Li returned to the kitchen.

"What happened here?" Wu asked again.

Ahmed thought quickly. They knew about the computers. That mes-sage had come directly from Hamid.

"The woman killed Karim. I arrived almost immediately afterward, too late to save him. Then the man came and"—his cheeks burned with shame at the recollection—"they took me prisoner and left me here. They have both computers," he said hopefully. "They've not been gone long."

"What are their names?" Wu asked as he pulled out his iPhone. Ahmed told him and a moment later Wu had a photograph taken of Jeff and Daryl at a computer conference in Las Vegas the previous year. She was stun-ning. "They are CIA?"

It occurred to Ahmed that these ruthless men might very well kill the couple for him. "I think so. They are highly skilled agents, computer ex-perts as well. I would take no chances with them."

Li set the glass down. Ahmed reached forward with his two hands now burning as the blood rushed back into them. By being very careful he was able to lift the glass to his lips and drink.

"Where can we find them?" Wu asked.

"A woman named Saliha Kaya is traveling to Ankara, Turkey, with an important message for my government. These CIA spies intend to stop her. They are probably at the airport right now."

"I need details of this Kaya woman."

"My phone," Ahmed said with a slight smile. "Everything is there. Even a photograph." He looked at Li. "May I have my computer, please?"

45

The morning flight from Prague to Ankara had left promptly at 11:45 A.M. Jeff and Daryl had missed catching Saliha by minutes.

"Now what?" Daryl asked, slumping in a chair. She glanced at her bandaged hand and made a face. It hurt like hell.

"We find the next flight, book tickets, then replace our phones."

Daryl looked at her stained pants with disgust. "I need to buy clothes and it wouldn't hurt me a bit to wash up. I look like a bag lady."

Forty-five minutes later they were booked on Lufthansa flight 1691 with a change of planes in Munich, then direct from there to Ankara. As for their needs, Prague-Ruzyne International Airport was one of the most modern and convenient in Europe. At an Apple Store, Daryl picked up a replacement iPhone. Not far away Jeff acquired an HTC Galaxy with the Windows OS he preferred.

While she went shopping for clothes, Jeff waited outside the store and configured his phone to access the high-security e-mail server he and Daryl used. In less than ten minutes he'd retrieved his e-mail, contacts, and calendar. The first message he sent was to Frank Renkin, giving him his new cell-phone number. Once Daryl was finished shopping she'd do the same, then was going to call Bridget directly with word she was safe and thanks for her help.

When Jeff decided he'd waited long enough he punched Frank's contact to dial his number. They didn't have a lot of time. Their flight was boarding in fifteen minutes.

Frank answered. "Yes?"

"Frank, it's Jeff. Daryl's safe, she's with me right now."

"Jeff! Thank God! Are you two all right?"

"We're fine except for some bruises." Jeff told Frank what happened. "We're at the Prague airport right now. We've booked a flight to Ankara. We have the mule's address there and hope to catch her." He gave Frank all the information they had on Saliha. "How dependable do you think the information about the Tusk patch is?"

"Wait a minute. Let's back up here. You say Daryl *killed* one of the kidnappers and left his body in a Prague apartment?"

"She didn't have any choice, Frank. It was either him or her."

"And you haven't called the police?"

"There hasn't been time and we lost our cell phones. We only just got replacements. We've been trying to stop Saliha."

"Let me think about this a minute." There was a long pause, then Frank resumed. "Look, this Ahmed is an Iranian agent for certain. We've had him on the radar for over a year. At this point though you know more about him than we do. What I'm about to tell you couldn't be any more secret so careful where you tell Daryl. The rollout for Tusk started on April 1, April Fool's Day. So far no sign of penetration. Frankly, I've suspected your abduction was related but from what you tell me that doesn't appear to be the case. We've found an ingenious way to jump the Iranian air gap. Your zero day Android vulns proved invaluable." Frank told him how it was planned to work. "With this UNOG mess there isn't any report. Right now our hopes are on Tusk but it will take time. I don't know if we have enough. The countermeasure is, of course, Chinese. We have no idea if it will work but their earlier versions I'm told have blunted the first two versions of our stuff. It's going to work at least somewhat, perhaps as good as your man bragged. I'm concerned about the delay in our current rollout. I'll meet with the lady running our show out there and my guess is she'll put some wheels in motion but you two are hot on the trail. I can't tell you what to do but if you think you can find this woman and get that code back without any danger to yourselves then you'll be doing us a great service. If there's risk, let those trained for this sort of thing handle it."

Frank assured Jeff he'd get all the information he could that might be of help and would text it as it became available. "Don't let anything happen to you two, all right? You don't have to save the world. There's always another way."

Just then Daryl walked out of the boutique with a mischievous smile. "Say hi to Frank." Jeff held up the phone. Daryl snatched it up and began talking. Jeff glanced at his watch, caught her eye, then held up ten fingers. "Got to go, Frank," she said. "I need to wash up and change clothes. See you guys soon."

She handed the phone back to Jeff. "Where's the ladies' room?"

Once she'd vanished behind the door Jeff considered calling Ulrich Spyri in Prague. The man had been very professional with him. He'd worked as hard as he could and in the end had taken the right approach. He'd not succeeded because Jeff had run out on him and he felt very badly about that.

But better to wait, Jeff decided. Better to get out of Europe first—just in case.

46

LANGLEY, VIRGINIA
CIA HEADQUARTERS
CYBERTERRORISM–COMPUTER FORENSICS DEPARTMENT
12:19 P.M. EST

Agnes Edinfield walked down the hallway, smiling to several subordi-
nates as she did, then entered her reception area. Her assistant glanced up,
nodded in acknowledgment, then returned to his computer. In her office
Edinfield set aside her notepad and papers, then entered her private restroom.

In the war on terror, as it was still known within the Company, there was
one positive: funding had improved. There'd been a time when she'd had to
scramble for every piece of her budget or to grab a position or two. Today it
was more a question of positioning herself to get a bigger slice of the pie.

Frank Renkin had come by her office earlier that morning and delivered
stunning news. First, a UNOG official had been murdered on the street
outside his home in downtown Geneva. She'd seen an alert on it earlier
but had not matched it to his earlier briefing. The ongoing manhunt had
been turned up dramatically. Interpol was requesting CIA assistance—
which meant data, not manpower as they were very sensitive about that
sort of thing. But there was a lot they were prepared to tolerate if the outcome was to their liking. You simply could not let officials be gunned down
at will, especially in Switzerland. A man believed to be an Iranian national
was the assailant and had been killed at the scene. Jeff Aiken had been
brought to the site and identified him as one of the abductors.

There was, regrettably, no word on Dr. Haugen and Edinfield had
decided that she could only assume Haugen was a loss. She didn't like the
thought of that but over the years she'd seen it often enough to know the

likely outcome. Those abducted were typically killed quickly unless there was a reason to hold them. She hoped there was one in this case but she couldn't see it. No, that lovely woman was almost certainly dead. Well, that's what came of association with risk takers like Aiken.

The second bit of news from Renkin had also been shocking. After identifying one of his abductors, Aiken had fled Geneva. Now why would he do that, especially when the Geneva police so obviously needed his assistance?

Which led Edinfield to rethink the unfolding events. How much of the story Aiken had told in Geneva could be accepted at face value now that he'd disappeared and was no longer cooperating with local authorities? It wasn't as if he was a professional agent being debriefed. They had no idea why he had gone or where. They'd needed him to examine photographs of suspects. Instead, he'd sneaked passed his police guard and vanished.

If this story Aiken had told was true there was no reason for him not to cooperate. The Swiss police were internationally known for their efficiency. Even Aiken should have understood that after the murder of a UNOG official the manhunt for Dr. Haugen and her abductors would take priority.

No, she concluded he'd left for his own reasons and those could not be good. He'd been holding something back, something he didn't want the Swiss police to know. His flight suggested guilty knowledge, perhaps even guilty actions on his part. Either that or he was acting as a lone wolf. Neither was a good sign. She wondered how many people were going to get killed before his luck ran out.

Two weeks earlier, Edinfield had received her first classified briefing informing her of the existence of Stuxnet3. It was being unleashed on Iran to stall once again its nuclear weapons program. At first, Stuxnet had existed in the Company only as an idle rumor. The concept was that their Cyber Warfare Center had, along with the Israelis, designed a transformative digital weapon.

She'd long wondered why they'd waited so long. Cyberweapons were used by America's enemies every day. The Chinese had certainly shown no hesitation in employing their considerable capability in attacking U.S. national security databases. She'd been told that once the United States crossed that threshold there was no turning back and no telling how much damage would be inflicted. The world was simply too dependent on computers to risk it.

But all that had changed with Stuxnet.

Given their expertise, she suspected that Aiken and Dr. Haugen had

done work on Stuxnet3. Part of her had wondered if that wasn't the real
reason they'd been abducted. And maybe, she now thought, giving Aiken
the benefit of the doubt, that was what he'd held back. American involvement in Stuxnet was a closely guarded secret, one he'd not have been able to
share with local police. At least she wanted to believe that of him even if he
tended to be a wild card in the field, a place where he had no business being.

Just then her mIRC-app chimed. She opened the secure message and
read. Aiken was now known to have flown to Prague where he'd rented a
car. An Iranian man had been found murdered in his apartment. Interpol
was considering whether this was connected to events in Geneva because
a young, rather tall Western couple had been seen by neighbors leaving the
scene. They matched the description of Aiken and Dr. Haugen.

She wasn't dead after all. That was a relief. But had they killed the
man? If this was one of their abductors they should have simply called the
police and told their story. Unless . . .

Edinfield needed to do something, and quickly, before this fiasco spi-
raled out of control. First, she sent an alert to her offices in the region, ad-
vising of the situation and that the couple likely possessed highly sensitive
information. They were to closely monitor events and police alerts, extend
all cooperation to local authorities to assist in finding them, even to act on
their own as circumstances dictated.

Her deputy was included on the alert and she sent him a separate message assigning him as coordinator of activities, to brief her every two hours
on events. Then Edinfield typed her reply to the message she'd just received.

Subject: Jeffrey Daniel Aiken

Local police should be advised that it is likely the man seen fleeing
the murder scene is the above subject. He should be detained and
held so we can question him. If Dr. Daryl Haugen is with him she
should be held as well for her own protection.

A. Edinfield

47

Ahmed had been too exhausted, physically and mentally, to do anything after the two Chinese men had left. Finally, he'd cleaned up before leaving the dead Karim in the apartment. He'd been careful to wipe everywhere he thought he might have touched. He wondered how long it would be before the body was found. A long time he hoped.

On his way to his apartment he'd stopped for lunch, trying to clear his head, thinking how he was going to report all of this to Hamid. The best scenario would be for the Chinamen to catch and kill the couple and while he thought that very likely he couldn't think of any way he'd learn about it early enough to help him.

What he needed was rest. A long rest. And a good story. The unvarnished truth was of no help to him.

After his fifth cigarette and fourth cup of espresso he decided to go home, no closer to an agreeable account of recent events than when he'd first sat down. As he entered the building he found it unusually quiet. He glanced at the dirty Armenian's door but the man didn't stick his head out as usual. Probably upstairs somewhere.

Ahmed hesitated at his apartment when he realized the door had been forced. Perhaps the Chinese had done it. He entered cautiously, then closed the door behind him. Stepping out of the kitchen was a very neat, rather diminutive, bearded man dressed in a dark gray suit with an open-collared blue dress shirt. "Do not be concerned," he said in Farsi, in a voice Ahmed was certain he recognized. "Take a seat. We must talk."

"Hamid," Ahmed whispered, suddenly more frightened than he'd ever been before in his life.

Hamid waited until Ahmed was seated on the small couch. He pulled a chair over and sat on it carefully. He examined Ahmed head to toe before speaking again. "I'm General Hamid," he said. "I require a detailed report from you. I want to know how you managed to get your two most valuable agents killed and how both the woman and the man you took managed to escape. I want everything, no tales. Most of all, I want to know why I've been compelled to expose myself like this to pick up after you."

Ahmed's mouth was suddenly so dry he couldn't swallow. He tried to speak and couldn't. Finally, his voice coming out more as a croak, he poured out the story without embellishment. It took most of an hour, and once he had to get water from the kitchen but finally it was done. He closed his eyes waiting for judgment.

"These Chinese men, you really think they'll kill the couple?"

"I hope so. Mostly they want their computers."

"Your courier, this Saliha, she is on her way, you say?"

"Yes," Ahmed said quickly. "She has the code on a key chain and is flying to Ankara as we speak."

"What schedule does she follow once there?"

Ahmed had questioned Saliha about this repeatedly until he was certain he knew every detail. "She will arrive late this afternoon and go to her mother's house. I have the address. She will spend the night since she has a very long drive across eastern Turkey the next day. As soon as the rental agency opens she will pick up a car and be on her way. She takes different routes so as not to establish a pattern. I've insisted on that. She will cross the border around sunset tomorrow and make the transfer an hour or two later. She has done this many times before without incident."

"There was no trouble with her?"

Ahmed paused, then said, "No, of course not."

"Tell me."

Ahmed licked his lips, then told Hamid what had happened, how much he'd had to promise to get her to go.

"She is not reliable this time; that is what you are telling me?"

"I . . . I think she is. She has always done what I've told her in the past."

"This woman, she is your lover?"

"It seemed the best way to tie her to me."

"Of course. And she is ugly so it has been a great sacrifice for you."

"No . . . no, she is not unattractive, I admit."

"It is vital this code gets through tomorrow night. The Zionist dogs and American infidels are trying to sabotage our program even as we sit here. We must make certain she is successful. You understand?"

"Yes. I can call her, tell her—"

Hamid raised his hand. "Don't be any more foolish than you have already been. Call her? What will that accomplish? No, we must go to Turkey, make certain this happens. You understand?"

Ahmed nodded.

"Good. Collect your things."

Wu leveled the SportCruiser LSA at 1,500 meters. He scanned the controls, then took in the vista all about them. Clear flying from here to Ankara, though they'd not arrive until after sunset. He would be landing in twilight so there was no margin for delay. His primary concern was a headwind, which would not only slow them but might require a stop for more fuel.

It was remarkable that the trail led back to Turkey of all places. He wondered if that was a good omen. Certainly expectations would be high for his success. While he had a strong signal he took out his cell phone and called his father, Mei Zedong in Beijing, who answered at once. Wu reported what had happened, leaving out the concierge.

"Turkey, you say? That is something. Fortune is with us. I'm giving you a number. This man is well connected. He can track cell phones, gather information, tell you almost anything you need to know. His tentacles are everywhere, and he is the one who wants these computers. You understand?"

Feng, Wu thought. From what Wu understood there was nothing in the world secret from Feng's people. If something existed in a computer he could get it.

"I understand."

"Take care."

Wu waited an hour before calling Feng, time for his father to have reached him. When they spoke he gave him all the information he had—names, cell-phone numbers, addresses. "I will need everything you can get from this information if I am to recover those items for you."

"You will have it before you land. Good hunting."

At the Prague airport Ahmed and Hamid learned they had missed the earlier flights to Ankara. The next wasn't until 5:25 that evening. Hamid booked it, then had Ahmed do the same. He didn't want the records to show them traveling together. They'd changed planes in Munich and that was where the trouble began. During the wait, security flooded the waiting areas of the airport. Sniffer dogs were brought in. Passengers were told to stay where they were.

"What is going on?" Ahmed asked.

"It appears there has been a terrorist threat."

"Not by us."

Hamid looked askance at him. "Don't ever say such things."

The first phase of the delay lasted over an hour. Hamid watched the unfolding confusion with dismay. Though he anticipated their connecting flight was being held on the tarmac, this was eating into valuable time. They should have arrived in Ankara around midnight and at the girl's location two hours later. That would have been ideal, to catch her in the dead of night. Now this.

"What will they do?" Ahmed asked more than once, feeling foolish but unable to help himself. Hamid had no way of knowing what was going to happen.

"Who can say? They will let us move on when they are ready."

But instead of ending, the crisis only escalated. As the delay entered the third hour, the public-address system ordered everyone to exit the terminal. Every passenger was to reenter and clear security again. The passengers from Prague and other connecting cities were enraged. They'd been screened before boarding and had never left the secure area. Why should they be screened again?

But there was no reasoning with authorities, certainly not German ones. Hamid and Ahmed joined the wide column of passengers that spilled into the area beyond the X-ray machines and body searches.

"What is this about?" Ahmed asked someone, as if another passenger would know more than they did.

"ETA, I hear." ETA was the Basque terrorist network. It typically bombed and shot Spanish police officers but from time to time it showed its reach by planting a bomb in a European city. Of all the nights for ETA to make such a ploy—this couldn't have come at a worse time.

"ETA," Ahmed told Hamid.

Why not? Hamid thought. *But they have no finesse.*

48

Saliha's mother was delighted to see her as always. But not long after her daughter had arrived, she asked if anything was wrong. Saliha had never come back so quickly from a trip.

"You are nervous. What is it?"

There was no question of telling the truth. The burdens of her life were almost more than she could bear. To share her problems would be needlessly cruel, however. It was her duty to lift the load from her mother.

"I am just tired. And I have this for you." She handed her all the money she would not need for the trip.

"So much? Can you afford this?"

"Yes, I can afford it. I had no time for gifts. But I'll get them something before I come back in two or three days."

"Your being here is all the gift we need. Rest. I will have dinner soon."

As the girls played, frequently glancing at their older sister to be certain she was watching everything they did, Saliha thought about her situation again. Clearly, time had run out for her in Prague and with Ahmed. She'd never been so frightened as when the American had her. Her instincts told her he was a good man but he'd been a desperate one and even good men do terrible things when they must.

She wondered how his chase had ended. Had he found his wife? Was she alive? Unharmed? Then she smiled grimly. Was his story even true? Maybe he was a Mossad agent after all, or CIA. There was no way to tell with those people. They were crafty, able to fool you into thinking they were someone else. She'd heard the stories since she was a little girl, seen the Turkish television shows. She knew she'd been very lucky to escape and was proud of herself for taking the risk when the opportunity had presented itself.

As for Ahmed, perhaps it was best she not try to collect her final payment. He probably wouldn't pay her anyway. Still, she didn't like the idea of giving up on the money. She'd taken, was taking, enormous risks for it. And he'd threatened her. She didn't like that. When a man treated her like that her instinct was to do the opposite.

So on the flight she'd considered not even delivering the thumb drive. Which was worse? Take it into Iran and hope Ahmed had not sent word ahead to have her arrested once she was across the border? Or throw it away and never return to Prague?

How many choices did she have? If she betrayed Ahmed, how far would he go to punish her? Would he find her in another country? She couldn't dismiss the possibility. He was some kind of secret agent, he had contacts outside of Prague; if he made it his business to find her, could she hide well enough? And how long a memory would he have? Could she ever feel safe? What about her family?

Just how important was what she did? Would they want to kill her to keep her from telling anyone about it? Ahmed had kidnapped the woman and her husband. At least she was more inclined to accept that as truth. Wouldn't he kill her? If not him, then others he knew.

She reviewed her options anew. She wasn't going back to Prague. The city wasn't big enough for her safety. Some of the girls she'd worked with were living in other cities in Europe—Rome, Paris, Berlin. She'd made no special effort to stay in touch but she had talked with two or three over the last few months. Better to visit one of them, get a small wardrobe, calm down, plan her next step. Yes, that was the better way.

What she could not do was go back to Prague, she reminded herself. Ahmed was there. She'd seen movies. She understood. You always get caught when you go back for things you can buy at any store.

None of which answered her question: what to do now? She puzzled over the decision even as she played on the floor with her brother and sisters. No answer came. Do it or not, both options were filled with risk. After dinner, as the girls bathed and she prepared for bed, Saliha's mother came up behind her and began slowly brushing her hair.

"I can do it," Saliha said, reaching up for the brush.

"I want to," her mother said. "*Ahneh* always said your beautiful hair was a Gift from Allah." She leaned down close and whispered in her daughter's ear. "But it is you who are the gift to us from Allah." Saliha couldn't speak she was so moved.

She'd go to Iran. What else could she do?

Wu maneuvered the plane for final approach into his usual Ankara airport. The slight headwind meant he was arriving later than he'd hoped. His legs were cramped and he desperately needed to urinate.

He'd watched with a sinking heart as twilight dissolved into night. He was now checking the petrol gauge every minute. He was dangerously low on fuel but didn't want to waste the time to land. He was certain he had enough.

It was a vast expanse of night beneath him; his depth perception was shot. He'd been cautioned several times by real pilots that night flying was as dangerous as it got. Disorientation was all too easy. Planes stalled without warning or eased into slow dives, catching the pilot unawares until it was too late. Maintaining pitch and yaw required constant monitoring of the instruments and sometimes flying the craft in a way that seemed counterintuitive.

So he'd been told. For all its virtues and suitability for his needs, the SportCruiser lacked the sophisticated instruments required to safely do what he was doing.

He'd thought about taking a faster commercial flight from Prague to Ankara, leaving the plane to be picked up later, but their passports had not been stamped on entry and it would have raised questions. There was also the matter of the body in Prague. He realized now he'd been too casual about that. If it was discovered and two Asian men were recalled as being in the building around that time, an alert for them would have been issued. Finally, it was very possible they were going to need this handy little airplane. It had proved itself very useful in the past in moving about Turkey.

A few minutes earlier Wu had called the airport and spoken to someone he knew. The runway lights were on, he was told, and there were no other landings or takeoffs expected, though caution was always advised.

As he nosed the plane down and cut back slightly on power, the air was suddenly choppy. The aircraft was rocked in a very unsettling motion. Li sat quietly beside him and Wu wondered if he knew just how dangerous this was. Like most passengers he probably assumed the pilot knew what

he was doing. Wu just wished that were true. The SportCruiser lacked
landing lights. He'd depend entirely on the runway lights for the landing.
He was terrified.

Wu had no real sense of how close the ground was. He could see the
runway lights in the distance and slowed the plane to just above stall. In
daylight he would not have been so cautious but now he wanted every advantage he could manage.

The craft buffeted again and he abruptly increased power. Maybe too
slow wasn't such a good idea. He glanced at Li who sat unchanged. Wu
nosed down more sharply to keep from climbing and the runway seemed to
rush at him. He should have practiced this before. There had always been
the chance he'd have to do this someday out of necessity. But the truth was,
it frightened him so much he'd not wanted to risk it.

Wu wiped a hand on his pants, then the other. His mouth was dry but
the bottle was behind him and he didn't want to take his hands off the control to grope for it. And this was no time for his attention to flag. One moment you were flying, the next you were falling. There was no in-between
with an airplane and the change could happen so quickly you had no time
to regain the sky.

The turbulence eased and he slowed once again. He was almost there.
He decided to overshoot the landing as he didn't need the entire runway,
just a small portion of it. No need to risk landing short. He lowered flaps
and felt that slight rise, which told him they were in place. He cut back on
the engine and felt the craft start to glide. There was a slight crosswind
and he compensated, realizing too late it would carry him to the side of
the runway. He hoped he landed before it swept him off the landing strip
altogether.

Over the first lights and very close to asphalt, he felt the ground effect
grip the craft. The SportCruiser seemed to hang in the air for a long
moment, unable to drop through the invisible plane that rode fifteen to
twenty-five feet above land. The plane all but hovered, he was now going so
slowly, then it happened—the plane dropped. He watched the lights to his
right and left and searched for the pavement, letting the plane ease down
ever so slightly, nudging it lower as if he didn't want to crush eggs beneath
him, watching the runway slide off to his right as the wind pushed him ever
leftward.

Then a wheel touched lightly down, followed a heart-stopping moment
later by the other. He cut power. He was on the ground. When he gunned

the engine to taxi it sputtered, coughed, then stopped. He was out of petrol.

It was just after 11:30 p.m. before Jeff and Daryl had cleared customs and immigration at Esenboga Airport, Ankara. Now that they could speak freely out of the crowding of the airplane, they sat at the first opportunity.

"Do we take a taxi or rent a car?" Daryl asked. The clothes she'd bought in Prague were a bit flashy but that was all the place had sold.

They had the address Saliha would likely stay at, her family home. They'd feared that she might already have left Ankara but they had to start there.

"I don't relish driving the streets of Ankara at night," Jeff said. "I've never been here before. I doubt I'm as exhausted as you are, but I'm very, very tired. A taxi is tempting."

"Then what? I'll bet this isn't a very good neighborhood we're going to, otherwise she wouldn't be living in Prague working in a nightclub. We can't just stand around. And you aren't planning on knocking on the door after midnight, are you? Remember, you scared this woman out of her wits."

"We take our chances with a car, then."

As Jeff located a Hertz counter and took what was available, Daryl bought bottles of water, candy bars, anything that looked of use to them. Half an hour later they were dropped at a parking lot. Jeff walked along the row of cars until he found theirs.

"It's a Fiat," he said. "It's all they had." The Fiorino 1.3 was red and completely unappealing. Squat, small, it had two doors but otherwise looked much like a panel truck.

"Doesn't James Bond drive a sports car or something?"

"You take what they have," Jeff said. "Get in. I'm told it's got navigation. You're in charge."

Jeff took the driver's seat, looked over the controls as he adjusted his seat, then groaned. "It's a manual."

"You can't drive a stick shift?"

"It's been a few years." Fifteen as near as he could recall.

"It's like riding a bike."

"Yeah. Easy for you to say."

Driving from the parking lot onto the highway was no easy task. He stalled the car twice and counted himself lucky. His main concern as he began to feel comfortable with it was that it would take too much of his attention once they were on crowded city streets. He needed to get the hang of this quickly. They were some fifteen miles from central Ankara on a modern highway. "How's it look?" he asked.

"It seems to be working all right. Just follow the directions. I told it you speak English." Daryl opened a candy bar and bottle of water. "You know, you owe your girl a few nice meals."

49

GENEVA, SWITZERLAND
UNITED NATIONS OFFICE AT GENEVA (UNOG)
AVENUE DE LA PAIX
11:57 P.M. CET

Henri Wille sat at his desk, the hallway outside utterly silent. He couldn't count how many nights he'd spent like this. Whenever dignitaries came to the palace he worked round the clock. But never before had he been involved in an abduction as well as the murder of an employee. He'd already given reports to the security committee and been told to write one in detail. That's what he was supposed to be doing now but he realized as he worked on it that events were still ongoing. He could write what had happened to the extent of he knew, but there was much he didn't know.

Not that the committee would care. Someone needed to take the blame and as head of security it was his neck on the chopping block.

Just before midnight Henri took a moment to reread the police alert on Jeff Aiken and Daryl Haugen. Spyri had told him the man had fled Geneva; that was the word he'd used: "fled." He'd been angry about it and baffled. A few hours later he'd called back to inform him that the Prague police had issued a pickup notice on the pair.

"She is alive?" he'd asked with relief.

"Yes, so it appears. I am greatly relieved. I never expected such a positive outcome."

"It is extraordinary. She'd been taken to Prague?"

"Yes."

"How did it happen?"

"I'm not certain. Details are sketchy, which is my polite way of saying they won't tell me."

"Do you know if the police found her?"

"I don't believe so but.I'm not certain."

"Did she escape?" The man had, why not the woman?

"I don't know. They are essentially, though politely, stonewalling me. I still can't understand why he left here without helping us first."

Henri thought about that for some time and was certain he had the answer. Aiken was a computer expert. It was very likely he'd done the job of the local police faster than they could move. The man had obviously gone to Prague since the municipal police there had issued the alert. The two of them were wanted for questioning regarding a homicide. The notice didn't say they were suspects but they might very well be. "What do you know about the dead man in Prague?"

"An Iranian."

"On a watch list?"

"You know DAP. It is a one-way street with those people."

"I suppose it's not important now. I'm just curious." He paused. "Do you think the man found her?"

"That doesn't seem likely, though I suppose that is probably why he went there. You have better sources than I do, Henri. Use them, then call me back and tell me what the hell happened."

Henri called his Interpol counterpart with the Prague police, a senior police official he'd met several times, and asked the same questions. There had been a link to Jeff Aiken. A tall Western couple had been seen leaving the building where the killing took place, he was told. Two Asian men had entered as well and left not long after.

"How was the body discovered?"

"Blood dripped into the apartment below."

"Is there any evidence putting this couple or the Asian men with the deceased?"

"No. It was just unusual for any of them to be there. The apartments are rented by Middle Eastern immigrants. We'd like to talk to them."

"What can you tell me about the dead man?"

"This is all confidential, Henri. The name on his Iranian passport was Karim Behzad. He was killed following a violent struggle. There were signs someone had been tied up. A neighbor reported seeing him and another man with the woman earlier. He'd thought she was drunk."

"What do you know about the deceased?"

"He worked as a waiter. We found two other passports hidden in the apartment."

"An agent?"

"Probably."

"What have you discovered about the Asian men?"

"Nothing much. Late twenties, early thirties. Well dressed. We've alerted local police to bring in any two men matching these descriptions that they encounter within the city. They may have seen something, they may have seen nothing, they may have killed the man. We don't know."

"I see. A 'tall Western couple' is not much of a description. Many Czechs would match it."

"It was unusual in that building as I say."

"How did you connect this pair described to you to the names Jeff Aiken and Daryl Haugen?"

"Yes, the prize question, my friend. You will owe me a drink after you hear the answer. We received a notice from our American friends giving us the names." CIA. No surprise there. "They urged us to pick up the American man for questioning, hold the woman if she is with him."

"Why would they want them held?"

"I can't say. They don't share their motivations with me. Perhaps they are employees; that seems likely. Maybe it's for their own protection. Right now their situation is the same as it is for the Asian men. We don't know if they are involved in the killing at all. We don't even know if it's those two. Different people altogether may have left the building. The Americans may have it wrong."

"Have you traced them?"

"Yes, they left earlier today on a flight for Ankara, Turkey, before the alert entered the Prague police computer system."

"Are you aware of any connection between Turkey and Iran in all this?"

The man laughed. "Only if I look on a map."

Henri read the alert once again and reviewed what he knew. The two Americans were kidnapped here in Geneva by three Iranians. The man escaped. One of the abductors murdered the UNOG official with whom they'd been working and had himself been killed by police. The other two had fled the country with the woman. She'd somehow gained her freedom in Prague. There was another dead Iranian there. The two were now wanted for questioning. Significantly, in Henri's opinion, they'd not contacted the police or the American embassy. Instead, they'd boarded a commercial flight to Ankara.

No, the pattern seemed clear enough to him. He took another look at the earlier Paris report. Afterward he sent a notice to be kept informed of unfolding events.

LAST DAY

THURSDAY, APRIL 16

FINANCIAL NEWS ANALYSIS

WHEN THE LIGHTS GO OUT—FOR GOOD

By Livingston X. Gooden—Financial News Analysis
April 16

Most of the electrical grid systems in the United States report repeated attempts at penetration by aggressive forms of malware. The attacks are pervasive and not directed at any particular company or region. Experts believe that every significant electrical grid system in the nation has at least some software implanted there by China, Russia, and other nations. Though this malware does not interfere with current operations, it is believed much of it is intended to transfer control of our electricity producing capability to a foreign power in time of emergency.

The electrical blackout in Yakima, Washington, one week ago, originally attributed to a computer malfunction, is now believed to have been the test of such a capability. "We have found no cause for the fourteen-minute blackout of the WAyk5 [Yakima] region," said a spokesperson with the company, who asked not to be identified. "We believe someone, somewhere, executed a kill switch as a test." Efforts to locate malware capable of such an event have thus far been unsuccessful but are ongoing. The only nuclear power station in the Northwest, the Columbia Generating Station in Richland, Washington, shut down for three hours as a safety precaution.

American power companies are rapidly converting to a system known as Smart Grid. This is designed to be customer friendly, allowing individual customers to directly access their account and regulate power into their homes and offices. Many companies view the rapid adoption of Smart Grid as a way to leave behind issues of penetration. Unfortunately, those in charge of the new system appear to have learned nothing. According to the Government Accounting Office, two-thirds of all Smart Grid systems have no special security measures and are as vulnerable to a Yakima-style attack as the old system.

Significantly, analysis of the most recent power grid malware's behavior reveals startling changes in purpose, according to Bruce Freeman of the Cyber Security Consortium in Seattle, Washington. "The code now permeating our national grid system is intended to stop the system at will. The new code also has the capacity to destroy infrastructure components," he said in a recent interview. "This is the equivalent to targeted bombing by smart bombs."

Should a cyber-attack be simultaneously launched against our entire national electric grid system, destroying components along the way, it would leave our military defenses and communications ineffective in time of emergency or war. Vast regions of the United States, perhaps even a majority of the country, could lay in darkness for weeks, even months. It would, in effect, turn the clock back to the nineteenth century.

50

Jeff opened his eyes and stretched in the driver's seat. It had been cold overnight and the morning was still chilly. The sun had been up for nearly an hour but they were parked in shadows, holding the car in twilight. He'd been so worn out he'd nodded off when he should have been watching. No police had knocked on the window during the night, and in the dark the red Fiat had not attracted notice. Other cars were parked just off the busy road behind him.

He was at the broadened entrance to an old and narrow street, mostly dirt, though ancient cobblestone sections still existed, exhausted from centuries of use. The street was coming alive as workers emerged from their apartments and set out for their jobs. Traffic on the road was picking up.

He twisted and looked behind him. Daryl was sound asleep. She needed it. The Fiat might be small by American standards but the area behind the two front seats was open and flat, just right for a tight bed. He didn't know how she'd managed the events of these last few days and maintained her sanity. By most standards she should be in a hospital right now. But except for the cut on her hand and the dark circles about her eyes, she seemed remarkably sound. He was surprised by the feeling of relief that overwhelmed him as he watched her, to the point that he felt a knot in his throat.

Jeff turned forward and looked back at the front door he'd been watching through the night. Saliha would likely be leaving soon, he thought. He could only guess how she planned to reach Iran. Driving was the most obvious but it was a long haul to the border and he had no idea of the condition of the highways. Someone might take her or she could go alone.

"Wake up," he said gently. "Need you bright and alert."

Daryl moaned, then rolled onto her back and opened her eyes. "You fell asleep, didn't you?"

"Only a little. She's still there. No harm done."

"You say. Maybe she already left."

"We'll know pretty soon. You need to get ready."

They'd agreed the approach was best made by Daryl, woman to woman. It had worked with the roommate. Perhaps if Saliha knew what she was taking she might be persuaded to give it up. She was a Turk. It seemed unlikely to them that she'd want neighboring Iran to have a nuclear bomb. Of course, she could be an Islamist at heart and might see it as a weapon for all Muslims, though given the history between Turkey and Iran Jeff couldn't see it. And, frankly, she'd not seemed political to Jeff in the time he'd been with her, just a girlfriend doing a favor for some extra cash and a chance to visit her family.

And he knew that Saliha really didn't want to make this trip. It occurred to Jeff they might just offer her money. If that was why she was doing it, perhaps they could just buy her off. But however it worked out, it was up to Daryl to make the pitch.

She opened the rear doors and climbed out, straightening her hair and clothing as she did. She rubbed her arms against the cold. She had a bottle of water she used to wash her face, then went to the mirror away from the street and worked on her hair for a long minute. She unwrapped a toothbrush and brushed her teeth, spitting afterward into the gutter. She looked at Jeff and smiled brightly. "All set."

She climbed into the passenger seat, dug into the bag she'd bought in Prague, and handed over a candy bar and fresh bottle of water. "Breakfast."

Jeff peeled off the wrapper and as he was taking his first bite, the door opened and out stepped a girl of about eleven. Another girl, perhaps a year older, came out holding the hand of a boy, around eight years old. Then there she was, standing in the doorway, talking to a woman dressed in black.

Saliha was outfitted for a trip, wearing denims and a light blue jacket, with a tan travel bag hanging from her shoulder. Her dark hair was held in place with a dark blue band. She and the older woman embraced, then Saliha leaned over and gave each child a long hug in turn.

She stepped away with a determined smile, gave them all a farewell wave, then set off down the street away from Jeff and Daryl. Jeff started the Fiat, then slipped the car into gear, remaining in first gear as he drove slowly over the bumpy road, more comfortable with the stick shift now though not yet proficient.

"Stop before you get to her," Daryl cautioned. "I'll get out and catch up with her on foot. Stay back or you might frighten her."

The street was suddenly very busy as more workers joined by young uniformed students poured out of the apartments. The street narrowed. A man cursed Jeff, raising his fist.

"What's that for?" he asked nervously. Was this a one-way street?

"Just a little closer, then stop." Daryl was silent, then said, "I think this street's closed to cars. Look around. This is the only one."

Jeff glanced in the rearview mirror, then ahead. She was right. Theirs was the only car. He braked to a stop and Daryl leaped out without a word. Jeff stayed as she briskly walked after Saliha. An older man wearing a dirty watch cap pounded on the driver window, shouting at him in Turkish.

Jeff looked at him and grinned. "Sorry. I'll only be a minute." He held up a finger as he watched Daryl closely. The man pounded again. Jeff searched for a way off the street. The shouting man was gesturing for Jeff to back up and he could see no suitable side street forward. A crowd was gathering, curious for now but if it turned ugly he was concerned that the noise would draw Saliha's attention and that it would block his view of events. He unrolled the window and killed the engine. "I don't speak Turkish. I'm sorry. What's wrong? Anyone speak English?"

"American?" the man shouted. "American?" Jeff nodded, uncertain what was going to happen next. The man turned and shouted to the gathered crowd. His face contorted as he looked back and shouted, "Go away! Go back! Go to America!" He pushed on the door. Others put their hands on the Fiat and began rocking it with increasing agitation.

Jeff started the engine, put the car in gear, and slowly began backing up, hoping he didn't run over anyone, now unable to watch Daryl.

Saliha heard the noise behind her but didn't turn around. Something was always happening on this street. She wished her family lived somewhere else but this had been the first house of her parents after their marriage and her mother refused to consider leaving.

She glanced at her watch. She'd get to the rental agency just after it opened. With a good day driving she'd cross the border by sunset. She'd never wanted something to be over before the way she wanted this trip to end.

"Saliha!" she heard and turned to see who was just behind her. It was a tall, very pretty woman with blond hair. There was a bandage on one hand. "Just a minute. We need to talk."

"What do you want?" Saliha said, not stopping.

Daryl hurried to catch up and started walking beside her. "My name is Daryl. You helped my husband find me. He got there in time and rescued me. I want to thank you."

Saliha stopped. "You? You are the wife?" She looked at her closely. "Did Ahmed truly kidnap you?"

"Yes, in Geneva, with two other men. When I fought with the man to get away, I was cut." Daryl held up her hand. "We need to talk. It will only take a minute."

Saliha stepped away quickly. She had no idea what to make of this. "I must go." Daryl ran up beside her. "How did you get here?" Saliha demanded. "How did you find me?"

"Ahmed told us your name and gave us the information."

"Ahmed? I don't think he would do that."

Daryl smiled. "I think my husband persuaded him."

Saliha laughed harshly. "I can believe that. Did he kill him?"

"Of course not."

Saliha looked at her with suspicion. "You are married to a very dangerous man, I think." She looked at her good hand. "Why don't you wear a wedding ring?"

"I . . . well, actually we live together. We're like husband and wife." Saliha looked at her skeptically. "You mustn't make this trip," Daryl persisted. "You're putting a great many lives at risk."

Saliha eyed Daryl suspiciously. "What do you know about a trip?"

"You told Jeff you were going on one, remember? I know you're going to Iran. I know you're taking something for Ahmed, something very bad."

Saliha stopped herself from looking at her purse where the thumb drive was. "What are you talking about?"

How to explain it? Daryl thought. *What words to use?* "The thumb drive, it has code on it. It's like a military weapon used against computers."

"You mean it attacks computers? Like a virus or something?"

"Yes." That wasn't the truth but what was really happening was too complicated to explain on an increasingly busy street.

The noise down the street was suddenly very loud and a car honked.

Saliha looked up. "Cars are not supposed to drive there," she said. "Everyone knows that." Daryl looked back with concern. "Your husband, he is in that car?" Saliha asked.

"Yes, we didn't know about the street." She looked back toward the crowd. "I think they're mad at him." Before she could say anything more Saliha was running from her, just as fast she could go. Daryl hesitated, torn between what was happening to Jeff and getting the thumb drive. She broke into a run herself, pursuing Saliha just as fast as she could.

Jeff had killed the engine twice. Backing up in such a small area with a crowd screaming at him and rocking the car, all the while trying to work the clutch and gas, keep the Fiat straight, and not hurt anyone was proving daunting. The reverse gear was higher than the first forward gear and it was giving him lots of trouble.

He kept moving backward, working at staying in the street, moving slow enough so as not to run over anyone. Fortunately the street began to widen. He backed beyond the apartment he'd been watching and as he neared the broad area beside the roadway he'd driven up on, the crowd came to a stop, including the man who'd pounded on his window and started it all. They were satisfied they'd driven him from their neighborhood.

Jeff reached the road, stopped, changed gears, then merged into busy morning traffic to put some distance between himself and the crowd. As soon as he could, he turned onto a quieter street and pulled over. He took out his phone and called Daryl.

The phone rang and rang, and finally rolled over to her new voice mail. "Call me," he said, then disconnected.

Next, he checked Daryl's location using their app. She should be with Saliha. He saw the location. He glanced around, then made a sharp U-turn and continued in the direction he'd been going. As soon as he found a major street turning right he'd go with it.

It was nearly six in the morning when Ahmed and Hamid landed in Ankara. The passengers were surly and in a rush, and the car rental agencies were either unmanned or overwhelmed. They'd finally rented a black Korean car, then driven toward the city.

"Are you certain she stays with her mother?" Hamid asked.

"She always stays with her mother."

Hamid had given him a tight smile. "You mean, that's what she tells you. For all you know, she has an old boyfriend here. You should not assume things, Ahmed. You were taught that, remember?"

Saliha? With a boyfriend? It was impossible. Of course, he'd had his afternoons with others but she wasn't that kind of woman, he was certain.

As they reached the outskirts of Ankara, Hamid made a call, then directed Ahmed to drive to a small café. He told him to wait while he went inside. Two minutes later, he climbed back in the car carrying a small gray travel bag.

Ahmed was driving while Hamid gave him directions from the navigation system. Even then, the obscure street was difficult to locate. "What is that?" Ahmed asked as they finally approached it. There was a street disturbance just ahead. A red car was lurching onto the road, its driver having some difficulty before he joined the traffic and drove away.

"This is the street," Hamid said. Ahmed turned, pulled to the side, and stopped. "It should be right here." Hamid climbed out of the car. Ahmed joined him, careful to lock up. The men set off down the street, looking for the address.

Hamid was a legend in the VEVAK. He'd been in charge of European operations for more than a decade and had been responsible for turning it into one of the most professional organizations on the continent. He'd removed the fanatics, brought in cooler heads, and exercised considerable discretion in selection of operations. His preference, it seemed to Ahmed, was the gathering of information. Overt operations were quite restricted.

No one knew his base of operations or his cover. Ahmed had heard rumors that he was ruthless in suppressing opposition within the Iranian ex-patriot community in Europe. From Ahmed's perspective, the most disturbing aspect of his tenure was his absolute ruthlessness when it came to failure. He was a field man, fortunately, so he was not without understanding, but if an agent truly made a mess of it, there was no homecoming.

Two things about his predicament concerned Ahmed. The first was that his latest operation had been a botch almost from the start. Though they'd successfully taken the couple, both of them had managed to escape. Karim was dead at the hands of a woman. Ali had successfully killed the UNOG official but it had cost him his life. That part of the operation, he suspected, was compelled by the man's escape. No, this had been a mess from the beginning.

Karim's body had surely been discovered by this time. The Prague police would be looking for witnesses and suspects. They'd certainly have the American couple's description, and that of the two Chinese men. Worse, someone might remember Ahmed or, despite his specific instructions, there might be a link in Karim's apartment to him.

No, he'd have to assume everyone in Prague was burned. He'd have to relocate, move the other two agents there. And all this would have to happen immediately. He might even be too hot to remain in Europe. He'd tried to think of a way to raise the subject with Hamid but it would only make matters worse. The man had not wanted to talk. He'd done his job with an absolute minimum of words.

Then there was the other part of this that more than troubled Ahmed; it terrified him. The fact that Hamid was here at all.

"This one," Ahmed said, glancing at Hamid for approval.

When he hesitated, Hamid said, "Go ahead. We haven't much time."

Ahmed knocked and a moment later Saliha's mother answered the door. *"Evet?"* Yes?

Ahmed smiled and spoke in English as he knew no Turkish. "I am Ahmed, from Prague. Is Saliha here?" He smiled.

Hamid didn't wait for a reply. He simply walked into the apartment, and pressed the woman back with his hand, sudden fear in her eyes. "Close the door," Hamid ordered, glancing over at the three children. "This won't take long."

The streets wandered in ways that Jeff found impossible. On the cell phone, the way from here to there seemed straightforward but there were any number of streets not on the screen and a great many of those turned out to be one-way. He was getting better with the clutch and gears but that was small consolation.

Then his phone rang. "Yes?"

"She ran. I lost her for a while but I finally found her. She's at a car rental agency. I'm across the street watching her. Can you get to me? I'll try and talk to her again when she comes out. You need to stay back, though. She's scared to death of you. I think she suspects you killed Ahmed."

"What?"

"Hurry." Daryl disconnected.

Jeff checked her cell location again. She was close and if he could just find a street that connected he'd be there in a flash. The problem was that traffic was getting worse by the minute. The vehicles mostly crawled with short spurts of modest speed. Pedestrians treated the roadway as a parking lot, weaving through the intermittently stopped and moving cars with casual indifference.

Most surprising, drivers seemed to have no sense that they were not alone on the street. Cars abruptly stopped while the driver looked over his shoulder to wait for an opening so he could change lanes, backing traffic behind him. Horns blared constantly and fists were waved through open windows. Though there was surely some measure of order to it, the streets looked chaotic to Jeff.

He moved his way to the right, searching again for a significant street that headed toward Daryl's location. The car behind him honked. There was a slight opening and Jeff moved toward it only to see the car off his right rear speed up to block him in. Jeff turned on the blinker, then steadily moved to the right. The other car could give way or they'd collide.

A moment later he felt the crunch.

They knew the pretty woman in the rental office. One of the young men was flirting with her and she flirted back briefly while indicating she was in a hurry. Daryl had been lucky to find Saliha after losing her in the busy streets. She'd worked systematically on the assumption she would continue in the same general direction. She'd spotted the rental agency and seen the dark-haired woman at the counter, glancing nervously over her shoulder every few seconds. Daryl had remained across the street, standing in the morning shadows.

Saliha emerged with the attentive young man, clutching papers. He smiled as he talked, leading her along the sidewalk. They turned up a driveway and though the rental cars weren't apparent from her location, Daryl was certain they were parked back there. She looked left, then right, then left, then right. Finally, she stepped onto the street and started weaving through the busy traffic the way she'd seen other pedestrians do.

Just as she reached the other side of the road a midsized black car drove by her. It slowed, and something about it caused her to move to the side of the sidewalk and seek cover with a group leaning against a cement retaining wall.

The black car pulled up almost entirely onto the sidewalk, stopping just short of the rental agency. Two men climbed out. One was wearing a dark charcoal business suit without a tie. He had a short cropped beard and luxurious hair. He was small for a grown man. The other was . . . Ahmed.

Daryl caught her breath. Ahmed. Here! How was that possible? He was *here*, on this street, at this moment, with her. The men entered the rental office, only to emerge a moment later. They walked quickly in the same direction as Saliha had headed. When they reached the driveway, they abruptly turned and ran back to their car.

Just then a car honked at the curb. She ignored it and watched the men climb into their car, then saw Saliha pull out of the driveway in a blue compact. The young woman looked both directions, then turned to her right. Ahmed and the other man pulled into traffic and followed.

The car honked again. It was Jeff. Daryl ran to the Fiat, which had a new, large dent on the passenger side, and climbed in. "Follow the black car!" she snapped. "It's Ahmed with another man and they're after Saliha. Hurry, Jeff! Hurry!"

51

Wu eased the SportCruiser off the runway with a sense of relief. He lifted the nose and relaxed back in his seat as the plane gained altitude. At last, he was beginning to feel that his endless stream of problems were behind him.

Li sat beside him as impassive as ever but Wu was warming to the man, feeling almost a kinship with him. He'd long suspected Li had been sent to Turkey to spy on him but it turned out he was being punished for an incident he didn't want to discuss.

Wu slowed the rate of climb to cut the engine noise and began his slow turn north. He was still exhausted despite his few hours' sleep. The long flight from Prague had just about done him in. He'd never imagined night flying was so demanding or isolating. There'd been times when he felt as if he were floating in space. He'd clung to what his meager instruments told him, even when their readings defied his senses. And they'd always been right. The frightening night landing had been almost too much for him. Looking back on it, he realized it had been closer than he'd thought at the time.

After settling Li in, Wu had gone to bed though still tense. When he finally dropped off, his dreams were unsettled, evading his memory each time he was awakened. He'd risen early and stepped into the shower, scalding water beating on his skin as he struggled to relax. After shaving and dressing, he checked his phone. The message from Feng told him that they'd located credit card purchases in Prague and had new cell-phone numbers for the couple.

Wu knocked on the spare bedroom door and saw that Li was ready. The men went to the parking garage to claim his Buick, then had driven to a small eatery Wu often visited. Over strong Turkish coffee he checked his iPhone and the locations for the cell phones again. He was not familiar with the area since it was a poor working-class district.

Now, as he inched forward in rush-hour traffic, Wu reviewed again the situation. The Iranian agent Ahmed had claimed this couple were skilled CIA agents, then he'd added they were computer experts. Feng wanted the laptops so Wu was confident the last part was true. Ahmed also said the woman had killed his associate so she at least must be trained and ruthless.

It all seemed improbable to Wu. Computer experts and skilled killers? The two just didn't go together.

Feng had forwarded to Wu a great deal of information overnight, so much that he'd read it this morning on his laptop during breakfast. Ahmed, it seemed, was the conduit for secret code being sent to Iran. Saliha was his mule. A vital patch had just been sent and she was carrying it into Iran. It was important she get through.

Wu thought about that. It wasn't his job but when he and Li got the computers they'd make certain the American couple were stopped. They couldn't be allowed to interfere.

Wu glanced at his watch. They'd moved perhaps ten meters in half an hour. There were all the signs of a serious blockage ahead. He checked the location again and cursed. Li looked at him. "They're moving away from us, leaving the city, I think."

"They are after the courier, then. They must have missed her."

"Yes. She'll be on her way to Iran. We've lost our chance to get them in the city."

"Perhaps it will be easier in a less crowded place."

"All right. We need a change of plans." Though he hated it Wu could think of no alternative. He turned the wheels sharply left and when the on-coming traffic left the barest of openings, he punched the gas. He cringed as his Buick smashed into the low concrete divide, then up and over it, the bottom dragging across it and sounding as if the heart of his car was being torn out. The cars braked and honked. He wheeled the car around, then joined the faster traffic.

"We'll stop at the safe house," he said, "and get what we need. Then we'll catch them from the air."

52

E80
TRANS-EUROPEAN MOTORWAY (TEM)
TURKEY
11:33 A.M. EET

Traffic was moderate on the E80 heading east, much heavier going the other direction. There were three lanes on this side of the divided highway.

Hamid could see the blue car ahead, a Ford it looked to him. "Don't lose her," he said. He didn't like repeating the instructions so often but if they lost the woman he had no idea how they'd find her again. After a few minutes he looked back at the side mirror. "There's a red Fiat following us. Do you see it?"

Ahmed, who was driving, did not. "No."

"Just keep doing what you are. I will keep an eye on it."

After a long pause Ahmed said, "Do you think the Americans have called in assistance?"

"Perhaps. The CIA has agents in Turkey but I don't think this is the way they would help. But there is also no reason for the car to be following us."

"Shall I test it?"

"Not yet. The border is far away and we have plenty of time. I could be mistaken. It could just be a coincidence."

They'd arrived too late at Saliha's mother's apartment. By the time they'd finally located the obscure street Saliha was gone. There had been no need for threats. Her mother claimed they'd just missed her and told them where to find the car rental agency she always used.

And they'd just missed her there as well, but as they followed the blue car she'd rented it was apparent she had no idea she was being followed.

For now, Hamid was content just to keep her in sight. After all, they knew where she was going.

Again he glanced at the boxy red Fiat behind them. Would the CIA actually use such a car? He shook his head in bewilderment at the idea.

Once Jeff and Daryl's car reached the divided highway marked E80, they calmed down. In explaining the fresh dent, Jeff had told her that changing lanes in Ankara called for more finesse than he possessed and that if he had occasion to drive there again in the future he'd rent an SUV in someone else's name.

Daryl expressed her frustration at not persuading Saliha. "This is a bigger job than I thought," she said. The woman was very frightened and not only of Jeff, it seemed. From what her roommate had said, Saliha was more frightened of what Ahmed might do than anything.

From time to time on wide curves in the highway they could see the blue car. The black Hyundai with Ahmed and the other man was tailing her as well. Traffic was not especially heavy but there were many passenger cars, overloaded pickups, and heavy semis heading east.

"Careful Ahmed doesn't see us," Daryl cautioned.

"Right. But I don't want to stay too far back," Jeff said.

"I checked. This highway goes all the way to the Iran border. She's not likely to leave it."

"We'll plan on that. She's also holding a steady speed of a hundred and ten kilometers an hour, just under seventy, which makes my job a bit easier."

"Boy genius," she said with a smile.

"It's on the speedometer." A minute later he said, "So . . . why is our favorite Arab here with his bearded friend?"

"Iranians aren't Arabs."

"You know what I mean."

"Unfortunately I do, Mr. Racial Stereotype. All I can think of is that he's concerned Saliha isn't going to deliver this final patch."

"He seemed satisfied she'd do it when we talked to him in Prague."

"Talk? Is that what you call interrogating a hog-tied man lying on the floor?"

"I never touched him."

"Maybe the bearded guy is a boss of some kind and wants to make sure everything goes smoothly."

"They might think she's betrayed them. That won't be good if true."

"Jeff, there's really nothing we can do except talk to Saliha when we get the chance. I don't like Ahmed being here. He's a killer. I haven't the slightest doubt he had every intention of killing both of us. We'd be dead now if we hadn't managed to escape. I don't need to remind you that this isn't what we do. We need a backup plan. Do you think Frank can have her picked up by the Turkish police or stopped at the border? This really shouldn't be up to us. Surely the Company has assets in place by now."

"Assets? Where'd you get that?"

"I read novels, I know how these spy types talk. And I worked at NSA, remember?"

"If the Company had anyone in the area Frank would have called. It's not like there's a lot of time for them to coordinate an operation against a moving target in the middle of the desert. He's not thrilled about us doing this but he sees the necessity since we're on her tail. As for Turkey, I don't know about cooperation. It's been moving more Islamist every year. The current government is pretty cozy with Iran. They aren't known to cooperate with America, or Europe for that matter . . . not unless there's something in it for them. Just a second. She's pulling off the highway," Jeff said. "Hold off on that call. The boys are following her."

"The red car is exiting with us," Ahmed said. "You were right."

"Be prepared. It's almost certainly the CIA, though we cannot rule out the Mossad."

At the mention of the dreaded Israeli agency, Ahmed's mouth went dry. To his knowledge he'd never encountered its agents but the stories he'd heard were bloodcurdling. Its exploits in Europe and the Middle East were terrifying in their daring and success.

"How is it possible for them to be here?" Ahmed asked.

"Why do you even ask the obvious? Two CIA agents questioned you. You gave them Saliha's name, didn't you? And her cell-phone number? You told them what she was doing?"

"I didn't. Really."

"Of course you did. That's why they are here."

Saliha preferred stopping infrequently on these trips. It was a long drive and every minute off the highway was a minute lost. But from long habit she'd established when and where she'd take a break. This town was one of many along the highway, red-roofed stone houses clustered together, the spire of a single mosque shooting skyward. Here, just off the exit, was a small, clean café where she could use the facilities and order a roll and coffee to go. She'd pick up some water while she could. She parked the Ford Fiesta beside the café, locked the doors, and went inside.

Ahmed slowed his car as he waited for instructions. "She doesn't know me," Hamid said. "I'll go inside, then follow her to the car. I'll get out here. I want you to park well in front of her. Watch through the mirror so she doesn't see your face. She's your girlfriend so she should be happy to see you but you've never come to Turkey before and your presence will likely startle her. I'll talk to her, then you come up and be certain to smile, Ahmed. This is a friendly gesture on your part. You want to help her out."

"She's smart. She'll know."

"Just do it. Now let me out."

"What about the red car behind us?" Ahmed asked as he braked to a stop.

"Here." Hamid reached into the gray travel bag he'd picked up at the café and handed over a Browning Hi-Power 9 millimeter. "It's single action for the first shot," he reminded him. There was a Spanish .380 Astra Constable as well, a much smaller though still heavy pistol. Hamid took that for himself, slipping it into his pocket. "We want no trouble. This is just in case they start it." Hamid stepped from the car, then casually walked to the café.

Jeff stopped the Fiat well back from the Hyundai. He saw the bearded man exit the car, then watched as it moved and parked some thirty feet in front of the Ford Saliha was driving. "Ahmed's driving," Daryl said. "I've never seen the other man before this morning. What do we do?"

"Wait and watch." He glanced beside him at the sound of a bell and saw a loaded donkey behind, led by a young boy.

Inside, Saliha smiled at the owner, who expressed surprise at seeing her again so soon. She ordered a large American coffee to go and her favorite sweet along with two bottles of water. While she was in the bathroom, Hamid entered. As he spoke no Turkish he ordered two coffees in English and pointed to several rolls, asking they be put in a sack for him. The man understood and had both orders ready by the time Saliha come out. She saw Hamid and smiled politely while reaching for the money to pay for her order.

She was not a beautiful woman, Hamid noted. She was pretty in a traditional Turkish way with a more prominent nose than he preferred and long, quite lovely black hair. She moved with a certain confidence rare in any Muslim country and he wondered if it was because she was from Turkey or if it was the result of her time in the West.

He gave the man more money than necessary, then hurried after the woman. He glanced to his left and saw the red Fiat well back. A man and a woman were in it, watching. He turned right and timed himself to reach Saliha just as she arrived at her car.

"Excuse me," he said, glancing over her to see Ahmed exit the Hyundai. "Do you know this area?" So close, he saw she was a good three inches taller than he was. That was, unfortunately, all too common in his life.

"No," she answered without suspicion. "I'm just passing through."

"Ahh. The same as me."

"You could ask in the café."

"I could but I speak no Turkish."

"I don't know if—"

At that moment Ahmed was immediately behind her. He placed one strong hand on each of her shoulders. "Hello, Saliha."

She turned and gasped. "What . . . what are you doing here?"

"Ahmed will ride with you," Hamid said. "I will follow. We just want to be certain you reach Iran without difficulty." He smiled. "All is well, I assure you."

"I . . ."

"Let's go," Ahmed said with a warm smile.

Once the two were in the car Hamid knocked on the passenger window. "Here," he said to Ahmed. "I bought you coffee and something to eat."

As the couple drove off, Hamid returned to the Hyundai. With a last glance at the red Fiat, he followed.

"They've kidnapped her," Daryl said.

"That's one word for it. I think they want to make certain she gets to where she's going."

Jeff followed the two cars through the town, then back onto E80 where Saliha in the lead car soon returned to her former pace.

"I don't see that there is anything we can do now," Jeff said. "They are dangerous men and there's no doubt the bearded one saw us."

"He doesn't know who we are."

"Somehow that fails to reassure me."

Daryl stared out the window. The countryside was rolling and green, shedding winter. The poverty was apparent everywhere she looked. The sky, however, was magnificent, an indigo she couldn't recall seeing before. "I'll call Frank while we still have a signal."

When she was finished placing the call, Daryl lifted the cell phone to her ear. She glanced out the window again. A small, white plane trimmed in silver was slightly behind them, pacing traffic.

53

Frank could not have been more unhappy. He'd not seen his family for a week. His wife understood and didn't complain, but it was still difficult. He talked with his daughters each day and they seemed to take it well, but with children you never knew.

Preparations for the Iranian nuclear test at the Kavir-e-Lut salt flats were well advanced according to the latest analysis of satellite imagery. Chatter intercepted by the National Security Agency confirmed high expectations within the Iranian military and among the ruling elite. The logistics were complicated but once every part was ready, transported to the site, and assembled, it wouldn't take long.

And so far there was no sign that Tusk had managed to leap the new air gap. Once it did it would spread like wildfire and this time it was designed to be a program destroyer, not an inhibitor. The satellite image of the fuel enrichment plant in Natanz was continually displayed on one of his monitors as he waited for confirmation of success. During occasional lapses in his frantic schedule, he'd find himself staring at the buildings and grounds, searching for some sign.

The target date for detonation was April 26, just ten days out. The UNOG report had been delayed and was the subject of wild speculation, some of which was now in the media. Its contents and conclusions had been cast in doubt. The consequence was that a military strike had been ruled out for the time being, leaving Stuxnet3 as the only remaining weapon. With this Chinese countermeasure on the way, its success was in doubt, and if it failed Frank didn't want to think of the way the world would be changed.

With the access Jeff and Daryl had given him, Frank was now continuously monitoring the cell-phone locations for the couple as well as that of Ahmed. According to Jeff and Daryl, Ahmed and Saliha were now in the same car. Any likelihood of Jeff and Daryl talking the woman out of the trip or getting the patch from her was all but gone.

Frank had attempted to get agents moved into action in Turkey and been shocked at the amount of red tape he'd encountered. One senior manager had even wanted to schedule a meeting to discuss his request. As a consequence he'd spoken briefly to Edinfield earlier, ostensibly to update her, but in fact to see if he could enlist her help in getting agents in place. Instead, she'd told him about her pickup order for the couple so he'd not wanted to risk revealing their location. They were in the hunt, on the very tail of the mule, while he had no idea if real agents could get that close in time. He didn't like it but it was up to them.

Which raised the most important question of all: So what if Jeff and Daryl pulled this off? The Chinese would just find another way, or for that matter they might simply e-mail the patch to Iran. Until now they'd used a mule but there were ways to send it digitally that were nearly as secure. With time running out and their mule intercepted wouldn't that be the logical move?

The question was all about timing. Somehow he had to find a way to delay the patch until after the air gap was jumped and the Trojan had time to do its work. He looked again at the growing file on Ahmed Hossein al-Rashid of Prague. He'd had a very able team on the man since his name first appeared. They'd accessed ASSET at the Italian border crossing the night Daryl was likely transported into the EU and they'd found the man's photo.

In the end, he'd settled on arranging to have an advisory sent to the Turkish government concerning Ahmed Hossein al-Rashid. He'd included the passport information and photograph. The advisory requested that Ahmed be detained and the Prague police notified because he was wanted for questioning in a murder there, and also by the Geneva police concerning his involvement in an abduction and killing of a UNOG official. He didn't know if it would help or not but it was something.

54

Daryl glanced into the sky. "That plane's still there."

"What plane?"

"There's been a small white plane following behind us almost from the start. I thought I said something about it earlier."

Jeff leaned down to look and spotted it off to their right flying low. "That's odd."

"It's probably just following the highway to wherever it's going."

"Maybe. Still, you'd think it would have flown past us long ago. I'd think an airplane would have trouble flying as slow as a car travels. Keep an eye on it." He glanced at his cell phone. No signal.

Half an hour later the blue Ford exited the highway, followed closely by the black Hyundai. Jeff glanced at the fuel gauge. "Pit stop, I think. We need gas as well and a stretch."

"Among other things. Make sure it's got a restroom."

Jeff watched as both cars ahead drove a short distance into the city then nosed into a large service station. It was situated amid rolling hills, the city itself thick with trees. He spotted three minarets, which he took as an indicator of size.

Saliha parked the car, then climbed out followed by Ahmed. The bearded man got out, giving Jeff and Daryl a look that seemed to say, "Stay where you are."

Which proved no problem. There was a small car rental agency across the street and a few blocks down, still within sight, a gas pump out front. "Think they'll sell to us?" he asked.

"Why not? You've got a credit card."

Keeping an eye on the two other cars Jeff went inside and found they would fill up his tank. There was also a restroom they could both use. When Jeff came out Daryl was standing beside the Fiat, staring into the sky. "That plane's circling. It's following us."

"Or them."

"Or all of us."

Jeff checked his cell phone, confirmed a signal, then placed a call to Frank. It rolled over to voice mail. "Frank, do you know anything about an airplane out here? We're on E80 more than halfway to the border, in a town I can't read the name of. Call back when you can."

"What do you think it's up to?" Daryl asked, watching the sky.

"I don't know."

"It can't be good."

"Probably not. Traffic will thin as we drive farther east. I wonder if whoever it is would try something then?"

"Jeff," Daryl said, "I have an idea. If I'm wrong it won't mean much; if I'm right it could make the difference."

Ten minutes later Daryl pulled in behind the Ford and Hyundai, driving the Fiat. Jeff was just behind her, in a newly rented Ford Fiesta, this one green. She planned to trail the other cars for a bit, slowly dropping back while Jeff moved in front of her, testing if the plane stayed with her. If not, she'd just close up and they'd work with two cars. If it did, she had other plans.

When Ahmed slid into the car beside her, Saliha was enraged and for a time her anger overwhelmed her fear. Why had he come all the way to Turkey? She was furious, so mad, she said nothing for a long time.

Then she began to wonder just how he'd tracked her down. He must have gone to her mother's place. How else could he have managed it? Had he threatened her? It wouldn't have been necessary. Her mother knew better than to resist a determined man. Saliha had even mentioned Ahmed to her once or twice, always in a positive way.

"Why are you here?" she demanded, startling Ahmed from his thoughts. "And just who is that little man with you?"

He smiled. "I'm here to help you. I told you before that this was important. Don't you want me here?"

"I can handle this on my own. This makes me think you don't trust me."

"I trust you, but . . ."

"He is your boss? Is that it?"

"Something like that. He doesn't know you like I do. He insisted we come just to make sure."

Saliha drew a deep breath, then released it in a sigh. She was in trouble. Why else would they go to all this effort and expense? They wanted this thumb drive in Iran today and they wanted to be certain she didn't change her mind. She shouldn't have said anything about this being her last trip. It had made Ahmed suspicious and brought in this other man.

She's continued thinking about this as they drove, not certain what she should do. She smiled, behaving as if everything was fine. A dark thought returned to her. When she crossed the border, would she be allowed to come back? Thinking of Ahmed with his false sincerity she suspected not. They'd sever her relationship with whatever she'd been taking, once and for all.

It occurred to her that she should start looking for a way out. She ran through any number of scenarios, then the most obvious came to her. These men weren't Turkish, and Turks were well known for defending their own women. If she had the chance she should take it. After all, she'd managed to get away from the American with no help at all. She'd toss the thumb drive at their feet and run. Let them take it into Iran. It was time she got to Paris or Rome.

Then she recalled the threat against her family. Had Ahmed meant it? Would he really go so far? What would the men he was working for do? But she had to try, she just had to. She wanted to cry.

The caravan below, as Wu was coming to think of it, had reached a more isolated region of Turkey. Traffic on the highway was minimal. What remained were the heavy semis, a few pickups, and a scattering of cars. Houses were far between, the country primarily rolling grassland with small scratch farms. It looked exhausted.

He'd picked up the Magic Dragon cell-phone tracker along with the weapons. Magic Dragon, as the device was known, made it possible for him to track any cell phone. It was especially effective from the air. It was simple to use and he'd taught Li within minutes. The device was the size of an iPad, but with old-fashioned knobs. What it did was emit a signal that mimicked that of a cell tower. The cell phone being tracked would then automatically *ping* the tower and report its GPS location whether the phone was in use or not. Magic Dragon had a range of up to two miles from above, less on the ground. It had allowed them to locate then stay with the cars below.

The morning weather had been clear but now dark clouds gathered overhead and gusts of wind rocked and buffeted the small plane from time to time. It would likely get worse as the day progressed and the ground warmed. If this were a pleasure flight he'd have turned back long ago. Li was looking a little nauseous though he'd not said anything.

Sometime earlier, Li had reported that Ahmed's cell phone was now appearing in the blue car. That had puzzled Wu until he'd thought to have him insert Saliha's number into the Magic Dragon locater and there it was, with Ahmed. They were in the car together. Ahmed's partner in the black sedan was following close behind.

"We need to get the red car away from the others," Wu said. "The computers will be in it. We want it off the highway and on a side road. Once there we should have no problem. I'm reluctant to do anything on a busy highway. We need to continue operating in Turkey when this is finished."

Li said nothing. He was now quite pale. Wu smiled to himself, having once been very airsick himself. He needed a break below, some change he could take advantage off. In the meanwhile they needed to be ready. "Check the weapon," he ordered.

Li nodded. He put aside the Magic Dragon, reached behind, and removed a HK G36, the assault rifle of the German army. It was best not to use Chinese-made firearms.

GENEVA, SWITZERLAND
UNOG
2:37 P.M. CET

Henri Wille received the notice over his secure Interpol e-mail system. Their American friends had sent a strongly worded "request" to the Turkish government that one Ahmed Hossein al-Rashid be detained. The Prague police wanted the man for questioning into the murder of Karim Behzad. He was also wanted by the Geneva Canton Police for the abduction of two Americans and his complicity in the murder of a UNOG official.

Henri smiled at the last. He wondered if the Geneva police even had this man's name. He leaned back in his chair and thought. Someone was pressing very hard. Though official wheels were turning Turkey was known for how slowly it moved in these matters. But there was another way. A better way.

For more than three years Henri had served as UN liaison on the TALOS project, intended to provide the European Union with the most advanced border security system in the world. With UNOG located just a few short kilometers from the EU, it had insisted they have a security representative on the committee.

His counterpart from Turkey was Attila Arif, a senior deputy in the General Directorate of Security in Ankara. Despite his ominous sounding first name, Arif was a congenial man, given to heavy drinking and relentless womanizing.

When he came on the line, he said, "My friend, Henri, it has been too long. We are not supposed to meet for another two months."

"I have a favor to ask, Attila."

"Just ask. If I can do it you know I will."

Henri told him what he wanted.

"Consider it done, my friend. Nothing could be easier."

55

Gholam Rahmani, known as Hamid, watched the Ford Fiesta almost in a trance, his mind far, far away. When will it all end? he thought. How long must it continue?

No wife, no children, no real life. He'd been a teenager the year the Shah fell. Now in his early fifties he wondered what jihad had really meant to him. Was the cost too high?

After his father vanished into Iran and he'd received just the one letter from his mother there'd been no word again. He'd assumed all his family dead. These had been very difficult and lonely years. Once the family rug business in Italy became prosperous it was only natural that he joined the Frente Democrático Iraniano, FDI. Now as executive director he was in position to know every opponent of the Islamic Revolution in Europe. Had anyone accused him of being a devoted son of the Iranian revolution his life would have been worthless. He was certain that no Iranian exile would initially believe it. Rahmani, they would say, had every reason to despise the mullahs and what had been done to his family. He would not support them and he'd never betray his Iranian brothers and sisters in exile.

In fact, convincing the Iranian intelligence service VEVAK of his sincerity had not been easy, since his reputation as an opponent had been so well established. But he'd persisted and in time they'd given him small assignments, which he carried out with precision. When he'd been ordered to kill the then executive director of FDI, a close friend and longtime mentor, he'd seemed to scarcely hesitate. Only after that had he been accepted and quietly ushered into Iran for special training, then given the field name Hamid.

In time he'd risen in responsibility. He'd subsumed every normal human response and emotion to his great jihad. The Prophet taught that every man is at war with himself and that he must first conquer the darkness within before he would make jihad on the enemies of Allah. He struggled every moment in Iran to conquer himself. The fate of his family had been unfortunate, he was told. Had his true loyalties been known they might have been spared. He must accept the most sincere apologies for his loss. And he had.

On his third trip to Iran, two years earlier, he'd been given a great gift, a visit with his older brother, Nader. It had been a joyous homecoming as each of them had thought the other long dead. They met in Tehran though Nader said he lived elsewhere, the city unnamed. Hearty, heavyset, gregarious as ever but now with gray hair, he told his younger brother that he was married with three children. "All daughters, alas." He'd trained as a scientist and did unspecified work for the government.

Rahmani had found family again. The third day of their visit, Nader had taken his younger brother far out into the country into the foothills of the Alborz Mountains in a borrowed Land Cruiser. There, the brothers had set up a small camp; they'd joked, eaten, relaxed. Then, at last, far beyond any possible ears, all pretense vanished as a heavy silence fell between them.

Rahmani broke it. "Our father and mother."

"They killed them both. Father simply vanished almost the moment he got off the airplane. An informer reported that mother had sent you a letter. She was arrested and disappeared."

"She wrote me of our brothers. And of our widowed sisters."

Nader closed his eyes briefly in sorrow as he murmured a prayer.

"I am allowed to see them from time to time. They are okay. Not happy, childless, unmarried, but okay. Perhaps they will let you see them."

Rahmani said nothing for a long time. "Can this really be our Iran? It is like a prison, my brother."

"It is not *like* a prison, it *is* a prison. Let me tell you about my work." Nader had then told him what he did at the Natanz Fuel Enrichment Plant. "We are preparing enriched uranium for our glorious Islamic nuclear bomb." Rahmani said nothing. "You are part of the revolution now, my brother. An important man, I am told. They trust you or you would not be allowed to see me."

"I tried to go on, to live a normal life. I had an Italian girlfriend in school. I wanted to marry her."

"You should have. A good marriage is a blessing. I am very fortunate."

"But we are having this conversation out here." Nader shrugged. "No, I could not marry, not with what I planned to do."

"And what was that, little brother?"

"The mullahs cannot last. They are too corrupt. Iranians will not tolerate a theocracy indefinitely. They came to power in a revolution, a revolution will sweep them away."

"Just as I thought. You were always the hard one."

Rahmani told his brother of his mentor, of the night he'd killed him. "I knew he was sick, though not how badly. I told him of my mission but that the price for acceptance was his death and it was too much. He held my hands and told me he was dying. He spoke of his dreams for our great nation, how the mullahs must be crushed. He told me I must pay whatever price was necessary, no matter how hard I found it. He told me he was proud of me. He asked for a week to visit family, to make his arrangements. He gave up his remaining few months so I could wage jihad against the mullahs from within. Still, it was very, very hard. He was a great man."

Rahmani stared across the land toward the mountains, inhaled the sweet fragrance unique to this region. "From where I am now I do them enormous harm. I've already largely neutralized their European operations. Several agents have been executed for failures I arranged. But this bomb—it will change everything. Even Iranians who do not support the mullahs believe Iran should have the bomb."

"Yes, it will give them many more years in power. And they will use it. Trust me. They will use it."

"When they do, the West will retaliate. They are not as weak willed as the mullahs believe."

"They are stupid men. So stupid you would be amazed."

"What more can I do? You have not told me your duties without a reason."

"Nothing right now. We are having many problems. This Stuxnet—I'm sure you've read of it—has caused much greater harm than is admitted. But they are preparing a new, secure computer center. Once it is operational they will accomplish wonders. Today, we must set up a secure means for me to communicate with you. When I know something vital, I will tell you. Then, if you can, you must act."

Rahmani was silent for a time, then, "If I am caught and tortured, what we have said today will come out."

"It is written, little brother. But like you, I will not rest until these bearded bastards burn in Hell."

"Allah willing," Rahmani said. His brother met his eyes and repeated, "Allah willing."

There had been no message after that and Rahmani wondered if Nader had changed his mind or perhaps disappeared. Scientists in Iran were reported to simply vanish from time to time. Then, on March 19, a month earlier, had come this message through the tortuous digital pathway they'd agreed to:

Detonation April 26. Enough fuel from FEP April 17 or 18. Stuxnet no longer delays. Supporting dox attached. Do what you can. Allah go with you. And with me.

His brother had taken a terrible risk in contacting him and forwarding the internal FEP documents to support his claim. While only such evidence would be persuasive to any meaningful power, it exposed him. Rahmani wondered if his brother could escape his fate.

Two days later, Rahmani delivered the information to the United Nations because he did not trust the Americans or British to do anything. But if UNOG failed to act, he'd threatened, he'd take the data to them, and if he had to he'd go public. Somehow, he would find a way to compel the world to take action.

Then this Chinese counter to any new version of Stuxnet had appeared. He'd risked everything giving his brother's documents to the UN. He continued that risk today. Ahead, Ahmed rode with the mule. Rahmani would stop her. That was why he was here. If he could do it and keep his position as chief of Iranian intelligence in Europe, so be it. If not, he was always in the hands of Allah, the Merciful.

"I have to go," Saliha said.

"Go where?" Ahmed looked confused.

"You know, in a ladies' room."

"Oh. Of course. You can pull over. It is not a problem."

"What do you think I am? A woman who squats on the side of a highway? There is a town up ahead. I stopped there once before. It has a café I can use."

Ahmed thought about it a moment. "All right."

They were now two to three hours from the border and Saliha had decided she'd only have two chances. One would be a stop well short of the crossing; the other would be at the border itself. She'd spent some time considering talking Ahmed into taking the thumb drive across himself. He was here, what did they need her for?

But that led to only one answer. Yes, they wanted what she *had* in Iran but they also wanted *her* in Iran. She slowed when she saw the sign. YAY-LACIK. It was not much of a town. The hills were more pronounced now with evergreen growth in the cooler climate.

Behind them, Rahmani slowed with the Ford. He glanced at his watch. Early for a break. The weather was turning nasty. The wind had really picked up and was blasting the car with considerable force from time to time. Sunset was at 7:30 p.m. and that was about when they'd reach the border. He needed to do something soon.

Behind them both, Jeff dropped well back, wondering how he'd pass unnoticed in such a small town.

Daryl had fallen far behind and the plane remained with her. She'd checked her cell phone to call Jeff but there was no signal. She had her spot picked out, Tercan Baraji, an enormous hydroelectric reservoir. The map showed a network of roads leading around it. She'd take in the sights while the other cars drove on. After an hour of delay she'd return to the highway and follow. Easy.

Ahead of Jeff the blue Ford pulled to a stop in front of a small café. There were a few tables and empty chairs. The black Hyundai stopped immediately behind the Ford. The diminutive man climbed out and stretched, looking back the way they'd come, not registering Jeff in his different car. Jeff saw the woman get out and go inside, followed by Ahmed. The bearded man remained without, smoking a cigarette.

Jeff turned into a narrow side street, then maneuvered until he was largely unseen from the other cars but had a clear view of the front of the café.

Daryl spotted the road to the lake and took it. A short distance later she looked up and sure enough, there was the little plane. She could feel the wind herself and wondered what it was like up there. Not pleasant.

Overhead, Wu had been fighting the SportCruiser for the last two hours. The pounding wind was playing havoc with the little plane. More than once he'd thought about just turning around but the red car was just there. And now it was by itself, away from the highway. He banked the plane and descended, maneuvering for the best approach.

Li had thrown up once earlier and apologized repeatedly for it. Still, he'd improved after that and though he looked wan he had the assault rifle between his knees, ready for action. These were CIA agents, certainly armed. Wu was taking no chances.

"Take them out," Wu ordered. "Careful with the car. We don't want computers with holes in them." Wu dipped the plane and cut speed even more. His main concern was a sudden downdraft. He doubted the craft had enough power to overcome anything too precipitous.

Li opened the window and cold air beat into the cockpit. He moved in the seat so he could aim the assault rifle. He had a one-hundred-round magazine with three more in the war bag. He slipped the weapon to full automatic fire.

Below, Daryl was concentrating on the road. If it deteriorated she planned to turn around and head back to the highway, then find another off road to follow. It didn't have to go to the lake. It could go anywhere.

Saliha stalled in the restroom. She'd counted on men being gathered here as they always were, but because of the weather there were only two sitting inside, both old. Even if they stood up for her, how far were Ahmed and the other man prepared to go? And once she tried to get away and failed, they'd know, and if she was wrong in her assessment she would certainly be their enemy from then on. She might not even live to reach the border.

Ahmed knocked on the door. "Let's go. It will be dark soon."

Saliha stared at herself in the mirror. She felt the knife in her pocket, knowing she hadn't the courage to use it. *You're a coward*, she thought. A coward.

As she exited the café she looked at the men. No, these wouldn't do. It had to be the border, she thought. There were guards there. They'd likely remember her. Yes, the border. That was the best place to escape. As for her family, she'd call and warn them.

Ahmed stood at the bar to pay for his soda as Saliha went outside. He glanced at the television. Startled, he saw two photographs of him, one from his passport, the other of him sitting in a car. *My God!* he thought. He stared in amazement and fear. The picture cut to a serious young woman reading from a script, then a telephone number appeared on the screen. He was wanted, here in Turkey, right now! He glanced quickly around. No one else was watching the television. He dropped a large bill on the counter and rushed out.

Fortunately, Hamid had stayed with his car. Saliha didn't notice Ahmed's anxiety as he slipped behind the wheel and joined her. She made a U-turn and drove back to the highway. Beside her, Ahmed stifled his panic. He'd have to avoid getting too close to the border. He needed to tell Hamid about this but when he did it would be just one more sign of failure. Perhaps after Saliha had crossed over and they had a success to enjoy. Yes, that would be the moment.

Just then, there was a distinctive sound Daryl had only heard once before—bullets striking very close to her. There were thuds across the front of the car and the distant sound of rapid gunfire. She accelerated rapidly.

The plane, she thought, *it's from that plane!*

Overhead, Wu gunned the engine, gained altitude and banked. "Any luck?"

"I shot across the engine to disable the car. If you can come in very low I'll go for the tires next."

Wu didn't like the sound of that. Low was not good. The plane was a lot safer higher up. He looked down and spotted the red car racing toward the lake. He gunned the engine to make a low pass but much faster, much safer than before as he had to catch the fast-moving car. "Make the most of it, Li."

The strong wind battered the plane and Li had trouble taking aim. As the car came in sight he squeezed the trigger but only let off a few wide shots. The plane just wasn't stable enough. "We need to make the car the target or give this up," he said. "It's too rough for proper aim." Wu gunned the engine and made a sharp turn to come around for another pass.

Daryl was frantically searching for somewhere to hide, a building of some kind or a natural protection. This road joined a broader, more improved road running beside the lake. She raced toward it, taking the turn hard, the tires screeching. She shifted gears, then gunned along the new road, picking up speed, wishing they'd rented something with more power.

Then bullets slammed into the car, the sound on the roof like very heavy hail.

On the highway Jeff glanced back repeatedly for sight of Daryl and the red Fiat. He couldn't get used to the idea of their being separated at such a time. It looked as if she'd been right about the plane; once she'd faded back he'd lost sight of it. It was possible it had flown on but if it had she'd have rejoined him by now, assuming the Fiat could catch up. Saliha was maintaining a quick pace.

He glanced at his phone. No signal.

Daryl weaved back and forth across the road, doing what she could to evade the plane and the bullets. Several had struck the car; one had gone through the passenger seat. Steam was coming from around the hood and the engine was making a terrible racket. Ahead was a cluster of squat buildings near the dam. She straightened out and risked a look for the plane. With a sinking heart she saw that it was coming around again.

Daryl downshifted, punched the accelerator to the floor, and the little engine screamed.

"Last pass," Wu said. "Empty a full magazine into the car, aim for the driver."

"Right," Li said as he reached behind him and extracted a fresh magazine, which he snapped in place.

Wu nosed the plane down and pushed the throttle full forward. The wind was less violent and he was willing to risk a lower pass, one certain to make the kill. Then he'd land on the asphalt road, recover the laptops, and they'd be on their way.

Li placed the rifle out the window and pressed it against his shoulder. Wu could see the buildings ahead but he'd catch the car before it ever reached them. When the car was in sight Li held the trigger down in sustained automatic fire, aiming as best he could directly at the driver.

Daryl sensed rather than saw or heard the plane. She yanked the wheel hard over. The Fiat tottered on two wheels as if it might go over but it held as her momentum drove her off the road onto the flat expanse beside it. The car came to an abrupt stop as the engine died.

Daryl looked anxiously out the window. The plane was making a slow wheel in the sky as it turned to attack again. She turned the key. The engine ground in a disheartening way and refused to catch. She tried again with no luck. As she turned the key a third time, she saw the plane coming nearly straight at her.

The car engine roared to life. She rammed the gear into reverse and shot backward onto the asphalt. She slammed on the brakes, changed gears, then punched the accelerator as she pointed the car for the buildings directly ahead. As she did she weaved side to side, alternating between braking and accelerating. Bullets slammed into the car. She felt a blow from above but no pain or other sensation. She hit the brakes hard, the car skidding to a stop. The plane zoomed past her.

"They stopped," Li said, pulling the rifle back in. "Maybe I got the driver."

Wu banked sharply, still at a leisurely pace for an aircraft designed to resist extremes. The car below was not moving. "Again," he ordered. "I think we have them."

But as he approached, his worse fear was realized. The wind pummeled the plane cruelly and as he slowed to give Li his best shot, they were caught in a sudden downdraft. It seemed to Wu that the plane was being pressed to the ground by a powerful, unseen force.

Daryl saw the plane coming at her. Light-headed, she turned the ignition again but this time there was no hope. The engine refused to even turn over. She jumped out of the car and looked back at the plane as it dropped even lower, like a fighter coming in for a strafing run.

Wu pushed the control forward for maximum power and fought to raise the craft but to no avail. He was being forced down relentlessly. "Pull up!" Li shouted, but it was too late. The plane slammed into the ground just in front of the red car in a violent crash that at once turned into a fireball, the flames engulfing the Fiat as the wreckage scattered immediately in front of it, some striking the front in passing.

Daryl had only made it a few yards when she felt the plane hit and she was knocked forward, engulfed in the horrible sounds of the crashing plane. Then there was silence, broken only by the sound of the flames.

She was out of breath and light-headed, struggling to stand up. When she looked she saw that her clothes were covered in blood. Unseen to her, men rushed from the buildings in response to the explosion. The violence of the explosion, flames, and ugly plume told them there were no survivors.

56

E80
TRANS-EUROPEAN MOTORWAY (TEM)
NEAR GURBULAK, TURKEY
7:19 P.M. EET

I need to change clothes before crossing the border," Saliha said. "You know how you Iranians are."

"Of course." Ahmed had cautioned her that first trip about what she must do. He was pleased she remembered because it was obvious she was upset. He'd never seen her like this, so withdrawn and anxious. Confronting her in Ankara had been a mistake. He wished Hamid had listened to him. Had they left her alone all would have been well. Instead, he was a wanted man in a foreign country. "I'll tell you where," he said.

This next part was going to be tricky. Ahmed didn't dare get too close to the border for fear of being recognized. But this had to go smoothly. He doubted Hamid would take the thumb drive across himself and he certainly wasn't going to suggest it. No, it had to be Saliha. That's what she was paid for.

They'd been driving through a mountainous region of Turkey for the last hour. The highway wound back and forth like a snake, crossing numerous bridges, large and small. The sun was dipping very low on the horizon. The leaves on the poplar trees flanking a stream bristled in the breeze, reflecting a final stream of fading sunlight. Some fifteen miles from the border they came on a gaudy truck stop. "Here," Ahmed said. "You can use the restroom."

Saliha pulled the car off to the side of the building, out of the path of the trucks fueling up. It was one of those modern structures, seemingly snapped together like a child's toy. She found it very depressing. In all her trips she'd never once stopped at this place.

She was exhausted as she went to the rear of the car and opened the trunk for her Iran-crossing attire. She'd tried to devise some scheme for the border and could come up with nothing specific. She'd have to see the situation, then respond to it. The only thing about which she was absolutely certain was that she was not entering Iran.

Rahmani pulled up beside the blue Ford and climbed out as Saliha walked past him, carrying a travel bag. She stared straight ahead, making a point not to look at him. He lit a cigarette and pulled his light jacket closely about him. It was cold.

"She is changing," Ahmed said. Rahmani nodded in understanding. "We are close to the border." Rahmani glanced at Ahmed and wondered why he was saying these things. They were self-evident.

Across the service area, Jeff drove to the opposite end of the building and killed the engine. He'd watched Saliha go around the station carrying a bag. He glanced along the side of the building and decided to risk an attempt. Before getting out of the car he checked his cell phone. There'd been no calls from Daryl and he was uneasy about the silence. Once, he had regained a signal and called her; each attempt had rolled over to voice mail. He assumed she was out of contact but took no comfort in the thought.

Ahmed and the other man were talking, each keeping a casual eye on the corner Saliha had gone around. Jeff slipped out of the car and walked by the side of the building, along the wall to the back. The ground dropped off sharply here and there was little space for him to move along. Excess concrete oozed from the foundation and was now frozen in a permanent curl. Loose rock and gravel made his footing uncertain.

Jeff edged along the back until he came to the far corner. A quick peek revealed two doors he took to be the entrances to restrooms. He waited for one to open, then he'd do what he could. It was more likely she'd bolt than talk to him.

"At the border," Rahmani said in front, "you will see her to the crossing." No such thing would occur, of course, but that was what Ahmed expected to hear.

"Hamid," Ahmed said quietly. "I must tell you something." Rahmani raised an eyebrow and Ahmed rushed into his story, telling him how he'd seen his photograph at the last stop, that he was certain he was wanted here in Turkey. "I cannot risk getting close to the border."

"Was my photograph on the television?"

"No, I assure you."

"Did you wait until the broadcast was finished to be certain?"

"I . . . I left. Saliha was outside and I was concerned someone might recognize me if I remained near the television."

Rahmani considered this new information. Events were moving much faster than they had a right to on their own. He and Ahmed should have been undetected here in Turkey yet someone knew enough to put out an alert for Ahmed, perhaps even for himself though he couldn't imagine that was likely.

Still, it was apparent that he'd dithered too long. He needed to act as soon as he could. The woman had to go because she'd seen him as an ally of Ahmed. Ahmed had to die because he'd know Rahmani had stopped Saliha. "Get the woman," he snapped. "We need to go somewhere private."

When Ahmed came around the corner, Jeff pulled back. He heard pounding on the door. "Saliha. Change later. We need to leave right now."

"I'm not finished."

"Forget it. Let's go. We're in a hurry."

A moment later Jeff heard the door slam, then Saliha complaining to Ahmed as the two went toward the front of the building. He moved as quickly as he could back the way he'd come, turned the corner, then sneaked a look. Saliha was getting into the Ford with Ahmed beside her. The other man had already started his engine and was watching them intently. As soon as the two cars pulled away he jumped into his car. To his surprise they turned away from the border.

"It's just up here," Saliha told Ahmed, gesturing lightly. "I don't know why I couldn't finish. It would only take a few minutes."

"Just go where you usually do. It is quiet, you say?"

"Of course. You think I undress in front of others?"

Two miles up the highway, she found the small road leading to her usual place by the stream and poplar trees. She exited, then drove slowly to the small, discreet clearing she always used. "Hurry up," Ahmed ordered.

"Oh? Now you are in a hurry?" Saliha climbed out of the car and opened the rear door where she'd left the bag. "Go join your friend. I don't want you watching me."

Ahmed opened his mouth to say something, then thought better of it. He went to Rahmani, who had just stopped and was getting out of the car. Ahmed told him she wanted privacy. "As if I never see her naked," he said. The two lit cigarettes and leaned against the Hyundai, smoking.

The sun had set and the place was cast in shadows. Saliha glanced about uneasily. The trees were a dark, ominous presence. The water bubbled around rocks and over stones, the sound cold, not cheery as it had been so often. She opened the trunk and lay her clothes neatly inside as she removed them. It was cold and she shivered in the breeze. She removed the ankle-length dark skirt and matching long-sleeved parkalike garment from her bag and slipped into them. She placed her denims and jacket into the bag. She picked up the head scarf and put it on, then closed the lid.

Rahmani glanced the way they'd come. "Did you hear that?"

"Just a truck on the highway," Ahmed answered.

"It sounded like a car on this dirt road."

"I heard nothing."

Rahmani had already slipped his .380 pistol into his jacket pocket and now he held it in his hand. He turned his attention from behind him to the woman as she returned. In a moment they'd both be where he needed them.

Jeff saw the two cars flash their brake lights, then turn off the highway. He came nearly to a stop as he watched them vanish amid trees and brush. He could see there was a stream down there so it was unlikely they'd gone far. He made the same turn, stopping almost at once, and backed the car into a thin spot amid the brush, the branches pressed against the car. He got out, carefully pushed the door closed, bumped it gently to seal it, then followed on foot. The dirt road curved slightly, blocking his view.

He heard the slam of a trunk before he saw the cars. When he spotted them the little man was holding a gun and waving it about as he barked orders.

This was nonsense, Rahmani thought. *Why am I talking? I know what I have to do.*

Ahmed looked confused as he followed orders and stood beside Saliha. What was Hamid up to?

Saliha, for her part, knew. She saw the look in the man's eyes—apprehension mixed with determination. When she saw the gun she had not the slightest doubt what was going to happen. She'd waited too long. "He's going to kill us," she hissed.

"What?" Ahmed glanced at her, then at Hamid. Realization washed over him in a cold chill. Of course. That's exactly what he was going to do.

Ahmed smiled. "Hamid. What is the problem, my brother?" he said in Farsi. "We have a duty to perform . . ." As he spoke he slowly reached for the Browning Hi-Power that had been sticking in the small of his back all these hours. Hamid might be highly trained, he might be the master of operations in Europe, but Ahmed saw how nervous he was. He only required an instant.

Rahmani was sweating. He was angry he'd hesitated at all. Ahmed was prattling on and on about nothing, then suddenly there was the gun he'd given him in his hand. Rahmani snapped off a shot but Ahmed dove away as he did. Saliha lunged to her right. Rahmani fired a shot at her, too, but knew he'd missed.

From the ground, Ahmed was raising his weapon even as he struggled to his knees. Rahmani fired again and again and again. As the bullets struck him, Ahmed fired but the shot went wild, his bullet ricocheting off into the distance. Then his arm lost strength and the gun fell. Ahmed wobbled on his knees for a moment, then toppled forward onto his face.

Saliha saw the first bullet strike Ahmed as she pulled up her long skirt and went running for her life toward the highway. She heard the other shots in quick succession. Then, in front of her, was the American. "This way!" he shouted. "I've got a car!"

The two of them ran the short distance to his car. She frantically jumped in as did Jeff. He started it up and shot out onto the dirt road, fish-tailing toward the nearby highway. The rear glass of the car shattered and he heard the zip of a bullet passing very near his head. Then he was on the highway accelerating as fast as he could.

"The other way!" Saliha shouted. "To the border. There are armed guards there!"

But it was too late. It was a divided highway with a deep cut between the two sections. Jeff was speeding back into Turkey.

———

Rahmani ran to his car and was quickly on the highway, racing after the Ford. He accelerated past two slow-moving semis as he steadily gained on the smaller car.

"Faster! Faster!" Saliha shouted. "I can see a car behind us. He's getting too close. Faster!"

Jeff glanced at the speedometer. Nearly ninety miles an hour. The highway curved and he was forced to slow each time, taking all three lanes to make the turns. He was more concerned with crashing than getting shot. He couldn't imagine the Hyundai was faring any better.

Rahmani had caught a glimpse of Jeff. Where had he come from? How was it possible for him to have traced them to this remote corner of Turkey? He thought about his cell phone. That had to be it. The CIA was tracking his cell phone. No, he suddenly thought, not his, but Ahmed's. Yes, that made sense. They'd been on to Ahmed; that was why his photograph was on Turkish television.

There was a lesson in this. He'd have to figure out how to carry a cell phone that couldn't be traced.

Jeff accelerated after every turn but his speed remained distressingly slow. For bursts he managed eighty or ninety miles an hour, but at the turns he'd drop to seventy or less. The car reluctantly responded when he accelerated. He raced past slower-moving traffic, flashing his headlights repeatedly to press a car out of a lane.

For all this, behind him Rahmani was slowly gaining.

Ahead, Jeff spotted a cluster of vehicles. He lifted his foot from the accelerator and slowed, searching for a way around the trucks and cars. Saliha was no longer shouting at him but had turned in her seat and was watching behind them, telling him every few seconds how close was the pursuing car.

"Who is in it?" he asked.

"The little man. Ahmed's boss, I think. He shot Ahmed. He was going to kill me."

They reached the cars and to Jeff's dismay he was forced to drop to just sixty miles an hour. The other car would be on them in seconds. He crowded his way up against another car and leaned on the horn, flashing his headlights. The car braked quickly three or four times to get him to back off.

Jeff looked to his left, then his right, to see if he could go off the road and get around a car and three semis moving bumper to bumper. The drops on both sides were steep.

"He's here," Saliha said, her voice suddenly rising an octave.

Jeff slammed on his brakes and the Hyundai was suddenly beside him. He wrenched the steering wheel to the side and banged into it hard, then harder still as he tried to force it off the road. The Hyundai dropped back and Jeff accelerated again, soon reaching the other vehicles. But now they'd thinned and he managed to weave his way through, only touching one of the passenger cars on the rear bumper as he passed him. With clear road ahead he punched the accelerator to the floorboard.

Saliha had dropped below the passenger seat but now that the car was running smoothly she climbed back up and peered again over the back of the seat. "I can't see him. I think he's blocked. Can you find a road off? Maybe we can take one and hide where he can't see us."

There were no exits. The only good news was that there were only occasional cars. Jeff was free to go as fast as the highway allowed. Still, the frequent curves forced him to slow again and again. Finally, Saliha said, "I see a car gaining on us. It's him, I think. Can't you go faster?" She jerked the head scarf off and threw it onto the backseat.

Jeff flew by a slow-moving pickup truck. The highway dipped and ahead was a long straight stretch.

"He's catching us!" Saliha shouted. "He's almost here! Hurry!"

Jeff saw the car in his rearview mirror. Just as the Hyundai was almost on him he again slammed his brakes. This time the car ploughed into him, clinging to his bumper, trying to flip him around. Jeff sped up but the other car closed at once, quickly pulling beside them. Again Jeff slammed into him then pulled to his left and hit his brakes. The Hyundai shot forward and now Jeff was behind him.

"Cross over here!" Saliha shouted. "There! See it?"

The divide between the two stretches was flat now. Jeff braked hard, spotted an informal crossing, and went over to the other side of the highway. They raced back toward the border. "Get into the town!" Saliha shouted. "There are guards. He will have to stop."

Jeff could hear a grinding in the rear of the car; metal pressed against a tire.

"Oh no!" she said. "There's a car coming after us. You have to go faster!"

But there was no going faster. It was as if something was pulling the Ford back, keeping it from speeding up.

"He's shooting again!" Saliha screamed. "He's—"

A wet mist splashed against the windshield and on Jeff, showering the side of his face. He looked over. Saliha had collapsed in the seat, a section of her skull missing.

Jeff slammed on his brakes and the Hyundai shot up to him. He looked over and saw the driver aiming a gun at him, his eyes wide in excitement. Jeff wrenched the wheel hard over and smashed into the car, hearing the grind of the sides, forcing his car against the other. He pressed harder, then harder, finally driving it off the highway. Jeff followed it to the apron, then fought to crawl back onto the asphalt. When finally he had control, he looked over his shoulder. He could see nothing.

The black Hyundai had shot off the highway, flying into one of the many small chasms over which they'd raced. For Rahmani, there was no time to think. At one level it all happened in slow motion, on another it was irresistible. He was trapped by the onward motion. He saw the rocky wall at almost the moment the car struck it. Then dark consumed him.

Jeff looked at Saliha again. There was no doubt at all. He slowed to fifty miles an hour to think what to do. Ten minutes later when he saw an exit he took it. He drove a few miles along a lonely road, pulled to the side, and stopped. Outside he stood sucking air, struggling to clear his mind and steady his nerves.

As the adrenaline faded, Jeff felt suddenly depressed and anxious. That young woman. He'd never seen anything like her death before. One minute she was struggling to live, the next instant her life was gone. Had he caused this? Was this all his fault?

His hands were shaking as he ran them over his face, struggling to regain control. Finally, on wobbly legs he went around the car and from the passenger door lifted the woman out, then dragged her into the brush. He lay her respectfully. He returned to the car, retrieved the scarf, and covered her face. Finally, he checked her clothing and located a thumb drive matching those he'd seen in Ahmed's apartment. He slipped it into his pocket.

There was nothing to bury her with and he wasn't even certain he should. Better he made certain she was found. He checked the rear wheels and managed to bend away whatever was rubbing against a tire. Back on the highway he checked markers and made mental notes that would lead someone to this spot.

With immediate danger past, he wondered where Daryl was.

57

MENLO PARK, CALIFORNIA
PG TECHNOLOGY APPLICATIONS
11:09 A.M. PST

The problems with the WAyk5-7863 grid in Washington State had brought matters to a head for Guy Fagan. He and his team had been working on a complex program that was designed to make possible an emergency override of an electrical grid in the event of a cyber-attack. At the minimum it was intended to prevent the kind of cascade that led to massive power outages. These were nearly always the result of an interruption in the delicate balance of supply and demand. As a safety precaution, power generators dropped out of the grid when too much strain was placed on them because of the abrupt collapse of electricity. The new program allowed such generating stations to remain in the grid without danger. It was potentially revolutionary—if it worked. It had in simulations. Only with its adoption would Fagan know if it performed as designed in the real world.

Though no one was saying so, the pressure he was under to release the new program suggested that someone had made an initial determination that the Yakima grid had been subject to just such a cyber-attack, and there were fears the malware that had caused it was implanted within other grid systems. His oversight committee had met earlier in the day. Fagan's team had carefully reviewed every simulation for them and it was decided the new program should be released. He was confident it would do what it was designed to do but if it did not, it would cause no harm. That had been a priority in the project from day one.

Approximately one-third of the electrical grids in the United States would receive the program within the next few minutes. Another third were expected to adopt it over the coming weeks.

"All right," Fagan said. There were five of his team in his office. "Here we go." He sent the program off, confirmed the message had gone out, then turned around to be greeted by grins and applause. "Good job, all."

"We've got cake and ice cream," his assistant said.

"I'd rather have a drink."

One of the engineers whispered, "We've got that covered."

As the software arrived at each operations center, it was opened. In some cases it was installed at once, in others it would be installed within days. It made no difference. The moment the program was opened, the Trojan Horse insinuated itself into their control system, concealing itself where no one looked, doing nothing for now. When the time was right it could call home and inform its creator that it was in place, that they had a backdoor into one-third of the American electrical grid, a backdoor through which any malware could be inserted, an opening for a full scale cyber-attack.

PEOPLE'S REPUBLIC OF CHINA
XINJIAN PROVINCE
URUMQI
PLA CYBER WARFARE CENTER
2:30 A.M. CST

We have successful penetration," the tech announced to his team standing behind him. "Five of the grids have already called home. The others should within a few hours. Congratulations to us."

There was a scattering of applause and wide smiles as he swiveled in his seat.

"Very good," Colonel Jai Feng said. "I believe there is refreshment waiting for you all."

"Won't you join us?" the tech asked.

"I cannot. But you have my congratulations." Feng nodded to all, then took the stairs back to his office. A success. Just what he needed. The silence from Beijing was ominous. There had been an initial expression of disapproval when his data-altering program had been uncovered at UNOG and Whitehall so quickly. He'd explained how that was inevitable once it was employed in such a cavalier way. But as was always the case even though his warning was true, or perhaps because it was, the accusations against him had been sharp.

And his hopes had been so high. Had he been given enough time that program could have been spread throughout the West. The havoc his team could have created would have been incalculable. No one would have trusted anything in their computers. True, his own people had made an error but that was something he could have overcome. Given time Feng was convinced this virus would be the most powerful tool he'd ever unleashed on China's enemies.

There'd been no word about the two laptops he'd wanted, no confirmation that his Stuxnet countermeasure had found its way into the new Iranian computers. He'd assured his superiors repeatedly that using a mule was unnecessary, that there were secure ways to send it by e-mail but he'd been overridden repeatedly.

"Colonel?" It was his aide.

"Yes?"

"Men here to see you."

"Men? What do you mean?"

In marched three men in suits, one of middle years, the others very young. Feng knew none of them but he knew immediately what they represented. "Ministry of Public Security," the lead man said. "Come with us, Colonel."

Feng lifted himself erect. He blinked as if struck, then blinked again. "I have just performed a great service for the party and our country."

Their faces might have been carved from stone. "Come with us, Colonel," the man repeated.

Feng hung his head. It was over.

58

NATANZ, IRAN
FUEL ENRICHMENT PLANT (FEP)
BUILDING J
1:07 A.M. IRST

After the body search at the entrance to Building J, Dariush Elahi went directly to his workstation to begin his night shift, nodding to a few co-workers on the way. Since the Stuxnet infection security had been significantly increased. Building J was part of the facilities expressly designed and maintained to create the ultimate air gap. No thumb drives or personal computers were permitted in this new facility. Cell phones were allowed but they had to be turned off and could only be used during breaks or at mealtime.

Before the acquisition of new computers and the creation of this secure facility, the program had been set back repeatedly. The failure rate of the 12,000 centrifuges spinning out enriched uranium had exceeded half and those that had not failed had nearly all produced useless product. The full scope of the disaster was known only within certain parts of the program. As senior engineer, Elahi was privy to such knowledge.

They were very close now, very close indeed. Promotions and bonuses had been promised at the time of success. Elahi could hardly wait. Projections from earlier that week said that some time in the next few days they'd have the quantity necessary for the first test. Then they'd see if the engineers had done their job and the bomb worked.

Elahi lay his cell phone down on his desk as he went to work. A few seconds later, Stuxnet3 made the wireless leap into his computer. This was a virgin system, which had never before been penetrated and the Trojan

Horse found a vast expanse of fertile digital space in which to seek, to expand, and to destroy. As the malware moved beyond Elahi's computer, it encountered itself spread everywhere, like an enormous spiderweb. In fact, there was almost no space left for it. The thirty thousand new computers within the air gap were utterly and thoroughly infected though until now the malicious network remained almost entirely dormant.

Now, having reached a specified critical mass and implanted itself in all the essential processes, Tusk initiated the sequence for which it was designed. And like a digital kamikaze, it set about destroying itself.

LANGLEY, VIRGINIA
CIA HEADQUARTERS
CYBERTERRORISM–COMPUTER FORENSICS DEPARTMENT
4:19 P.M. EST

There had been no word from Turkey since the advisory that an arrest notice had been issued for Ahmed Hossein al-Rashid. Since Agnes Edinfield had had nothing to do with it, she wondered just who had. The only information she possessed for now was that it originated from the General Directorate of Security in Ankara. She'd asked her man in Ankara to learn how it had come about.

There was, as well, no word about Jeff Aiken or Daryl Hagen. She wondered if they'd succeeded. Or were they dead in a ditch somewhere in Turkey?

She was tired. She closed her eyes, wanting very much to go to sleep. Instead, she read the cable once again. China had been informed that the United States knew of the Stuxnet3 countermeasure and that there would be hell to pay if they attempted to give it to Iran again. All this had taken place through back channels, but in her experience these were usually the most effective.

In his office, Frank Renkin was again watching the Intel sat in geosynchronous orbit over the Indian Ocean. For some two weeks, one of its powerful sensors had been directed at the fuel enrichment plant in Natanz. This was the primary target for Tusk. From this angle there was nothing special about the place. Most of the facility was underground but what was above was a series of square and rectangular buildings roughly organized around a rotary motorway.

The Israeli time estimate for penetration and activation had been six to ten days. The clock was fast running out on that and the plant would reportedly soon be ready with enough fissionable uranium for a nuclear test. Activity at the test site remained frenzied and several prominent Iranian officials were on their way there for an inspection tour. Company interpretation was that they wanted to see the bomb go off.

Edinfield wandered into his office. "I'm leaving. Anything?"

Frank wondered how she knew. Well, you couldn't keep something like this a secret for long from professional spooks. "There have been some tantalizing trickles of information from FEP that suggests penetration. The program is designed to make preparations and activate when a specific level of saturation has been achieved to produce maximum effect."

"How'd you jump the air gap?"

Frank smiled. "Classified." *It was Jeff Aiken,* he wanted to say but could not. He looked back at the screen. "I've been watching this thing for two weeks now with no sign."

"Will you know from the screen?"

He smiled. "Oh, yes. I'll know."

"We think China's going to back down on the countermeasure you were concerned about."

Frank had reported his call from Jeff, confirming the mule had been stopped. "How'd you manage that?"

"With the events of the last few days we've got enough evidence that they've been helping the Iranians to go public. They don't want that getting out, certainly not with the international condemnation and sanctions that would bring . . ."

"Think it will stop them for good?"

"For a while. What's that?"

Frank looked back at the screen. "That's it!" Suddenly he was no longer tired. "It worked! By God, it worked!"

In real time, with a very slight stop-action motion, Frank watched one explosion after another. In one building, the windows were blown out, followed by a large section of the roof. In two others, the roof came off at once. Then from the ground about the structures, enormous plumes of smoke and dust emerged, confirming explosions underground.

Frank sat transfixed as each of the enrichment facilities was destroyed. They'd be getting radiation readings soon but they weren't really necessary. Tusk had already shown itself to be the most powerful Trojan Horse ever unleashed on an enemy.

"A virus did that?" Edinfield asked in awe.

"Yes."

"This will change everything," she said.

"For them and for us."

59

ERZURUM, TURKEY
ATATURK UNIVERSITY HOSPITAL
10:53 P.M. EET

"How're you doing, trooper?" Jeff asked.

Daryl was sitting upright in a hospital bed. "I'll live. I've got a new scar or two, unfortunately."

"Just as long as you're okay." After leaving Saliha's body, he'd checked his cell phone again and there was a message from Daryl telling him she was in the hospital in Erzurum. She wanted him to come as soon as he could. On the way, he notified Frank of Saliha's death, confirming he had stopped the countermeasure from reaching Iran, and given him the markers so someone could find her body.

"My wild-goose chase turned out to be more that I bargained for," Daryl told him, as she related the story. "The power plant workers saved me. We should do something nice for them. And for Saliha's family."

"I'll call Frank. Maybe he can pull some strings."

She glanced toward the hallway. "I'm going to have to talk to the police about the airplane." Daryl closed her eyes. "I'm really tired, Jeff. So very tired."

"We'll be home soon."

Her eyes popped open. "What happened to Italy?"

MEMORANDUM

Date: July 3
From: Rhonda MacMillan-Jones
Deputy Director, Cyber Security
National Security Agency
To: Admiral Braxton L. R. Compton
Chairman, Joint Chiefs of Staff
Pentagon
Re: Confirmation

It is estimated that the success of Stuxnet3, Operation Tusk, has set back the Iranian uranium fuel enrichment program at least five years. A detailed report will follow. We have confirmed the executions of fifteen scientists involved in the nuclear weapons program. The hunt is on for more "traitors," as they are known.

On a sober note, the April 9 blackout of the Yakima, Washington, power grid WAyk5-7863 now appears to have been the result of a targeted cyber-attack. We believe it originated from the PLA in China.

In follow-up to my previous communication the extraneous software embedded within the U.S. Pacific Fleet Command computer structure has been largely removed. I say "largely" because fresh malware of unknown origin has been located. We remain uncertain of the level of penetration of USPFC at this time.

You have on your desk the latest estimate of cyber penetration of the DOD.

You've asked for the status of certain individuals:

- Colonel Jai Feng, director of the PLA Cyber Warfare Center, vanished from sight, then was publicly executed last week for treason. He has been replaced by a director known for his close ties to the so-called Patriot Hackers.
- Mei Zedong, deputy first state counselor of the Communist Party, has been demoted and now serves as deputy director of a potash factory in Qinghai province.
- Henri Wille, director of security at UNOG, has retired, under pressure.
- The source of the Iranian nuclear information to the United Nations, Nader Rahmani, was one of the scientists executed following the destruction of Fuel Enrichment Plant in Natanz.
- Lloyd Walthrop of the UK Foreign Office has retired and is reportedly writing a book. The subject is unknown.
- Agnes Edinfield has been promoted and placed on the list to receive the Medal of Freedom when she retires.
- Frank Renkin, director of the Cyberterrorism–Computer Forensics Department, has likewise been promoted with expanded responsibilities. As an aside, he is the proud father of a baby girl the couple have named Daryl.
- Jeff Aiken and Daryl Haugen continue working from their home in Georgetown. Both declined offers to return to government service.

cc: CoS, POTUS
        NSA, White House

INTERNAL DISTRIBUTION ONLY
SECRET

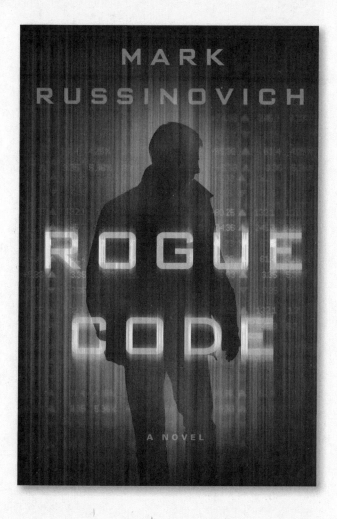

Trojan Horse • *Rogue Code* (Available May 2014)
Operation Desolation (short story)

THOMAS
DUNNE
BOOKS St. Martin's Press